UP AND DOWN
WITH
KATE

Kay Chorao

Dutton Children's Books • New York

For Deedee

Copyright © 2002 by Kay Sproat Chorao
All rights reserved.

Library of Congress Cataloging-in-Publication Data
Chorao, Kay.
Up and down with Kate / by Kay Chorao—1st ed.
p. cm.
Summary: Kate's fantastic grandmother, who always guesses correctly what
Kate has drawn, leaves Kate a special gift before moving away.
ISBN 0-525-46891-9
[1.Grandmothers—Fiction. 2.Family life—Fiction.] I. Title.
PZ7.C4463 Un 2002
[E]—dc21   2001047085

Published in the United States 2002 by Dutton Children's Books,
a division of Penguin Putnam Books for Young Readers
345 Hudson Street, New York, New York 10014
www.penguinputnam.com
Printed in Hong Kong   First Edition
1 3 5 7 9 10 8 6 4 2

E
CHO

CONTENTS

POT

Mama had a big blue pot.

It held Papa's tree.

But not today.

It was empty.

Kate looked at the pot.

It had blue dragons and blue trees.

Kate touched the pot.

Mama would say, "No, no."

But Mama was not there.

Kate looked inside.

She saw birds flying.

She bent over the pot

to look at the birds.

Then she fell in.

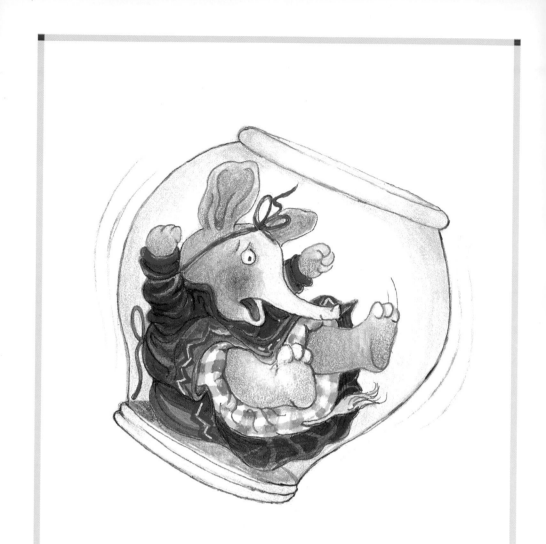

The pot wobbled.

"Oh, oh!" cried Kate.

The pot rolled over.

CRASH!

Kate tumbled out.

"Now you are in trouble,"

said George.

Kate was scared.

She ran outside.

Papa was just coming inside.

"CAREFUL!" said Papa.

He was holding a big package.

"Come in and help us,"

said Mama.

"No," said Kate.

Tears ran down her face.

"I am bad.

I broke the pot," she cried.

"That old pot was cracked,"

said Mama.

"It leaked," said Papa.

"We got a new one."

Mama dried Kate's tears.

Mama and Papa opened

the big package.

Inside was a new pot.

It had flowers and pink clouds.

"Pretty," said Kate.

Papa planted his tree in it.

Papa let Kate water the tree

all by herself.

She was very, very careful.

BEACH

Papa drove everyone to the beach.

"Swim time," said Mama.

"No," said Kate.

"Don't be afraid," said Papa.

"It will be fun," said Mama.

"Unless the crabs bite," said George.

Kate put one foot in the water.

"Crabs!" yelled George.

Kate fell back.

"Ha-ha, just fooling!"

yelled George.

Kate was mad.

"Go away," she cried.

Kate sat in the sand.

"Swim away," she said.

"And never come back."

Kate built a sand castle.

She looked up.

George was gone.

"Oh, oh," said Kate.

Kate splashed into the water.

"George!" she called.

Kate kicked and splashed.

George heard.

He ran to Kate.

"You are swimming,"

yelled George.

"Hooray for Kate!"

said Mama and Papa.

ARTIST

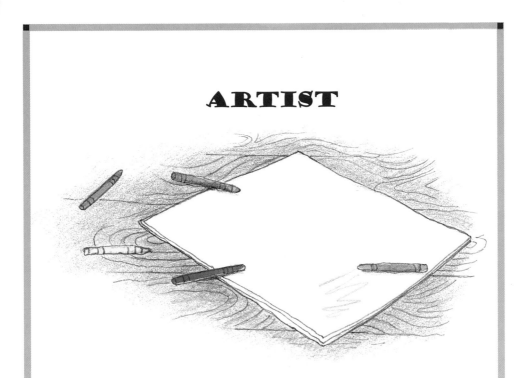

Grandma gave Kate

paper and crayons.

"Be nice and quiet," she said.

"Grandma needs a nap."

"I will be an artist," said Kate.

"A quiet artist," said Grandma.

Kate began to draw.

She drew with green.

"Grass," said Kate.

She drew with red and

purple and yellow.

"Flowers," said Kate.

She drew brown lines.

"Fence," said Kate.

Mama came in.

"What a pretty dragon,"

said Mama.

"No!" said Kate.

Papa walked by.

"What a bright horsey,"

said Papa.

"No!" cried Kate.

George looked.

"Scribble," said George.

"No, no, no!" cried Kate.

She ran to her swing.

She stayed there all alone

for a very long time.

Grandma found her.

"You made a beautiful drawing," said Grandma.

"It is not a dragon or a horsey or scribble," said Kate.

"Of course not. It is a garden,"

said Grandma.

"Yes!" said Kate.

"Anyone can see that,"

said Grandma.

"I am an artist," said Kate.

"Yes," said Grandma.

"You are my own quiet artist."

"I know," said Kate.

Then Grandma pushed Kate high
on the swing.

And her toes almost

touched the leaves.

"Whee!" said Kate.

NECKLACE

Grandma and Kate looked out

the window.

Wind blew leaves off the trees.

Clouds raced across the sky.

"It is growing cold.

Soon I must leave," said Grandma.

"No," said Kate.

"I will get you a surprise.

Then you won't feel sad,"

said Grandma.

Kate sat on Grandma's lap.

"A necklace?" asked Kate.

"Is that what you want?"

asked Grandma.

"Yes," said Kate.

"My friend Rose has one.

It is made out of beads."

Kate loved Rose's necklace.

Soon Grandma had to leave.

Papa drove her to the airport.

Kate cried.

She ran to her room.

There, on her bed,

was a little box.

Kate opened the box.

"Oh, no," cried Kate.

"I wanted a necklace."

"It *is* a necklace, Kate," Mama said.

"But I wanted fat beads in

  bright colors," said Kate.

"Like Rose's."

"This necklace has a secret,"

said Mama.

Kate looked at the little gold heart.

"Secret?" she asked.

Mama opened the top.

Inside was a picture of Grandma.

Mama put the gold chain

around Kate's neck.

"Now Grandma will always

be near you," said Mama.

Kate smiled.

She opened the little gold heart.

"Come back soon, Grandma,"

she said softly.

The New Reich

THE

NEW

REICH

Violent Extremism in Unified Germany and Beyond

MICHAEL SCHMIDT

Translated from the German by Daniel Horch

PANTHEON BOOKS   NEW YORK

All rights reserved under International and Pan-American Copyright
Conventions. Published in the United States by Pantheon Books, a division
of Random House, Inc., New York, and simultaneously in Canada by
Random House of Canada Limited, Toronto. Translated into English from
the unpublished German manuscript by Michael Schmidt. Copyright © by
Michael Schmidt.

Library of Congress Cataloging-in-Publication Data
Schmidt, Michael.
    [Neue Reich. English]
    The new Reich : violent extremism in unified Germany and beyond /
Michael Schmidt ; translated from the German by Daniel Horch.
        p. cm.
    ISBN 0-679-42578-0
    1. Violence—Germany. 2. Radicalism—Germany. 3. Germany—Race
relations. I. Title.
HN460.V5S3613 1993
303.6'0943—dc20   92-43378
                                                           CIP

Book Design by Fearn Cutler

Manufactured in the United States of America
First Edition
9 8 7 6 5 4 3 2 1

Contents

This book is dedicated to the cause of moral courage

Acknowledgments

I WOULD LIKE TO THANK THE FOLLOWING PEOPLE, whose moral and professional support made this book possible: the French translator; a kind colleague who put his material at my disposal and who helped me with quotes and contexts but, for various reasons, must remain anonymous; and the staff of Lattès, the French publisher. I am also grateful to Birgitta Karlström, without whom there would never have been a film, much less a book. Finally, very special thanks to a good friend, Graeme Atkinson.

Foreword

NEO-NAZIS—IN THE FALL OF 1988 I BEGAN, GINGERLY, to investigate this subject. Half a year later it was my only interest. My goal was to produce a film that would show present-day Nazis as they really are. By the summer of 1991, I had amassed over 110 hours of raw footage; two years of research and months of filming had to be condensed into just sixty minutes. The result, *"Wahrheit macht frei,"* (Truth Will Make You Free)* has since been shown in sixteen countries; in some places, many times.

By the spring of 1992, I had another goal: a book that could provide more background and context than a film possibly could. For those who prefer to look away and deny the truth, this too can be dismissed—as was the film—as "nothing new." Certainly I do not make any claim to completeness. On the contrary, these are but fragments of an iceberg. No one has yet seen it all. But what I have seen is enough to terrify me as surely as any nightmare.

Michael Schmidt   Paris

January, 1993

*The film's title is a slogan of the neo-Nazi revisionist movement and is itself a play on *"Arbeit Macht Frei,"* the sign that hung above the entrance to Auschwitz. This film is available from Filmmakers Library, 124 East Fortieth Street, New York, N.Y. 10016.

I

INSIDE THE SCENE

The Second
Revolution

THE HEAVY DOORS CLICK OPEN AND I LOOK CAU-
tiously down the aisle of the courtroom. A slim man dressed in
black, the defendant, is in mid-sentence: ". . . I am indeed a
National Socialist, and I publicly acknowledge it. . . ."

I am in the right place. Not Munich circa 1924, but the state
court in Frankfurt am Main in the spring of 1989. The bailiff's head
appears and I quickly flash my press card. With a wave he directs
me to the spectators' bench. There are only two other visitors in the
courtroom. One shakes his head repeatedly with disapproval as the
defendant continues his arguments; the other is zealously taking
notes. The trial concerns neo-Nazi propaganda, which is forbidden
under German criminal law. The defendant is Michael Kühnen, who
is charged with writing inflammatory documents that glorify violence, praise the Third Reich, and deny the historicity of Nazi war
crimes.

One example is an article in the journal *NS-Kampfruf* (National
Socialist Battle Cry), where Kühnen's work often appears. Complete with imperial eagle and swastika, this "Combat Publication of
the National Socialist German Worker's Party" is designed to look
like a mainstream newspaper. To the right of the logo, next to the
date, the number *100* is printed in brackets, denoting the centenary
of Adolf Hitler's birth. The article reads:

"Soon after 1918, historians and researchers around the world were quick to establish that Germany had not wanted a war. . . . But after 1945, and up to the present day, the situation has been completely different. . . . Today a revision of the 'War Guilt Question' and a withdrawal of Germany's enemies is neither planned nor imagined. The morality of a victor-nation whose people managed to build atom bombs and use them against human beings is being enforced. . . . The frg [Federal Republic of Germany—lowercased in the original] and the other German states are political entities of inferior authority. . . ."

It is a historical fact that the Nazis began the Second World War. It is also a historical fact that the Americans dropped the first atom bomb. The author of this article suggests that this was an immoral act but prudently keeps silent about an otherwise readily quoted fact: namely, that the Germans themselves were working feverishly on rocket and nuclear technology, right up to the last moment, hoping to change the course of the war with the help of a "retaliatory weapon"—the atom bomb.

According to another article: "History does not repeat itself in exactly the same form! Therefore we neither strive for a copy of the Third Reich nor do we let references to the alleged atrocities of the past make an impression upon us. . . ."

These documents, which dismiss systematic genocide and crimes against humanity as "alleged atrocities," are published by the NSDAP-AO, which is based in Nebraska. NSDAP is the original name of Hitler's party (Nationalsozialistische Deutsche Arbeiterpartei—National Socialist German Workers' Party); AO stands for Auslands- und Aufbau-Organisation (Foreign and Development Organization). The NSDAP-AO has become known through its worldwide mass-mailings of neo-Nazi propaganda. And as I would soon learn from the man sitting in the defendant's chair today, there is far more to it than propaganda.

Kühnen's seat is in the middle of the courtroom. Again and again he reaches for his mirrored sunglasses on the table before him and fiddles with them while he speaks. He seems pale, especially so given his dark hair. But he calmly and skillfully takes advantage of every possibility to make a political statement; his dedication to the cause of National Socialism is clear.

The court and the district prosecutor are anxious to present the case against him soberly and carefully. This is not easy, since Kühnen is constantly aiming for effect. An associate judge asks him to explain his high regard for the totalitarian "Führer principle," with its focus on a single leader, and by way of response Kühnen talks about his military service. When the judge, irritated, asks what the army has to do with it, Kühnen sees his chance.

"Well," he says, "I don't know how *you* imagine the army, but when a company is at the front, the soldiers are certainly not going to take a democratic vote on whether or not to attack."

There is general laughter, and the district attorney and judges grimace in embarrassment. The court secretary, who seemed to have fallen asleep, is startled awake. Kühnen, enjoying his triumph, gazes out at the audience. The mood lightens and even my head-shaking neighbor grins briefly. Kühnen's lawyer, Herr Loebe, laughs sardonically. Laughter makes it so easy to forget the past. I flip through my notes. Colleagues told me confidentially that Loebe's firm had also handled business in Germany for Josef Mengele, the notorious chief doctor at Auschwitz.

My information about Kühnen himself is sketchy. He was born in 1955 into a middle-class family, was raised a Catholic, and has been politically active since the age of fifteen. Kühnen was even, briefly, a Maoist, and he stands by his past.

"Today I still consider Maoism to be a sort of Chinese National Socialism," he explains to the court.

It is tempting to write off Michael Kühnen as an unrealistic, radical crackpot. But no one in this court underestimates him and, sad to say, his record shows that they are right not to. Of his eighteen years in the extremist movement, he has spent seven and a half in prison, mostly for crimes like those he is accused of today. The charges are not restricted to propaganda, but also include "defamation of the state," "wearing a forbidden uniform" (the brown shirt of the SA, with belt buckle and ammunition), and even assault and battery. Kühnen has always been a ringleader, a dangerous man—the sort of person my instincts and better judgment would ordinarily have kept me far away from.

Nevertheless, I am, through a strange chain of events, sitting here, trying to get to know him. Like millions of other Germans, in the fall of 1988 I watched a profusion of special televised reports commemorating the fiftieth anniversary of Kristallnacht—the Nazi regime's prelude, on November 9, 1938, to the merciless persecution of the Jews, which would end in the historically unique mass extermination of millions of people. Like many others, I was certainly moved. But, then, I thought, ah well, this is all in the past. One report, though, changed my mind completely. A certain Dr. Fritz Hippler, a white-haired old gentleman, appeared on the screen and explained that simple envy was the motive for the persecution of the Jews: the Nazis envied the talented and wealthy. And then the program showed an excerpt of a film Hippler had made for Joseph Goebbels: *Der ewige Jude* (The Eternal Jew), a smear film that compared Jews to rats. I couldn't understand it, how could this man speak so calmly?

That got me started. Reading everything I could find on the Third Reich, I soon came across books that were even more shocking, in particular *Die kalte Amnestie* (The Cold Amnesty) by Jörg Friedrich and Ingo Müller's *Die furchtbaren Juristen* (The Terrible Judges). The first describes the reintegration of Nazi criminals into postwar German society, and the second discusses those judges and lawyers who issued verdicts of terror during the Third Reich and who were either allowed to continue their legal careers uninterrupted or were treated mildly by their "colleagues" in the Federal Republic. Thanks to legal technicalities, even the worst offenders received mercy instead of justice. For example, in March 1957 the state court in Stuttgart sentenced Dr. Günter Venediger to two years' penal servitude for acting as an accessory to murder. As the Gestapo chief in Danzig, Venediger had murdered four English prisoners of war. The verdict stated: "Perpetrator regarding the execution of these four officers in Danzig was Adolf Hitler, the former Führer and Chancellor. He acted illegally and with criminal intent."

This brazen miscarriage of justice disturbed me deeply. What, I wondered, were those old Nazis up to these days? And the ones out yelling "Germany for the Germans!" today—were they just chips off the old block? These are the new Nazis, I thought, a sentiment that grew and grew in me. I would feel guilty myself if I did not do something to fight them. But what could I do?

Months later, here in Frankfurt, I am studying the defendant. Neither of us experienced the National Socialist reign of terror directly. Yet Kühnen is the very model of the unscrupulous and fanatical *Führer* whom millions followed into suffering and disaster.

For months now I had been researching the neo-Nazis, together with Graeme Atkinson, the European editor for the English newspaper *Searchlight*. Graeme is also an adviser to the European Parliament's Committee of Inquiry into Racism and Xenophobia in Europe and has devoted his life to investigating such activities. In the course of his work he has often disguised himself and infiltrated neo-Nazi groups. Today, for the first time, I am meeting an actual representative of the neo-Nazis. According to Graeme, Michael Kühnen is an important, if not central, figure in the German scene. During a pause in the hearing, I approach the defendant, who doesn't bat an eyelash. I almost have the impression that he expected to speak with me, and he agrees immediately to an interview after the next session.

Four days later, near the courthouse, we met at a café on a busy commercial street. Kühnen is sitting in the back of the room, behind a barrier of flowers, where we won't be disturbed. He is not alone. A maternal-looking woman—around fifty, small, with short dark hair and a friendly face—is sitting with him. She was a witness at the trial today, and in the courtroom one got the impression she was no more than a casual acquaintance of Kühnen's. She "didn't know" the answers to most of the questions she was asked. In reality she is a key figure in the movement. Her name is Christa Goerth and she is the chairwoman of the HNG (Hilfsorganisation für nationale politische Gefangene und deren Angehörige e.V.—Relief Agency for National Political Prisoners and Their Dependents), an important neo-Nazi umbrella organization. Only later would I discover the HNG's real mission. Today Goerth does not interest me nearly so much as Kühnen. Yet I am struck by her ability to argue on topics that create interest and attention, and that perhaps even win sympathy: "Nuclear power is a crime no matter what! It's just so irresponsible to let hundreds of power plants keep running, every day and every minute producing all that poison that can never, ever be disposed of or controlled."

Amazing, I thought. Neo-Nazis against nuclear power! What will the Greens make of this?

Goerth notices my interest and continues.

"It is just such an enormous crime that, really, only with all possible force and might—you know, a gentle excursion just won't work here, only killing will." Maybe the Greens don't need to know about this after all.

Kühnen agrees with her enthusiastically. He examines me closely while Goerth gushes about energy policy. Then, with considerable didactic skill, he shows me just how seriously he and his movement must be taken.

"I think our chances are good," he says. "This system is not solving any of its problems, and problems that aren't solved and are continually put off only get bigger. And the longer they're put off, the more likely it is that one day the living conditions of the masses will become so dire that mass discontent will result. And then, when they are totally discontented, when they are in the mood for rebellion and revolution, the masses will follow those who have carried on the most credible, lengthy, consistent, and firm opposition."

Kühnen speaks forcefully. In the mirror behind him I notice that other guests are looking over at us. Kühnen glances around before continuing more quietly, though no less forcefully.

"And so, right now I see my task as nothing less than to make sure that everyone who is halfway interested in politics knows that this alternative exists. Then, when the crisis situation arises, they will remember it. I am completely certain of it. But I can't make any predictions as to when the time will come."

In 1923, Hitler and a few supporters attempted a sensational putsch. Although it failed, by mythologizing the event and using his trial to spread propaganda he brought himself to the attention of the entire population. Sentenced to five years' imprisonment, Hitler was released after just nine months. And ten years later he was in power. His "logic" was similar to that now used by Kühnen, who has brought the past into our time.

In Germany, these days, one often hears that "Bonn is not Weimar." This expression is generally employed to dismiss warnings of the growing danger to German democracy from the radical right. But such a slogan is a hollow reassurance, for the tactics of the right are almost unchanged. Again we see the clever method of spinning political capital out of popular discontent. Earlier, the principal watchwords were "the yoke of Versailles" and "the influence of the Jews." In 1989 Germany's division and "the foreigner problem," and in 1991 Maastricht as "Versailles without a war" and "the refugee problem," served the same political purpose. The right-wing parties all advance the same arguments. The pronouncements of the REP (Republicans), the NPD (National Democrats), the DVU (German People's Union), and the openly neofascist FAP (Free Workers' Party) differ only in their degree of clarity and radicalism.

"The Republicans say what many people think, and I say what many Republicans think." Kühnen sits opposite me, and his searching eyes register every one of my reactions. Now and then he playfully twists his silver chain bracelet. He drinks "Spezi," a combination of Coca-Cola and orange soda. He thanks me but refuses my cigarettes, preferring his own menthol brand. His cigarette glows as he inhales deeply, and then he continues.

"Just two days ago I had a small meeting in Bielefeld. Half the people there were members of the NPD and the DVU and the Republicans. One man extremely active in the local Republicans came up to me. He said, "I'm a Republican, I belong to the party. I hope that I can use it to accomplish something for my ideas, but naturally I can't say that to the Republicans.' "

In the background is the sound of glasses tinkling and jazz music. Kühnen flicks the ash off his cigarette and stares at me. "And these people are happy that there are men like me around, that there are platforms, publications, and other opportunities to express themselves. Our existence allows people who are otherwise constrained by their moderate contexts to preserve a sort of internal radicalism. Because they can see that others express it openly. And we profit from the fact that the overall societal atmosphere then changes. It makes a difference whether you advocate an idea as a small minority . . ."

Kühnen has clenched his hand into a fist on the tabletop. He turns it slowly around and spreads out his fingers. It looks like a flower blooming, or like a hydra's mouth opening. ". . . or whether you know that you're in a psychological situation where ten percent vote 'national.' "

Kühnen had been convinced for some time that with reunification the course would be set for a "Greater Germany" racial policy. He would, unfortunately, be proved fatally right. In September 1992, a nationwide survey (conducted by the INFAS Institute, which is located in Bad Godesberg) made the alarming discovery that 51 percent of all Germans were sympathetic to the slogan "Germany for the Germans." In 1989, these words were the exclusive chant of the neo-Nazis.

I tell Kühnen that I'm planning to write a novel and therefore need certain background information. "Though my preference," I add, "has always been film."

He takes the bait instantly. "Yes, film is naturally much more interesting!" he says enthusiastically. He knows that television appearances can have a much greater effect than books.

As Graeme and I decided earlier, initially I will just promise to think about it. In the future it can only help if the film is considered Kühnen's idea, and not mine.

I bring a video camera to our next meeting, which, like the first one, takes place right after a court session. Once again Kühnen is not alone. This time he is accompanied by Thomas Brehl, his occasional deputy, who has appeared today as a witness for the defense. After his exhausting performance, the first thing Brehl needs is a beer; judging from his looks, this is often the case. When I learn that he organized a military sports camp, I wonder how he could ever force his huge, protruding beer belly into a uniform. His face is bloated and red; no wonder, since he's drinking bottle after bottle of beer in the morning. Brehl has no trace of Kühnen's class and charisma. On the contrary, he fits perfectly the stereotype of the "ugly German." He is only thirty-two but looks forty-five. With a coarse mustache on his upper lip and short, parted hair, he looks like a miniature version of Ernst Röhm.

Röhm was head of the brown-shirted SA. Hitler's intimate friend, though controversial in Nazi circles because of his homosexuality, he ultimately became a victim of his own political partners. In June 1934, on the "Night of the Long Knives," Hitler had Röhm and much of his staff killed. The SA, which had already been eclipsed by the SS, no longer fit his plans. Kühnen and Brehl, however, are partial to the SA, considering it the more romantic and revolutionary of the two outfits, a "pure" Nazi battle troop. The socialist revolution Röhm had once called for, the second revolution, was now overdue. The first revolution had been the "national" revolution waged in the battles Hitler and Röhm fought together, when Röhm and his SA brownshirts cleared the way for Adolf Hitler's NSDAP leading to the seizure of power in 1933.

Most people remember the SA primarily as vicious gangs of thugs who, bludgeoning everything and everyone in their way, fought bloody street battles with the communists. Sensing my antipathy, Brehl thanks me but refuses to participate in the interview.

Together with Graeme, I had prepared an extensive list of questions for my conversation with Kühnen. Now we are sitting, Kühnen and I, in a park near the Frankfurt courthouse. His alert eyes keep moving back and forth between the camera and me. Like Hitler, Kühnen used his stays in prison to pursue his favorite hobbies: he wrote manifestos and read voraciously. But his favorite author is not Hitler. He raves about Nietzsche and science fiction. His own book is called *Die zweite Revolution* (The Second Revolution). Like *Mein Kampf,* this manual for followers was written in prison. These parallels would contribute to the "Kühnen myth."

Kühnen confirms that he has contacts among the Republicans as well as several international connections. When Graeme and I subsequently analyze his remarks, we discover to our astonishment that Kühnen is extremely accurate with regard to his accomplishments and activities; our search for lies or exaggerations is fruitless. The situation is quite different, however, when it comes to the history of National Socialism. For example, Kühnen puts forward the thesis that the Nazis did not start the war. His proof is a facsimile of an English newspaper, The Daily Express, from March 24, 1933. "JUDEA DECLARES WAR ON GERMANY," the headline proclaims. The facsimile comes from the Deutsche Nationalzeitung, the house organ of the radical-right DVU, and the headline is apparently enough to shift the war guilt onto the Jews. Kühnen himself must know better, since this sensational charge is refuted in the article itself, which refers to a call for a trade boycott of Germany because of its increasing repression of the Jews.

Kühnen hates democrats and accuses them of hypocrisy, dishonesty, and selfishness. Like Hitler in Mein Kampf, he makes no secret of his intentions. He openly admits that "all the methods of democracy must be used in order to eliminate it." He takes pains to infiltrate the Republicans and other right-wing parties in order to win over their memberships. His success is mixed, and it is fine with him that these parties, for tactical reasons, officially distance themselves from him. He is, nonetheless, disappointed with Harald Neubauer. According to Kühnen, Neubauer's seat in the European Parliament has "made him a bit of a megalomaniac. And such a hypocrite. After all, he was once thrilled to be allowed to join us."

Harald Neubauer? The Republicans' second-in-command, Franz Schönhuber's crown prince, a member of the European Parliament? "Yes, that's the one." Kühnen leans back. A hint, no more. Later I will learn more on this subject, but first I am to attend an "action" Kühnen is planning.

The Langen train station is completely typical; it could as well be in any other small town. Express trains to Frankfurt and Darmstadt rush by without stopping, and newsstand customers are greeted by name. The station is special only for one unfortunate reason: grim-looking men in bomber jackets regularly assemble there. If you risk going there at the wrong time, you will soon understand why Langen is called the "capital of the movement"—that is, among certain circles, and always with a wink. The wink is because the true "capital of the movement" remains Munich, Hitler's original base of operations.

Across the street from the station is a family restaurant and diagonally across is an Italian one. In the latter, the waiter greets select customers with an outstretched arm. Mussolini sends greetings.

I arrive in the morning, at nine o'clock sharp, with a rented Opel and a rented film crew. Since Kühnen is nowhere to be seen, we decide to watch the gathering of boot-wearing Germans from a distance. When we look around we discover another Opel. Its passengers are, like us, watching attentively.

"The police, definitely!" guesses the cameraman, sounding relieved. "At least now nothing can happen to us."

He's right. So now I can take the chance of speaking to these guys, since it's already gotten quite late. (As I would observe again and again over the next few years, punctuality is not the neo-Nazis' strong suit.) One young man in a brown shirt looks important as he gives orders and looks around suspiciously. I politely introduce myself and discover that he is in command here. He informs me that "nothing will be filmed until the chief comes," and with that I trot back to my car like a wet poodle. Not two minutes later, I hear knocks on the side window. "Police! Your identification papers, please!"

Since anyone could come along and demand that, we ask him for *his* credentials. While we each examine the other's service papers and press card, respectively, I try to speak with the officer. He isn't very forthcoming, but I do learn that the brownshirt I'd just spoken with is connected to a certain Gerald Hess. The policeman adds that Hess is already known to them, though not these others, and that Kühnen is also going to come, and that Hess is just a little thug, and that he, the officer, wonders just what we are after here. Then he disappears into his Opel.

In the meantime, another twenty neo-Nazis have turned up.

Finally Kühnen arrives in his car, a red Opel. He is in full uniform, with brown shirt, black pants, and mirrored glasses—"fascist glasses," as the cameraman calls them.

Everything happens all at once. Half of the group disappears, not wanting to be filmed. Then what's left of the group starts off in cars. Kühnen is in front, followed by a yellow Opel with a Cologne license plate, then us, and finally, at a polite distance, the Opel with the officer we'd spoken to, followed by yet another unmarked police Opel. After all the conspiratorial exchanges, this column of Opels moves from village to village in the most banal fashion. We stop at regular intervals, but there are no assaults, no robberies, and no murders. The Nazis distribute their leaflets ("Germans awake! Foreigners out!") as we shoot film and the police take photographs. An equable ratio of ten Nazis, three journalists, and six policemen. It's simply laughable.

Three years later, the laughter will have left me for good. By then, right-wing extremists had killed thirty-four people. Refugees' homes had gone up in flames, and the police escort was no longer a handful of officers but entire task forces that nevertheless would still hesitate to intervene—not least out of fear of themselves being beaten by an overwhelming number of hate-filled thugs.

I would be there to witness it: how youths are indoctrinated, how the hard core is sworn in for street battles, and how hate seems to escalate without limit.

II

INSIDE THE EMPIRE OF
HATE

A VOICE BOOMS FROM THE LOUDSPEAKERS: "FROM THE start of man's existence, rats have followed him as parasites. Their homeland is Asia. From there they migrated in giant hordes through Russia and the Balkans into Europe." An alarming net of lines spreads over the screen as the brown rats flood through Europe. Cut. The same lines appear, but this time they represent the migration of the Jews.

"That can't be!" The young man next to me is outraged, indignant at the Jews' "insolence" in spreading out like that.

The image flickers on the screen while the spectators in the darkened room sit spellbound. Now and then someone curses loudly. On the screen rats run toward us.

"Wherever rats turn up," the narrator explains in a sober authoritative voice, "they bring destruction with them. They destroy goods and foodstuffs and they spread disease: leprosy, plague, typhoid, cholera, dysentery, and many others. . . . They are cunning, cowardly, and cruel, and they generally appear in great hordes. Among animals, they represent an element of treacherous, subterranean destruction, just as Jews do among men."

The swarm of rats is juxtaposed with a group of, presumably, Jewish faces. Because we've just seen the rats, in closeup these people suddenly seem treacherous by association, and most spectators mutter sounds of disgust. One man even shakes with horror.

The music becomes disagreeable, grating. As if all this weren't enough, the narrator adds a final touch: "These physiognomies conclusively refute the liberal theories of the equality of all who bear a human countenance."

Among the audience, agreement is general—as it probably was in 1941, when *Der ewige Jude* (The Eternal Jew) played in Berlin's biggest movie theater. But once again, in 1990, this movie, along with *Jud Süss* (The Jew Süss) and *Juden sehen dich an* (Jews Look at You), is part of a standard indoctrination program. The viewers are schoolchildren and apprentices, young workers and journeymen, between fifteen and twenty years old. Gerald Hess has gathered these new followers in his home. They had responded to leaflets or were brought along by comrades. For many it is their first meeting. Along with Kühnen, Gerald Hess and his father, Wolfgang, are prepared to iron out any possible uncertainties and translate the message of *Der ewige Jude* for the present day. I can hardly believe it, but the film has the intended effect.

"I didn't know much about the Jews," says one young man, acne still blooming on his cheeks, "I'd heard they were just businesspeople. But that they're *that* kind of people . . ."

Another has not yet mastered Jewish ritual. "They slaughter pigs," he declares firmly, "but the way they torture the animals—I think that's shit."

Obviously the scenes in which cattle are slaughtered have made a deep impression on him. In closeup, a Jewish butcher smiles into the camera as he whets his knife; the next image is of a deep cut into the animal's jugular. Thus the cruelty of the Jews is reinforced by a scene that even Goebbels, who commissioned the film, would show only to select audiences.

The skinhead next to me demands brutal vengeance: "Someone should cut the Jews' throats so that they bleed to death."

A girl nods approvingly as her boyfriend comes to an infuriating realization. "That is total animal torture!"

"They're pigs, all of them!" says the lanky teenager with peach fuzz on his upper lip.

One youth, who has thus far restrained himself, demonstrates how successful this indoctrination is. Perhaps seventeen years old, he doesn't look even remotely violent; indeed, he shyly, shame-facedly hems and haws as he fiddles with his glasses and finally remarks, in a faint voice, almost to himself, "Now I can at least imagine, even though I wasn't born back then . . ."

Gerald Hess encourages him: "In principle, you can apply ninety percent of that to the present day."

Gerald's father is conscious of my camera's presence as he asks in his deep, strident voice, "What does this film say to you?" The question is superfluous. Wolfgang Hess is in his forties, and with his tattooed arms and three-day beard he cuts a rather brutal figure. He is sometimes unemployed, sometimes a roofer. He is an anti-Zionist—not, he claims, an anti-Semite—and a weapons expert. He is also an ex-convict. He is the suspicious and cunning old fox, but also a comrade and paterfamilias. His youngest child is just two years old, and the mother, his girlfriend, could almost be his daughter. Both mother and baby are almost always present whenever he makes an appearance.

Wolfgang Hess is the head of the Anti-Zionist Action, and culti-vates contacts with neo-Nazis in South Africa. Moreover, he handles logistics when venues for meetings need to be found. Today he takes on the role of expert on Zionism. He is sufficiently radical to win recognition, but cunning enough not to get caught too often by the police in the process. As Wolfgang Hess babbles on about the Jews—"In politics and economics, everything is *Jews!*"—a feeling of resignation washes over me.

This indoctrination film, which had sparked my first serious investi-gations into the past, produced the same effect on me as before. The text, which practically explodes with hate and is completely false, was written by a Dr. Eberhard Taubert. Not only was he never condemned for the film, but after the war he continued to work for the federal government and, as of 1980, for the army's Division of Psychological Defense.*

---

*See Kurt Hirsch, *Rechts von der Union* (To the Right of the Union), p. 453. Among his other activities, in 1933 Taubert was a judge on the People's Tribunal, where

As for the "creator" of *Der ewige Jude,* its production chief, Dr. Fritz Hippler, will later boast in his memoirs of his friendship with Walter Scheel, a former president of the Federal Republic of Germany. As a propagandist, Hippler was in demand as a publicity manager—and not just by right-wingers but also by the liberal Free Democrats.

Hippler later developed literary pretensions. In 1985 he published a book, *Meinungsdressur* (Opinion Trainer) in which he wrote: "Without a doubt, the Negroes of Africa never had it worse than in the brief period after their liberation. In places where their situation is actually better than before, namely South Africa, the progressives inform them that their misery is intolerable and incite them to a 'struggle for freedom.' " Today Hippler writes for such "national" newspapers as the reactionary, extreme-right *Nationalzeiting* and the *Nation,* a "political magazine for Germans" that describes the world wars as "two campaigns of annihilation against Germany" and celebrates the new "German dominance in the European community."

Hippler and Taubert, film director and publicist to the Reich. Punishment has passed them by, as it has so many others. Their seeds have been sown back, and even now they thrive and spread—and their best tool remains slander. And still they are completely unpunished fifty years after the film's production—despite the war, despite the Constitution, despite democracy.

> And no matter what enemy comes with force and cunning, stay forever true, you comrades . . .

---

he shared responsibility for handing down numerous death sentences; and in 1939–40 he was involved with Nazi propaganda in the occupied Eastern territories. Yet in 1955, a high official in the Federal Interior Ministry insisted that "Taubert is the man we need."

Shrill whistles drown out the rest of the song, with the aid of a police helicopter that roars just above our heads, as the "National Camp" assembles in a small Bavarian town on August 19, 1989. Those who aren't whistling are yelling: "Nazis out! Nazis out!" Around five hundred disciples of Hitler, both young and old, are marching through the narrow streets of this small town, waving flags; many wear brown or black shirts. An equal number of counterdemonstrators are on the outside, keeping the same pace. In between are white-helmeted policemen. The inhabitants of the adjacent houses gape at this spectacle. One older woman has made herself comfortable, resting on a cushion on her windowsill, looking down curiously at the long train of demonstrators, which presses its way through the town with deafening noise.

"No more of that—understood?" A nightstick-wielding policeman yells loudly at a skinhead who had tried to leave the march to attack a counterdemonstrator. Fights erupt again and again between the two groups, and the police separate them as quickly as possible. The *Antifa* (short for "antifascists") are here to show the Nazis that their public appearance will not be tolerated. Colorfully dressed punks with garishly dyed, extreme hairstyles terrify the citizenry in their own way, and it's no wonder they come to blows with the Nazi skinheads. Many of the antifascists, however, look rather respectable. And despite the mutual hostility, there are occasional discussions, though they generally collapse into all-out brawls.

"My grandpa was also in the war, but he told me a different story!" a young antifascist in an army parka yells over the barricades to a white-haired marcher.

The old man waves his miniature, black-white-red paper flag with the imperial symbol and sings: "Fatherland, we are coming!"

With a resigned "Oh, God!" the young man turns away, holding his head in his hands.

The day's slogan is "Rudolf Hess—martyr for Germany," and his picture is featured on hundreds of the marchers' placards. We are in northern Bavaria, in the town of Wunsiedel, not far from Bayreuth. Adolf Hitler's deputy is buried here. In May of 1941, Hess flew to England on—in the words of the neo-Nazis—a mission of peace. In fact, his only intent was to secure an armistice with England that would allow Germany to finish off Russia undisturbed. When his naïve, unauthorized plan failed, Hitler declared him mad. He remained a prisoner of war until he died in 1987 in Berlin-Spandau, the Allies' military prison, the sole survivor of the Nuremberg trials. Suicide was the official verdict, though the neo-Nazis raised accusations of murder. Martyrs make much better legends than suicides.

What is certain is that Rudolf Hess lived for ninety-two years, and that he has turned Wunsiedel into a place of pilgrimage for the radical right that has achieved international significance. I hear scraps of Spanish, English, and French. It is the first time I've seen foreign neofascists, who are taking this opportunity to meet their German comrades. Members of the British Movement are here, along with the French FNE (Faisceaux Nationalistes Européens) and the Spanish CEDADE (Circulo Español de Amigos de Europa). I also see supporters of the banned VMO (Vlaamse Militanten Orde), led by the Belgian Bert Eriksson, and members of the Dutch ANS/NL (Aktionsfront Nationaler Sozialisten—Gau Niederlande).

Similar meetings take place annually in the Belgian town of Diksmuide and in Spain. In 1990, the Wunsiedel march turned into one of the biggest international assemblies, though most of the news media failed to acknowledge it. Neofascist comrades from Spain and France will address the gathering, but still no one pays any attention.

Time and again, I'm harassed by the organizers, who don't like filmmakers or photographers. They prefer to stick their hands in the lens or to stand with their backs to the camera. But later, after we've gotten to know one another, the same organizers would protect me from their own people. I would then be obliged to come to the unpleasant realization that bystanders considered me to be one of the Nazis. More than once I would come close to being drawn into a brawl, but that isn't surprising.

I once had a comrade,
he was the best there was . . .

larly is a ritual. Hainke himself does not drink excessively, but he understands what he calls "my boys' needs." Then, though a little bewildered by my forwardness, he agrees to let me film his tattoos. "I have these all over my upper body." He gestures with a circular motion.

"Well, then," I say, "off with that shirt!"

"What, here? In front of all these people? Forget it!"

"Sure, where else?" I say, already unpacking my camera.

Excited by the idea, Gerald Hess suggests we go upstairs. No sooner said than done. We find a small space in a corridor, Gerald finds two chairs, and Thomas Hainke, *Gauleiter,* lifts his shirt over his head to show me a magnificent display, the masterpieces of a tattoo artist: dragons, spiderwebs, eagles, and the Grim Reaper; in between, a coat of arms, naturally in black-white-red, and on the shoulder, the superfluous legend: "skins."

Hainke leans forward in his chair as I come close with my camera. Then I stop, suddenly, at the sight of a deep, circular scar, still blood-encrusted, on his shoulder.

"A bottle," he explains. "A punk."

No question: Hainke is a militant. It's not for nothing that he's called the "boss skinhead." One of Michael Kühnen's most active followers, he doesn't try to avoid difficulties; his troops are tightly organized and feared by foreigners and leftists alike.

In the future, whenever we meet, I will ask him about his newest wounds. It becomes a kind of game between us. But despite his violence, Hainke is an earnest young man who is conscious of his own contradictions. A year later he played a key role in the plan to send a neo-Nazi mercenary unit into the Gulf War, and established contacts with the Iraqi Embassy in Germany. He also made repeated trips as a mercenary to Croatia, which has a tradition of fascist cooperation, to fight in the Osijek area "for the preservation of the white race against Serbianism." Afterward, he proudly showed off the military award he received "for shooting sixteen Serbs."

Hainke is a rock-solid National Socialist, and has been since he was thirteen, when he joined Kühnen's organization. Like most young neofascists, he is strengthened by his sense of social rejection. He is frequently fired from jobs, something even he can understand.

He wants to go his own way, yet he aspires to be a powerful leader one day. "Of course we also have good contacts with the Republicans and with the NPD, the DVU, all that," he explains calmly, just as Kühnen did a few weeks before. Hainke speaks carefully. From time to time he presses his lips together or raises his eyebrows, especially when talking about his arrests or his fights. "Something almost always happens with punks or niggers," he says contemptuously. "When we meet on the street, you just don't cross to the other side. But then it's over pretty quickly. Either them or us . . ."

Hainke sits in front of me, his shirt now pulled down. Gerald Hess has sat down next to us on the floor. The atmosphere is confidential, almost intimate.

But when I ask how I can reach him in the future, he gives me Christa Goerth's telephone number. He does not forget for a minute that I am one of his enemies, like all outsiders, like all "democraps." Like all who are not his friends.

The Waldfrieden is a remote country pub near Wunsiedel. About thirty-five exuberant people have assembled in the rustic parlor's dim light to drink, cheer, and sing. The few who are not part of the assembly look on peaceably. After all, we are very close to Bayreuth, Wagner's home. In these parts, people have a soft spot for music, especially if it's German. And what's being sung today is more than German. A sturdy Austrian, around thirty years old, with nickel-rimmed glasses and short-cut hair, has pulled out his guitar. He strikes up the tune of the pop song "Pretty Belinda," but the text to the song has been changed:

The parliament, it's a shame,
in twenty years it'll be a gas chamber.
You can't do anything by talking,
and gas makes—pretty corpses.

And then we'll be the only rulers,
and then they'll all weep to death from woe,
the Jews, the others, all the ripe ones,
they're destined to be—pretty soap.

Look out, brother, we're coming again
and we're mowing down the red rabble.
Look out, brother, 'cause now comes the revenge,
the Jew shall perish, and Germany will arise.

These neo-Nazis want to be undisturbed, though the proprietor, the three other guests, and the waitress act as if these ghastly happenings were normal. The giant beer glasses and Bavarian platters with sauerkraut are routinely served.

Most wear SA-style brown shirts or other parts of the uniform. Their haircuts are short: in the so-called helmet cut (just above the ears), or in skinhead-style. Some of the younger ones look like extras in a bad film; with defiant chins and glassy eyes, they're parodies of themselves. When they bang their fists on the table in time with the marching songs and beer slops out of their glasses, it looks like a beerhall during Oktoberfest, though with a slight costume change, to be sure. But it's much more than that: these are like resurrected fossils of the Third Reich, with insignia on their sleeves, swastika patches, leather shoulder straps, and the determined expressions of the Hitler Youth. Their repertoire extends from new brawling songs to old Nazi anthems to medieval folk music.

As the atmosphere becomes increasingly boisterous, I do my best not to provoke trouble. Gerald Hess introduces me and I am allowed to film an interview with Gottfried Küssel. I set up my videocamera and put a small tape recorder on his table. He is the "regional head of the Eastern Borderlands," which is what the Nazis call Austria. His fleshy face indicates that the job doesn't require him to starve. In fact, Küssel is not just fat, he's massive. The same goes for his features: his cheeks are huge compared to his nose and mouth, whose gentle curve stands in strange contrast to his angular chin.

"I am not a fascist!" he declares. "I'm a socialist, but not an international socialist. I'm a *national* socialist." That much is evident; but when I ask him, nevertheless, about international contacts, he admits to knowing "American nationalists." He thinks for a moment, then adds: "We are also in contact with representatives of the Black Muslims."

"Black Muslims?" I say. "Aren't those blacks?"

He doesn't give any names, but claims to be negotiating with the second-in-command of the Black Muslims. They share the same goals: the radical separation of blacks and whites, no "racial mixing."

Intolerance is an essential part of radicalism; tolerance is interpreted as weakness. Therefore it isn't very surprising that right-wing radicals should support the most intolerant and brutal of any stripe. Le Pen, in France, joined the German neo-Nazis in supporting the dictator Saddam Hussein. Other "models" are such bloody figures as Pol Pot and Ceausescu, as well as Libya's Muammar al-Qaddafi. Küssel, then, will cooperate with people whom he otherwise views as "racially inferior." Politics does make strange bedfellows.

"Speaking of Africa, the black population's anti-Semitism is growing noticeably. . . ." With this he launches into the thoroughly familiar theory of "an international finance conspiracy." I sometimes have trouble seeing his eyes through the glare on his eyeglasses. Nevertheless, he studies me with a rather mocking gaze. When he stops to think, he sometimes lifts up his head and puffs out his cheeks; when he's finished thinking, the trapped air rushes out with a light *phhf*. He shakes his head disparagingly when he regards a question as inappropriate.

"The Negroes," he finally concludes, "are gradually figuring out that these guys' noses are more crooked than normal, and that they've got a homeland in Israel."

"Oh," I say wearily, "the Jews."

"Naturally," he responds cheerfully. "The Jews, of course!"

When I ask if he knows any Jews, Küssel looks at me with compassion. Since he lives in Vienna, he explains, it's normal to know a Jew or two. He is unable, however, to cite a single bad experience he's had with a Jew. And since I've constantly heard the expressions "kike" and "Jew scum," I ask whether his hatred is based on something beyond the personal.

"I am an anti-Semite," Küssel says, as if this were entirely reasonable. His nostrils twitch as he awaits my reaction.

It looks funny, and I become incautious. "What would you say if I told you I was a Jew?"

Küssel's eyes narrow for a moment. I realize too late that my question was foolish. He answers instantly and archly: "With your permission—Küssel," he says, then leans his head to the side condescendingly and waits for me to introduce myself in return. "One normally introduces oneself before a conversation," he adds.

So my correct response, as a Jew, would be: "Good day. My name is Schmidt, Jew." But I am not Jewish, and I hasten to tell him so. I have since asked myself why. Cowardice? Insufficient moral courage? Simple fear? Presumably a little of each.

Küssel has now become suspicious, and sizes me up as if he can tell from my nose or ears whether or not I am a Jew.

I prefer to shift the conversation back to his contacts in Africa. When I ask what kind of blacks work together with neo-Nazis, he says, "They are representatives of national political organizations, and they are on track to . . ." He has come to a standstill. He thinks for a painfully long time, and then adds: "I can't say right now, I can't tell you the name. . . . He's a world-famous freedom fighter." Anticipating my next question, he says, "It's not Mandela."

Hours go by. It's getting late, and the majority are already drunk. It's then that I notice that the cassette is missing from my tape recorder. By now I've also had my share of beer, and so I grow bold. I take Gerald Hess to the side and complain about the missing tape.

He promises immediate clarification, and within two minutes Berthold Dinter, a former SS man, stands up and begins to speak. It occurs to me that he helped organize the Wunsiedel march. He now makes it known that the journalist Schmidt has had a tape stolen. Herr Schmidt was invited here and deserves to be treated as a guest. Furthermore, Herr Schmidt is a decent fellow, *almost a comrade,* who has eaten and drunk with the rest of us—he did not sing with us, that much is true, but that may certainly come later—and one does not steal from a comrade! Yes, it is a case of "robbing a comrade, and in my day the case was completely clear: if you steal from a comrade, you should be hanged!"

Well, I think. This is getting pretty interesting. Still, it would be enough for me if someone just discreetly gave me back the cassette. I look around the room trying to guess who the thief might be. Certainly not any of the four Dutchmen to my right; they didn't even notice that I was making a recording. Next to them sits a group of men in SA uniforms, but earlier on they had been completely open with me, though it's true they're now stone drunk. To their left is a table of Hitler Youth imitators; it could be one of them, but why? I look to my left, where I was sitting earlier. Küssel's table is deserted except for the empty tape recorder, which sits reproachfully in the middle of the table. Küssel and his companions have moved to the other corner, from where they observe the course of events with interest. He agrees that the theft was "not good." The two skinheads at my table don't voice their opinion.

It would be best to forget the whole affair, I think, rather than risk bad feelings. But it doesn't work out that way. Peter Ziehl, nicknamed "Pit," stands up. He's already mighty drunk, as are most of the others. They look annoyed as they listen with glassy eyes. What does the damn democrap here want, anyway? Pit stokes this change of mood. "You say this journalist here is our guest? Fine! But . . . around here you have to behave. The journalist is making a film. That's fine too. But . . . did he ask any one of us what we thought about it? Next he records everything. And now he's missing a tape. Well, that's not good. But it's also not the end of the world. And someone just said—he's a comrade. But a comrade doesn't bitch like that!"

My stomach is cramping up.

Pit has come to his conclusion. "He's no comrade. He's just trying to make trouble among us. And the man who does that should be hanged!"

Then everything happens in slow motion. A few look at me with hate in their eyes, while others go on talking as if nothing had happened. My temples are throbbing, and slowly I slide my hand into my jacket pocket, hoping to find my car keys. Suddenly I realize all the mistakes I've made. The car is parked in the wrong place. I'm sitting too far away from the door. I'm alone, not a soul knows where I am. There's no trace of Gerald Hess. Meanwhile, Pit lights himself a new cigar and awaits the effect of his appeal. Would I even make it to the car? Should I pretend I'm just stepping out for something, or is it better to run away as fast as I can?

I'd never go there alone, my lawyer had said. *Don't drink too much!* Graeme had warned. But no one had prepared me for this.

It becomes quiet, and I realize that everyone is staring at me. I must say something, immediately. And it has to be perfect.

"Well," I begin, "there are a couple things I'd like to say about this. . . ." Sweat is breaking out all over me. I'm almost angry over losing control of the situation. What can happen to me? They certainly won't hang me. Or will they? Too many witnesses. And not because of a cassette. All right, then. But I could easily end up in the hospital if I don't think of something fast. *Don't be intellectual!* Graeme had said.

At least that wasn't hard. "I came here all alone, and if I really wanted to make trouble, I'd certainly go about it differently. But seriously . . ." *Shit,* I think, am I trying to tell a joke? The two skins at my table show no reaction. It's amazing how indifferent people can seem, or maybe I'm not seeing it right.

Maybe, I think, they'll react if I bring "honor" into it. "I came here alone because I had the impression that you could be trusted! And I would be very disappointed if it turned out now that your enemies were right"—disappointed! that's a good one!—"and you are not men who can be trusted."

Now a few are nodding thoughtfully, and suddenly Gerald Hess appears. He announces that we'll work all this out among ourselves, and then takes me outside into the corridor. He'll do his best, he promises, if only to uphold the reputation of himself and his comrades—"if that's still possible." Waiting by the door, I realize I've left my camera inside, along with all the tapes; and if that gets stolen, this whole expedition was a waste.

After a few unbearable minutes, Gerald comes back and shows me an audiocassette. "Could this be your tape?" When I nod, he looks relieved and presses it into my hand. "But I can't tell you who stole it."

"Oh, God," I say, "I don't even want to know." It's obvious that it could only have been Küssel, who didn't want his songs immortalized after all.

> A Jew stands in the woods,
> all quiet and still,
> then comes a German tank
> and runs him into the hill. . . .

These lyrics, sung to the melody of a children's song, were perhaps the high point of his performance.

"I knew immediately who it was," Hess says. "But I'm *not* going to tell you, all right? He had his reasons, and I just stole the tape back from him."

Gerald has another surprise for me: he has arranged for me to spend the night in the inn. The whole group is sleeping there, and after a glance at the clock—it's two o'clock in the morning—I thankfully accept his offer. The only catch is, I do not get my own room. I'll have to share quarters with Gerald and another comrade. Actually, that's all right. This way we'll be able to talk a little longer. So we drink one last beer and then go upstairs, where our roommate is already snoring loudly. A shiver runs through me when I realize that this third man is Pit. After I've recovered from the shock, I think for a moment—it's too late to turn back. There's nothing to be done but stow my gear in the closet and lie down on the bed. Gerald has two more bottles of beer, and as we toast each other, I have, for the first time, the feeling that I have found someone in these ranks whose entire life does not revolve around *Nation und Führer*.

Sleep is out of the question, since Pit could wake up anytime. It's four o'clock, my shoes are on, and we're still talking. For two hours

Gerald and I play a game of question-and-answer; we are both opponents and partners. He wants to know more about me, just as I want to know more about him. We're both acutely conscious of the position we find ourselves in: neither can say very much because, as we both know, anyone who isn't a friend is an enemy. But we both look for points of contact, shared values. So when Gerald asks me about my other work, I lie to him; he must not find out that this is my first journalistic experience. I babble something about stories on animal experimentation, and he's satisfied with that.

Gerald is twenty. Like his father, he works as a roofer. At twelve he was already in the Viking Youth, a rightist organization that leads children and teenagers, boy-scout style, onto the neo-Nazi path. Since it involves minors, this group is kept strictly out of public sight. He has been a follower of Kühnen for two years and, because he's industrious and reliable, he is already the *Bereichsleiter* in the state of Hessen.

Why is he a neo-Nazi? What attracts him? Is it habit, indoctrination, predisposition? I know that Gerald has been in a lot of fights, though he won't admit to liking violence. By way of evasion, he offers the stock slogans of nationalism and fascism—"Be obedient, be brave . . . Believe, obey, and fight"—but soon realizes that jargon won't work at this hour. It was, in any case, only a half-hearted attempt.

"Why," I ask, "do you have so much hate inside you?"

"What do you mean by *hate?*"

"You were singing earlier that Jews and blacks weren't people, that you've got to smash them up . . ."

"But that was just a joke!"

The regular snoring coming from Pit's bed has a calming effect.

"But you wouldn't make that joke if you accepted Jews and blacks as human beings."

"That's not what it's about."

"No, that's exactly what it's about!"

Gerald is silent, and for a moment I'm afraid that I've gone too far. But that's not the case. Emotions long repressed burst out of him. He is suddenly furious and wants me to understand him. "No one accepts us, no one!"

He is continually faced with repression, Gerald tells me. He's a sociable guy, and so he looked for friends and camaraderie. The Viking Youth offered him that. Of course, it also familiarized him with the "enemy": communists, and, even worse, democrats. He learned that he was not free. The "democraps" supposedly oppressed everyone who thought differently, especially those who loved their people—the "Nationals." "We're not even allowed to express our opinions!"

I don't understand. "How's that?"

"If, for example, I'm of the opinion that there weren't any gas chambers at Auschwitz, I'm not allowed to say it in public. I'd be punished for it."

I sip my beer. I need to be careful about what I say, but I have to say something. "And that's how it should be. Because simply by saying that, you inflict new, deep pain on the Holocaust survivors. Think about it: it's more than an insult. It's like if someone said to you, 'Your parents, they didn't exist, you're the offspring of a lie.' "

"But there *was* no Holocaust, that's all just propaganda." Gerald answers quickly and certainly, as if rehearsed. I notice that he has his doubts, but he will not admit to them. He wants to believe there never were any gas chambers. (Only much later will I learn why he and his comrades cling so bitterly to their denial of the Holocaust.)

I now understand that he's caught in a vicious circle: once a Nazi, always a Nazi. Not because it's so wonderful, but because you can't simply step out of the spiral of violence and hatred and repression. Prohibitions can be tempting. Arrests follow, then hearings, then frustration, violence, more arrests, more frustration, more violence. The battle lines and enemies are fixed and clear: the leftists, of course; the police; the state security forces; and the Verfassungs-schutz (the internal intelligence service), known in Nazi slang as the *"Schmutz"* (dirt)—the enforcers of the detested democracy, which supposedly gives the leftists more breathing room than the rightists. Gerald will not admit that, in reality, the exact opposite is true. He feels abused, ostracized, and misunderstood.

Gerald is fascinated when I tell him about my favorite film, Luis Buñel's *L'Age d'or*. He doesn't know that soon after the film's premiere in the thirties, right-wing radicals ransacked the movie theater, and I don't tell him. But from my description Gerald immediately recognizes the movie's anarchic and anticlerical traits; he especially likes the scene in which Catholic priests "pray until they are skeletons."

Suddenly, he deduces from my love of this surrealist movie that I must *also* be opposed to the state. And he wants me to admit it. When I remain silent, he provides an explanation: "You can't admit it, of course. But you think a little bit like we do. If that's your favorite movie, you must think a little bit like we do!"

When I don't answer, he leans back. After a moment, I say, "I want to know what you people are really like. I think National Socialism is nonsense, and I'm afraid that you're dangerous. But you can convince me otherwise about that if I'm wrong."

Now Gerald is uncertain. On the one hand, he naturally wants people to fear him and his men. But on the other hand, everyone needs a little sympathy. "You know," he admits, "there aren't many reporters that speak with us like you do. There also aren't many who take as much time as you do."

Pit, who briefly had been quiet, now starts snoring again full tilt. Gerald stares at me, his eyes growing bigger and bigger, almost as if he wants to hypnotize me. With a calm, inquiring tone he asks, "Why are you doing it?"

In the future he will ask me this a lot. And he will always get the same answer: "Because it interests me. I believe it's important to find out who and what you really are."

His gaze now seems to bore right through me, and he doesn't expect an answer to his next question. "You're pretty damned curious, aren't you?"

From this point on, Gerald Hess will be, along with Kühnen, my most important contact in the movement. I visit him frequently, and our long conversations reveal he isn't as rigid in his worldview as he seems. He detests violence, viewing it as an expression of helplessness, and wishes that all men could live in peace with one another. He is really an idealist who makes horrible concessions to his environment. At some point I get the idea of trying to pull him out of it. The idea is not "to turn him around," but simply to help him put his respect for humanity into practice and get out of the scene.

My attempts will not succeed. Gerald Hess will not survive the next year.

III

"Before Us Lies Germany"

The former grounds of the great Nazi rallies, the Luitpoldhain in Nuremberg, are nowadays a popular excursion site for families. The parklike environment is spacious, and there is a small lake, and playgrounds, and promenades. A locale heavy with history, and with edifices—of which the city is no longer proud, and which many would rather hide. But the colossal stone grandstand with towers on the side and a sort of mega-balcony in the middle is simply too big. The gigantic relics of power decay slowly. They were, after all, "built for a thousand years."

But if you know your way around, you can even find a memorial and an informational display beneath the motto: NEVER AGAIN FAS-CISM, NEVER AGAIN WAR. In front of the giant grandstand is a marching ground the size of several football fields. A half-century ago, Hitler celebrated the climax of the Nazi Party's annual rallies here. Today it is quiet. All the same, given the overpowering proportions of the place, it isn't difficult to imagine the roars of masses of people crying "Heil!" when the Führer appeared. This very sound comes out of the loudspeakers of the video display set up in a small hall at the back of the grandstand. It is part of the memorial, with the exhibition "Fascination and Violence." The educational video runs nonstop, all day long. Over and over, Hitler's voice, bomb explosions and sirens, cheering masses and marching music fill the room, vibrating back off the high walls with an eerie echo. In between these bursts of sound, the hall is so quiet that visitors' footsteps sound harsh in the room. In a whisper, a father explains the meaning of the pictures to his small son. Others watch the video for a while before proceeding through the rest of the exhibit.

A government employee is present to answer questions, and to maintain the memorial's silence and dignity. He reaches for the telephone instantly when he notices the new group of visitors. They stand in a perfect semicircle in front of the video screen and watch with interest. He dials for the police and whispers hurriedly into the phone.

"Victory for Germany . . ." Hitler booms.

"Then I know: you are joining the ranks! And we know: before us lies Germany, in us marches Germany, and behind us comes Germany . . ."

These last words are not coming only from the loudspeakers, because some of the neo-Nazi spectators recite them along with the Führer. These young people know the words of their idol by heart. For those who still don't quite understand the significance of their paramilitary outfits, what happens next comes through loud and clear. The song in the documentary, now played to warn and to educate, sticks in your mind insidiously.

> We walk into the future, man for man.
> We march for Hitler through dark and danger . . .

Not two lines are sung before the young men join in. The father takes his young son by the hand and hurries out of the room, but even outside, the song echoes after them:

> . . . with the flag of youth for freedom and bread.
> Our flag floats in front of us,
> our flag is the new age.
> Our flag will lead us to the end of time.
> Yes, our flag is greater than death.

The police arrive ten minutes later. The report, which I later examine, reads in part as follows:

> On 8/20/89, at 3:45 P.M., the police station Nurem-
> berg-South was notified. The garrison at Pegnitz 12/15
> apprehended the group of people behind the stone grand-
> stand. The individuals were detained for purpose of iden-
> tification and held until identity was firmly established.
> The individuals were of German, Austrian, and Dutch na-
> tionality. Since the witnesses could identify neither those
> individuals who displayed the "Hitler-salute" nor the
> ringleaders, the individuals were released, between 4:45
> and 5:20 P.M. The detained individuals included . . .
> Schmidt, Michael. . . ."

I'd never been arrested before, and it's a strange feeling to suddenly become a suspect. The police begin by searching for weapons. And I somehow must have done something wrong, because after I identify myself as a journalist, I'm the first to be frisked. Küssel and his men enjoy that immensely. The police examine my identification and conclude: "You are Herr Schmidt. . . . So what are you doing here?"

The neo-Nazis are not impressed by the detention. First of all, they're used to this sort of thing; and second, they know that nothing generally comes of it. And if an arrest actually does lead to a trial, or even to a conviction, they can usually count on the same lenience that—traditionally, one might say—the former Nazi crimi-nals enjoyed. It is sad to discover, after intensive research, that few judgments against right-wing extremists approach the severity of the sentences received by leftists. The exception is Michael Kühnen, who served relatively long prison terms for his illegal propaganda activities. But for most judges, it seems, the Weimar era—when this "paralysis on the right side" was already a trademark of the courts—serves more as a model than as a warning.

One could at least expect that now, after the Rostock riots of 1992, the judges would follow the politicians' declarations and "finally strike with a strong hand." But the old practice continues, and right-wing offenders are continually afforded the benefit of such extenuating circumstances as drunkenness or youth. Also, they are generally charged and sentenced as "isolated perpetrators," regardless of their connections to neo-Nazi organizations. Yet it is precisely these connections that are the source of the terror. In any case, for them it is always an honor to come into conflict with the law. After all, Adolf Hitler was once in jail, and it was there that he quietly dictated the story of "his struggle" to his secretary, Rudolf Hess.

Consequently, it isn't surprising that the neo-Nazis no longer hide. Unlike this rather casual incident in Nuremberg, most public appearances are carefully arranged demonstrations from which, it is hoped, followers will draw strength and inspiration. These are the actions—when shown on television, usually together with reports on firebombings and the desecration of graves—from which the organizers expect their best propaganda successes. These hopes are even in part justified, although the sight of uniforms and speakers from the radical right does not, by a long shot, instantly transform the viewers into comrades-in-arms, as some television editors obviously fear.

And then there are the events at which journalists are not so welcome. Meetings at which no value is placed on propaganda effects and where participants act nervous if anybody looks like "press." Meetings where, at the first sign of a camera, the respectable-looking gentlemen with graying temples instantly unfold newspapers in front of their faces. Within weeks of the incident at Nuremberg, I would witness exactly that.

The Black Stallion Restaurant, in a village near Fulda, in North Hesse, looks as if it were designed for such a meeting. The central location makes it easy to find, the village is big enough that the participants' cars aren't conspicuous, and small enough that any unwanted visitors can be spotted. There is a spacious hall next to the small dining room. The food is tasty and inexpensive. The proprietor has nothing against this assembly on his premises. "After all," he says while pouring a beer, "they're going to meet somewhere."

They belong to almost every neo-Nazi splinter group, and they have found their way here today to hold a private assembly. Kühnen is here, and Wolfgang Hess in jackboots and Nazi belt buckle. Thomas Hainke has come with Christa Goerth. Berthold Dinter is already talking spiritedly with a respectable-looking man in a dark suit, and Christian Worch shows up with his intimate friend Thomas Wulff, nicknamed "Steiner" (Stony).

Many others, about sixty of them, are completely unknown to me, even though I've been researching the scene intensively for over a year now.

You could really call this a meeting of big shots, since, as I discover, leading activists from the entire extreme-right spectrum are present. The invitations were issued by the HNG, one of the most important neo-Nazi organizations. Christa Goerth, who had accompanied Kühnen when we first met, is on the executive committee of this body, which is, on its surface, a legitimate association with a large roster of registered members. But its membership lists can be quite misleading, because, as the HNG is an umbrella organization that includes a variety of rival, and even enemy, groups, it is uniquely able to provide them with a neutral ground (usually secret) on which to meet. Here they can agree upon concerted actions and strategies in the spirit of common cause. Officially, however, the HNG concerns itself with aiding "political prisoners," to whom letters are written and visits paid to demonstrate solidarity and loyalty, and not least of all, to keep them supplied with the latest propaganda material.

For the neo-Nazis, it seems to be an honor to serve a prison term as part of "the battle for the reestablishment of National Socialism." In this regard, I recall that at Kühnen's trial, the presence of his girlfriend Lisa's brother had such a soothing influence on him. "After the revolution, a record as a political prisoner will look very good. . . ." The old folks will remember: the lower the NSDAP membership number, the greater the Nazi. Likewise today, the earlier the prison sentences, the higher the honor.

In addition to its members and contacts throughout the right-wing, the HNG also has, as Kühnen later tells me, important international connections. There are sister organizations in the United States, France, and Belgium,* and HNG contact people can also arrange foreign and domestic financial support for individual "actions." German and French members of the secret organization KKK (Ku Klux Klan) are supported in prison, as are confirmed terrorists from the right-wing underground.

I'm genuinely curious about what I'll hear at this meeting. More than anything, I am astonished at how many positively respectable-looking elderly ladies and gentlemen arrive, one after the other. What's more, they seem to get along wonderfully with the brutal-looking skinheads in combat boots.

While my cameraman sets up his equipment, I step into the room. Though Christa Goerth has invited me, I'm scarcely inside when an elderly man plants himself in front of me. "You are the gentleman from the press?" he asks, several gold teeth gleaming.

"Yes," I answer, unsuspecting.

"Out."

He is so unambiguous that I obey without delay or protest. Then my cameraman tells me about an alarming conversation at the next table: evidently, one of those old guys offered a skinhead 250 marks to "neutralize the camera and crew." We therefore retreat outside, where we can at least copy license plates. In case anything happens,

---

*United States: COFPAC (Committee for Free Patriots and Anticommunist Political Prisoners). France: COBRA (Comité Objectif Entraide et Solidarité avec les Victimes de la Répression Antinationaliste). Belgium: HNG (Hulpkomitee voor Nationalistische politieke Gevangenen)

we would have some idea as to who was involved. Fortunately, nothing of the sort happens.

For Christa Goerth it's all "very embarrassing." Her explanation—"It just so happens that there are people here who have had some very bad experiences with the press"—is the same, word for word, as what Christian Worch and others tell me. It sounds rehearsed, and I don't believe a word of it. I do succeed, however, in steering Michael Kühnen into our car for the ride back. I was already thinking that the day was a waste, but Kühnen is talkative and excited. He just reached an agreement with one of his archrivals, so from now on their groups will work together. During the two-hour drive, I learn a few other things, some of which contradict earlier assertions that it is a purely political battle being fought.

It has gotten dark. The cameraman is driving and Kühnen is sitting next to him; from the backseat, I have a good, constant view of Kühnen's profile. Kühnen enjoys being driven. He is relaxed and smokes his beloved menthol cigarettes while he talks. I can even bring up the subject of weapons.

"Officially, we don't have any weapons hidden away. But at the same time, you can count on every responsible comrade having a hideout where there are certainly also weapons."

"But what are the weapons supposed to be for?" I ask, as innocently as possible.

"And to think, you're normally such a clever little bastard. You should be able to figure out that we're no backyard gardening society. But at the moment there's certainly no need, since everything's going so astonishingly well for our cause. On the contrary, I've even instructed the comrades for the moment not to carry around guns or anything like that."

This frank admission gives me the courage to ask about a subject heretofore unmentioned. "And the money?" I say casually.

"What do you mean? For the weapons or—?"

"No, in general."

Kühnen becomes hesitant, but finally admits that finances are a "complicated chapter." That much I believe, since Kühnen is always happy to be taken out for a meal. For everyday affairs, he says, his organization is dependent on members' contributions and donations. He also explains that some people traffic in drugs, mostly with connections in South America. This is a flagrant contradiction of the official line on drugs, but it doesn't trouble Kühnen: "If the junkies want to shoot up until they die, we don't stop them. And if it helps the cause, I don't care where the money comes from."

Then there are also wealthy comrades who can occasionally effect larger purchases. Christian Worch, for example, is the scion of a wealthy family. Funds also flow in from the NSDAP-AO in the United States, and from other groups—but, Kühnen explains, "they only give when they're convinced their money will be utilized effectively."

"What sort of groups are they," I ask.

"I can't tell you."

"ODESSA? South America?" I ask Kühnen almost matter-of-factly.

After the Second World War, many SS men escaped arrest and trial with the support of the Vatican and the International Red Cross, as well as the American military secret service, the CIC (Counter Intelligence Corps). Few left without the necessary traveling money. The escape routes went through Austria, Italy, and Switzerland to South America and the Middle East, but also to Spain and Scandinavia. Because these routes were created with the help of high officials in the Catholic Church, the war criminals themselves called it the "Vatican line." The American espionage community, which took advantage of the SS and Gestapo officers' useful knowledge while protecting them from arrest, had another name for it: the "rat line." For their own part, the SS men who had thus achieved security founded a relief agency variously called "Spider" or ODESSA (Organisation der ehemaligen SS-Angehörigen—Organization of Former SS Members), which became widely known through Frederick Forsyth's novel *The ODESSA Files.*

"Spider," as Graeme Atkinson had explained to me, also developed an organization within Germany: the HIAG (Hilfsgemeinschaft auf Gegenseitigkeit—Mutual Aid Society), a group we will come to later. In any case, rumors and myths surround this secret society, though most neo-Nazis simply deny its existence.

Kühnen just shakes his head. "I really can't tell you," he says, almost apologetic. But after a short pause he continues: "ODESSA doesn't exist any more. But . . ."

I decide to try to help him. "But of course there's still money there . . ."

"Mmm, but we don't have much influence on its distribution. There are certainly people around who came out of precisely those ranks. But even *if* we do get any money from them, it's only for specific, isolated actions, and they expect results."

"What kind of money?"

"For example, for large-scale poster and pamphlet distribution, you could say around ten to fifteen thousand marks. It's never more than forty thousand marks."

"And for weapons?"

Kühnen turns to look at me. He has just confirmed the existence of a successor to the legendary ODESSA, and that it occasionally funds the neo-Nazis. Obviously, drug dealing and weapons purchases conform to the picture of his movement that he would like to present. Changing the subject somewhat, he tells me that my work is important. I ask him why.

"Your footage will be worth a fortune after the seizure of power. No one has filmed us as much as you have, and documentary material from our time in opposition will be much in demand," Kühnen says jokingly.

I laugh, never having viewed the matter in quite that light. Kühnen knows that the chances of that happening aren't the best. He becomes solemn. "But your film could also become more valuable in another way. Who knows? But it's certainly possible that in a few years some of the people you're filming now won't be so easy to film."

"Why?" I ask, confused.

"Perhaps they'll be hunted as terrorists and have gone underground," he says. After a brief pause he adds: "Hmm. It's certainly conceivable. But thankfully things haven't gotten that bad yet."

Naturally I'm curious as to which of his "comrades" Kühnen sees as potential terrorists, but he won't say a word. He realizes that he's already said too much and tries to change the subject.

Then he says, almost mockingly, "It's lucky you're just making a movie. If you were writing a book, I'd already be having second thoughts. You could be dangerous: bit by bit, you're learning a whole lot about us. Maybe too much."

IV

SOMETHING NEW IN
THE EAST?

"THUS THE MOVEMENT IS ANTIPARLIAMENTARY. EVEN its participation in a parliamentary institution can have only the purpose of perpetrating its destruction, of eliminating an institution in which we observe one of the severest symptoms of mankind's decline." So wrote Adolf Hitler in *Mein Kampf*. And of course, that is precisely what happened.

After the Nazi dictatorship's collapse, the Federal Republic of Germany created a Constitution that, supposedly, would make a repetition of that reign of terror forever impossible. Yet in such a task it is easy to fail: one article of that document, the only one that really interests the neo-Nazis, offers them a parliamentary loophole. Article 146 was originally written with reunification in mind, but it's possible to interpret it differently: "This basic law shall lose validity on that day when a constitution freely chosen by the German people enters into force."

January 1990. About a hundred extremists are gathering in a back-alley bar outside of Bonn. Getting in, however, is like opening a succession of locks. We meet first at a rest stop on the Autobahn, where we receive directions to the next rendezvous. With this procedure it can take hours before the gathering is complete, but the organizers can be relatively certain of shaking off, or at least wearing out, undesired pursuers. Christian Worch is an expert in this tactic (after all, his model is Reinhard Heydrich). At these events, Worch gives instructions written in a precise, military style, complete with site plan and area map.

The occasion for this spectacle of conspiracy is the convention of the Deutsche Alternative, a "national protest party" founded in May of 1989 as an advance organization of the NSDAP-AO. As Kühnen explains it to me, its goal is the legal seizure of power, and then the elimination of the basic law by way of Article 146. So long as the NSDAP is banned as a party, it will remain an illegal underground organization, the NSDAP-AO (based, as noted earlier, in Lincoln, Nebraska). The AO, as it's called for short, is divided into a system of cells, which means that most members do not know one another. Communication with the "Central" in Lincoln is also handled, as in a secret society, with code numbers and cover names. Very important contacts even have access to "clean" addresses— that is, addresses the police don't know are pertinent. All of this makes infiltration and surveillance by the authorities difficult at best, and usually impossible.

Since both the NSDAP and the AO are banned in Germany, advance organizations are required in order to reconstruct the party. Their only purpose is to get around the ban. When one of these advance organizations is also banned, the members just switch to another, usually founded on the eve of the latest new ban. These organizations include the FAP (Freiheitliche Arbeiterpartei—Free Workers' Party), DA (Deutsche Alternative—German Alternative), NL (Nationale Liste—National List), and many others. When, for example, the ANS (Aktionsfront Nationaler Sozialisten—National Socialist Action Front) was banned, the same activists later reformed as the NS (Nationale Sammlung—National Union), which was subsequently also banned.

At that point, the DA took over and became especially active in what formerly had been East Germany. Later, in December of 1992, the DA is also banned—but it really doesn't matter. Even if all parties are outlawed, another level exists that for lack of official membership cannot be forbidden. This group has the lapidary name

Gesinnungsgemeinschaft der Neuen Front (Community of Partisans of the New Front—GdNF) and is a "community of convinced and professed National Socialists whose aim is the repeal of the ban on Nazis and the refounding of the NSDAP as a legal party," according to its self-description in the underground paper *Die Neue Front* (The New Front).

Many political analysts tend to focus on the differences between the individual groups, and the confusion this creates is precisely the organizers' intention. And at the same time, this exercise can lead to judicial hairsplitting, which at trials can tip the balance toward acquittal. But if you are unwilling to be fooled, plain logic is sufficient: the Nazis' core organization is and remains the NSDAP, and all the other front organizations—whether the AO, NS, NL, NO, or FAP—exist only because the NSDAP is illegal. Through them, the Nazis can carry on legally and the "democratic" road to power remains open to them. Banning such organizations doesn't have any effect; work is temporarily slowed, but the personnel doesn't change one bit. For example, there is an advance organization called Initiative Volkswille (Initiative: People's Will) with a single member, who happens to be Michael Kühnen.

Most of those present today belong to one or another of these organizations. One of the older men in particular catches my attention. Sitting two tables away and talking excitedly with his youthful neighbors, he is an extraordinarily repulsive figure, with giant, jughandle ears and thick glasses that magnify his blue eyes. His thick hair is cut very short, and his mustache is also sharply trimmed; on his chin is a strip of beard, almost "musketeer-style," but wider. He is slim and his dress is refined, clearly expensive. I move in order to see him better, and watch him through the heads of the others. Like a secret agent, he looks around continually; when our gazes meet, I look away and sense that now he is also examining me. My tablemate doesn't know who he is, so I ask Kühnen, who tells me he's a comrade from the Netherlands, a man named Et Wolsink.

Wolsink! I'd heard quite a lot about this Dutchman from my colleague Graeme Atkinson, who never neglected to include this

piece of advice: "If you ever meet him, be careful. He's bad news."
Graeme had written several articles about Wolsink for *Searchlight*.
For all that, no one had ever succeeded in interviewing or filming
him. Without expecting it, I might succeed in doing so. Kühnen
makes the necessary arrangements. Trying to be as inconspicuous as
possible, I fiddle with the tape recorder as if it were the most natural
thing in the world. I move to a seat farther to the front.

Heinz Reisz, whom I've known for a while, is standing there,
easy enough to recognize with his gray hair, thick walrus mustache,
and broad shoulders. He is from Langen, and his main job is to brief
journalists; in fact, most interviews with Michael Kühnen take place
in Reisz's apartment. In private he is friendly and even has a sense
of humor. He sees the microphone in my hand and winks. Perfect.
The recordings have now been officially approved, and it's highly
unlikely that anyone will give me any trouble. As always, Reisz's
speech is vigorous. Indeed, he is a parody of a Nazi speaker, what
a schoolboy would imagine Nazi speakers to be: loud, aggressive,
bellowing.

"Friends, I want to make this brief. You can march separately,
but you must strike as one. . . ." He even quotes Bismarck:
" 'The prerequisite for any national politics is the courage to see the
truth.' And the truth is: we are one nation, we remain one
nation and . . ."

The rest of his sentence is lost in the applause and cheers of the
hundred or so supporters. Reisz winks roguishly at his comrades,
and suddenly there erupts a rhythmic *Sieg Heil! Sieg Heil! Sieg Heil!
Sieg Heil!* The skinheads scream like a machine gone mad, and with
so much emphasis on the *"Sieg"* that it sounds completely different
from the well-known, choral *"Heil"* chanted by the masses of the
Third Reich.

Heinz Reisz's speech contains nothing new. It's as if he copied
it out of a dictionary of nationalist oratory. But he makes up for
this with the vigor of his presentation. As he speaks, the mood in-
tensifies:

"Who among us has not yet sat in jail, who has never had to pay
his dues to world Jewry? Who has not yet endured the terror of
persecution?"

The skinheads nod enthusiastically; then Reisz gives them strength:

"All of that shall not shake us. We answer with a single sentence: Many enemies, much honor!"

Now Wolsink has stood up. While Reisz accepts the applause by making the Hitler-salute, Wolsink comes to the front.

"For our comrade from the Netherlands, a threefold 'Sieg . . . Heil! . . . Sieg Heil! Sieg Heil!' "

I would never have believed that a hundred people could be so loud. The organizers were wise to choose such a remote spot for this event.

Wolsink speaks in a thin, feminine voice. "Dear comrades, after the storm that my comrade Heinz Reisz has unleashed here, my words are merely those of a poor speaker. . . ."

He's got that right. Wolsink has a marked Dutch accent and frequently jumbles his words. One nevertheless senses that this man is a true believer. Graeme has told me that he had been an officer in the SS. But now, standing about five yards away from me, Wolsink seems to me to be too young for that. I guess his age at sixty-five, at most, which means that in 1941 he was only fifteen, too young to serve in the SS. I learn later that he volunteered for the SS at the age of sixteen, using a forged birth certificate.

I make sure that my tape recorder keeps working while Wolsink speaks. He refers to a series of house searches that the Dutch police undertook recently. They discovered weapons and propaganda material and made several arrests. "You know roughly what we went through—it was nothing important!"

This is very much his style, but is this understatement or does he really consider it unimportant? Wolsink describes the event with a cynical smile.

"Well, I can give you the details. We didn't suffer too badly. They ransacked our houses, they stuck us in a cold cell for seven days, and yet they got very little out of it. A whole lot of noise for nothing . . . The Gau Netherlands within the completely Zionized Netherlands, our ANS Netherlands, remains standing, remains with Michael Kühnen . . ."

That gets a round of applause. So, Wolsink belongs to the ANS.

The National Socialist Action Front (ANS) was banned in Germany, but in Holland the NSDAP-AO continues to be represented under this name. Wolsink has to pause, waiting for the euphoric howl of "Küh-nen, Küh-nen, Küh-nen" to run its course before he can go on.

"It is with the greatest satisfaction that I hear that the German Alternative is now blossoming more than we ever expected, perhaps more than we in the Netherlands can ever do, save through a revolution! But we, too, will go home this evening or tomorrow morning with renewed strength and we will swear it: we will stay true to the chief, up to the end! *Heil Hitler!*"

Wolsink now gives the Hitler-salute as the boys again bellow their aggressive *"Sieg Heil"* over and over.* His salute looks as though it's second nature. How naturally this veteran maintains the traditions of the Third Reich! I suddenly have the feeling that I'm in another world, whose existence I couldn't have guessed at just a year before. A world where Hitler is honored—in all seriousness. Where in secret, conspiratorial circles, men and women pursue a single goal: the destruction of democracy and the reestablishment of dictatorship, with all means and might. This is no Romanticism but rock-solid determination.

Then another begins to speak. It is Walter Matthaei ("Captain Walter"), a former hero of the SS and, after the war, a leader of CEDADE in Spain. (The Circulo Español de Amigos de Europa is one of the most influential neo-Nazi organizations in Europe.) This slim, almost gaunt man speaks with a Rhenish accent. His lips are strikingly large, the lower lip so curved that it looks as if he's always about to smile. Despite the many wrinkles, his face has something youthful about it. Matthaei is already very old, and sick. Despite his attempts to sound resolute, his speech is rather tedious—until, that is, he finally, and energetically, assesses the present situation:

"Here in the heart of our continent something is forming once

---

*Since the Hitler-salute, with outstretched hand, is forbidden in Germany, the neo-Nazis often get around this ban with the *Widerstandsgruss,* or "resistance salute," in which only thumb, forefinger, and middle finger are spread out, forming a *W.* This is also called the "Kühnen-salute."

again, something that throughout history has become a powerful force for order again and again. It is: the sacred, our Reich.''

Matthaei's entire body begins to shake as he reaches his conclusion:

''What we want is this mythical concept of a force for order in the heart of Europe, and that, above all else, is what urges us on. If it costs a lot of money, and even if it costs some of us pain and blood, we do not care. The Reich, that is our religion, that is what we have sworn ourselves to.''

Those sentiments go over well with the boys. To tell the truth, even I sense the power of the group, the dynamics of sworn blood brothers, and it feels sinister. A five-man delegation of skinheads from the still extant East Germany sits at the next table. They are from Dresden and this is their first Western event. They sit with a rapturous gaze, like figures in a Leni Riefenstahl movie.

As I look around, observing faces that could not be farther from the Aryan ideal, Wolsink catches my eye again and again. He looks strangely unimpressed, and I have the feeling that he doesn't like all this hot air. It is, for him, a tiresome exercise. This sense grows stronger when, after the assembly, I'm talking to Wolsink, and Pit, the roofer, joins in unexpectedly. The same Pit who wanted to hang me for sowing dissension at Wunsiedel. And now, flushed with beer and mythology in this backroom ambience, he again has a brilliant idea:

''All right, the thing I don't understand is—what exactly do we have against the Jews? I mean, they're just people.''

In a thick Hessian accent, he presents this plain and simple logic. The only unclear part is whether he's bringing this up despite or because of his obvious drunkenness.

Wolsink looks at Pit with an expression of astonished disgust mingled with amusement; his eyes, opening wide, examine the roofer through thick glasses. Wolsink abruptly interrupts him, his tone soft but biting.

''My dear''—he hesitates briefly before continuing—''. . . comrade. You are speaking the language of a liberal, of a humanist. What you are saying is humanism. But listen, and listen well: those ideas are completely wrong.''

No one fails to notice that Wolsink addresses Pit with the formal *Sie* instead of the informal *Du*, which everyone else has been using. He stares at Pit, who cannot stand up to it for long. Silenced and embarrassed, he pulls a cigar out of his jacket pocket as an awkward silence sets in.

Then Wolsink turns to me and says, "What do you want from me? I am completely uninteresting!"

I reply as innocently as I can. "You're part of the older generation, an eyewitness. And the younger ones venerate you. I think that's very interesting."

"There are many who are much more interesting than me. I am old and sick. You won't be able to get much out of me."

Is Wolsink being coy or simply cautious? I decide to go on the offensive. "But you're the liaison man for England," I say. "That's an interesting subject."

Wolsink looks at me suspiciously, his eyes growing bigger and bigger, and I get the feeling that he's just as tense as I am. Without letting me out of his sight, he now speaks in Dutch with Tonny Douma, who's sitting next to him. Tonny and I have known each for a while—since we were arrested together in Nuremberg—and I hope he's putting in a good word for me. But since I don't understand the language, I'm not really sure what's going on. Then I hear him mention the word *"Searchlight."* Wolsink is damned clever, and I must steer him away from this as quickly as possible. So I explain to him that I'm doing long-term coverage, not ordinary journalism, and that an interview with him would be very important.

Wolsink twists his mouth mockingly. "Yes," he says, "for you, perhaps. Look here, I am entirely unimportant. And about my connections with England . . ." Here he switches from German into English. "No, I won't talk about it. Do you speak English? It's so hard for me to speak German."

Good manners require me to respond in English, but I must be careful not to speak it too well. I don't want to feed his suspicion that I am somehow connected to *Searchlight*, that hated English newspaper.

Kühnen had described the "problem with *Searchlight*" to me

earlier, though he had no idea I was working with Graeme Atkinson. The leading activists (and only they are authorized to give full-length interviews) divide journalists into three types: first there are the "sensation hounds." These are especially popular when money is short, as they pay cash for information, interviews, and appearances; and because they hurry from one story to the next without bothering to do much research, they can easily be manipulated. Next come the "acquaintances." They research at length and publish reports regularly. Each is an expert in his own way and is—for tactical reasons—"neutral" or "objective," with more or less good contacts to "the scene." I was considered to belong to this category. The third type are the *Dreckschweine*—the filthy swine. These journalists refuse to censor themselves and have no interest in neutrality. For them, fascists are unacceptable; their goal is unequivocal opposition. As a result, "they don't help the propaganda one bit," and if they were to present themselves openly, their health, and perhaps even their lives, would be seriously endangered. Kühnen gave examples:

"Günther Wallraff and that Gerhard Kromschröder from *Stern*. And especially the people from *Searchlight*. They are really against us, and so for them there'll be no mercy."*

Wolsink is obviously worried that I might be a *Dreckschwein*. I start to explain how it is that I know he's the liaison man for England. Then I remember that an article about Wolsink was published in some Nazi paper, and it's possible that his connection with the British National Socialist Movement was mentioned there. That's the solution:

"I've already read plenty of interesting things about you in *Neue Front*. All I really want is to confirm what's already been published. As you know, I've been working for quite some time already on this film—about Michael Kühnen and so forth."

---

*Gerhard Kromschröder wrote for the German newsmagazine *Stern,* among others. For his reporting he often goes undercover, sometimes impersonating a neo-Nazi. On the basis of his report on a meeting of former SS members, one of the participants, Otto-Ernst Remer, was indicted and convicted for slandering the memory of the deceased.

Wolsink reflects briefly. We've been treating each other courteously, and he apparently sees no reason to be rude to a possibly friendly reporter. "Herr . . . Schmidt—I don't give interviews. But if that's what the chief wants . . . please. But I will not talk about my connections!"

What the hell. It's certainly worth a try. "What kind of connections are these, the ones you don't want to talk about?"

"I will not talk about my contacts in America and South America, and in South Africa and Australia and in England."

This is amazing! Presumably, the important thing for him is not to say *who* his connections are. However, after we find out *where* they are, we should be able to figure out the rest easily enough. But he remains coy, pretending that he's not at all important.

"You mentioned *Searchlight* before," I say, "and I've already heard a few things about it. Do you know the *Searchlight* people?"

Wolsink grimaces. "Zionists. Otherwise insignificant."

For the Nazis, of course, all those who oppose them are "Zionists." "What about that guy from the National Front," I ask Wolsink, pretending not to know that Hill was actually from the British National Party. "He was from *Searchlight,* right?"

"Hill. We could liquidate him, but he's not important enough."

For years Ray Hill was a leading activist in various neo-Nazi organizations in England. In the late seventies he changed sides and began working closely with *Searchlight.* Officially he remained an activist, and on the highest European levels, at that. As a mole, Hill supplied both the authorities and *Searchlight* with important information. Then he was let in on the plan for a bombing, right in the heart of London during the mostly black Notting Hill Carnival— something after the fashion of the 1980 explosions at the Bologna train station (eighty-five dead) and the Munich Oktoberfest (thirteen dead). The plan was aborted and Ray Hill had to flee, since only he could have been the "traitor" who told the authorities.

It wasn't only English Nazi groups that were hit by the exposures. The clandestine net throughout Europe had suddenly become visible. And to this day the Nazis do not know whether and where other moles are still working, perhaps planted by Ray Hill years ago.

Wolsink spoke of "liquidating" Hill. When I ask about it, he hurries to explain that by this he didn't mean murder. I nevertheless wonder what else it could possibly mean. In the *Lingua Tertii Imperii,* even "special treatment" means execution.

For the moment, I sense, this will have to be enough. But I arrange with Wolsink to continue this conversation later, in Amsterdam. And with Kühnen's approval, he promises to give me an on-camera interview. He hands me his visiting card with a telephone number, and we agree on the code I should use when I call—on January 13, the date of our first meeting.

February 1990. It is three months since the Wall fell, and the German Democratic Republic (the DDR—Deutsche Demokratische Republik) is on the path to democracy. A difficult path. The euphoria of new-won freedom will soon fade into depression as the unemployment rolls shoot up, when the glorious promises of reunification prove to be unfulfillable.

Michael Kühnen bases his strategy on popular discontent, recognizing the potential for protest early on. He concentrates on two issues: first, the development of cadres in the East; and second, the promotion of his Deutsche Alternative as a legitimate political party that could attract the disappointed, discontented, and disoriented.

On February 14, 1990, leading neo-Nazi activists from the East are gathering in Fechenheim, a suburb of Frankfurt. But this meeting takes place not in Frankfurt an der Oder, near the Polish border, but in Frankfurt am Main, in the West.

Interestingly, most of the participants have never seen one another before. They come from different cities throughout East Germany: Magdeburg, Halle, Dresden, Rostock, Cottbus, Frankfurt/Oder, Berlin. Up to now, cooperation between the individual groups has rarely, if ever, existed. That is about to change.

About forty young men are in the side room of a bar called the Napoleon, sitting at a long row of tables that have been pushed together. Ready to take Kühnen's instructions to heart, almost all of them are wearing green bomber jackets and combat boots. Some have carefully parted and cut their hair to Hitler Youth specifications; others are skinheads. What they have in common is an aura of brutality. The blond boy with the bad skin, for example, who continually juts his jaw forward, as if in imitation of Mussolini. And the tattoos on the neck of a skinhead at the same table leave nothing to interpretation: HASS (hate) is the clear message, its jagged S's just like SS runes.

Since this is a secret meeting, I am permitted to take only a few pictures. And when I try, about half the people present either leave the room or show me their backs. Nor do I learn much more about what's being discussed. The agenda of the "First Coordinating Meeting—East" is so secret that I have to wait outside during the negotiations. Nevertheless, I have no doubt that they will reach agreement, arrange to exchange information, and think about how to hasten the development of an underground structure. Sooner or later, I'm also certain, I'll learn about this conference, but without running the risk of appearing too nosey.

But how was it possible for such a meeting to take place so soon after the Wall came down? Why didn't the Eastern Nazis know each other before? And who made the connections? For that matter, how could it come to this in the first place—in a state that steadfastly proclaimed in its Constitution that "German militarism and Nazism have been eradicated" in its territory? Hadn't the leadership of the DDR been raving for years about its youth, who had proved themselves "worthy of the heritage of the best sons and daughters of the German people, the aspiration to freedom and justice over war and fascism"?

Hadn't Erich Honecker's wife, Margot, in her capacity as minister for education, announced during the Ninth Pedagogical Congress in East Berlin in June 1989, just five months before the Wall fell, that "the seed that our country's educators have sown, and continue to sow daily, [had] sprouted"? What kind of seed has sprouted there in the East? Or did everything spill over from the West?

I vaguely remember newspaper articles reporting anti-Semitic graffiti in East Berlin in the eighties, long before the Wall came down. Now and then I would hear about draconian punishments for skinheads, which were considered an expression of the antifascistic character of the DDR as a whole. It would take a long time for the small pieces of this mosaic to fit together, but the resulting picture wouldn't match the DDR's self-image as "antifascist bulwark" one bit.

In 1987, for the first time, the DDR leadership had to admit that militant skinheads were active within their boundaries, carrying out atrocities against those who looked or thought differently. The occasion was a brutal attack during a concert in East Berlin's Zions-kirche. This church in the borough of Prenzlauer Berg not only hosted a leftist environmental library, but was also a popular rendez-vous for East Berlin punks. On the evening of October 17, 1987, a punk concert ended abruptly when about twenty-five skins broke down the church doors with their heavy boots and stormed in, armed with chains and yelling *"Sieg Heil,"* "Jew swine," and "This sort should be gassed." They thrashed the place and seriously injured several audience members. The police knew about it far in advance, and had posted three personnel carriers and five squad cars nearby as a preventive measure. But by the time they moved in, the skins had already vanished.

For days, the East German media were dead silent about the political background of the attack, referring only to "rowdiness." The incident finally led to the first trial against skinheads in the DDR to be covered by the media. Six weeks later, four suspects, all in their early twenties, were convicted of "rowdiness" and "rioting" and given sentences of between one and two years. By DDR stan-dards this was mild punishment, and it was met with sharp criticism. The state prosecutor appealed, and upon retrial, eight months was added to their sentences.

These judgments were barely handed down when, in the same borough, the Jewish cemetery on Schönhauser Allee was defaced. (By March 1988, it would be ravaged a total of five times.) Two hundred and twenty-two gravestones were damaged, some beyond recognition. Once again the police did not intervene, even though every single window in the back of the Prenzlauer Berg police station looks out directly onto the cemetery. In the writ of indict-ment, the state prosecutor wrote, with remarkable openness, that the youths had shouted "increasingly loud fascist and anti-Semitic slogans under the influence of alcohol and mutual encouragement." And no one in the station heard a thing?

But the sentences handed down on July 5, 1988, to these perpetrators, some of them only fifteen years old, were harsh. The longest was six and a half years. For the judges, the case was clear-cut: the youths had modeled themselves on "fascist and neo-Nazi role models transmitted by Western media." Period. The DDR media reported the trial with an unprecedented comprehensiveness. But then, this was the same time that the government was negotiating with the Jewish Claims Committee over symbolic reparations payments, a necessary step to pave the way for American economic aid.

Despite the intentionally spectacular trial, however, there persisted a wide range of racist and anti-Semitic activities, including acts of violence. So it should have come as no surprise that once the Wall fell, not only were two states unified, but also two well-organized neo-Nazi movements. In Oranienburg, for over three years, a group attacked people in trains, restaurants, and on the street without disruption. In Wolgast, near Rostock, the SS-Division Walter Krüger counted respected citizens, including teachers and civil servants, among its members. In Erfurt, a girl was violently branded with a Jewish star. In Königs-Wusterhausen, skins attempted to physically force one of their victims to admit that he was Jew. In May of 1988, two Africans on a train from Riesa to Elsterswerda in the Dresden district were attacked; one of them, a man from Mozambique, was thrown from the moving train and seriously hurt. The perpetrators were merely sentenced to probation for negligence and attemped bodily injury.

Assaults on foreigners had been recorded ever since the DDR ended its "foreigner-free" phase at the end of the sixties. From 1983 on, the police knew about organized skinheads, or so-called Nazi punks. They also knew about the anti-Semitic slogans of the Berlin Stasi-Club BFC Dynamo's soccer fans. After the stiff sentences, the neo-Nazis operated more cautiously and secretively. They changed both their appearance and their strategy. A net of tiny groups sprung up across the entire DDR. Their orderly appearance, their discipline, and their will to achieve, both in the workplace and during their free time, made them welcome members of the Communist Party's youth organization, the FDJ, especially as supervisors. The supervisor's job was to ensure "a healthy atmosphere, order, and discipline wherever young people spend their time or gather for political celebrations." So says the official handbook of DDR social organizations.

To learn to ensure order, the young men trained at the paramilitary Gesellschaft für Sport und Technik (Society for Sports and Technology) or in the gyms of the Deutsches Turn- und Sportbund (German Wrestling and Sports League). There they rehearsed close combat against foreigners, punks, and leftists. While the Stasi (short for Staatssicherheit, the East German secret police) concentrated on such opposition forces as the peace movements and antifascist associations, these young "fascho-skins" maintained their own sort of order on the streets of the DDR. And as the skins terrorized punks and other maladjusted youths, they could even count on a measure of popular approval. Many factors created this fertile ground for racist and anti-Semitic activities: insufficient attempts to come to terms with the past; latent racism, exacerbated by the presence of foreign residents, particularly the contract workers from allied socialist states; and the anti-Zionist state doctrine.

The young East German Nazis were supported by their Western comrades, and not just ideologically. Couriers brought supplies like baseball bats, combat boots, and Imperial German war banners over the border without difficulty. These contacts, after the Wall fell, would provide the basis for East–West cooperation. After November of 1989, many of the neo-Nazis active in the DDR simply continued their activities without interruption. Two of the defendants in the Zionskirche trial turned up as leading members of the Nationale Alternative (NA), an East Berlin group that quickly became associated with Kühnen. In Cottbus, Eastern skinheads with similar records form the core of the local Deutsche Alternative.

Yet it is another dubious group that forms the principal link between East and West: the "political prisoners" in the DDR who were bought free by the West German government—"freed within the

framework of the . . . government's special efforts in the humanitarian sphere,'' in the jargon of the Federal Republic.

The big business of trading so-called political prisoners for de-
pendable West German cash began in 1963. Over the next twenty-
six years, the Federal Republic spent 3.5 billion marks on these
"special efforts." It bought freedom for almost 38,000 prisoners,
rejoined 2,000 children with their parents, and enabled 250,000
people to emigrate to the West. Ludwig Rehlinger, the former
under-secretary of state for intra-German affairs, casts light on this
"commerce in people" in his book *Freikauf* (Bought Free). Rehlinger is an expert on the subject, indeed, he was in charge of the
negotiations with the DDR from the start and, in 1963, worked out
the flat rate of 40,000 marks per person. "If you are serious about
morality, you sometimes have to swallow a lot," he comments on
these dealings.

Prices did not remain frozen, however. In 1977, almost 96,000
marks—more than double the original sum—had to be turned over
for each prisoner. In his discussion of the obstacles to freedom
purchases, Rehlinger lists the preferred offenses: "fleeing the republic"; "subversive activities"; "agitating against the socialist state";
"asocial behavior"; and "assemblies criticizing the system; . . . a
broad palette of all imaginable activities, which ideological regimes
all over the world view as odious, which they fear, and which they
persecute in order to retain power." Prisoner purchases were in full
swing right up to the end—1,450 in 1986, 1,840 in 1989.

It cannot be claimed that the East chose to make neo-Nazis
"available," but it is true that the résumés of many Western
neo-Nazis begin in the East. They were generally either expelled as
criminals or sold to the West. Few actually escaped. The band led
by Nuremberg neofascist Karl-Heinz Hoffmann, founder of the
eponymous military sports troop, is a catch basin for former DDR
prisoners. Ralf Rössner, Hoffmann's security chief, comes from
Sondershausen, in Thüringen. In 1971 he was sentenced to three
and a half years' imprisonment for attempting to flee the country.
He spent the last nine months of that sentence in solitary confine-
ment, until, in 1974, just after his eighteenth birthday, he was sent
off to the Federal Republic.

In the same year, the Federal Republic paid 50,000 marks to free the political prisoner Uwe Behrendt. This future colleague of Hoffmann had been condemned to twenty months' imprisonment for attempted flight. Soon after his arrival in the West, he went to Tübingen and joined the extreme-right Hochschulring Tübinger Studenten (Academic Circle of Tübingen Students). The organization was led by Axel Heinzmann, who was also bought out of a DDR prison. Through it, Behrendt made contact with Hoffmann and finally murdered—"as an individual perpetrator," according to the authorities—a Jewish publisher and his girlfriend in December 1980. The Hoffmann-related activists Uwe Mainka and Rudolf Klinger also come from the DDR. Their paths to the West remain unclear.

Arnulf Winfried Priem's story, on the other hand, is no secret. In 1968, the Federal Republic bought the twenty-year-old Priem out of a DDR prison, where he was serving time for neofascist activity. Barely arrived in the West, Priem ran as a candidate for the Baden-Würtemberg state parliament on the NPD ticket, switching in 1971 to the DVU. But party work wasn't enough for this neofascist rocker with long hair and a black head band. In 1974 he founded his Kampfgruppe Priem in Freiburg, to fight for "the reestablishment of the German Reich." Three years later he moved to Wedding, a borough of Berlin, where he became the "actions leader" in the illegal NSDAP's local committee. In his *Kampfprogramm* (Battle Program), published in 1980, he urged the "sterilization of people with hereditary diseases." After numerous probations, in 1983 he was finally sentenced to eighteen months in jail. Today, Priem is the leader of the motorcycle gang Wotans Volk (Wotan's People). Priem was Kühnen's contact man for the neo-Nazis of East and West Berlin and could be seen at nearly every demonstration in East Germany. At present he is the Berlin regional chairman of Deutsche Alternative; once that party is banned in December 1992, he will be able to switch over to other NSDAP-AO advance organizations.

Deutsche Alternative would never have achieved the importance it had before its ban without the cooperation of active DDR neo-Nazis, former DDR neo-Nazis bought free and then schooled in the

West, and Western neo-Nazis. Its chairman, the twenty-seven-year-old Frank Hübner, was imprisoned in the DDR in 1984 for "illegal contacts." He spent fourteen months in the Bautzen prison before the Federal Republic bought him free on April 3, 1985. The federal government also bought his older brother, Peter, who'd been imprisoned for founding a neo-Nazi military sports troop. The brothers then founded a "youth group" military unit in Frankfurt. Frank, who had been retrained as an office assistant, joined the DVU. Still a DVU member, Frank participates with his brother in the Nationale Sammlung in Langen, a troop that includes Heinz Reisz, Gerald Hess, and Michael Kühnen.

Everyone was enthusiastic about Frank Hübner, his appearance and his bearing; and the collapse of the Wall catapulted him swiftly to the top of the internal neo-Nazi hierarchy. Together with his brother, he went to Cottbus as soon as he could, bringing a huge amount of propaganda material. There he renewed his contacts with the East German neo-Nazis Karsten Wolter and René Koswig, and by December of 1989 they had already founded a DA regional association. Frank Hübner invited the Cottbusers to Frankfurt, where together with the Western comrades they worked out a basic framework for future strategy.

Rainer Sonntag had been deported by the DDR as a criminal. Like the Hübner brothers, Sonntag gained a foothold in the West with the Nationale Sammlung, and then went to Dresden after the Wall fell to continue his neo-Nazi activities. The Hübners and Sonntag form the most important links between neo-Nazis in the East and the West. Peter Hübner is the team leader in Langen, while Frank became the undisputed chief of the Deutsche Alternative.

Another DDR native, the twenty-six-year-old Roman Dannenberg, is Hübner's right-hand man and the party chairman for Saxony. Dannenberg had been arrested for extreme-right activities in the DDR and deported to the West. There he joined the NPD and eventually became a parliamentary candidate. Dannenberg came to the DA through Heinz Reisz, and after the Wall fell he moved back to his home town of Hoyerswerda. In September of 1991, neo-Nazis in this coal town attacked a refugee home to general applause. After a day-long siege, during which the police moved in only hesitantly, the refugees were transported out of Hoyerswerda, though not before their bus was pelted with rocks and the windows broken. What Dannenberg and his pals achieved in Hoyerswerda was what Kühnen, Hess, and Reisz had long been planning for Langen: to make the city "foreigner-free." Just as *gauleiters* once eagerly reported to their Führer that their regions were *judenfrei,* so can Dannenberg now boast that Hoyerswerda is *ausländerfrei.*

The positions of the "purchased" or deported DDR neo-Nazis in the West demonstrate how smooth the relations are between the extreme-right parties and the militant groupings. But the question remains open as to what the Federal Republic had in mind when it liberated active neo-Nazis for sums between 50,000 and 90,000 marks. And why were they then permitted to continue their activities in the West without a hitch, and later to expand into the East? In fact, these extremists of Eastern origin and Western experience were, from an ideological viewpoint, useful to the Federal Republic. As early as the 1970s, the conservative daily *Die Welt* floated the theory that the DDR had infiltrated the West German extreme right, hoping to support the extremists in order to damage the Federal Republic's reputation. West German neo-Nazis as Soviet agents, Eastern control of Western neo-Nazis . . . these were examples of "socialist dirty tricks."

Such a theory certainly doesn't explain the motives for buying the freedom of these specific prisoners. However, these purchases did establish the personal groundwork for excellent cooperation between neo-Nazis from East and West.

March 16, 1990. Berlin is once again Germany's capital. The borough of Steglitz had been a stronghold of Hitler's NSDAP, and it is here, in the Elefant restaurant, that activists from all parts of Germany and Austria meet today. As usual, the beer flows freely, and this is the proprietor's only comfort. He had expected a boring political gathering and is open-mouthed as he watches cars full of bomber-jacketed skinheads arrive.

Not everyone comes by car; as always, there are rendezvous and checkpoints at the train stations, where familiar faces greet you and a contact phone number is provided, just in case. The message on the answering machine is: "You have reached the main educational office of Wotans Volk. . . . Your call will be returned. Speak after the machine gun." Then you hear the gunfire. If the caller leaves the right name or code word, he will be called back and guided onward via telephone.

A section of the hard core surrounding Michael Kühnen and Gottfried Küssel sits today in the Elefant, but there are also some new followers—about a hundred and fifty people in all, many with the SA look of brown shirt and belt buckle. Tattooed skinheads and girls from the Deutsche Frauenfront (German Women's Front—DFF) with black skirts and stern expressions are also present. About half of them are from the DDR. Heinz Reisz from Langen is here, and Gerald Hess as well.

Kühnen's new girlfriend, Lisa, greets me happily. Her name is actually Esther, but in these circles Lisa goes over quite a lot better. She is a cheerful, pretty girl with dark, medium-length hair, about nineteen years old and an "enthusiastic National Socialist." After all, she is the DFF's *Führerin*.

The Nazi scene is really a completely male society, with all the attendant elements of male chauvinism, militarism, and homosexuality. Outbursts of homophobia, when they occur, frequently spring from simple rivalry. In such cases, the denunciation of another's homosexuality (real or imagined) is essentially insincere and serves simply to mask one's own cravings for power; the goal is to humiliate rivals, and thanks to the narrow-minded views of many followers, this tactic is frequently successful. The considerable percentage of gays, especially in leadership positions, corresponds roughly to the percentage of homosexual functionaries in the Third Reich.

Also as in the Third Reich, the role of women is intentionally limited to particular spheres. The Deutsche Frauenfront thus stands in the tradition of the NS-Frauenschaft (Nazi Women's Union). Their "work topics" include not only the traditional "family politics" and "preservation of racial purity," but also, since the accident at Chernobyl, nuclear power. The DFF's few members are mostly partners of neo-Nazi activists—such as Christian Worch's ex-girlfriend, Ursula—and the organization probably exists only to "prove" that the neo-Nazis aren't misogynists. Essentially the DFF is meaningless. Women constitute only about a fifth of the scene, and it is the men, homosexual or not, who determine its direction.

"Terror" is written in blood-red letters on the shirt of one bald-headed fellow. Next to him Frank Hübner wears a black tie with his white shirt, and others have also dressed respectably, with bourgeois charm. At the same time I see labels like *"Gau Hesse"* or *"Vienna"* sewn onto brown shirts in Nazi-style script. A few wear simple, checkered flannel shirts, popularly known as "woodsmen's shirts," but referred to here as a "worker's shirt." Above the shirts they wear workers' caps or army surplus caps with long visors.

"We are here in Berlin, we are in the capital of the Reich . . ." booms Gottfried Küssel in his Austrian accent, and at least in this he is similar to the Führer. Before him sit the faithful on rows of long benches. Having made it here through the checkpoint system, they listen to Küssel speak about the hard reality of the "political soldier." In the Third Reich, the "political soldier" was the heroic selfless fighter, an image that was somehow supposed to justify the war's mindless bloodshed. Today they still picture themselves in this same way. And hard reality could certainly burst upon them at any moment, since the *Antifa*—the antifascist leftists—have mobilized and greatly outnumber them. If they managed to discover this place, a wild mass brawl would be inevitable. The waiter knows this too. He serves the beer nervously, trying to hide his terror as Küssel stands and bellows:

"We know that we do not only have friends in this world. The world is full of enemies. And if they do not want to be our friends, then they must be our enemies. And that's just fine. Because then they have to reckon with our united might. And then they have to count on getting thrashed every once in a while. And then they can't stand out on the street yelling 'Death to fascists' and then get all upset when we actually come and give them a beating. . . ."

Küssel's voice almost breaks. He stands there like a boulder, powerful, massive, violent. His index finger, which he periodically raises for emphasis, strays up and down. Then he clenches his fist again and gestures with his entire forearm, like a boxer. His audience roars its appreciation. His speech is low on content, but all the more aggressive for that lack, which is exactly to their taste.

"If our German racial soul would boil for once! It's still just lukewarm, it's got to get hot, it's got to boil! It must burn with love. . . ."

Now Küssel himself turns ecstatic as his words pound the room. "Together we are intolerable. We are intolerable for the system in the East and in the West. And let us remain intolerable, let us remain faithful, let us hunger for victory and never be satisfied with less! Let us remain faithful, rock hard: you in the East, we in the West, we in the Eastern borderlands, and—before you can blink— we will move on to Breslau, we will move on to Königsberg. And I want to see Gorbachev on his knees!"

A charlatan? A clown? A madman? An actor? Or a dangerous agitator who plays on the hates and fears of the "disorientated"? Küssel is no isolated case, but only one of many.

In May 1990, the neo-Nazis are already working at full speed to develop advance organizations and, above all, the Deutsche Alternative. I hear more and more hints of a secret plan, and it is around this time that I meet again with Gerald Hess.

"It will be public sooner or later anyway. But until then—not a word that you got it from me!" With that, Hess presses an envelope into my hand. After much toing and froing, I have in my hand the document that contains the tactics behind the underground work. I blink at him.

We're sitting in his apartment in Langen. Gerald has put two bottles of beer on the table by the couch. His one-room apartment is on the thirteenth floor of an ugly skyscraper near the train station. Photographs hang on the walls: Gerald and Kühnen. Gerald and Lisa. Gerald in uniform. Gerald and his comrades. Memories. Then the obligatory portrait of Adolf Hitler. He sometimes hangs a swastika flag next to it, whenever it isn't needed somewhere else, or confiscated by the police. Across from the couch is a giant wardrobe, and next to that a kitchenette and glass doors leading to a small balcony.

Gerald Hess and I have become almost friendly. I genuinely like him and have been thinking for some time about how I can arrange to get him out of the scene. I'm waiting for a signal from him. But today it seems more like he's awaiting a sign from me, an indication that I want to join his organization. He'll have to wait a long time for that.

I pull the document out of the envelope. A runelike "W," for *Widerstand* (resistance), has been drawn on the first page. Underneath, in giant gothic letters, "DIE NEUE FRONT." The typed document is dated "21.1.1990/101," the "101" indicating the number of years since Hitler's birth. Underneath the date is written:

EASTERN REGION
EASTERN WORKING PLAN

I look at Gerald skeptically. "And how is it you're giving this to me now if it's so secret? It was already published a while ago, wasn't it?"

Gerald lights a cigarette. "Want one?" he asks, offering me the pack before answering my question. "In principle, yes, but only internally. And you always said I could trust you."

True. But what I had meant was that I would help him if he wanted to get out. I read on about the development of the movement in the DDR: "Behind all legal activity must stand a steel-hard, ideologically sound cadre unit." And then: "The outside should be told as little as possible about the cadre and its ideological stance. The cadre shall remain underground."

The NSDAP-AO advance organization Deutsche Alternative would be the legal superstructure. In addition, "a separate DDR party program for the DA in Central Germany will be worked out, the formulation of which must be moderate enough to allow registration as a legal political party."*

---

*The extreme right refers to the DDR as "Central Germany"—the implication being that Poland is, in fact, an "Eastern German" territory, to be reclaimed in the future.

For a party program to be written in this moderate tone is nothing new. Yet upon careful examination, striking similarities emerge between the platforms of the DVU, or the Republicans, and that of Hitler's NSDAP.

The twenty-five-point program of the NSDAP (announced in 1920) held, for example, that "Whoever is not a citizen may only live in Germany as a guest and must be subject to foreigner laws." The DVU couches this same notion in more democratic terms: "The DVU candidates support policies that allow foreign youths to retain their national and cultural identity as well as to remain part of their people, thus keeping open the road of return to their homeland." It is easy to imagine what kind of headaches this compromise language must have required. After all, it must still communicate what the leader of the DVU, Dr. Gerhard Frey, states concisely in his speeches: "Germany for the Germans!"

The same is true for the Republicans, whose demand is more specific: "Immigration ban for foreigners. Exceptions allowed only within narrow margins." The Deutsche Alternative document concludes that "There are too many foreigners in the country. The DA opposes any primitive xenophobia, but it also opposes—in agreement with the large majority of the German people—the massive settlement of self-contained foreign racial groups." In order to remedy this situation, they demand "not a 'foreigner ban' or a 'foreigner limitation,' but a humane, yet thorough-going, repatriation."

The Eastern Working Plan is quite direct, however, about how modest their goals are at the start: "First developmental goal is one hundred party members in the DDR (at the moment there are nine . . .)." But within a year, the DA will have hundreds of members, and the ranks of other right-wing organizations will have grown just as explosively. (In June 1991, 2,000 neo-Nazis march through Dresden because one of their ranks was shot in a fight with a pimp.) And these numbers don't include the Republicans and the DVU, whose memberships in 1992 exceeded 50,000.

The rest of the Eastern Working Plan discusses the deceptive maneuvers needed to develop legal party organizations, to attract members, and to spread propaganda. It includes the advice to "take part in demonstrations and attempt to radicalize them without isolating oneself,'' an approach that will later be followed in the attacks on asylum-seekers—which in Hoyerswerda and Rostock will degenerate into out-and-out pogroms.

Gerald Hess has slipped a cassette into his tape player and turned the machine on; it's the "Horst Wessel Song."* The bad sound quality and the buzzing speaker make it sound a little flat, almost comical, but suddenly I realize with terror that I'm humming along. Somehow I've stopped thinking about what lies behind these songs, some of which are damned catchy. Once or twice I even found myself whistling the melody to "Vorwärts! Vorwärts! Unsere Fahne flattert uns voran" ("Onward! Onward! Our Flag Flies Before Us") in the shower!

I have been working on this subject exclusively for over a year, and now I sense I'm on the verge of losing my distance. Everyone who knew about my project warned me about exactly this. I realize that I enjoy visiting Gerald, and that some of my visits were not in the least bit necessary. Even my initial horror at this "world of hate" has occasionally faded into an almost pleasant eeriness, an acclimatization I wasn't aware was taking place. My easy manner with the neo-Nazis is no longer feigned; we know and respect each other. At the same time, I realize that my own circle of friends has shrunk to a handful of intimates.

It has come time to review my situation. I have one other problem: finances. All my reserves and savings are gone since, for security reasons, I have not wanted to sell my story piecemeal; nor

---

*Horst Wessel, the son of a parson, joined the SA in 1926 and worked his way up to "Sturmführer." Wessel, who earned his living as a pimp in Berlin, was shot to death in a prostitute's apartment in 1930. The Nazis exploited his death for propaganda, naturally keeping silent about the actual circumstances. Goebbels fashioned the Horst Wessel myth, and numerous movies and plays were written about him. A primitive marching song that he had written a few years before ("With flags raised high . . ." etc.) was renamed the "Horst Wessel Song" and made into the "hymn of the movement." It later became, for all intents and purposes, a second national anthem.

have I found a producer for my film yet. A contract for a thirty-minute TV report gives me a reprieve of two or three months, and Graeme Atkinson gets me occasional research assignments from foreign TV stations. But my financial situation is essentially unchanged. Again and again I have to borrow money from friends and relatives, with no end in sight. Should I, as one friend advises, put the whole thing on hold and wait until the subject becomes more "topical"?

Gerald watches me curiously. I'm not sure how long I've been sitting there brooding. He has turned off the music and is sorting through his mail. When I reach for my cigarettes, he silently gives me a light. Gerald realizes that I have problems. We sit and smoke for a while without saying a word.

Finally he rouses himself to say, "You're not doing so well at the moment either, are you?"

I nod. I decide to take a month off.

Four weeks later, in June 1990, I am in Cottbus, where the first fruits of the Eastern Working Plan are apparent. The Deutsche Alternative is holding a team meeting in the back room of a musty restaurant. The twenty-year-old Karsten Wolter bites his lip. His well-proportioned Aryan features look more and more uneasy. Although his head does stand proudly above the collar of his brown shirt—to which an SS death's-head has been affixed—farther down his body language is saying something quite different. He's trying, as inconspicuously as possible, to signal for moderation. Toward that goal, he waves his left hand, downward, again and again. But that does as much good as his imploring look. Through my camera's viewfinder I see Wolter giving up. For a moment he gazes up at the ceiling. The corners of his mouth twitch. He takes a breath, and then—he doesn't say anything.

I move the camera slowly away from him to the center of the room. Wolter's followers are arranged at a long table, and they haven't the least intention of restraining themselves. On the contrary, the expressions used by the forty or so neo-Nazis become stronger, their voices louder and their faces angrier. The present assembly is supposed to be showing me its desire for justice and order—the simple, benign goal DA wants the world to believe it supports. But this sham is in the process of crumbling; the party's program is too lax for its own members.

The apprentice with the thick glasses doesn't care that the Eastern Working Plan was formulated moderately for tactical reasons. "You all can blab whatever you want," he hollers straight across the restaurant. " 'No violence initiated by us,' " he quotes the party document contemptuously. "Listen—I'll be the first to knock the niggers flat if they talk to my girl!"

Wolter looks imploringly at his three colleagues, who along with him represent the leadership cadre.

René Koswig, born in 1966, is the team leader, a big man with thin lips and broad shoulders. "Quiet, now!" he roars in his Brandenburg dialect.

Everyone obeys, and Wolter tries to salvage the situation. With a dogmatic tone he says what he often has to say—"We will stand up for the safety of our people!"—and then looks quickly over at me. He wants to make sure my camera is recording all this. "Some people misunderstand when—"

"What are you talking about?" someone yells.

"Everyone knows that we do not initiate violence," Wolter says, and it's easy to see that even he doesn't believe it.

But his colleague from the leadership cadre produces a Solomonic solution: "But if we are attacked," he says, "we are naturally going to defend ourselves!"

The others approve, and there is general merriment. He grins broadly and again presents a disturbing view of teeth that can only be the result of bad food, bad care, and a bad dentist.

Cottbus is in the East, near the Polish border, just next to Hoyerswerda. The DDR still exists, but its demise is certain. The figleaf of state-ordained antifascism is already gone. As one can see, it didn't help anyway.

René Koswig is an ardent Nazi, and his list of prior convictions proves that this was true long before he'd come in contact with the "imperialist West." However, in the summer of 1991, he and Karsten Wolter took advantage of the presence of a television team from Süddeutscher Rundfunk to stage a confrontation with their former judge for her "unjust verdict."

In the main hall of the Cottbus district court, the judge and the condemned faced one another again, this time obviously for the television crew. Koswig and Wolter glare reproachfully as the judge explains the case against the two neo-Nazis. Suddenly the roles are reversed and the judge is required to defend her judgment. The camera documents her hand-wringing with a close-up as she says, uncertainly, "I can't deny that at the sentencing we couldn't completely block out the thought: 'Let's stamp it out at the start.' " As if she should be ashamed of it.

It was a great day for Cottbus's neo-Nazis. And good propaganda too, since these scenes in the film *Deutschland erwache* (Germany, Awake) furthered the impression of Communist injustice. According to Frank Hübner, the reporters paid 750 marks for the Cottbus Nazis' cooperation—"for drinks and so forth." I didn't believe him, but Michael Kühnen told me the same thing two weeks later. "It happens a lot," he says, and thanks me for the meal I've just treated him to. I shake my head. I don't yet know that, some time later, I myself will pay for an interview with a man on the run from the law.

Frank Hübner and René Koswig pull the strings behind DA's activities. They are quick studies, and one presumes that in the future they will act less ladylike when it comes to using violence. Koswig considers himself part of an elite. He denies the reality of the Holocaust and is straightforward in his hatred of Jews.

I ask him what he would say if it were proved that Jewish blood flowed in his veins. Koswig leans back. His hands, covered with tattoos of spiderwebs, open gently. His eyes become smaller as he shifts his head to the side.

"If anyone tried to tell me I was a Jew, I'd break his neck!"

On October 20, 1990, the Dresden sky is overcast. It's only a week or so after Germany's reunification. Today I've decided to invest my last financial resources and rent an expensive film team. The occasion is the first neo-Nazi march in Eastern Germany since reunification. Sadly, it won't be the last, but premieres always seem somehow "historic," especially when they have to do with fascists. I also want to see how the population and the authorities will react.

Will there even *be* a march? Of course there will. As always when Christian Worch has a hand in the organizing, this action will enjoy impeccable legal arrangements. In any case, I'm curious what the head of the police detail will say when he realizes exactly who is in attendance. This march was registered by an otherwise completely undistinguished individual by the name of Edgar Meyer. The tactic is always the same: an activist unknown to the authorities will file for a permit under some neutral purpose—say, "demonstrating for social justice"—and add that a prominent figure will give a speech, so there will also be a rally. He'll claim that he's still waiting for acceptances, so the speaker's identity is still uncertain. Thus the permit is approved.

If their colleagues in the Verfassungsschutz haven't warned the Dresden authorities about this trick, the security forces will have a surprise in store for them today. The motto will not be "social justice," but "Germany for the Germans"; and the "prominent figure" is none other than the organizational chief of the NSDAP-AO, Michael Kühnen.

The tension rises, though the event won't start for some time. We came way too early in order not to be late, and use the extra time to shoot the city in general and do a few interviews on the street. The last of these is with a stocky man, about forty years old.

"Are you afraid of neo-Nazis?" I ask him.

"Nope," he says.

"How come?"

"Why should I be? I'm a German, aren't I?!"

He leaves us standing there. The cameraman, the sound engineer, and I just look at each other, amazed.

A short time later the main train station is swarming with skinheads, hooligans, neo-Nazis of every stripe. We learn that there's also a soccer game today, which explains the hooligans. The police are already in the process of surrounding the square in front of the station, but inside there isn't a policeman in sight, only hard-core Nazis. Even from the outside you can hear them roaring, again and again: "Germany for the Germans! Foreigners out!" And, equally often: *"Sieg Heil! Sieg Heil! Sieg Heil!"* When Michael Kühnen arrives, accompanied by Lisa and two bodyguards, there is no more room for doubt about the precise nature of this event. Christian Worch, Thomas Hainke, and Gottfried Küssel have already sent their supervisory teams into position.

Curious what the police chief will make of all this, I find him about thirty yards from the main entrance of the train station, where the skinheads are making the Hitler-salute and yelling *"Sieg Heil!"* Police Commissioner Wunsch has a friendly, round face, friendly even beneath his "combat" helmet.

"I really find it astonishing," I say, "that neo-Nazis are permitted to demonstrate like this in Dresden!"

Wunsch shows himself to be Constitution-minded. "This is a lawful assembly, registered according to the statutes governing assemblies. So far I'm satisfied that it's perfectly legitimate. Tell me—where do you see neo-Nazis?"

What? They're swarming all around us. I try again: "Excuse me, but what are you saying? I don't think I understood you."

"It's exactly as I told you."

I try to imagine just how dumb this policeman thinks I am, then decide it's time for fundamentals: "So you think those aren't neo-Nazis? Or will that only appear later?"

Wunsch insists on the nonexistence of what's happening before our very eyes. "No one here has done anything to identify himself as such, in the sense that—"

"Yes, but people are yelling *'Heil Hitler'* all over the place!"

"Where?" he says. Then he looks around, puffs out his cheeks a little, and shrugs his shoulders, as if he can't make out—right in front of us—the men stretching out their arms in the Hitler-salute. The press is photographing everything, but the skinheads act as if there weren't a single policeman in sight—even though the Hitler-salute is a criminal offense. I notice that my cameraman is still filming the police commissioner, so I narrate the scene to him.

"There in front, even for the photographers, they're making the Hitler-salute. That's unambiguously neo-Nazi, isn't it?"

"I still have not noticed any such thing, I must tell you!"

Cut. That's enough. Especially since I next catch Police Commissioner Wunsch standing together with Michael Kühnen and Rainer Sonntag. In the hall of the train station I record the following conversation, during which Wunsch is completely surrounded by Kühnen's followers:

"You can hold your assembly over there," he informs Kühnen warmly. "And I would offer you the same route back, if you approve." Kühnen does approve, and Wunsch continues: "then you'll be able to count on me. And then I would suggest . . ."

After so much cooperation, Kühnen now asks, with interest, "What was your name again?"

"My name is Wunsch."

"*Wunsch* is good!" says Kühnen with a smile.*

"Yes indeed. Police Commissioner Wunsch," the officer adds, for precision's sake, as Rainer Sonntag enters the conversation.

Sonntag, a round-faced, somewhat squat man with thinning hair and a cast on his "playing hand," really doesn't look like a karate champ. But he makes no secret of his hopes for violence. "If the leftists try to get aggressive, we're not going to let them get away with it."

"If you expect excesses," Wunsch says, "well, that's what *we're* here for."

But Sonntag has no intention of being deprived of his pleasure. "All right, but we'll do it together."

Wunsch accepts Sonntag's impudence—just like that. (At this point it should also be noted that Sonntag, who is also an occasional informer for the Dresden police, has excellent contacts within their ranks.)

Commissioner Wunsch doesn't seem to care about anything except a smooth course for the demonstration. He turns again to Kühnen. "Then it's agreed?"

Wunsch is German for "wish." (Translator's note)

"Yes, we agree," says Kühnen, visibly astonished at such gracious treatment.

But Wunsch has something else to say. "Then we will keep ourselves at as great a distance as possible, and I would ask you not to feel restrained by the police officers. . . ."

And so it happens that about 500 neo-Nazis can march from the train station to the Semper Opera. Herr Wunsch's wishes are put into practice: a row of police officers marches along like cheerleaders in front of the Nazis, while Karsten Wolter marches so closely behind them with his imperial flag that the green-uniformed guardians of the peace seem to be waving the banner themselves. Either the police have not yet noticed this provocation—which has Christian Worch a bit worried—or, more likely, they don't regard it as such.

"Germany for the Germans! Foreigners out!" resounds through the center of Dresden, as well as: "Breslau, Königsberg, Stettin— cities as German as Berlin!"

Some of the skinheads immediately put their first demand into practice. They veer off from the demonstration and go to "cut up some Chinks." In other words, they randomly beat anyone they see who looks Vietnamese, and they're able to do so almost undisturbed by the police. As their voices ring out in unison—"We don't want any Jew swine!"—the police march placidly alongside and only once reprimand these public agitators. How fortunate, I think again and again, that I am able to record all this with my video camera.

Thus, so soon after reunification can Kühnen and Küssel hold a rally in front of Dresden's Semper Opera. The Leipzig "Monday demonstrations," through which the citizens of the DDR peacefully forced the end of communist rule, are scarcely one year old when Gottfried Küssel begins his speech to the young Nazis with this distortion of recent history: "It was this same revolutionary German youth that went out into the streets in the former DDR. This same youth that also began the demonstrations here in Dresden that finally led to the unification of the BRD and the DDR." As if it were the Nazis who had caused the Wall to collapse.

If democracy has a chance, it is said, it is only because of responsible citizens. So today my last hope is reserved for the citizens of Dresden. But how do they react to this demonstration? The majority stare at the chanting train of boot-wearing extremists with remarkable apathy. Their indifference is such that you can't really tell if it's caused by fear, repulsion, or silent sympathy. Shockingly few comment at all, except perhaps for one indefatigable antifascist who keeps yelling "Nazis out!" He wears a brown leather jacket, but his long hair and three-day beard set him apart from the rest of the bystanders. Surprisingly, no one supports him. Out of about a hundred passersby on this street corner, he is, without a doubt, the only one saying anything against the Nazis. Their response, even though he's alone, is a chorus of "Leftist Pigs!"

A moment later I notice a young girl in a leather jacket who seems angered by the "Foreigners out" chant. She shakes her dyed red hair, and I'm sure I mishear her when she yells indignantly, "Do I maybe look like a nigger, or what?"

It turns out that she's upset only because she thought the fascists were lumping her together with the foreigners. Given the way she hurled the word *nigger,* she probably could join the neo-Nazis without any problems.

Then there's the elderly gentleman who surely lived through the reign of National Socialism. "What rabble!" he curses sullenly. And then, to my astonishment, he adds this bold counterpoint: "They belong in a camp, all of them!" The correct description followed by a faulty prescription.

Much later, while editing the film from this Dresden sequence, I use none of these three reactions. Within the context of this event, they are too likely to convey a false impression of public response. We use, instead, a shot of another bystander's reaction. In the cutting room we nicknamed her "our treasure," and she certainly deserves our thanks. Sad to relate, I witnessed only this one such response to the Dresden demonstration.

There she stands, with dirty blond hair and a disgusted expression. She is around forty; the man accompanying her, clearly her husband, may be a little older. Both of them are watching as the demonstrators chant away: "Germany for the Germans! Foreigners out! . . ." With one hand she makes a gesture in front of her face, showing the Nazis that she thinks they're crazy.

Her husband, apparently fearing reprisals, vainly tries to move her away from the camera. It must have been this same reflex that half a century ago made it possible for Jews to be beaten, abducted, and carted off before the studiously unobservant eyes of their neighbors. Fear for one's own skin makes moral courage so rare. The older ones must still remember that oppressive feeling, the need to go unnoticed, "no matter what"—first by the brigades of SA thugs before the seizure of power, and later by the Gestapo as widespread arrests reduced to nil the courage to protest.

"We'll get you all!" So runs one of the neo-Nazis' favorite chants. The younger generation might better understand the full reach of this threat when I quote the feelings of another woman, a seventy-year-old. Shielding her mouth with her hand, she told me, "If I protest now, and then one day they come into power, then I'll have a 'previous record.' Our politicians, it's easy for them to make speeches about 'moral courage.' They've got it easy. They can just take off and leave. But me, where am I supposed to go?"

"We'll get you all!" is intimidation that works even *before* they come into power. It is a basic, insidious principle, a prerequisite of totalitarian rule. You don't have to be terribly brave to curse democracy; marching Nazis were able to silence good citizens prior to the Third Reich—and neo-Nazis count on the same reaction today. It's all too human a failing, and fascists exploit it without scruple. In this way the Nazis claim the support of the "silent majority," which makes resistance to right-wing extremism and xenophobia all the more important. At such protests in the winter of 1992, hundreds of thousands of Germans showed that the real "will of the people" is exactly the opposite of what the Nazis imagine it to be.

Still, in 1990 the people of Dresden simply looked on indifferently. That's why this one bystander, "our treasure," is so special: she does not let her husband pull her away, and instead she loudly proclaims what she thinks: "This is madness! The young people who grew up here, how on earth can they be so crazy and talk such nonsense? I can't understand it!"

V

How to Become a Martyr

GERALD HESS SITS DIRECTLY ACROSS FROM ME. WE have found a quiet spot in the most remote corner of the pub. The room is jam-packed with right-wing radicals of every sort, and the proprietor of the Alte Mühle, near Hamburg, is not in the least pleased with this clientele. I don't pay any attention to him; the pinched face of a deceived host has long since become a familiar sight for me.

"Listen, Gerald," I whisper, "you know that what I want to do is report about you like you really are."

Gerald wrinkles his forehead. "Yes—so?"

"But I can't do it," I whisper reproachfully.

"Why not? What's wrong?" Gerald too is whispering.

"I'm not allowed to film here!" I explain.

The British historian David Irving is expected to appear shortly and give a speech before an audience carefully selected by Christian Worch, who is acting under instructions from a certain Ewald Althans of Munich, the organizer of Irving's German tour. However, since the audience today includes Michael Kühnen, Irving demanded that journalists not be admitted. Irving, who, under the motto "Truth will make you free," denies the existence of gas chambers at Auschwitz, wants to prevent the accurate documentation of his friends and contacts.

"If it's true that Kühnen and Irving are meeting here," I say to Gerald, "then it's got to be wrong that I can't film it just because Irving's worried about his reputation—don't you think?"

Gerald thinks for a moment, then admits that he agrees with me completely. And it so happens that inside of ten minutes, with Kühnen's permission, something is decided that sounds unbelievable and must be kept secret from the others: I am going to film David Irving with a hidden camera, and Gerald and one of his friends are going to help me do it.

Soon afterward we're outside. It's dark, and the lamps by the entrance cast a pale light onto the surroundings. With Gerald's dark jacket pulled over my head, I crouch behind the two neo-Nazis while Gerald wedges the lens of my camera between his arm and torso. Then we wait as inconspicuously as possible, a short distance from the entrance. Finally Gerald whispers, "Watch out! he's coming!"

"More to the left!" I whisper back. Gerald and his companion carefully turn to the left while, still hidden, I follow the shadows of people about twenty yards away through my viewfinder. I curse my trembling hands, which blurs the picture slightly; but it's not every day that I film with a concealed camera. "Is that him?" I ask quietly.

"I think so," Gerald answers.

Wonderful! Now I can make out the outlines—Kühnen, and next to him the tall figure of Herr Althans, various others, and then Wolfgang Hess. Christian Worch comes out and issues commands. And there he is: Irving! I have him, in the company of people he never wants to be photographed with. Now he's speaking with Christian Worch.

"Hey, they're looking! Watch out!" whispers Gerald, getting nervous. No one knows how the others would react if we were discovered, and Gerald's nervousness is infectious. I'm already trembling so much I can barely hold the camera still.

"If they notice something now," Gerald announces, "we'd better get the hell out of here."

"Just one more moment!" I say, trying to zoom in on Irving.

"We have to stop, they're looking. Please, finish up!"

Okay, I've got it all on film. I press a button on the camera with my thumb to turn it off, and then I almost have a heart attack: I've just turned it on! I did see Irving through the viewfinder, but I didn't get him on film!

Despite the mishap, the evening in Hamburg was a success in another way. Our unusual collaboration created a strong bond between Gerald and me. He likes the idea of "pinning down that hypocrite for once"; and I like the idea that Gerald can think that way.

On July 21, 1990, we meet at one of his group's "comrades' evenings." Afterwards he gets into my car and we drive to a pub in Langen, where we can talk in peace. I need to talk, because I've had some problems. A few days earlier, in the small town of Maintal, near Frankfurt am Main, a massive police force had prevented an interview I'd arranged with skinheads to discuss neo-Nazi computer games. The police had, to my great annoyance, arrested the skinheads before I could get to the agreed-upon meeting point.

Gerald tells me that the father of one of the skinheads belongs to the center-left Social Democratic Party (SPD) and is friends with one of the policemen—also in the SPD—who participated in the arrest. And so, Gerald thinks, one party member probably asked the other to do him the favor of somehow preventing his son from appearing on television, since he had learned of his plan to give an interview.

This is a precarious theory, but Gerald suddenly becomes very serious. The waiter puts two beers on the table. Gerald takes one of my cigarettes and thinks. A slot machine chimes behind us. A couple is standing behind us playing darts, and I sit there listening as a dart hits the target periodically with a dull thump. "You've got to watch out!" Gerald blurts. "Don't you understand that there are police spies among us?"

"And how does that affect me?"

"Very simple. Then the police know what you're planning. And if they don't like it, you're in trouble. You'll see."

Now I'm genuinely alarmed. "Who's the informer?"

Gerald takes a drag on his cigarette, then shakes his head. "I don't have any proof, but of course we know who it is. More accurately: who they are. But I won't tell you the name, because . . ." I wait tensely until he finally continues: "It's really none of your business," he says.

Something here seems completely illogical. "If you know there's a spy," I say, "why do you let him keep working with you?"

Gerald grins broadly. "There's no better way to fool the pigs and the *Schmutz*. The comrade receives selected information—but it doesn't always have to be right."

I order another beer and for a while we sit quietly facing each other. Actually for about as long as it takes for the beer to arrive. I toast Gerald, but he doesn't react.

"You know I like you," he says. "But I just don't trust you anymore!"

I turn hot, then cold.

"We've known each other for over a year now and I still don't know *what* exactly you have in mind. No one before has ever filmed us as much as you. And you know things even *I* didn't know about. About organizations abroad, for example. You know them all, names, locations, all of that. The comrades are slowly getting suspicious because you're not finishing your film. And I wonder where you get all this information about us! Who *are* you?"

"I'm Michael Schm—"

"I don't believe you! Are you from the *Schmutz* or the *Antifa*? You're certainly not a normal reporter."

I notice I'm sweating. Gerald is now deadly serious, and my answer needs to be convincing: "You know damn well that if I were from the Verfassungsschutz or an antifascist I wouldn't tell you. I can only ask you to trust me and to believe me: I am neither a policeman nor a left-winger. Besides, if I were in the *Schmutz,* why am I having all these problems with the police?"

"That could also be a trick!" he says.

Gerald now sees himself surrounded by enemies, agents, informers, false friends. (Of course, he's not completely off the mark, as we'll soon see.) But finally I'm able to reassure him, and he opens his heart to me: he has money troubles, problems with his girlfriend, he feels overwhelmed. He's sick of doing all the organizational work himself, while the others only show up for "actions" or drinking bouts. The political police, he says, are pressuring him, perhaps hoping to make him cooperate. And he's angry with one of his comrades. He won't tell me who it is but says that, in any case, he can't trust him anymore. Because "he's also an informer."

Meanwhile, Gerald has finished his seventh beer and is getting drunk. I pack him into my car and drive him home. If he needs someone, I tell him, he can always turn to me. Gerald thanks me, presses my hand, and says, "Maybe.   We'll see."

Five days later he's dead.

Heinz Reisz called with the the news that Gerald was found shot to death.

"It's true," the desk officer says in response to my panicked phone call to the local police precinct. "I can confirm that tonight a suicide took place in Gerald Hess's apartment. For us this case is already closed."

In answer to my next question, he tells me that an autopsy and related investigations will confirm the course of events established by the police—"or else they won't. But in this case I'm sure they will confirm it!" he promises me.

I don't understand how he's so sure, but he should know what he's talking about.

Then I call Wolfgang Hess. For me at this moment, he isn't a neo-Nazi but simply the father of a child.

"Sure, that fits their picture perfectly: Gerald Hess commits suicide!" He's bitter and can barely control his voice. "After all, it was only a dirty little neo-Nazi! That fits their cliché all right! Of course that kind has to commit suicide—with his sick brown brain!" Wolfgang Hess is shattered. His son was still living when he found him. Gerald died in his arms, parts of his lungs still hanging from his chest. The weapon was a sawed-off shotgun, fired from the lower left at the front of his torso.

"My son has been murdered!"

A flyer by Michael Kühnen appears soon after, under the heading "THE SUPREME SACRIFICE FOR GERMANY": "It was a voluntary, conscious martyr's death for Germany. Comrade Gerald Hess wanted to send a signal. . . . So far as we know, Gerald died by his own hand. But he was nonetheless murdered: his murderer is the ruling system, which not only offers our national youth no values or ideals, but also persecutes and torments them. . . . His murderers are the cowardly, self-satisfied bourgeoisie. . . ."

So Gerald is treated, as was to be expected, as a martyr. Even his comrades agree with the verdict of suicide, and for the moment only his father believes he was murdered.

But this changes when Kühnen issues a special edition of the underground newspaper *Die Neue Front*. "Even if the documents left behind suggest a voluntary, political martyr's death, it also must not be hidden that there are riddles about this death. . . . He was found with a knife wound on his leg and red bruises on his face. Where did these wounds come from? The police, moreover, have acted strangely and tried to close the case prematurely, to avoid public attention. Only a murder charge . . . brought further investigation into motion."

A police search later uncovered a letter that supplies some information about the relationship between Gerald and the "informer" he no longer trusted: the man with whom he had so many problems. Dated "24.8.1990 102 JdF" (that is, the 102nd year of the Führer), the letter is from Michael Kühnen to the Dresden neo-Nazi Rainer Sonntag. Its language is straightforward: "Many here in Langen believe that you shot Gerald. There are also rumors that you were in Langen during the time in question. It would already be difficult, after you left us so unceremoniously and spoke out against us on television (to say nothing of the money you owe many comrades) to readmit you honorably. Gerald was especially unyielding on this point. . . . If you had anything to do with Gerald's death, it will come out, sooner or later. And you can surely imagine what our stance toward you will be then, since Gerald was one of our best. . . . On the condition that you had nothing to do with Gerald's death, you have my approval to teach your comrades loyalty toward me and our organization, to distribute our propaganda material, and for you and your comrades to join one of the advance organizations. . . ."

. . .

Who, then, is Rainer Sonntag? As a powerfully built, pugnacious eighteen-year-old, he was hired in 1973 by the criminal police in his home town of Dresden as an "unofficial collaborator." His duties included the "prevention of illegal border crossings." He had completed school only with difficulty and never finished his apprenticeship. At this time, Sonntag was a gambler and a drinker, and he quickly learned his way around the demimonde of the city on the Elbe. In the same year he was convicted of attempting to flee the DDR and sentenced to a year and a half in prison, where he earned privileges as an informer. After his release, jail terms for theft followed.

In 1986 he was deported to the Federal Republic as a criminal. In the West German reception center in Giessen, he claimed to have been a political prisoner. Sonntag moved to Langen and quickly made contact with the Kühnen circle, which wanted his help in making that small town "Germany's first foreigner-free city." In the municipal elections, Sonntag ran in the number-three position on the list of Kühnen's Nationale Sammlung (NS). The party's campaign paper, Der Sturm (The Storm), published this description of him: "Known for his direct manner and his untarnished political devotion to Germany, he quickly wins the ear and attention of his listeners. He knows the social and spiritual problems of his (and our) compatriots in Central and East Germany."

As chief of NS's internal security, Sonntag harassed foreigners and was finally tried for assault and battery and the possession of illegal weapons. Shortly before the election, on February 9, 1989, NS was banned.

In "his direct manner," Sonntag had by this time learned how to earn quick cash in the West. He earned his living in the neighborhood around Frankfurt's train station, as a self-described "slut protector." As a whorehouse bouncer he could hone his fighting skills. His attempts to finance his expensive lifestyle out of his comrades' pockets failed, and he took advantage of the destruction of the Wall to move back to Dresden. Although he was already on bad terms with Gerald Hess, from whom he'd stolen almost six

thousand marks, he prided himself on his good connections with Michael Kühnen.

In Dresden he quickly succeeded in gathering a troop of young neo-Nazis around him. Sonntag—who loved to drive around in his Japanese all-terrain vehicle, and who always had a German shepherd at his side—was also prominent in the establishment of various neofascist groups in Dresden: the Schutzstaffel-Ost (SS-East), the Verband der Sächsischen Werwölf (Association of Saxon Were-wolves), and the Nationale Widerstand Deutschlands (German National Resistance—NWD). Sonntag had grand plans for the NWD, the "party of law and order," which was prepared to fight against "society's deterioration." In March 1991, under the flag of the NWD and with banners proclaiming that "Dresden Will Not Become a Bordello," about 300 extremists and skinheads marched through the streets of the city, protesting unemployment, drugs, prostitution, and crime. The erstwhile "slut protector," Sonntag, marched at the front.

With time Sonntag became presentable. He held conversations with the state security forces, and Dresden's Special Commissioner for Foreigners invited him to talk about the plethora of racist attacks in the city. Nonetheless, he remained controversial among the Eastern neo-Nazis. As a Western import, he was frequently watched with suspicion; he talked too much and was considered a con man and a loudmouth.

Sonntag realized it was time to prove himself in action and announced plans to develop his own antidrug police. "We want to protect our children from this devilish junk," he dictated into the notebooks of the local journalists. Then he went after con artists in Dresden's commercial promenade. There, on Pragerstrasse, three-card monte players, most of them foreigners, earn their living off of Germans' confidence that they can't be fooled. Suckers who'd been ripped off applauded enthusiastically when Sonntag and his pals bludgeoned Hungarian card dealers in several "cleanup actions." As a publicity stunt, he even chained one to a lamppost before handing him over to the police.

The police had no objection to such assistance. One good turn deserves another, and Sonntag emerged untarnished from a series of

personal investigations and detentions. The high point of police-Nazi cooperation in Dresden, city of culture, was reached when a police officer went so far as to chauffeur Sonntag's men to their engagements in his private car.

With their cleanup operations against gamblers, illegal street vendors, and prostitutes, Rainer Sonntag's band cultivated the approval of the Dresdeners. "I am the eye, ear, and mouth of the people," Sonntag boasted to reporters. Yet while he joined the battle for "Germanic purity" against foreigners, drug trafficking, crime, prostitution, homosexuality, and leftists, the neo-Nazi was also running protection rackets. A group of Vietnamese cigarette vendors was paying significant amounts of money. in order not to be smacked around by Sonntag's band of thugs. While his supporters demonstrated against pornography, he was receiving protection money from brothels.

On the night of June 1, 1991, this double strategy became his undoing. On this night, barely a year after Gerald Hess was shot-gunned to death, fifty members of Sonntag's NWD gathered in front of the Faunpalast, a movie house in central Dresden. They were mostly dressed in black, their heads shaved, and they wore heavy combat boots. Their leader, Rainer Sonntag, had gathered them there for an "action against prostitution," to "flatten" a nearby brothel on Moritzburgerstrasse. His actual motive was to punish a brothel owner for refusing to pay five-figure protection money. But Sonntag's plans would come to nothing.

A little before midnight, a black Mercedes coupe glided up. A passenger jumped out, and a verbal dispute developed into a fight. Then the man pulled out a sawed-off shotgun, and Sonntag was hit fatally in the head. Blood-covered, he fell onto the sidewalk while the gunman raced away in the Mercedes.

After his comrades recovered from their shock, they covered their leader's corpse with an imperial war flag and vowed "blood vengeance" for the death of Rainer Sonntag. Since the immediate perpetrator was not available, they went off to "fuck up some foreigners." The hunt for Vietnamese and three-card monte players continued into the next morning. A day later, the brothel on Moritzburgerstrasse was destroyed. A few days afterwards, an Interpol investigation turned up two men in Bangkok, ages twenty-four and twenty-five, both well known in prostitution circles, who were then arrested as suspects in the murder.

The controversy over leadership in Dresden is buried along with Rainer Sonntag's death. The entire German neo-Nazi scene agrees to use his death as a rallying point for the movement in the East. This is perfect propaganda. Finally, a comrade has been shot on the open street. True, he wasn't murdered by a political opponent—but, as with Horst Wessel, a small-time pimp can be turned into a great martyr.

Kühnen's letter following Gerald Hess's death is forgotten, as is the rumor that Sonntag had sold the shotgun to his own murderers only three weeks before they used it to kill him. Forgotten as well are Sonntag's criminal activities, his services as an informer, and his robbery of his comrades.

Almost all of the major neo-Nazi organizations prepare a demonstration in Dresden for the occasion of Sonntag's burial. The city's mayor, Herbert Wagner, a Christian Democratic, grants approval for the gathering, explaining feebly that he really can't ban a funeral march—despite his earlier promise to Aviv Shir, an official at the Israeli Embassy, that he would never again permit neo-Nazis to hold a rally in Dresden.

Finally, on June 15, 1991, about 2,000 neo-Nazis march through Dresden. The banners read: "Rainer Sonntag—Martyr for the Reich." Arms fly up to give the Hitler-salute as marchers pass the Faunpalast, and cries of *"Sieg Heil!"* resound. The police again stand by placidly, and many citizens applaud, though surreptitiously. Heinz Reisz reaches back into his bag of fascist clichés—"Sonntag died like a soldier"—and theatrically swears revenge by the graveside. Sonntag, he says, was "butchered in Dresden by assassins, just as Dresdeners once were by Allied bombs."

This spectacle is repeated after charges are dropped against the two pimps arrested for Sonntag's murder. The judges rule this a clear-cut case of self-defense, and their discharge feeds the growing legend of the martyred Nazi. Sonntag even has a song devoted to him:

> The Wall fell, the country was free.
> He knew that the time to fight was here.
> For German order, German right, Rainer would always fight.
> We Dresden comrades always stood at his right.
> For German faith, German heart,
> Flowed Rainer Sonntag's hero's blood.
> The day of revenge will find us ready.
> Forward for the Fourth Reich, for a better age.

But if Gerald Hess and Rainer Sonntag were not true martyrs, neither were they true National Socialists. Deep inside Gerald's soul were humanitarian feelings that in the long run might have saved him. But Sonntag? What more need be said?

The spate of deaths, however, is not yet over. The next victim has known his fate for some time already. He knows too that his death will set off a power struggle within the neo-Nazi movement.

During my research, Michael Kühnen had opened doors for me that remained closed to many others. Since his tactics were based on publicity ("Before one can become loved, one first has to become known"), this was hardly surprising. But I still wonder if Kühnen hadn't also hoped that my work would become a cinematic tribute to his "fight for freedom," with him, naturally, as the hero. Only this, I think, can explain why he gave me entree to Küssel, Worch, and others, thus allowing me to learn more than was necessarily good for him or his movement.

Even before we met, Kühnen knew how little time he had left. He'd been HIV-positive for some years, and reports of his infection were circulating as early as his prison term that ended in 1988. Since that time, despite visible weight loss, he has countered further rumors with vehement denials and alternate explanations. Indeed, Kühnen remained active for an astonishingly long time, doggedly carrying out his physically draining activities. As his model, Adolf Hitler, once did, Kühnen sees his end approaching yet is determined to fight on. In contrast to Hitler, his is a particularly personal battle, and Kühnen knows well that a victim of AIDS does not make a suitable martyr. Yet he has no choice: he will work on until he can work no longer, and then he will hope for a quick end. During his last television interview, in January 1991, he is emaciated and speaks in a hoarse voice.

Kühnen purchases a house in the small town of Zimmern, in Thüringen, where he lives out the last months of his life with his girlfriend, Lisa. Though his suffering is now progressing rapidly, he doesn't disclose his disease to Christian Worch, his most intimate friend, until the beginning of March 1991. By then, as Worch tells me on the day of Kühnen's death, he was "in such a fragile condition that confirmation was really no longer necessary."

On April 11, 1991, the police arrive at the house with a warrant for "driving without requisite insurance," and Kühnen is put under arrest. But he is in the terminal stages of his disease and no longer capable of walking or even standing. After the police doctor has declared him "absolutely incapable of imprisonment," Kühnen is sent to the municipal hospital in Kassel. Fourteen days later, on April 25, 1991, Michael Kühnen dies from the consequences of the immune-deficiency syndrome.

Thus ended, according to Christian Worch, "an era of political development . . . that will not come again." That much is true, since Kühnen's "weaponless politics" goes with him to the grave. After a series of terrorist attacks in the early eighties, he altered his tactics and ordered his people to conduct the struggle more with propaganda than with armed might; he called it the "phase of political provocation." But this official renunciation of violence proved unpopular, and along with the controversy over Kühnen's homosexuality, it led, in 1986, to a split in the movement that continued up to his death. Although temporary truces were often arranged, a real agreement was never reached.

Fractured by these rivalries, the disparate leadership now has an opportunity to change its tactics in secret. And before long, the results are apparent. The successor chosen by Kühnen himself is Gottfried Küssel, who spends as much of his time on the road in the former DDR as he does home in Vienna. As he moves from place to place, a wake of hate and violence follows behind him. After Küssel or his deputies begin to organize in a town, it remains quiet for about three weeks. Then the riots begin. Soon the assaults, beatings, and brawls in the cities of the East are too numerous to count. The police usually have no idea where or how to get information about these acts of violence, and the strikingly racist attitudes of many police officers don't help matters; in fact, attacks on blacks and Vietnamese are frequently investigated only halfheartedly. As for Küssel & Company, the ones pulling all the strings, they've naturally been elsewhere for a good long time.

Michael Kühnen's death was a severe blow to my investigations. His successors have little trust in me and I am obliged to step back from the scene. What I see from now on is a continuous change in leadership, but with no visible change in the state of affairs. What is different, though, is that there are now more of them: many more young people are joining, and they are openly advocating violence.

It has to be said that Kühnen's death, like Gerald Hess's, hit me on a personal level. After an intensive period of investigation, in which both of them provided me with many insights into this world of extremism, it would be wrong to deny the human closeness that developed in the process. There were moments when the borders blurred and sympathies emerged, especially in my relationship with Gerald Hess.

Perhaps it is excessive to describe a twenty-one-year-old as having a hard shell and a soft core, but Gerald Hess frequently demonstrated deeply humane feelings and sometimes despaired of the contradictions and violence of his chosen movement. True, his indoctrination was so complete that he frequently censored himself. But in the long run—or so I hoped, at least—he might have abandoned the neo-Nazis for good. Whether or not my hope was justified will never be known. It was, perhaps, more a subjective wish than an objective assessment: a straw of humanity that I could clutch and which made my dealings with the Nazis bearable.

Whoever knew Michael Kühnen personally can attest to his readiness to cooperate and his easy openness, as well as to a certain integrity that was sometimes difficult to reconcile with the stereotype of the rabid Nazi.

The late Jewish poet and author Erich Fried, an avowed enemy of right-wing extremism, carried on a lively correspondence with Kühnen that began when both were invited to participate in a television talk show. The relationship between them got so close that in 1984 Fried visited him in prison and offered to testify in Kühnen's defense. He issued a public explanation of this offer: "I wrote the following: that in our discussions he was not only an honorable debater, but also anything but obdurate or unwilling to learn. And that after this meeting I would trust him with my life at any time. That was my impression. And I have no choice but to stand by it." This opened Fried up to the criticism that he had been seduced by neofascism; and while this position is understandable, it precludes a more discriminating interpretation. From my own experience, I can confirm the core of Erich Fried's statement: Michael Kühnen had personal integrity, and he was trustworthy, qualities quite divorced from his political views. And yet, whether one should, as a result, have conceded to him the right to promote National Socialism is a completely separate issue.

Michael Kühnen will come up, repeatedly, throughout the course of this book, although he is not its primary subject. The experiences I'm about to describe do not always follow chronologically; rather, they are for the most part organized thematically.

VI

GUNS AT THE READY

THE RAIN BEATS HARD AGAINST THE RENTED BMW's windshield, but Jo has got the gas pedal on the floor, and I'm on the verge of a heart attack. Jo is one of the cameramen who sometimes helps me, and he likes to drive. In fact, he can go all night without stopping. Right now he's enjoying bouncing along the bumpy East German Autobahn through rain and wind, pushing the Trabbis over to the right lane.* I'm already familiar with his driving style; it's why I chose the backseat. Sophie sits in the front, her hand clutching the dash as Jo blows past the gesticulating Trabbi drivers at 110 miles per hour.

Sophie is from London, but to me she is a gift from heaven. Her production firm gave me a paid research assignment just when I was running out of money. Sophie is the firm's reporter, and she wants to learn as much as possible about German neo-Nazis. She's come to the right people for that. She knows it and occasionally winks at me, to let me know that she knows it—but not too often, because we have one of them in the car with us. Frank Hübner, the future party chairman of Deutsche Alternative, is sitting next to me in the back. We were in Cottbus to film a meeting, and he's going back

---

*Trabbi—nickname for Trabant, the name of the small, low-quality automobiles manufactured in the former DDR. (Translator's note)

with us to Wiesbaden, where he lives and where Sophie has set up base.

Hübner has high cheekbones, but this is easy to miss since his face is rather chubby. He looks rather like a baby, only not so fresh; his lips are well-blooded, if thin. He is not a big man, and traces of baby fat make his body seem harmless. But he makes up for this by relating stories of neo-Nazi martial-sports clubs. That, apparently, is where one gets hardened.

"Worch is the worst dictator there!" Frank Hübner stretches out in the backseat as he recalls his last military training. "He and his group always have to be the best, or else he's not happy. And that man has a real commander's voice in his body. Man!"

We're happy to listen to him. As yet, Hübner has little of the whining, "party chairman" manner he will later develop. On the contrary, he acts very indiscreetly, often blurting out sensitive information. He speaks enthusiastically of the tent camps and military training in the Lüneburg meadow. Now things are "really getting started in Central Germany." Appropriate locations have already been chosen—"where no one'll bother you, understand?" Of course. And who organizes these drills and trains the boys? . . . Hübner is at least clever enough not to go into these details. But then he spits out: "There's a lot of practice ammo from the army." That's something to pursue, but we're about to drop him off at his apartment, so I just thank him for the conversation.

"Of course, of course. And if you ever want anything, all it takes is a call!"

We wave to each other, and I realize that Hübner's intrusively friendly manner rubs me the wrong way. Forget him, I think, he's unimportant. What a slime. This turns out to be a fatal misjudgment, at least in terms of his importance. Because in less than two years, under Hübner's leadership Deutsche Alternative will develop into one of the most militant and terrorist of the advance organizations. By then, Hübner will give interviews with a cold smile and a self-confidence that knocks me off my chair, especially when I think back to Cottbus, where he'd stammered before the camera, "We stand here before the former palace of Prince Pückler in Cottbus." And on September 4, 1992, I finally have to live through the sight of Hübner on television with Manfred Stolpe, the Social Democratic state prime minister. Stolpe shakes hands with Hübner and sits down to talk with him as if he were discussing quotas with the unions. At this point I am forced to admit it: I had completely underestimated Hübner. I should have paid more attention to him back then, and not only when he was talking about military games. On December 9, 1992, Hübner's Deutsche Alternative is banned by the interior minister of the Federal Republic of Germany. With that he has become an official enemy of the state, the highest honor for a hard-core neo-Nazi.

But even without him, my investigations turned up a few interesting facts.

"Hurrraaah, Hurrraaah!" bellows the fat man in the camouflage uniform. Then he goes on the attack. As the colored pellets fly from his training weapon, I decide it's time to take cover. Twigs crack as he works his way through the mixed forest.

"Are you crazy!" a voice suddenly booms out of the undergrowth with a strong Viennese accent. "The enemy's on the other side!"

"Oh!" The fat man corrects his line of fire. Of course, had this been an actual war, he'd be history. So he's taking part in military exercises to make sure that that doesn't happen.

Near Vienna, in a remote part of a private forest in Langenlois, the faithful followers of NSDAP-AO functionary Gottfried Küssel are training—"nightstick training," "close combat," and sometimes even firing live rounds. But because I'm present (along with a second cameraman), the neo-Nazis restrict their paramilitary exercise to "paint-ball" games, in which one uses an air gun to shoot opponents with colored pellets. The red pellets can look pretty realistic, and a blond fellow who got shot in the head has to laugh at me before I can stop staring, horrified, at his gigantic "wound."

The only thing martial sports have in common with real sports is that in both of them people move around. Otherwise, they're deadly serious. And yet I can recall a statement made by Franz-Josef Strauss, former prime minister of Bavaria (quoted in the Social

Democratic press service on October 1, 1980): "My God, if a man enjoys strolling through the country on a Sunday with a backpack and in battle fatigues with a belt buckle, then he should be left in peace." His misunderstanding is symptomatic of the ways that the danger of right-wing terror is minimized and denied. The strollers Strauss was speaking of were members of the Hoffmann martial-sports troop.

Their commander, a graphic designer named Karl-Heinz Hoffmann, had often declared that he wanted to "save young people from spiritual and physical neglect, thereby performing a task supported by the Bavarian Constitution." The authorities, and, above all, the Bavarian interior minister, happily believed him and treated him benevolently. Hoffmann and his troops, outfitted with military equipment, did not limit their mischief to the woods around Nuremberg, yet they still had nothing to fear. Thanks to his good connections, especially among the police, he regularly learned of impending house searches in advance. Meanwhile, the courts ignored his ties to Belgian, French, Italian, English, and American neofascists, instead treating him as a harmless "gun enthusiast."

Nearly all the leading figures of the illegal NSDAP-AO passed through Hoffmann's martial-sports camp, and his bands of thugs raised havoc throughout the entire republic. Nevertheless, only months before the federal Interior Ministry banned the troop, at the end of January 1980, Bavaria's interior minister, Gerald Tandler, gave the neo-Nazis his approval, finding that "Martial sports are not in themselves criminal."

After the ban, Hoffmann transferred his activities to Lebanon, with the help of the PLO. In 1981 he was arrested on charges of counterfeiting, intimidation, grievous bodily harm, and for infringements of laws governing on weapons and explosives. For these offenses, in addition to numerous cases of deprivation of liberty, he was finally sentenced, in 1986, to nine and a half years behind bars. He was then forty-eight years old. As a model prisoner—able quickly to adapt to the prison's authoritarian system, and entrusted with errands by the thankful wardens—Hoffmann was freed in 1989, despite the fact that he had in no way "altered his beliefs," as he openly admitted to television reporters.

The trial against Hoffmann turned up horrifying details about life in his camp in Bir Hassan, in Beirut. There Hoffmann had established a reign of terror that provides a perfect example of neo-Nazi brutality. Members of his troop were treated with bestial cruelty and tortured with glowing bayonets. Kai-Uwe Bergmann, a twenty-year-old from Hamburg, did not survive his ordeal. Hoffmann and his deputy camp commander had laid a burning coal on his stomach, whipped him, and then beat him with everything they had. The reason: Bergmann had disobeyed Hoffmann's no-smoking rule several times. His corpse was never discovered. The punishment handed out to his tormentors was rather less severe. The troopers Franz-Joachim Bojarski, Walter-Ulrich Behle, and Uwe Mainka got off with sentences ranging from nineteen months' probation to two years and nine months' imprisonment. These follow-up trials were hardest on Horst Röhlich, a printer from Heidelberg, who got four and a half years. At Hoffmann's orders he had printed not only the camp's "battle paper," *Kommando,* but also 800,000 dollars' worth of counterfeit money, with which Hoffmann had hoped to finance his terrorist activities.

And the murder of the Jewish publisher Shlomo Levin and his companion, Frieda Poeschke? In Erlangen, on the night of December 19, 1980, these two were shot to death—only a few miles from Hoffmann's home. A pair of sunglasses belonging to Hoffmann's girlfriend was found at the scene of the crime, and the weapon used was one that had already been confiscated from a Hoffmann intimate five years earlier, only to be returned shortly thereafter. In the view of the state prosecutors, Hoffmann had delegated the murder to his close friend Uwe Behrendt, the motive being "militant radicalism of a fascist nature." The court, however, decided that Uwe Behrendt had acted as "a solitary perpetrator." How lucky for Hoffmann that Behrendt had died in Lebanon in the summer of 1981. Suicide, according to Hoffmann.

Then there is the matter of the bombing at the Munich Oktoberfest on September 26, 1980, in which thirteen people died and over 200 were injured. Once again, the tracks lead straight to Hoffmann. But none other than Hans Langemann, chief of Bavaria's Verfassungsschutz, gave him an alibi. According to his testimony, Hoffmann was in Neuburg all day, under observation by his agency. Hoffmann himself, however, claimed to have spent the entire day in Nuremberg and produced several witnesses to that effect.

This would not be the only complication in the investigation. Investigators quickly decided that the attack was, again, the work of a single culprit and that Gundolf Köhler, who had been fatally injured in the explosion, must have been the perpetrator. To be sure, he was a member of Hoffmann's military group, but his motive was determined to be personal, not political: the result of a fight with his girlfriend. Evidence and testimony suggesting that Köhler hadn't acted alone was quickly dismissed, and his involvement in the neo-Nazi scene was never thoroughly examined. Testimony that directly incriminated Hoffmann was disqualified by the investigators as "alcohol-inspired nonsense." Experts ruled out the possibility of a single person building, deploying, and detonating such a heavy bomb, but the investigation was nonetheless discontinued in 1982 with the pithy remark: "Concrete evidence for the participation of another party does not exist."

Now back to 1990, in the Austrian forest. Here Gottfried Küssel has his paramilitary band firmly under control; Hans Jörg Schimanek, a good-looking man with light blond hair, is responsible for the formal instruction. He has had mercenary experience in Surinam and also, apparently, in Croatia. Up through the mid-eighties he was a career soldier in the Austrian army, a drill instructor stationed in Vienna. Then weapons began to disappear from Vienna's Maria-Theresa barracks and, after a judicial tug-of-war, Schimanek was dismissed. The Vienna state prosecutor had characterized him as something of a coward, but he is certainly adequate for today's exercises: "Left . . . turn! No, that was not right."

The troops stand rigidly in a row, and Schimanek positions their feet with the tips of his boots. Küssel stands in the background and benevolently inclines his head, which is covered with camouflage paint. The quiet of the forest is broken by birdsong and Schimanek's commands.

Should Schimanek ever be at a loss, Reinhold Kovar can always help him out. Kovar, with his neat mustache and Hitler Youth haircut, is standing beside me. The green-and-brown camouflage stripes on his face look very professional, as well they might, since Kovar is a corporal in the Austrian army.

Unit strength is fifteen men, two women, and one dog. With the exception of the dog, all are members of VAPO (Volkstreue Ausser-parlamentarische Opposition—The People's Loyal Extraparliamen-tary Opposition).* VAPO is the NSDAP-AO's advance organization in Austria.

There are martial-sports groups in almost every place where there are neo-Nazis. The privilege of documenting Küssel's "defensive exercises" is courtesy of Michael Kühnen; until he interceded, Küssel refused to allow me to film.

I had originally wanted to film such activities with Christian Worch, but when I asked him about it on the telephone, he played dumb. Only when I told him that Kühnen had referred me to him did he admit having anything to do with military games. But a film, he said, would be out of the question. At first he justified his refusal with the old complaint about bad experiences with the press. Yet when I pressed him, he came out with the truth: "Several active army soldiers participate in these exercises. And you can imagine just how much they'd like someone from the press taking pictures."

I certainly could. Worch's sorrow is hardly sincere when he expresses his regret that I cannot, unfortunately, document this aspect of the "national fight for freedom."

On November 12, 1992, the German Defense Ministry announces that over twenty incidents "with a right-wing extremist back-ground" have been reported that year, and that three people have been murdered. By February 1993, the number of incidents has

---

*The name is a playful allusion to the APO (Ausserparlamentarische Opposition—Extraparliamentary Opposition), which was a popular leftist student movement in the 1960s.

risen to eighty. And in Kiel-Holtenau, the ministry reports, "three officers and an ensign" threw a training grenade at a refugee shelter; the fact that "no one came to harm" isn't very reassuring.

"Getting hold of weapons is not a problem. Never has been," Küssel says at home after the military exercises. He has made himself comfortable on his couch, though his eyes betray a nervous restlessness that is in strange contrast to his massive figure.

The corners of Küssel's mouth curl as he explains the "obvious." "Every army in a civil war has weapons. Even people who didn't know where to get them got them the moment they truly needed to. It's really not a problem."

Gottfried Küssel is dangerous, as is Christian Worch. The difference is that Worch, a notary's assistant, knows how to answer thorny questions with such extreme caution that even a lengthy interview with him reveals nothing. Both of them, in fact, often amazed me with their presence of mind. They can make decisions and adapt to new situations within seconds. I could easily imagine Worch in the editor's chair of some newspaper, responding instantly as circumstances required; it's the logical result of years of experience with the enemy.

In the summer of 1990, Worch and Küssel organized the administration of a house in East Berlin seized by neo-Nazis. At that time, says Worch, "a hand grenade cost a bottle of vodka." The Soviet Army was in the process of leaving Germany, and in all the confusion Russian soldiers were able to sell huge quantities of weapons and explosives. Worch would remind me that he didn't say *he* had bought any. And he probably didn't; he was certainly smart enough to let others do that sort of thing.

I learn in 1992 that Worch has inherited a sizable legacy, and one can assume that he will use it to acquire the means to carry on with his intrigues, if not undiscovered, certainly unpunished. With enough money—as Hitler understood early on—you can direct the revolution while remaining in the background.

On January 7, 1992, Gottfried Küssel is arrested in Vienna for "crimes of renewed National Socialist activity." This offense, which formerly would net a life sentence in Austria, now brings only ten years. If this law were strictly enforced, Küssel and his followers would have been locked away for life a long time ago. Küssel has been a member of the NSDAP-AO since 1977, which he confirms for me in front of the camera. He has intimate relations with Ekkehard Weil, the Berlin-based terrorist who set off a series of bombs in the early eighties, including one in Simon Wiesenthal's house, which Küssel describes to me as "a firecracker, just to scare him a little."

Meanwhile, the Austrian judiciary considers itself humane. They feel strongly that one cannot imprison an adolescent for life just because he flourishes a swastika sticker one time. Their antifascist laws, however, were not created for such cases, but to ensure that incorrigible, violent, ardent, and organized Nazis would not get a second chance. Since Küssel and his comrades fit all of these criteria, it's only natural to wonder when they will feel the full strength of the law, which up to now has never been applied. For his part, Küssel should be able to appreciate the value of draconian punishment; he himself has announced that after the seizure of power he would reestablish the concentration camps, in order to "make the entire government understand, once and for all . . . where the mistakes lie."

In any case, Küssel's successors—in Vienna the militant Gerhard Endres (nicknamed "Earp"), and in Salzburg the highly intelligent Jürgen Lipthay—are already prepared to carry on his work. Küssel is in no way irreplaceable, and as long as well conceived laws are not enforced, an end to neo-Nazi activity is not in sight. And then, one day, their "basic idea and guiding principle," as presented in Die Neue Front, could once again become a bitter reality for us all: "Everyone participates—no one is responsible."

VII

THE FÜHRER'S
BODYGUARD

AGAIN AND AGAIN, THE FORKED TONGUE EXTENDS OUT
from the giant boa's mouth, searching. Snakes look at you with
astonishing indifference. They really don't even look, they just feel
their surroundings. The creature is about eight feet long, and its
middle is thicker than a powerful man's arm. At the moment she's
very mellow and has rolled up most of her gorgeous brown and
gold-flecked body onto her owner's lap.

"And this is little Trudy," says the white-haired gent lovingly,
patting the snake's slim back as if it were a German shepherd. He
has one of those, too. And cats. But they aren't in the room right
now because of little Trudy, the boa. There's no doubt about it:
Otto Riehs, Knight of the Iron Cross, is an animal lover.

"Like Adolf Hitler!" the seventy-year-old declares proudly.
"He was also a real animal lover. And in general: if you're a
nationalist, it's impossible *not* to be an animal lover, since, after all,
we love nature. And so we also love the races, since races are also
part of nature. So we really are nature lovers, but not like the
environmentalists, who are just against neo-Nazis."

He prefers the Republicans and recently tried to initiate a correspondence with the party chairman, Franz Schönhuber, "so that
German policies might finally be established. . . ." But Schönhuber
is clever. This former SS man has also served as department head of

the Bavarian State Radio Station and chairman of the Bavarian Journalists' Union. He knows exactly how Otto Riehs must be answered if the liberal press is not to prove an alliance with the Nazis: "Herr Schönhuber . . . highly appreciates the fact that you, a highly decorated man, have told him your convictions." Or: "He asks you to understand his political course and his need to differentiate himself from right-wing parties. In this hour, so crucial for our country, he begs you to contribute to the consolidation of the party for the good of the whole."

Trudy couldn't care less and is much more interested in the fist-sized piece of black foam rubber on the tip of my microphone. She moves toward me with a scary determination, thinking this dark shape might be an appetizing mouse.

Riehs, who has just laid out the Iron Cross he received for his bold attacks on Russian tanks, notices my emerging panic and pulls Trudy back. "A dear little animal, eh?"

Otto Riehs was born in Bohemia, once part of the Austro-Hungarian empire. Hitler "liberated" these Sudeten Germans soon after the annexation of Austria. At the time, many countries had fascist leaders who collaborated with Hitler and inflamed public sentiment at home; in the Sudetenland, it was Konrad Henlein. Since Otto Riehs was an eyewitness, I ask him what it was that his people were liberated from.

"From the Czech yoke," he says, as if everyone knew this.

But how, exactly, were they oppressed?

"Well, we weren't allowed to wear white stockings!"

And that was enough to justify an invasion?

White stockings, Riehs benevolently explains, happened to be the symbol of Konrad Henlein's movement, and were forbidden as an expression of National Socialist sentiment.

So it really wasn't the Sudeten Germans who were liberated, but the local Nazis, who took revenge by deporting every Jew they could get their hands on. They also treated many innocent civilians so mercilessly that after the war, after a brief internment, all Sudeten Germans—Nazis or not—were thrown out of the country by the Czechs.

This also happened with the Pomeranians, the Silesians, and

others. Since then, these expellees, along with those who could not live with the outcome of the war, formed "expellee associations" and "homeland societies." In part, these organizations keep alive the old traditions, which in itself is not objectionable; but they also regularly call for the return of their "lost territories." Thus the motto "Silesia remains ours!" The circulars of some of these associations print maps of "Germany in the Boundaries Justified by International Law," reflecting the borders of 1937, or even of 1939, which include large portions of Czechoslovakia, Poland, and, Austria, along with several smaller territories. It is typical of this way of thinking that many expellees' children also consider themselves "expelled."

Otto Riehs is not only an expellee, he is also an amateur video enthusiast. After he has detached himself from Trudy's loving embrace and returned her to her equally large companion behind glass, he proudly shows me his recordings of one of his "homeland society's" recent meetings. There were, as was to be expected, plenty of national costumes, flags, and speeches. He graciously fast-forwards through most of it; and then come the songs, including "Deutschland über alles." Several participants have raised their arms in the Hitler-salute.

It's all very nice, but I'm after something stronger and I know Riehs can help me find it. After all, I met him through Michael Kühnen. Riehs is his representative in Frankfurt am Main, and a hero of the neo-Nazi movement. So I ask if he knows General Remer, Hitler's bodyguard and the man who crushed the conspiracy to assassinate Hitler in July of 1944.

"Otto-Ernst? Of course I know him!" At my urging, Riehs reaches for the telephone and calls Otto-Ernst Remer. After a brief greeting, he hands me the phone and I have Remer on the line.

His voice is certainly old, but no less resolute for that. As I explain my hope to film an interview with him, he interrupts: "How old are you?"

"Um, twenty-eight," I answer, disconcerted.

"And your name?"

"Michael Schmidt."

"And what do you want to ask?"

A few months later I'm sitting opposite him. Otto-Ernst Remer has a narrow, chiseled face with sporty glasses and a high forehead.

"For you, Hitler was a democrat?" I ask.

"Yes, he was. He was fundamentally a democrat."

Now retired, Remer has dressed up for the occasion. A costly Tyrolean jacket with leather straps gives him a smart, youthful appearance, in spite of his tie and heavily starched collar. Born in 1912, he is tall, slim, and obviously in excellent shape. I sense his age only when he gets excited; and since his stroke, his doctor has forbidden him to become agitated. His wife, Anneliese, diligently watches over him—"Isn't this a little too much for you, Otto-Ernst?" she asks anxiously, again and again—but when it comes to politics, Remer is hard to restrain. After all, he is personally responsible for defending German values: his personal newsletter is called *Recht und Wahrheit*—Justice and Truth.

Today is my third visit to Remer's home; his wife and pet collie already know me. But once again we can't just simply record the interview. As before, a censor will intervene. The cameraman and his technician hook up their cables and set up the lights and cameras, and then they wait. If you deal with Remer, you quickly discover that he's inseparable from a man named Karl Philipp. This makes everything a little complicated, because Philipp, our "censor," is a difficult man. He should have been here long ago, but . . .

The cameraman occasionally raises his eyebrows and looks over at me. I'm in the side room where Remer, to kill time, is showing off old recordings of himself on the news—"There I am! . . . There I am again!" I can only shrug my shoulders in reply. He's a good cameraman and doesn't become impatient, which is exactly what I need right now.

At our first interview, Philipp demanded a contract stipulating that publication would be permitted only after his review; otherwise we would pay a penalty of 100,000 marks. That interview, of course, was never broadcast, though Philipp is prepared to permit us another interview. But we can't start filming until he is present to approve the questions.

After all, Remer has been condemned frequently for his statements. An example from testimony before the Kaufbeuren district court: "The defendant Otto Remer next stood up at the table, took out his lighter, let some of the gas escape, and sniffed at it. He then asked: 'What's this?' After a brief pause for effect, he explained that it was a Jew nostalgic for Auschwitz." When I ask him about this statement, Remer vociferously denies having said it and calls the *Stern* reporter Gerhard Kromschröder, who had confirmed the quote before the court, "a filthy pig."

However, Remer cannot restrain himself from calling Stauffenberg's circle "scoundrels, . . . traitors to the people . . . and bastards."* Since in the Federal Republic such declarations are criminal offenses, he and his advisers decided upon advance censorship for our interview. A clear necessity, since Remer froths at the mouth whenever he talks about "shit-democracy" and its "damned muddle of parties."

Thus, at the previous interview, one of Remer's advisers sat next to him, and whenever Remer started on one of his tirades, made a scissors motion with his first and second fingers. "Snip, snap, cut, cut!" he said with a smug grin.

The bell rings, and Frau Remer opens the door.

Smiling, Karl Philipp pushes past the Remers' affectionate collie. Remer had just lauded him to me as an "outstanding man. My successor! We have great plans for the future!" But he really doesn't look the type. In fact, this medium-built fifty-year-old with

---

*Claus Schenk Graf von Stauffenberg (1907–44) was a key figure in a group of officers who became convinced that Hitler would fail in his war aims and bring Germany to absolute ruin. Their attempt to assassinate Hitler, an operation codenamed "Valkyrie," was unsuccessful when the bomb set by Stauffenberg (on July 20, 1944) only wounded Hitler and the subsequent coup attempt was crushed, in part by then Major Otto Remer, who remained loyal in the period of confusion following the blast. Most of the resistance fighters were arrested and, if not immediately shot under martial law, executed after a show-trial.

thinning hair looks a bit like a pastor. His appearance is altogether bland. You have to observe his slightly round face for quite a while before you can discover anything on the order of a feature.

He informs me, dryly, that he too is a journalist.

"And amateur historian," he adds. He then produces a flyer from his briefcase. It perpetrates the infamous numbers game—long familiar to insiders—by which the total of six million Jews murdered by the Nazis is "proven," step-by-step, to be "only" between 40,000 and 300,000, depending on the version.

I want to return to the subject of his livelihood, so as a fellow journalist, I inquire about his professional activities.

"I write articles," he says, and looks as if he's wondering whether one really can live off that. But Herr Philipp doesn't need to: Christian Worch already gave me enough of a clue when he told me that Philipp was an "honorary consul." And where has His Excellencey been posted? Worch suggested that the Fiji Islands would be a good place to start.

Philipp looks at me inquiringly. Does he know that I know? I might not be able to read minds, but I can read what's in the German Travel Bureau's "Touristik-Kontakt" (vol. 26, page 503): "Fiji Air Ltd. . . . Managing Director Karl Philipp." And then (on page 528): "Solomon Airlines . . . Managing Director for Europe: Karl Philipp. Assistant Director: Anita Philipp."

So he's married. And in fact there's something about his wife in Pomorin and Runge's 1979 book *Die Neonazis Teil II* (The Neo-Nazis, Part II); in a photo caption on page 98 it says: "Karl Philipp, NPD regional chairman for Darmstadt . . . to his left his girlfriend: she photographs antifascists and, if the police come, claims to be an English tourist."

So, they speak English and are cosmopolitan, which is certainly an advantage for missions outside of the Reich. Thus one can read the following about him in the French *Tribune Nationaliste:* "The British National Party (BNP) held its most successful annual rally ever when its members . . . met in London on Saturday, October 12, 1990. At very short notice, due to the injustice of the ban against Manfred Roeder who was stopped by police in Jersey and escorted back to Germany, German speaker Karl Philipp addressed the rally

with a most enjoyable and interesting talk about the reunification of
East and West Germany and the growing awareness about the truth
surrounding the alleged gassing of six million Jews during the
Second World War.''

Of course! Philipp's hobby is denying the mass murders in the
National Socialist concentration camps. And he's clearly playing on
an international field now. I'd love to get Otto-Ernst's views on the
gas chambers, but Philipp decides that, regrettably, Remer cannot
be asked about this, nor about neo-Nazis, David Irving, Remer's
time in the Middle East, arms trafficking, or any other subject that
might prove "emotionally draining.'' I am, of course, not surprised.
Remer would become nasty. Or, as another censor put it, ''He's
just a soldier! We're cutting this out . . .''

I am determined, however, that today not a second will be cut.
After all, we're not in the Third Reich. Besides, it's well known that
Remer played a large role in putting down the rebellion of July 20,
1944. And that the Führer personally rewarded him for it: from
then on he was Hitler's bodyguard.

Philipp nods benevolently. This we can speak about.

"Looking back,'' Remer says, ''I can only say that in my entire
life I never met another individual of Hitler's stature. I still have him
before my eyes today. That wasn't just anybody—that was a great
man, the sort that's born perhaps once in a hundred years. And
historians today can tell all the lies they want!'' His voice becomes
terse, and he speaks as if making a formal declaration: ''Hitler will
be a permanent factor in German history.''

Who would argue with that?

Shortly after German history's permanent factor put an end to his
own life on April 30, 1945, the war also ended for Otto-Ernst. He
describes his last meeting with the Führer in his book, *Kriegshetze
gegen Deutschland* (The War Slander Against Germany). According
to Remer, the Führer sent him on his way with the following words:
''In an honorable decline lies the seed of ascent.''

Robert Wistrich's *Who's Who in Nazi Germany* describes how, in
the last days of the war, Remer ordered his division ''to break

through to the south, in the direction of Dresden,'' while he himself took off ''in civilian clothes over the Elbe river into the west, where American troops had already arrived.'' He clearly preferred to leave the dreaded fate of a Russian prisoner-of-war camp to his soldiers; he had bigger plans for himself.

By saving himself, Remer could help the ''seed of ascent'' develop. He and his comrades therefore founded the Sozialistische Reichspartei (Socialist Reich Party) in 1949, and two years later, in the 1951 regional elections in Lower Saxony, it received a spectacular 11 percent of the vote. But these impressive National Socialist rumblings were banned as unconstitutional in October 1952. That same year he was sentenced to three months' imprisonment for slandering the memory of the resistance movement—he called it a ''stain on the honor of the German officers' corps.''

To avoid imprisonment, he went into exile: to Egypt, where people then had a little more sympathy for the Nazis, and soon the Middle East became for Remer a second home. He was the friend of anyone who was the enemy of Israel, from the Grand Mufti of Jerusalem to Gamal Abdel Nasser, whom he served as security adviser. In Egypt he also developed into a major arms dealer. In Syria and in Lebanon he was a welcome companion for Alois Brunner, Adolf Eichmann's assistant and one of the most sought-after war criminals. (Brunner is reported to have died in Syria in December 1992. He was never punished for his crimes.) Brunner and Remer were—and Remer still is—in contact with the Institute for Historical Review, in the United States, whose goal is to convince the public that the Nazis' war crimes and mass exterminations are all propaganda lies. (More on this organization later.) In the 1950s, Remer visited Germany but returned to Egypt to expand his weapons business, the Orient Trading Company, a firm based in Damascus. At the start of the sixties, Remer was again in Germany, cultivating business connections for the Middle East.

In 1981, Otto-Ernst Remer returned to Germany permanently. Presumably driven by nostalgia, he christened his new political organization the ''Remer Brigade,'' in memory of his ''Escort Brigade of the Führer.'' Remer now strives to link his Middle East contacts with German and European right-wing extremists—for

example, with such people as the French terrorist Mark Frederiksen, a member of the neofascist FANE, the group held responsible for the bombing of a Paris synagogue on October 3, 1980, in
which six people died. "I've certainly had many connections and
I've gotten to know many people. These things were always important to me. But I'm also not an idiot. I saw that nothing was possible
at the time, that you couldn't even speak about it—until now,
suddenly overnight the tide has turned, and with it prospects have
opened whose end we cannot even glimpse."

Remer hopes to work with fascist organizations in Russia, such
as the anti-Semitic PAMYAT movement, but he has bigger ideas. In
a 1990 paper for the Institute for Historical Review, Remer claims
to have met with the Soviet ambassador to West Germany, Valentin
Falin. He then sent a memorandum regarding German–Russian
cooperation to Moscow, and discussed it, allegedly, with representatives of the Soviet Embassy. Though a bitter rival of Kühnen,
Remer also looks at all possibilities for "German politics." He
stresses this notion again and again: "Not left, not right, just
German." I will have to go to other sources to inquire about the
significance of this remark, since Karl Philipp won't permit any
questions about neo-Nazism. Remer himself says only that "No one
can accuse me of even faintly having the ambition to be a communist
or something like that. And another thing I want to make clear:
about National Socialism, I was never in the party."

I was still trying to figure out why he's denying what no one in
the room has accused him of when he explains: "I have always been
independent. I have my own ideas." And then he propagates them.
Remer, who wants to convince me that he has no contact with
neo-Nazis, that he doesn't even know what neo-Nazism is, proves
himself plainly to be what he always claims others are: a liar.

In fact, in an internal neo-Nazi videotape, Otto-Ernst Remer is
quite visible standing next to Thomas Brehl, Kühnen's deputy. And
the speech he gives to the gathered neo-Nazis of the FAP is equally
unambiguous: "In your difficult political struggle, more difficult
even than the one we once fought, you must be determined, you
must become a disciplined, responsible fellowship that cannot be
separated, an elite to form the foundation of German youth."

Remer and Philipp, I feel, are two people whom we will continue to meet in my investigations.

Graeme Atkinson reminds me of something Michael Kühnen said in our first conversation—that "the overall societal atmosphere is changing." How can it have happened that right-wing extremists are once again presentable? What kind of atmosphere is this, what kind of society? What is the state of the nation?

II

THE STATE OF
THE NATION

VIII

THE END OF THE
POSTWAR ERA

WE GERMANS HAVE BEEN THINKING A GREAT DEAL
recently about our national identity, but our concrete knowledge of
German history is shockingly inadequate. The survivors of the last
"People's Tribunals" can still tell the younger generation the real
meaning of phrases like "special treatment," "Action Reinhard,"
and "T4." But they are not asked very often, and in my own school,
I learned far more about chivalry than about the mechanisms of the
Third Reich. Which is not to say that chivalry is unimportant; but
we cannot accept as a matter of course a curriculum that teaches the
Middle Ages in tremendous detail while hurrying through the period
between 1900 and 1950 in just a few months. As a consequence,
only the end results are studied in detail; the causes are glossed over,
if they're even mentioned at all.

In the same way, our society and our politicians have failed to
account for the Third Reich. As a result, the virtual banning of this
subject from public discourse is already wreaking a bitter revenge.
If so many know so little about the Third Reich, it becomes possible
for a new generation of Germans to consider nationalism chic.

It is imperative that we understand why, even today, certain
older Germans wince when they hear the words *deportation* and
special action. But time is passing, and with it the generation that

experienced this period directly. The postwar era is coming to an end.

"We are the people! We are the people!"

It is the end of September 1989 and thousands of people are chanting rhythmically in Leipzig, the "city of heroes." There, in the square behind the opera house, thousands of East Germans gather every Monday to support the opposition's call for "actualized socialism," and to let loose their pent-up anger over the communist regime. Each week more and more people come to the dimly lit square, until finally the space can't contain all the demonstrators— more than a hundred thousand. The peaceful revolution, as the media would later call it.

Gradually other chants are heard. "We are the people" is a fundamentally democratic phrase, urging the greater participation of the citizenry and opposing authoritarian tendencies. At the end of October come the first calls of "The Wall must go," and on the first Monday after November 9, 1989, the day the Wall was opened, the Leipzig choruses cry "Germany, united fatherland" and "We are one people." Those who still chant "We are the people," the ones who began the upheaval with the words of Rosa Luxemburg ("Freedom is always the freedom of those who disagree"), are quickly outnumbered by those who simply crave the wealth of the West and have always felt victimized by the system to which they'd passively accommodated themselves for over forty years.

Black, red, and gold flags now predominate in Leipzig's Opera Square. The people are inflamed by the promises and enticements of the West German politicians, by the "welcome money," by the tropical fruit, the video recorders, the stereo systems. Drunken skinheads mingle among the demonstrators and revel in the growing nationalist mood. Enter the West German right wing, eager to exploit this change in mood. By the middle of December 1989, the Republicans are distributing flyers at the Monday demonstrations in Leipzig and other cities in the DDR, demanding "immediate reunification," as well as, ludicrously, an "end to 'overcoming the

past' ''—as if it had ever really begun.* Party chief Franz Schönhuber, a former Waffen-SS man, expresses his excitement in an
interview with the *Quotidien de Paris:* "For us the DDR is the source
of renewal."

On February 5, 1990, the DDR's parliament forbids REP (Republican) activities in its territory, but the police ignore the ban with
sullen indifference. Bavarian REP functionaries in private cars cart
their propaganda material over the border by the ton and distribute
it to enthusiastic East Germans. Following a demonstration of
150,000 people at the end of January, the REPs announce the
creation of their first base in the DDR, the Central Leipzig Regional
Committee. Franz Glasauer, the deputy Bavarian party chairman
from Landshut, and Reinhold Rade, the REP's DDR coordinator
from Bad Tölz, quickly convert the bar of the hotel on Lisztplatz
into a party hangout, covering it with flags, party posters ("Socialism Is Shitism"), and stickers. Seventy sympathizers crowd into the
bar, applauding Glasauer enthusiastically as he proclaims that "Pomerania and Silesia belong to Germany," demanding a "Europe of
fatherlands," and railing against "sham refugees." This last point
goes over especially well.

Candidates rush to volunteer for the committee elections. Without any urging they take the microphone and introduce themselves.
One claims that his "heart beats for Germany and the party,"
another is volunteering so that "we can get rid of foreigners here,"
and another stammers that his goal is to "join the Republicans and
stand up for them." The last, a painter, wrings his hands as he
searches for the right words: "I want to do everything for the party
. . . [pause] . . . commit myself . . . [long pause] . . . and I'm also
for a unified Germany and . . . [pause] . . . yes and . . ." Unable
to think of anything more, he hands back the microphone. Even so,
it's enough to get him elected.

Franz Glasauer is happy to have the formal business behind him,
since this day is really about symbolism: "With this new local

---

Vergangenheitsbewältigung: literally, "coping with the past"—the German term for
the process of facing up to the horrors of the Nazi era. (Translator's note)

committee, the Republicans are the first real all-German party that
is active in the DDR without auxiliaries or subsidiaries.''

Soon after the committee elections end, masked counterdemonstrators put an end to the Republican celebration by thoroughly
trashing the bar. The proprietress wails that she really had only
thought about the extra business the Republicans had brought her,
then just shakes her head at the ruins of her establishment.

The Republicans are not the only ones who come from the
golden West to show the "Easties" the facts of life. Representatives
of the Nationalistische Front (Nationalist Front), the NPD, and the
Patrioten für Deutschland (Patriots for Germany) mingle with the
discontented of the DDR. The newspaper *Wir Selbst* (We Ourselves)
from Koblenz recommences publication after a year-long shutdown
purely because of the upheaval. The *Wiking-Jugend* (Viking Youth)
distributes copies of the Deutschland Hymn with all three verses.*
Members of the Freiheitliche Arbeiterpartei (FAP) have come with
their leader, Friedhelm Busse, who has numerous convictions for
violating firearms and explosives laws. In print and in discussions
they demand a "free Germany, free from oppression, communism,
and foreign meddling.''

In the meantime, opponents of these groups (and foreigners) lead
a dangerous existence in the Monday demonstrations. A week
before the new REP committee's founding, they were condemned
as "Stasi children" and "Stasi swine" and chased clear across the
city under the slogan "Reds out of the demo.'' By now, about 2,000
neo-Nazis and skinheads are participating in the mass demonstrations for a "united fatherland.'' They form organized blocks and,
unresisted, carry their imperial war flags or REP party banners at the
front of the marches through the streets of Leipzig. They chant
"Goebbels, we love you!'' "Germany for the Germans!'' "Foreigners out!'' "Gysi and Modrow, up against the wall!''† and sing

*The first verse *("Deutschland, Deutschland, über alles . . .")* is forbidden in the
Federal Republic, whose official national anthem is the third verse: *"Einigkeit und
Recht und Freiheit . . ."* (Unity and justice and liberty . . .).
†Gregor Gysi and Hans Modrow: members of the Communist Party's successor in
the DDR, the Party of Democratic Socialism (PDS).

the "Horst Wessel Song." They besiege foreigner hangouts, break the windows of gay bars, and burn church flyers and information sheets. Long before the official reunification, neo-Nazis from East and West have unified on the streets.

Until the day itself—October 3, 1990—the DDR is host to a plethora of assaults on foreigners, refugees, Jews, punks, and Communists—anyone who looks or thinks differently. Scarcely any major soccer game goes by in these weeks without xenophobic riots. As a rule, the East German police merely look on. The same happens on July 8, when Germany narrowly wins soccer's World Cup in Italy on a penalty kick. The final whistle has barely sounded in Rome's Olympia Stadium before the hunt for foreigners begins in East Berlin and other East German cities. The boundaries between normal citizens and radicals blur completely. As bystanders cheer, Lebanese are chased through the tunnels of East Berlin's Alexanderplatz train station and then beaten up. In the course of the evening, about 500 skinheads gather in Alexanderplatz. Equipped with German flags, imperial war flags, and baseball bats, they pursue their favorite hobby—"cutting up chinks," as they, along with large parts of the DDR population, contemptuously term the Vietnamese. They celebrate Germany's championship and randomly knock down everything that looks un-German. Franz Beckenbauer, the national team's coach, fans the flames with his provocative boasts: "We're number one in the world. No one will beat us for years to come. I pity the rest of the world, but that's how it is."

After three long days in the newspaper archives, I'm certain of one thing: if the soccer fans are happy, the politicians line up right behind them. Of course, the politicians also know the wisdom of Günter Grass: "In this era," he wrote, "whoever thinks about Germany and looks for answers to the German question must also think about Auschwitz." They know that foreign countries are watching reunited Germany very closely; they know where German dreams of superpower status can lead; and they know that foreign countries hear the undertones loud and clear when Chancellor Helmut Kohl declares that after reunification, "We will be, not only in number but also by every other standard, the strongest country in Europe.''

That's exactly what worries the English, the French, the Poles, and all the others. They fear that what Germany could not win in two world wars—predominance in Europe—will now be achieved by its economic strength. In England the expression "Fourth Reich" is heard. Margaret Thatcher's adviser Nicholas Ridley even mentions Helmut Kohl and Adolf Hitler in the same breath. *Newsweek* reports that by annexing the DDR the Germans have won a capitalistic "blitzkrieg"—a word that entered the English language in 1939, under ominous circumstances.

At the formal reunification, the government strives to allay suspicions of renewed nationalist ambitions, emphasizing, rather, Germany's commitment to European responsibility. The speakers are painfully careful not to commit any faux pas in this historic hour. But Helmut Kohl and Lothar de Maizière, the DDR's prime minister for the last six months of its existence, are more forthcoming in their televised addresses on the eve of unification. "For me, a dream has now been realized," Chancellor Kohl declares, but he would not "forget the past because of his joy." To imagine that by "the past" he means the Nazi reign of terror, which in fact led to Germany's division, would be to miss the mark, and by a lot. No, he is *not* talking about the millions of Jews killed, not even about the Second World War. Not a word about those things. In this hour, of joy, this victory celebration for the Federal Republic's market economy, the German chancellor is talking about those people "who suffered so much from Germany's division." In Kohl's vision of the past, the Germans were the true victims of all this history. He is talking about how "families were brutally separated, political dissidents were imprisoned, and men and women were shot by the Wall." This, he stresses, must "never be repeated, and therefore we should never forget it."

De Maizière doesn't do any better. After babbling about how "unity was won with the heart," he then turns to the past. "We know very well what the past has inflicted upon us," he begins, as if Germans were helpless, innocent victims of an inevitable fate. "We do not want to repress the past, we must face her honorably and responsibly," he continues, and that sounds good. "But she must not be part of our future." Okay, now I get it: he's not talking about German history between 1933 and 1945 but about the last forty-five years. While de Maizière—who will soon be revealed as a Stasi informer and forced to abandon a promising political career in united Germany—looks with "joy and confidence in German unity," the past cannot be allowed to intrude. After all, "We stand at the start of a new era."

The majority of German media also seize upon unification as an excuse to put an end to thoughts of the past. Since Helmut Kohl has announced the end of the postwar era, why continue with these annoying memories of the Nazis? Instead, we can start "overcoming" the communist era; it's a lot more fun, and we've certainly had practice.

On unification day, the tabloid *Bild* informs its millions of readers in a banner headline that "THE TRUE GERMANY HAS ARRIVED." This special issue, with a token price of ten pfennig, wishes "Germany happiness and prosperity" now that the "misery of German division" is over. It began, according to *Bild,* with the raising of the "red flag above the Reichstag on noon of April 30, 1945." So, the liberation from National Socialism was the start of all the problems, and "the tragedy of broken hearts" began with the Russian capture of Berlin. And all blame for that lies with a single individual: "Adolf Hitler, the man who led Germany into catastrophe." And since that's the case, we really don't have to be ashamed any longer!

Why bother to think about the past at all? The day after the triumphant ceremony in the Berlin Philharmonic, the *Bild* headline read: "GERMANY! MY GOD, HOW BEAUTIFUL IT IS." According to the editorial on the following page, "Everything is different. We are experiencing the grace of zero hour." The future lies before us, the past has been erased, swept away by the "peaceful revolution," and unification heals all wounds. After all, as Lothar de Maizière said in his speech, "We stand on the threshold of a new era."

Attempts to free Germany from the burden of its history have been going on for years, and now this seed planted so long ago has finally sprouted.

IX

THE NATIONAL
IDENTITY CRISIS

I STILL REMEMBER EXACTLY HOW HELMUT KOHL, IN HIS
first statement as chancellor in 1982, promised he would devote
himself to Germany's "spiritual and moral renewal." And I remember Alfred Dregger, former CDU parliamentary delegation head,
urging the country "to step out of Adolf Hitler's shadow."* And
I remember Franz-Josef Strauss, the CSU party chairman and Bavarian prime minister who on Ash Wednesday, 1988, spoke his mind
in Passau's Nibelungen Hall: "We must step out of Adolf Hitler's
poisonous atmosphere. We must once again become a people that
does not walk with the stoop of a convict of world history but with
the upright stride of confident citizens who are proud to be German." They were all concerned with reestablishing a national identity, with putting an end to this walk of repentance, this incessant
remembering. After all, those were just twelve years in the civi-
lized, millennium-long history of Germany, right?

The brief period during which Willy Brandt could win election
under the motto "Dare to have more democracy" was long gone.

*Alfred Dregger, Christian Democrat, was mayor of Fulda until 1970, then CDU
state chairman in Hesse and a parliamentary delegate. He belonged to the CDU's
ultra right-wing "steel-helmet faction," and was general secretary of the party
until 1991.

Afterward, Germany once again had *Berufsverbote*—people forbidden to practice their profession; the word signifies a German specialty, and among specialists it has entered into English and French *(le berufsverbot)*. Basic democratic civil rights were sacrificed to internal security, which some saw as endangered by the Red Army Faction's terrorist activities. Willy Brandt had to make way for Helmut Schmidt, a Social Democrat whom many conservatives said was "really in the wrong party" an expression of their respect. After him came Helmut Kohl and his call for "spiritual and moral renewal."

Where will this new journey end?

Archives do reward patience: I come across a newspaper article from 1977. An "Auschwitz Congress" took place on August 6 in Nuremberg, the preferred city of right-wing extremists looking to meet in a historic locale. The declared goal was to "refute the lie of the century—that multitudes were gassed at Auschwitz." The *Nationalzeitung* provided headlines like "HITLER—GENIUS OR MADMAN? NOW THE TRUTH COMES OUT," and "6 MILLION GASSED JEWS—THE LIE OF THE CENTURY." The event's organizers were the former SS man Thies Christophersen, who in 1973 published *Die Auschwitz-Lüge* (The Auschwitz Lie), and Erwin Schönborn, who had distributed flyers offering a 10,000-mark reward for "every incontestably proven 'gassing' in a 'gas chamber' of a German concentration camp." The flyer added that "We will not accept concentration-camp survivors from Poland, Israel, or the U.S.A."

Hold on, I think. What have I just found? All these Nazis, the ones living eternally in the past, they certainly don't represent the mood in Germany.

We will learn more about these people later, but first let's take a look at one man I would meet again and again. I had failed in my first attempt to film him (from a hidden vantage point), but I would later succeed. The man is David Irving, the English historian to whom *Der Spiegel,* the renowned newsmagazine, devoted an entire series in 1978. Under the title *"Das Ende einer Legende"* (The End of a Legend), the magazine published advance excerpts from Irving's biography of Field Marshal Erwin Rommel, the "Desert Fox" who fought for Hitler in Africa. Thus a magazine, otherwise so proud of its duty to enlighten, helped Irving achieve wide recognition. A man who argued, in his book *Hitler's War* (1977), that Hitler had for a long time known nothing about the extermination of the Jews. A "historian" who even then claimed that concentration camps were "indispensable for political education," and that "Hitler created a Germany with equal opportunities for those who work with their hands and those who work with their heads. . . . [He] reestablished the nation's faith in the future, [and] all the cancerous symptoms of industrial conflict—strikes, drunkenness, pretended sickness—became phantoms of the past."

The editors of *Der Spiegel* knew who they were dealing with— they had reported on *Hitler's War* in detail in the fall of 1977. And now, in an internal "house bulletin," they introduced a man who doesn't even have a degree in history as a "British historian," and celebrate him as a "master at tracking down previously unused sources." Before the *Spiegel* series, Irving had already appeared at radical-right congresses and lectured on "Betrayal and Resistance in the Third Reich." And now, thanks to *Der Spiegel,* this author and his ideas enter the respectable mainstream.

Surely something else must have been going on. In the middle of the 1970s a bona fide Hitler fad swept through the Federal Republic. In 1973, Joachim C. Fest's biography of Hitler appeared, and a film version followed four years later. In 1978 Sebastian Haffner, a highly respected political journalist, published *Anmerkungen zu Hitler* (Notes on Hitler). Both books became bestsellers and the movie was a box-office success. Fest (who soon after became coeditor of the *Frankfurter Allgemeine Zeitung,* a major daily newspaper) had wanted to study Hitler's historical importance without blinders or taboos. He praised Hitler's "revolutionary ideas of 'renewal,' of transforming state and society into a conflict-free, militantly closed 'national-community.' " And, in his opinion, a comparison with other politicians of the Weimar Republic showed that Hitler was "certainly the more modern phenomenon."

In an editorial in the *Frankfurter Allgemeine* on January 9, 1974, Fest praised Alexander Solzhenitsyn, whose *Gulag Archipelago* had just been translated into German. According to Fest, Solzhenitsyn had not been afraid to say that "Hitler's extermination of the Jews was the repetition of that principle of terror, first applied in the Soviet Union, that does not ask about guilt or innocence, but instead punishes membership in a particular group with deportation and extermination." With that, Fest anticipated a controversy that he, as copublisher of the newspaper, brought to the fore in 1986.

The historian Ernst Nolte, who in 1986 would also play a major role in the debate, had already made Hitler and National Socialism merely relative evils with his 1974 book *Deutschland und der Kalte Krieg* (Germany and the Cold War): "Indeed, every significant state of the present that set itself an extraordinary goal has had its 'Hitler era,' with its atrocities and its victims, and the ramifications for the rest of the world varied only according to that country's dimensions and situation." So the systematic extermination of millions of Jews is placed in a series along with other horrors. Even though it was the result of an official program entitled "The Final Solution to the Jewish Question," put into action with all of Germany's resources and exemplary bureaucracy, with "German thoroughness," tenacity, and discipline—and maintained right up to the end, when Germany was fighting a war on all fronts yet still utilizing much of its transport capacity to deport Jews.

Haffner devoted a third of his *Anmerkungen zu Hitler* to fascism's "achievements and successes." For example, the emancipation of women made "great leaps forward" under Hitler—an interpretation possible only if you have a thoroughly sexist concept of women's emancipation. For Haffner, Hitler was "without doubt a socialist—in fact, a very effective socialist." It is painful for me to read such words from a figure like Haffner.

The historian Hellmut Diwald, who in 1990 would write the preamble to the Republicans' party program, also published a book in 1974, the *Geschichte der Deutschen* (History of the Germans). According to Diwald, Hitler was not a racist anti-Semite and the Holocaust was merely an act of vengeance, its "basic points still unclear." This book also became a resounding success.

In such an atmosphere, who could be surprised when, after the Majdanek judgment in 1981,* the *Frankfurter Allgemeine* completely misrepresented the judiciary's treatment of the Nazi regime and wrote: "The National Socialist criminals had to face a court, but the communist ones hold offices in their countries, receive titles and medals, and some are fêted at banquets in the West."

A new climate was created, in which such opinions could be expressed in bestsellers and respectable editorials, and which naturally lessened the resistance to such propagandists as David Irving. These "revelations" initially create confusion, as they're meant to; they break apparent taboos in order to make room for "new" ideas.

Alfred Dregger, in a June 1983 speech on the state of the nation, declared the following: "Between 1965 and 1975 a break with the majority of our traditions occurred. These traditions belonged—and belong—to the substance of our national identity, and this break directly affects the unity of the nation. German identity as a whole has been pushed into the twilight. Moreover, German history has also been examined simply to ask how it could lead to National Socialism. This has had the result of devalorizing German history as a whole. Since then there has been a trauma in our self-assessment. We have now achieved a political turning point that we hope to transform into reality, and the measure of our success will depend, not least of all, on our ability to reestablish our national identity within the identity created by our values." In other words, in order to "cure" German national identity, the "trauma" of the Nazi era must disappear.

Thus it was entirely fitting for Chancellor Helmut Kohl, on his trip to Israel in 1984, to claim for himself, as representative of postwar Germans, the "grace of a late birth." It was also entirely fitting that on April 25 of the same year, the magazine *Quick* ran a

---

*In July 1942, the Nazis established an extermination camp in Majdanek, Poland, where at least 200,000 people were murdered. The state prosecutor's office in Ludwigsburg finished its investigations in 1962 and handed the proceedings over to Düsseldorf. Thirteen years passed before the trial finally began in 1975. After six years, verdicts were handed down in July 1981. For proven participation in 17,438 murders, one defendant received a life sentence and the other seven were sentenced to a combined total of only 46.5 years in jail.

story on "The Power of the Jews." The article poses the question "How is it that 6 million American Jews control 209 million non-Jewish Americans?" and then explains that the Jews "control public opinion," since ABC, CBS, and NBC are "run by Jewish directors." Thankfully, writes *Quick,* the Americans are free to debate this question impartially; for the Germans, however, "a really objective, impartial discussion of this subject is made impossible by the burden of recent history." It was exactly this burden that *Quick,* with a readership of over a million, wanted to remove. All means justified this end, including defaming the State of Israel: "Their nostalgia-state costs America's Jews approximately an extra $300 million a year in donations." An outcry of indignation from other German newspapers and magazines was conspicuously absent. Just as no one complained when, after the neo-Nazi terrorist attacks on refugee homes in 1991, *Quick,* in a telling distortion of the facts, reported that "LEFTIST ANARCHISTS AND STASI-RABBLE STIR UP HATE."

In 1984, Chancellor Kohl received the Medal of Honor of the Expellees' Federation as a reward for declaring territorial issues to be "open." At the yearly conference of the Christian Democrats' youth organization, a motion by the executive board to affirm the permanence of Poland's western border—the Oder–Neisse Line—was defeated. In December 1984, the Federal Press Office still published a calendar that described the territories east of the Oder and Neisse rivers as being "under Polish administration."

The following year saw the beginning of a chain of events that attracted attention far beyond Germany's borders. In 1985, Hermann Fellner, the spokesman on domestic policies for the CSU faction in the Bundestag, gave his anti-Semitism free rein and declared that "the Jews are always quick to speak when money is jingling somewhere in German pockets."

Then, on May 5, 1985, Chancellor Kohl and U.S. President Ronald Reagan strolled together across the military cemetery in Bitburg where over 2,000 deceased Wehrmacht and SS dead are buried. This official state visit, which turned culprits into victims, caused storms of controversy even before the fact. Jewish groups and war veterans in the United States protested vigorously against Reagan's appearance and the attendant rehabilitation of SS criminals. The German reactions to these protests spoke for themselves. In Bonn, officials said an American withdrawal could lead to a "severe setback for German–American relations;" Kohl's spokesman, Peter Boehnisch, explained that the issue was not "which particular individuals the Bitburg cemetery" contained. As I read the newspaper articles, I asked myself why the government did not diplomatically choose another cemetery. But Boehnisch obviously wanted the SS men to be mourned, since he stressed that it should "be possible to make a gesture of reconciliation and friendship through such a visit."

The *Frankfurter Allgemeine,* while feigning some understanding for the Jewish protests, nevertheless cautioned that "Insightful people should warn certain Jewish circles against letting horrible memories move them to push certain ideas too far. . . . Israel's fate depends upon the defensive capability of the West, which in turn depends upon the Western countries' moral unity. If the Federal Republic were forced out of this community, then the constellation of strategic arrangements that also protects Israel would lose its cornerstone." In other words, stop reproaching Germany or Israel's security may be on the line.

Shortly before Reagan arrived in Bitburg, Fritz Ullrich Fack, the newspaper's copublisher, stepped into the fray with an editorial entitled "A Pile of Debris." In it, he commended President Reagan for having the "right instinct about how to act. But his country contains a powerful media machine that nurses a habit of persecution down through generations. The instigators are grateful for any opportunity to revive the caricature of the monstrous German and to open old wounds. They do not even hesitate to categorize the dead this way and turn their own president into a puppet in the process." In death, so the editorial continues, all are equal; it doesn't matter who were the perpetrators or who the victims. And this from one of Germany's biggest and most influential newspapers.

Der Spiegel also joined the disturbing debate. In his editorial *"Bitte* *kein Bit!"** publisher Rudolf Augstein asked, "Who, for heaven's sake, could have an interest in commemorating May 8, 1945?" He then provides the answer: "Of course, the Soviets have a genuine political interest. They hope to prolong memories of the past alliance in order to drive wedges between their present enemies." But the Soviets are not alone: "The Israelis also have . . . a genuine political interest. They want to keep alive memories of German guilt for the sake of material and military aid."

Yes, of course. If it has to do with money, naturally the Jews are involved . . .

However, Augstein goes on to say, "The celebration of May 8 is absurd, since the date signifies not only the liberation of millions, but also the enslavement of millions. Do we really still have to hold a seminar about who killed more people, Hitler or Stalin?" Therefore, liberation from fascism is not a sufficient reason for a celebration.

In the meantime, Alfred Dregger had written an unambiguous letter to fifty-three U.S. senators: "When you urge your president to forsake his planned noble gesture at the Bitburg Military Cemetery, I must interpret it as an insult to my brother and my comrades who fell in battle. I would like to ask you whether dead soldiers, their bodies already decomposed, can be refused a final honor? I ask you if you see an ally in the German nation, which for twelve years was subject to a brown dictatorship and which for forty years has stood on the side of the West?"

Indeed, Reagan did choose to stand by the people who had been "subject to a brown dictatorship." He found the anticommunist alliance against the "Evil Empire" of the Soviet Union more important than the Jewish protests in his own country; 250,000 people in New York alone demonstrated against his Bitburg visit. So he marched with Kohl past the forty-nine graves of SS soldiers, accompanied by a sole trumpeter playing "I once had a buddy . . ." The entire spectacle lasted only six minutes, but they were six minutes of enormous symbolic content.

*"*Bitte kein Bit!*": "Please, no Bit!"—a reference to the advertising slogan for a German beer, Bitburger Pilsner *("Bitte ein Bit!").*

Meanwhile, the police had divided the city of 12,500 inhabitants into heavily patrolled security zones and kept the Jewish demonstrators well away from the two leaders.

In a speech following the visit, Reagan made his opinion clear: "Forty years ago we fought a great war to liberate the world from the darkness of evil. . . . It was a great victory, and today the Federal Republic of Germany, Italy, and Japan belong to the community of free nations. But the battle for freedom is not yet over, since today a large part of the world still suffers from the darkness of totalitarianism." Thus the old enemies are united in anticommunism, and the crimes of former opponents no longer matter; anyway, the crimes of the present enemy render them merely relative.

And what did the German chancellor have to say? In order to spare himself the awkwardness of bringing up National Socialism by name at the cemetery, Kohl chose the expression "totalitarian rule." This made it possible for him, as the German philosopher Jürgen Habermas later pointed out, "to present himself and us to the American president as the oldest fighters against communism." A memorable day in the history of postwar Germany, and many more would follow.

I still remember May 8, 1985, perfectly. Back then I was completely uninterested in politics, but I was transfixed nevertheless. West German president Richard von Weizsäcker had just given a much-admired speech, printed verbatim in many newspapers, on the collapse of the Third Reich forty years before. At first I too was impressed, but a closer reading changed my mind. Weizsäcker did address the Nazis' inhumane system and reminded us of its millions of victims. But he also emphasized that Hitler had supposedly delegated the execution of their crimes to a select few, a small circle of fanatics. In the end, he said, "Other people became the first victims of a war started by Germany, and then we ourselves became the victims of our own war."

Still—and soon even this would not be taken as a matter of course—Weizsäcker spoke unequivocally of a war started by Germany. He pleaded for remembrance, without which reconciliation is impossible. The point now, he said, is to "take advantage of the opportunity to put an end to a long period of European history.'' There it is again: putting an end to it.

Weizsäcker's speech was scarcely over when Kohl became the first chancellor in twenty years to attend a meeting of Silesian expellees. At the last minute, the organization altered its motto from ''Silesia remains ours'' to ''Silesia remains our future within a Europe of free peoples.'' The change was purely cosmetic. Forgiving the German past always goes hand in hand with straightforward territorial demands, a fact that Alfred Dregger underscored at an expellees' rally: ''It is also true that Hitler's crimes neither justify nor excuse the crimes of others. . . . No crimes should be kept secret, not even those of the victors. . . . We must understand that the concentration camps of Hitler and of Stalin, the expulsion of the eastern Germans and of the eastern Poles, and the deaths of millions of German soldiers and of their opponents were all part of one and the same catastrophe.''

Prior to this speech, it had been rare for an important German politician to compare Hitler with Stalin, or to equate perpetrators and victims so unambiguously.

In 1986 that would change. A year after Weizsäcker's speech, the *Frankfurter Allgemeine Zeitung* reprinted an essay by a Washington lawyer named Franz Oppenheimer. Entitled ''The Danger of Drawing False Conclusions from the German Past: The Seductions of a Collective Obsession with Guilt,'' the piece had originally been published in *The American Spectator*. Hitler's seizure of power was a ''historical fluke,'' according to Oppenheimer, and only ''a small minority'' of the the Nazis were ''rabid anti-Semites.'' Anti-Semitism had not been any more prevalent in Germany than elsewhere. ''Hitler was practically alone—even within the Nazi hierarchy.'' Therefore, the vast majority of Germans ''were no more guilty of Hitler's crimes than others were of Stalin's yesterday, or of dear Mr. Gorbachev's today.''

Six months later, Chancellor Kohl would create an international commotion by comparing Mikhail Gorbachev to Joseph Goebbels, the Nazi propaganda minister. Kohl initially denied having done so, but on November 6, 1986, *Newsweek* published a transcript of his tape-recorded remarks. Gorbachev, Kohl said, was never in California, never in Hollywood, but he knows something about public relations. Goebbels also knew a few things about PR.

Clearly, something was in the air—as I discovered again and again in my search through the archives. What was the point of these continual comparisons and the relativization of Nazi crimes?

With Oppenheimer's essay, the *Frankfurter Allgemeine* had started what would later be called the "battle of the historians." The newspaper had been roused to action by Elisabeth Noelle-Neumann, a member of the Allensbach Polling Institute and the chancellor's own poll-taker. Her study on "National Sentiment and Happiness" had determined that Germans had less pride in their nationality than any other country in the world. Germany, she claimed, was an "injured nation," whose people had to endure the "humiliation" of occupation, and who, because of their past, did not feel confident enough to feel national pride. "The lack of a collective concept of a nation weakens a country, both internally and externally," and for this the poll-taker blamed the historians: "In Germany the extreme of self-humiliation has been sought. The population is never told that in no free election did a majority ever vote for Hitler. Our overzealousness continues to distort the picture."*

Michael Stürmer, the chancellor's adviser on historical matters, took Noelle-Neumann's feelings to heart in the pages of the *Frankfurter Allgemeine* on April 25, 1986: "In a country without memory, anything is possible. The poll-takers warn us that loss of direction and a search for identity are siblings." According to Stürmer, Germany's future belongs to "those who replenish our memory, form ideas, and interpret the future."

---

*Elisabeth Noelle-Neumann was hardly part of the "resistance" in the Third Reich. She was a journalist for the newspaper *Das Reich*. A 1941 article about America, is an example of her work: "To reach blindly for the Jew who must be hiding behind the *Chicago Daily Times* is like sticking your hand into a wasps' nest. After forty simultaneous stings, you stop paying attention to the individual wasps. Jews write for the newspapers, own them, and have monopolized advertising agencies . . ."

The newspaper's publishers did not have to be told twice. They printed article after article in an attempt to rework Germany's history for the sake of its future. Ernst Nolte's article of June 6, 1986, "A Past That Will Not Pass Away," is one example. I allow myself the comment that even the title interprets as a *burden* that which should be seen as an *obligation*. Under the subtitle "The Gulag Archipelago and Auschwitz," the historian asks: "Did not the National Socialists, did not Hitler himself, perhaps perform an 'Asiatic' deed only because they saw themselves and their people as potential or real victims of such an 'Asiatic' deed?" Nolte goes on to ask rhetorically: "Was not the 'Gulag Archipelago' more basic than Auschwitz? Was not the Bolsheviks' 'murder of a class' the logical and factual forerunner of the National Socialists' 'murder of a race'?"

The truth has finally come out: the Nazis had actually been victims, and for that reason alone did they become perpetrators. Everything that happened in the Third Reich was done as a preventive measure against the expected Communist crimes—and pardonable, since criminal law defines this as self-defense, and self-defense is not a crime. As to the question of who began the war, a year earlier, in an essay published in England, Nolte argued that Chaim Weizmann, as president of the Jewish Agency, had practically declared war on Hitler in September 1939. The war had just begun, with the invasion of Poland, and Weizmann declared that the Jews stood on the side of England and the other democracies. Thus, according to Nolte, Hitler was "entitled" by virtue of Weizmann's statements to treat the Jews as prisoners of war and to intern them. (This, of course, was the same case Michael Kühnen had made in our second interview in the park near the Frankfurt courthouse, when he even produced a Jewish "declaration of war" from 1933.)

"We have the moral right, we have a duty to our people to destroy this race which wants to destroy us." So said Heinrich Himmler in a speech to SS squad leaders in Posen on October 4, 1943. And the difference between Nolte's statements and the following by Himmler is not at all clear: "In this battle with Asia we must accustom ourselves to a necessity: the rules and the customs of past European wars, so dear to us and so much closer to our nature, must be condemned to obscurity.'' Himmler pounded this sentence into the heads of his generals on May 5, 1944, in Sonthofen. In a war with ''Asia,'' ''Asiatic'' deeds are naturally permitted; this would seem to be the original of Nolte's justifications.

But Ernst Nolte was not a lone voice. In April 1986 *Die Welt,* an important daily newspaper, printed an advance excerpt from Andreas Hillgruber's book *Zweierlei Untergang: Die Zerschlagung des Deutschen Reiches und das Ende des europäischen Judentums* (Two Kinds of Ruin: The Destruction of the German Reich and the End of European Jewry).* In his book, Hillgruber described ''the desperate and self-sacrificing efforts of the German eastern army and the German navy in the Baltic, which tried to save the population of the German East from the Red Army's orgies of vengeance, from the mass rapes, the arbitrary murders, and the indiscriminate deportations.'' He spoke of the ''army of Greater Germany'' and its ''defensive battle,'' as if this army had not invaded the Soviet Union before being pushed back.

On July 31, 1986, the historian Klaus Hildebrand was given the privilege of continuing the *Frankfurter Allgemeine*'s sanitation of German history. ''As research continues,'' he wrote, ''we now see that Hitler's Reich was certainly not conquered for the sole purpose of liberating, taming, and enlightening the Germans. The Soviet war objectives and, to a lesser degree, those of the British and Americans were often highly independent of that purpose.''

In the middle of August, Günther Gillessen asked the following question, again in the *Frankfurter Allgemeine:* ''The war of the dictators—did not Stalin want to attack the German Reich in the summer of 1941?'' In addition, Gillessen continues, Hitler's attack gave Stalin the opportunity ''to ignore the war's complicated antecedents

---

*Note that the Reich was ''destroyed,'' while European Jewry merely ''ended''—a euphemism I later heard used by neo-Nazi leader B. E. Althans. In an interview on Swedish television, he claimed that Hitler hadn't repeatedly spoken of ''exterminating'' the Jews. ''No,'' Althans said. ''He spoke about the end of European Jewry.''

and present it as a war to defend Russia, as the Great Patriotic War.'' Later Soviet leaders then tried ''to convert Russia's heavy loss of life and materiel into a special obligation for peace that Germany should owe the Soviet Union and to use this debt in international relations and propaganda. . . . This policy's continuation will become more difficult once the events of 1940–41 are clarified.''

By now it was time for Joachim C. Fest to enter the debate. In an article called ''The Indebted Memory,'' he posed the rhetorical question of whether ''mass executions committed by shooting people in the head, as were normal for years during the Red Terror, were something qualitatively different'' from the extermination of the Jews. Fest doesn't stop with Russia, but points also to Algeria, Vietnam, Cambodia, Chile, and Argentina. The idea that Nazi crimes were unique, he wrote, ''is ultimately also put into question by the fact that Hitler himself repeatedly cited the practices of his left-wing revolutionary opponents as lessons and models.'' Fest pointed out that he counted himself among the ''pessimists'' rather than the utopians who still believe in man's goodness. But for the pessimist or the realist, ''Auschwitz shrinks to the status of a 'technical innovation.' '' And to this, Fest concludes, no special guilt can be attached.

In the *Frankfurter Allgemeine*'s lead editorial on September 6, Kohl's adviser Stürmer wrote of the beginning of the Cold War that ''without knowing it, America had entered into the legacy of the German Reich.'' Thus the U.S. Army was the successor to Hitler's Wehrmacht in its ''defensive battle'' against communism. With that statement, the chancellor's historian underscored the very point Kohl and Reagan had attempted to make in Bitburg: that the common interest of fighting communism can exonerate the past. This idea encourages historical revisionism of an entirely different sort, but we'll come to that later.

In 1986, the opposition to Nolte, Hillgruber, Stürmer, and Hildebrand was led by Jürgen Habermas in the weekly newspaper *Die Zeit,* by Heinrich-August Winkler in the daily *Frankfurter Rundschau,* and by Hans-Ulrich Wehler in his essay *''Entsorgung der deutschen Vergangenheit?''* (Excusing the German Past?). The Battle of the

Historians also cast long shadows abroad. The *New York Times Magazine* devoted a cover story to it in November of 1986: "Erasing the Past—Europe's Loss of Memory in Face of the Holocaust." The Hamburg lawyer and publicist Heinrich Senfft, from whose 1990 book *Kein Abschied von Hitler* (No Farewells for Hitler) I took many of the quotes above, wrote of the controversy that "Since the German citizenry now want to stop living with the stain of the 'Holocaust,' the blame is generalized and internationalized until we finally arrive at the point our president had already reached on May 8, 1985: that we all ultimately are victims."

The right wing of the Federal Republic was highly satisfied with the result of the Battle of the Historians. True, they had not won it, and the majority of historians continued to disagree with them, but they had created a great deal of interest in their positions. As *Criticòn,* an intellectual magazine close to the extreme-right Republicans, summed up the affair: "Nolte and Hillgruber provided important impetuses for a more balanced and thus more just view of recent German history. A slow but visible change really does seem to be taking place in public opinion within the Federal Republic."

In the middle of November 1986, on Germany's Memorial Day, the Christian Democrat Alfred Dregger called for a "community of fate" in which "we must reconcile ourselves with one other, with our history and with the fate of our nation."

Soon after Dregger's speech, Wolfgang Schäuble, then the chancellor's secretary, encouraged the "expellees" to continue to press their pecuniary claims against the Soviet Union and Poland. Schäuble later became minister of the interior and is now the head of the CDU/CSU parliamentary faction. On a December 1992 segment of the TV newsmagazine *Kennzeichen D* (Mark D), he was shown speaking before student fraternities in traditional dress in the castle of Eisenach: "The Germans . . . here in the east of Germany, as we now say, even though it's really in the center of Germany . . ." He was interrupted by thunderous applause. Knowing that he'd scored a bull's-eye, he reached for his water glass and drank very slowly, satisfied by the popularity of an understated but clear hint that history has not had its last word. According to Schäuble, who certainly isn't regarded as a firebrand, Eisenach lies "in the center of Germany." It's not necessary to say anything more, since everyone in the hall understood exactly what he meant. Königsberg, Pomerania, and Silesia might not belong to Germany now, but that can change.

Back to 1987.

Right after the new year, Chancellor Kohl made a public reference to the "political prisoners in the DDR's concentration camps." Interior Minister Friedrich Zimmermann (CSU), who had earlier explained that he viewed fascism as a mere "word in political polemics, used above all by Communists," called the DDR "the biggest prison camp in the world." The final escalation was reserved for Otto von Habsburg, a CSU delegate to the European parliament and the son of the last Austrian emperor; since 1973 he has also been president of the ultra-right Pan-Europa-Union and a member of the Freedom for Rudolf Hess Committee. Said Habsburg: "The so-called German Democratic Republic has not only set up concentration camps, it is itself a single, giant concentration camp."

Half a year later, Otto Hennig, under-secretary of state for intra-German affairs, in an address to the Schlesische Jugend (Silesian Youth), gratified his audience by stressing that the division of Germany and the expulsions had affected "almost exclusively the innocent." As for the territories on the far side of the Oder–Neisse border with Poland, he declared that one "does not gain the right of settlement through illegitimate occupation." This time the German media didn't even make a fuss. On the contrary, such remarks were unextraordinary by 1987—a victory for the "moderate" historians and the right-wing radicals. Slightly later, Hennig concluded that next to the "protection of unborn life," the reestablishment of a "healthy national self-confidence" was the most important issue for German conservatives.

The speech that Philipp Jenninger, president of the Bundestag, gave on the fiftieth anniversary of Kristallnacht, on November 9, 1988, reflected perfectly the current political environment. He babbled about fascism's "fascination" and attributed Hitler's anti-Semitism to "childhood misery and adolescent humiliations, the ruined dreams of the failed artist, the displacement of the unemployed and homeless tramp, and the obsessions of a man sexually disturbed." The German people, Jenninger claimed, were largely passive in the pogroms of fifty years before, and many were horrified.

Jenninger was ultimately forced to resign, but the ambitions of other distorters of history could no longer be checked. The Battle of the Historians would proceed to its next stage after the destruction of the Wall.

X

Of Those Who Deny
and Those Who
Incite

Upon reunification, the question of how to deal with the past took on even greater urgency. If anything, the revisionists now had new momentum. The collapse of the DDR as well as the approaching Gulf War and the discussions over the new, greater Germany's world role seemed to lend themselves perfectly to the attempt to clean up a shameful history. Exactly a week after official reunification, *Frankfurter Allgemeine* commentator Eckhard Fuhr made an optimistic prediction: "Auschwitz will not remain a standard of condemnation at which Germans reflexively lapse into intense self-analysis."

Politicians and historians rushed to analyze the failed system of the DDR, and many observed with horror that the Communist regime was not only being compared to the Nazi reign, but judged its equivalent in the spirit of the old formula "red equals brown." My research gradually began to weary me, since it was so discouraging. History was being rewritten on a far greater scale than I had imagined possible.

Soon after reunification, the Bavarian interior minister, Edmund Stoiber, called the DDR politician Hans Modrow a *"Gauleiter."* Former East German author Jürgen Fuchs told *Die Welt* that the Stasi had caused an "Auschwitz in our souls." *Die Welt* journalist Enno von Lowenstern referred to the DDR leadership as a "political murder machine," and to Erich Honecker as "the greatest German murderer and war criminal." Hitler, of course, was Austrian, but Lowenstern's claim seemed odd nevertheless. He also coined new phrases, such as "Aryanizing in red," to describe the DDR's land-reform program in the four years after the war. *Frankfurter Allgemeine* commentator Friedrich Karl Fromme, looking back at the history of the DDR, declared: "Neither will this injustice vanish in the satisfaction of reunification, nor can it be made relative through a comparison with National Socialism."

Between March and October of 1990, the West German government reacted with paranoid sensitivity to any foreign attempt to disrupt the frictionless annexation of the DDR. The internal opposition has long since been reprimanded and excluded from the consensus. Günter Grass, for example, received no end of scolding for his statement that "whoever thinks about Germany and looks for answers to the German question must also think about Auschwitz." He was called the "nation's self-proclaimed pessimist," and accused of "instrumentalizing Auschwitz" in order to restrict the German people's right to self-determination.

In July 1990, historian Michael Stürmer, writing in the *Frankfurter Allgemeine,* warned that "In every demonization lies the danger of a self-fulfilling prophecy, and in every discrimination against Germany the danger of a separate path." Woe to anyone who dared discriminate against Germany. In September, the chief correspondent of *Die Welt,* Herbert Kremp, gave free rein to his superpower fantasies: "The Germany of the future stands as a superpower before the ruins of Eastern Europe, and the shambles extend deep into Russia." German soldiers had once made it that far—but that was before the division of Germany.

As always when it comes to excusing German history, Ernst Nolte was near at hand. The DDR, he claimed, though "much too small and dependent" to wage such wars itself, nevertheless "endorsed at every opportunity all of those forgotten wars of aggression through which the Soviet Union came into existence." Nolte went on to compare Auschwitz with Bautzen (a Stasi prison), the Gestapo with the Stasi, and the six million murdered Jews with—now, here's a coincidence—the "six million Stasi victims."

In January 1991, Nolte repeated his five-year-old thesis from the Battle of the Historians: "So 1933 should no longer be seen as a discrete, epoch-defining year, but rather as a hostile imitation of that much more important Russian year, 1917." Nevertheless, he added, one "can and must continue to speak of a singularity with regard to the later National Socialist extermination measures, for although the extermination was relatively smaller, it had, for groups declared foreign, a more revolting character than the quantitatively greater Soviet class-liquidation." Oh, if only Hitler's butchers had murdered with a little more aesthetic sense, not so revoltingly, then they would have spared us Germans so much trouble! After all, we *are* talking about a "relatively smaller group." The six million murdered Jews a small group? Of course, there are those who whisper that it wasn't even six million, those who chip away at the figures. But more on that later.

In February 1992, Nolte publishes the culmination of his thesis in the *Frankfurter Allgemeine:* "But the DDR was also the state Hitler feared when in his early speeches he spoke again and again about 'Bolshevism's bloody morass' in which millions of people would perish; and the DDR was the state all the countless 'bourgeois' organizations had in mind when they told themselves and others that Hitler, the 'people's chancellor,' had saved Germany at the last minute from the 'abyss of Bolshevism.' . . . The people who feared and hated the DDR before its actual formation were not all wrong." It would appear that a historian who publishes in mainstream German newspapers, and whom Chancellor Kohl occasionally quotes, is claiming here that the Nazis were "not all wrong," is suggesting that Hitler merely fought a preventive battle against Bolshevism, and is using the future experience of the DDR to justify the earlier actions of the Third Reich.

Unbelievable! Where is the outcry from the historians, or the government's apology to National Socialism's victims? Nothing of the sort is heard. On the contrary, Nolte's colleagues jumped on the bandwagon. Arnulf Baring, another historian often featured in the pages of the *Frankfurter Allgemeine,* announced that we Germans, because of our attempts to overcome the past, have "thrown our entire pre-1945 history onto a trashheap that we must now struggle to sift." His conclusion is clear from the start—"We are now witnessing the return of Germany"—and he immediately questions whether Germany's renunciation of nuclear weapons "is really supposed to be forever." Baring subsequently received a letter of support from *Der Spiegel* publisher Augstein, who opined that he could imagine situations in which Germany would have to "obtain nuclear weapons in spite of existing treaties."

At the same time, a circle of young historians led by Rainer Zitelman in Berlin suggested that Hitler not only thought of himself as a revolutionary but actually was one. As a social and economic "modernizer," he supposedly fought for "more equality of opportunity within the national community," strove for "egalitarian tendencies within social policy," and created the rudiments of a "welfare state." Hitler "already had a basic program against unemployment before Keynes had even finished explaining its causes," and he also "concerned himself with ecological questions in a startlingly modern way."

It can't get worse than this. Or *can* it? In the fall of 1992, Jörg Haider, the Austrian chief of the extreme right Freiheitliche Partei Österreichs (Austrian Freedom Party), praised the Nazis' "orderly labor policies." In July of 1991, Wolfram Engels, publisher of the liberal weekly *Wirtschaftswoche* (Business Week), urged us to break the "taboos" since "the economic history of the Nazi era is especially interesting," citing a "stirring" growth rate of nearly 10 percent. "Can we renounce a recipe for success simply because Adolf Hitler once used it?" Evidently not. "After all, we do not also renounce participation in the Olympics, or German shepherds, or choral singing."

As early as 1985, Martin Broszat, the director of Munich's Institute for Contemporary History, had already declared that the crimes of the Nazi era should not mean that "the numerous efforts at modernization should lose their historical significance simply because of their link to National Socialism." By regarding this modernization outside of its brutal, inhuman, and necessary context, are we not coming dangerously close to the frivolous idea that Hitler also had his good side? Yes, he did build autobahns and fight unemployment, but didn't these actions help the Nazis cement their domestic rule and form their "national community"? Can you really call organizations like the Federation of German Maidens or the Nazi Women's Union "emancipatory"? I can't do it. But then, I'm not a historian hoping to win praise for serving the cause of German national identity. For me, it's difficult even to quote a sentence such as: "The Third Reich was an extraordinarily modern state, in many ways Europe's most modern state"—from the book *Deutschland, was nun?* (Germany, What Now?), edited by Arnulf Baring.

On January 15, 1991, the UN ultimatum for an Iraqi withdrawal from Kuwait expires. As military intervention becomes inevitable, the question arises: What to make of the greater importance of Germany? The *"Wende* historians"* rush to find an answer. Joachim Fest criticizes the "moralistic, special role which seems nowadays to please Germans so much" and regrets the lack of political and military action befitting a new world power. Journalist Eckhard Fuhr stresses that Germans can "no longer simply invoke their historical trauma and rest upon their historical guilt."

The rush is on to shove German history into obscurity. I have come to expect this from certain quarters of the media: from *Bild,* naturally, as well as *Die Welt* and the *Frankfurter Allgemeine.* But suddenly, what do I see? Is that *Der Spiegel* pulling up to join the pack? Every week this newsmagazine uncovers minor and major scandals in politics, scholarship, and business; it often determines the subjects of the Sunday news programs and the Monday newspapers; it has a reputation for being incorruptible and absolutely honest. Yet now *Der Spiegel* is publishing the David Irving series.

*Literally, the "turning-point historians"—so named because of their close attention to the events leading up to the fall of the Berlin Wall and German reunification. (Translator's note)

Should I revise my opinion of this newsmagazine, which Augstein claims "has toiled to enlighten for forty-five years"?

I decide to reexamine its coverage over the past two years, and I'm quickly stopped short, in the second issue of 1990, by Augstein's essay "Zero Hour." The man who once jumped at the chance to point out the errors of Nolte, Hillgruber, Stürmer, and Hildebrand now seems converted: "Whether the Germans may, should, or must forget the past is not something that can be determined by command. Nolte's approach, the center of the so-called Battle of the Historians, was actually philosophically correct, even if one does find the whole debate somewhat superfluous." We're off to a good start.

The face of Communist Party chief Gregor Gysi, complete with worker's cap, peers at me from the cover of the next issue. Beneath his portrait is the headline "THE STRING-PULLER." Gysi is attacked because he opposes the immediate annexation of the DDR, and because he would rather save something of socialism rather than jump ship to collect a reward. Gysi is supposedly a "trickster who uses the honest cap as camouflage," a lawyer submerged "in classic legal dialectics" who "radiates refined intellectual coldness but frightens away the East German working masses." Gysi warns "with perfect demogogic methods against a supposed danger from the right," while he "impudently helps himself" to the Communist Party's property, "which really belongs to the people." A prototype of the portrait on the cover can be found in the Jewish Museum in Frankfurt am Main. Here a Nazi propaganda poster portrays a "typical Jew" in much the same way, and with an identical caption: "The String-Puller." It's certainly possible that the staff of *Der Spiegel* knew nothing of this Nazi poster, and one could protest that this particular article was just a slip-up. Yet the cover picture does cast Gysi in a shadowy light, making him look, in fact, shadowy.

The news media are not alone. Only six weeks before, Kohl's spokesman, Johnny Klein, had publicly blamed "international Jewry" for a change in the program of the chancellor's visit to Poland. And a week before *Der Spiegel* published Klein's comments, Franz Schönhuber, the former SS man and head of the Republicans, gave a speech in which he urged Heinz Galinski, the chairman of the committee of German Jews, "to finally stop with his slander of German patriots." At a REP party convention in the Bavarian town of Rosenheim, he spoke as follows: "Shalom, Herr Galinski, it's time for you to finally leave us in peace and to stop talking your nonsense. We do not want to hear it any longer, we cannot hear it any longer, and we will not allow ourselves to be humiliated any further. You are to blame if contemptible anti-Semitism should once again come to this country."

Der Spiegel is really just part of the trend. I'm not even talking about anti-Semitism; something completely different disturbed me as I looked through the magazine. I read on, and find another article by publisher Augstein in July of the same year; it is entitled "Deutschland und die Deutschen" (Germany and the Germans). In it he reduces the entirety of the Nazi era to a "historic case of bad luck." The bad luck was that "after 1918, an unsuccessful, hate-filled Viennese postcard painter"—not a German, thank God—"made the Jews responsible for the lost world war and convinced the very differently inclined Prussian-German generals to join him. . . . Prussia–Germany was no more anti-Semitic than France or Poland, for example. . . . The real guilty party was . . . Adolf Hitler." Here we go again. If only one man was guilty, then it's merely a logical conclusion to turn the murder of millions of Jews into the "decreed extermination of the Jews." Historical revisionism, pure and simple. The neo-Nazi Gottfried Küssel has already recognized this and turned it into a practical slogan: "Everyone participates—no one is responsible!"

In the summer of 1992, the career of Joseph Goebbels himself is serialized in Der Spiegel, and diary entries he wrote for propaganda purposes are presented to an audience of millions. It doesn't bother Der Spiegel that François Genoud—a Swiss banker, a self-proclaimed "critical National Socialist," and the owner of the rights to the personal writings of the Reich's minister for popular education and propaganda—pockets huge royalties in the process. Nor does Genoud's role in the neofascist scene trouble the Hamburg publisher. In Switzerland he was a founding member of the shadowy neo-Nazi organization Europäische Neuordnung (New European Order), and Otto-Ernst Remer calls him "my best friend."

In the fall of 1991, refugee homes in Germany, from Hoyer-swerda to Saarlouis, are torched. The cover of *Der Spiegel* on September 9 seems calculated to fan racist sentiments by announcing "THE ONSLAUGHT OF THE POOR: REFUGEES, TRANSFEREES, ASYLUM SEEKERS." The picture is of an overflowing boat—and the REP refrain "The boat is full" has hit the big time. In an article entitled "Skinheads, Robbers, Burglars—Are the Police Capitulating?" the magazine proceeds to describe Hamburg's Karolinen district, where, apparently, "violent Gypsy children terrorize most of the older natives. The Germans are developing a 'horrible hatred' out of fear, until even nice, peaceful people want something like a citizens' militia." The article comments on "gangs of delinquents" comprised of children with black hair and dark eyes, on "giant clans with hordes of children," and on "lunatics on the loose, everywhere."

In the November 14, 1991, issue of *Quick,* Manfred Hart pulls out all the stops: "They are foreign, dark . . . people who don't speak our language. People who have come to seek their fortunes in Germany." Hart conjures up a picture of sinister refugees making specious claims of political persecution. The headline is both inevitable and truly unbeatable: "IF I WEREN'T A POLICEMAN, I'D BE A SKINHEAD."

With its Gypsy story, *Der Spiegel* is somewhat ahead of its time. A year would pass before the right-wing youths of Rostock would take their hatred out on defenseless refugees for days on end, setting fire to a house inhabited by 150 Vietnamese.

With its issue of April 6, 1992, *Der Spiegel* is perfectly in tune with the apparent popular sentiment in Germany. The day after the electoral successes of the Republicans in Baden-Württemberg (10.9 percent) and of the Deutsche Volksunion (DVU) in Schleswig-Holstein (6.6 percent), *Der Spiegel* treats these regional elections as part of the fight against the supposed "flood of sham refugees." The word ASYL (asylum) is spelled out in huge letters on the magazine's cover, and underneath is the slogan of the REP and the DVU: "The politicians have failed." The picture shows an incalculable horde of "foreigners" pushing through an open gate, coming straight at the viewer. An electoral poster for the REPs or the DVU could not have been better designed.

Der Spiegel naturally offers explanations for the attacks on foreigners and refugees. In issue after issue, sociologists and other experts on West German youth interpret the racist crimes as youthful protest, denying them any connection with extreme rightist politics and presenting the criminals themselves as aimless, lost, unemployed, homeless victims. "It would be fatal simply to classify the recent riots as right-wing extremism," announces education professor Klaus Hurrelmann in an interview. Apparently the youngsters involved in the assaults "can't express themselves verbally very well," and their "real motive is a deep-rooted insecurity." The next step would probably be to excuse the perpetrators as victims of an "irrepressible play instinct." I have personally witnessed many neo-Nazis shaking with laughter over such analyses.

In the summer of 1992, *Der Spiegel* continues its attack, though couched in intellectual language, against the Romanians, who are by this time the most persecuted refugees in Germany. Citing "anti-Gypsyism"—since Germans complain about thefts, harassment, fights, panhandling, and chaos wherever Romanians turn up—the magazine laments the fact that "precisely this nonconformist people of nomads, the most difficult of all immigrant groups to integrate, now constitutes the largest contingent" of refugees. "The seemingly archaic behavior of these immigrants clashes with the norms of average Germans."

At this point, not much separates *Der Spiegel* from the *National-zeitung* (National Newspaper), which portrays itself as the champion of the average German: of "natives angered to the boiling point by refugees," of "taxpayers sucked dry," and of the "numerous German victims of crimes committed by foreigners." Its headline for August 28, 1992, reads: "VIOLENCE AGAINST FOREIGNERS—A RECIPE FOR GERMANY?" An appeal for new pogroms lurks behind that question mark. The xenophobic violence in Rostock supposedly represents a "warning" sent by the citizens to tell the "establishment parties" in Bonn that they must end the "growing flood of mostly criminal foreigners pouring into the Federal Republic of

Germany.'' Because ''the German people are not prepared'' to tolerate ''this galloping invasion of Gypsies'' any longer.

By the end of November 1992, foreign newspapers are full of reports on the horrors inside Germany—and it becomes too much, even for the former general secretary of the Christian Democrats, Heiner Geissler. In view of the 4,500 racially motivated crimes reported since the start of the year (in which eighteen people were murdered and 800 injured), he declares that ''the real cause of these crimes lies in the radical right's reacceptance into the mainstream.'' Someone—and a Christian Democrat at that—has finally gotten it right. Not only is this a question of a ''healthy national identity,'' but of refugees and reunification as well. ''The soul of the nation has grown twisted in the debate over foreigners,'' Geissler continues, going on to speak of the unleashing effect of the ''unfortunate discussion about asylum-seekers.'' This debate has been a major topic for years, not only in local bars, but also among mainstream politicians and in the media. In this way, the ''foreigner question,'' the basic issue of right-wing radicals, was made acceptable. Moreover, as restraints were lifted, young neo-Nazis could act out the little man's dreams and escape practically scot-free.

I remember clearly the Frankfurt municipal elections of 1989. I was living in Darmstadt at the time, and was often in Frankfurt. The Christian Democrats of Hesse began their offensive two weeks before the election with posters protesting the ''Abuse of Asylum,'' ''Sham Refugees,'' and ''Voting Rights for Foreigners.'' They were trying to emulate Mayor Walter Wallmann, who in 1985 had proclaimed ''You have foreigner problems at hand'' in his successful campaign. So the Hessian metropolis was flooded with CDU posters that bore the same messages as the literature of the NPD and the REPs: ''We Are for a Frankfurt Open to the World but Against Abuse of the Right to Asylum''; ''The SPD and the Greens Want to Bring More and More Refugees into the City!''; ''Home, Future, CDU''; and ''Watch Out, Hesse! CDU, Now More Than Ever!'' But the voters understood, and some preferred to vote for the original instead of the imitation. The NPD won 6.6 percent of the vote in Frankfurt and entered the City Council with seven delegates, two of whom had demonstrable connections to Michael Kühnen and the NSDAP-AO. One of them said it plainly to my camera: "I am a National Socialist." In other communities and districts, the extreme right's percentage of the vote reached double digits.

No election since has passed without an argument over the constitutional right to asylum, and no summer without the great asylum debate. This situation would intensify after unification. In the parliamentary campaign in the fall of 1990, the Christian Union parties (CDU/CSU) chalk up their first success. The forces within the Social Democratic Party who defend the constitutional right to asylum begin to crumble. Oskar Lafontaine, the party's candidate for chancellor and prime minister of the Saar, considers a restrictive amendment "necessary." The number of refugees continues to increase, which isn't particularly surprising: after all, Eastern Europe is collapsing; multiple ethnic conflicts are erupting; Yugoslavia is sliding into civil war. The demands for quotas now grow louder within the SPD, and even from the Greens. Elections take place in Bremen, whose SPD mayor, Klaus Wedemann, tries to take a stand by refusing to accept any more refugees. The extreme-right DVU reaps the benefits. On September 20, they receive 6.1 percent of the vote, and in Bremerhaven they get 10 percent.

The debate reaches a new level. The Bavarian CSU proposes to restrict the refugees' right to due process and adopts nearly all of the entire REP program. During the summer, Bavaria's interior minister, Edmund Stoiber, had already urged that the category of political asylum be changed from a constitutional right to that of a "mercy." Shortly thereafter, Volker Rühe, then CDU general secretary and now defense minister, sent a detailed memo to party members in city councils, state parliaments, and the Bundestag, urging an intensification of the asylum debate in order to win a majority for a constitutional amendment.

The right of asylum is debated in numerous articles in the newspaper *Bild*. "REFUGEES IN THE COMMUNITY—WHO'S SUPPOSED TO PAY FOR THEM?" asks one headline. On August 7, 1991, in "A

Report on a German Problem,'' millions of readers are asked to ''Imagine this situation: A man rings your doorbell and asks to come in. He says that he has powerful enemies who want to take his life. You give him shelter. But you quickly learn that the man wasn't persecuted at all; he only wanted to live in your house. What's more, he behaves very badly. He hits your children, steals your money, and wipes his shoes on your curtains. You would like to get rid of him, but you can't. This is the reality of German asylum laws in 1991. The house is the city of Frankfurt, and the man is a Yugoslav who in the underworld is known simply as 'Cento.' ''

In the fall of 1991, the Saxon town of Hoyerswerda becomes "foreigner-free." Instead of fighting the neo-Nazis with all the power of the state, the police evacuated the refugees. Earlier, they had done nothing to protect the refugees, ostensibly because of a personnel shortage. But when militant antifascists (*Antifas*) mobilize, hundreds of police who were strangely unavailable when the radical-right mob went wild suddenly sweep in to encircle them.

Hoyerswerda triggers a series of assaults and riots. Chancellor Kohl swears to the international community that Germany is a "country friendly to foreigners" and will remain one. The debate over asylum is not pushed to the side, however.

Politicians view the violence as confirmation that the fears and needs of the population need to be taken seriously, and argue that the best way to prevent the extreme right from gaining strength is to amend the Constitution and seal Germany's borders. In the meantime, attacks on foreigners, refugees, Jews, the homeless, and the handicapped increase in frequency and, more importantly, in brutality.

By October of 1991, the extreme right can smell victory. The CDU, CSU, FDP, and SPD have negotiated a deal to speed up the asylum screening process, but without providing the necessary personnel. Consequently, hundreds of thousands of undecided cases pile up. While this chaos is clearly the fault of the government, it still serves as marvelous ammunition for the movement to change the Constitution. Fantastic *Bild* headlines come one after the other: "LIVING SPACE REQUISITIONED: FAMILY MUST TAKE IN REFUGEES"; "GERMANY'S MOST UNBELIEVABLE HELP WANTED AD: REFUGEE HOME SEEKS GERMAN CLEANING WOMAN"; "REFUGEES NOW IN SCHOOLYARDS"; "EMERGENCY! REFUGEE TENT CITY IN HESSIAN PARK." Assaults are now part of the daily routine. In Rostock at the end of August 1991, right-wing extremists attack a boardinghouse for foreigners and the Central Reception Office for Refugees in Mecklenburg-Vorpommern—in both cases to the sound of popular applause. Thus emboldened, they instigate street battles with indecisive, hesitant police. One hundred and fifty Vietnamese are lucky to escape a fire set by neo-Nazis—only a day after the SPD announced its readiness to amend the Constitution.

Two weeks later, in an interview with the *Frankfurter Rundschau,* former chancellor Helmut Schmidt, a Social Democrat, announces that it was a mistake to have "diligently, and with all available methods, absorbed foreign workers into the Federal Republic." The notion of Germany turning into a multicultural society is completely wrong, he says. "You cannot belatedly turn Germany, a country with a thousand years of history since Otto I, into a melting pot. . . . These communities cannot support that. And society will degenerate." Helmut Schmidt, long my favorite politician, is worried that "we are de facto being overrun," and now is adopting such Nazi terminology as "degeneration." Statesmanlike as always, he predicts instability if we continue "to let half a million foreigners into Germany every twelve months."

In the middle of September, Federal Interior Minister Seiters celebrates the conclusion of a treaty with Romania that will make it easier to deport those denied asylum. The treaty's elegant title is "Repatriation of German and Romanian Citizens," but in fact no Germans are affected. Further, Romania also commits to admitting people without valid papers. Romanian associations in Germany speak of a "mass deportation" of over 40,000 and remind the Federal Republic of its obligation in light of the Romany murdered by the Nazi. Although such criticism is ignored in Germany, foreign countries react indignantly. English and French newspapers term it a "deportation treaty," while Seiters refers to it merely as an "effective step toward stemming illegal immigration." But in September, in *Bild*, he does acknowledge that "now we're deporting." To Seiters, the Romany are all "sham refugees," despite the persecution and pogroms in Romania, and despite the fact that in Germany only 0.1 percent of Romanian refugees—as opposed to 16 percent in France—are granted political asylum.

The Bavarian CSU continues to urge the repeal of the right to due process. The Bavarian prime minister, Max Streibl, chooses to enjoy the waters at a spa rather than join President Weizsäcker and Chancellor Kohl in a rally for the inviolability of human rights; REP chief Schönhuber subsequently declares his respect for Streibl. Yet only a few days earlier, Kohl had spoken of "a deep crisis of confidence in our democratic state." And he wasn't referring to the firebombings and xenophobic tendencies that are now part of everyday German life, but to "the immigration of foreigners [that] has created too great a burden."

Stoiber, the Bavarian interior minister, thinks that it might be necessary to close Germany's borders "with conscious disregard for the Constitution." At a CSU party convention in November, he's among friends. Environmental minister Peter Gauweiler decries the "explosive mixture" called multiculturalism; he thunders against the idea of "united men with united faces." One delegate receives prolonged applause for a speech that includes this trenchant metaphor: "The law was passed in 1949. I'm in the automobile business. Does anyone here think that we could sell a 1949 model today?" And for Otto Wiesheu, the Bavarian under-secretary for education, political persecution alone is not sufficient reason to grant asylum: "We in the CSU are also politically persecuted, by the Greens and the SPD, but that doesn't make us eligible for asylum, not by a long shot."

At the beginning of December, the great asylum agreement is finally reached. The constitutional provision remains intact but loses all practical significance. Only those who do not pass through a "secure third country" on the way to the Federal Republic have the right to apply for asylum from inside Germany. Since all neighbors, including Poland and Czechoslovakia, are conveniently declared secure, refugees can now only come to Germany via airplane, parachute, hang glider, or boat. The constitutional right has been rendered meaningless. Interior Minister Seiters is now looking into the possibility of using the army to seal off Germany's borders.

At the same time, working groups and other organizations in favor of cooperating with the extreme right spring up inside the CSU, whose chief, Theo Waigel, has already declared that the 1994 elections can be won only "at the right of the center." These groups now demand a straightforward rejection of the multicultural society and argue against the "foggy concept of a shapeless European unity stew," preferring instead "a Europe of fatherlands." Gerhard Mayer-Vorfelder, the finance minister of Baden-Württemberg, says it straight out: "The man who knows what's being said in the local bars will have the majority behind him." Then he indicates just how low he plans to stoop: "We don't have to constantly strew ashes over our heads just because we're Germans."

The conservative and right-wing CSU members attempt to achieve with their "Germany Forum" the spiritual and moral renewal Kohl promised them years before. This has yet to come about, even though Kohl announced—in his official chancellor's address on January 30, 1991, the anniversary of Hitler's seizure of power—that "Germany has come to terms with its history. From now on it can openly assume, and even expand, its role as a world power."

Still the rightists in the Germany Forum are not satisfied. What else can they want?

So we have now "come to terms" with our history. In that case, on October 3, 1992, the anniversary of reunification, why not also celebrate the first launch of Hitler's V-2 rockets in Peenemünde? And why not bill it as the "fiftieth anniversary of space travel?" This is obviously the brainchild of Erich Riedl, the under-secretary of state for economics. The ceremony is ultimately canceled, but Riedl calls the international protests an "absurdly hysterical reaction."

However, in June of 1992, when Queen Elizabeth proposes to unveil a memorial for Sir Arthur Harris, the Royal Air Force general, there is a furious protest in Germany. *Der Spiegel* says of Harris that he organized the "first prenuclear mass murder from the air." *Die Welt* calls him an "architect of extermination." Harris considered his airborne offensive the only feasible way of weakening Germany, both physically and psychologically, in order for an Allied invasion to have a chance of success. The German media systematically denounce him as a "butcher" even though he accomplished in Germany nothing more than what Goering's Luftwaffe had tried to do to English cities. Those who ask for "total war" have to live and die with the consequences—in this case, the deaths of tens of thousands of innocent civilians in the destruction of Dresden.

On May 9, *Frankfurter Allgemeine* editor Günter Gillessen even tries to rehabilitate the Luftwaffe. Pretending that Guernica and Coventry never existed, Gillessen writes that the Nazi Luftwaffe, in contrast to Harris, kept "on the whole, to the traditional distinction between civilian and military targets" and "tried to spare noncombatants." After mayors from the numerous cities bombed by the Luftwaffe write letters of protest, even Foreign Minister Genscher joins in the debate over the memorial, remarking that "The project is one designed to open old wounds."

The "expellee" rallies on Homeland Day in the fall of 1992 also contribute to the historical revisionism. The motto, interestingly, is: "For justice and historical truth." The Thuringian Regional Committee nevertheless finds it necessary to explain that "The main goal will be for Germany to escape the prescribed role of the repentant sinner and to reattain a healthy self-confidence. Even in a unified Europe, one without borders, communal and national identity will provide the framework of justice and order. In this order, the expellees finally want their right to self-determination and their right to have their homeland realized." In other words, the Eastern territories should be reoccupied.

·   ·   ·

"Whenever some Jewish cemetery gets desecrated, the New York Times gives it a headline," grumbles a Cologne television editor upset by our film, "Wahrheit macht frei." And as these desecrations become more and more common, Chancellor Kohl nevertheless takes the opportunity in March 1992 to meet with Austrian president Kurt Waldheim, controversial the world over because his wartime record has recently come to light. Kohl angrily dismisses criticisms from the Jewish World Congress, saying, "As chancellor I will decide whom I meet in Munich together with my friend Max Streibl. I don't need any advice."

On the night of November 22, 1992, a Turkish woman and two Turkish girls in the Schleswig-Holstein town of Mölln fall victim to a fire set by organized, right-wing extremists. The family has lived for many years in Germany; the girls were even born here. After a year full of brutal racist attacks, this incident changes the official attitude toward right-wing extremism.

Shortly before the Mölln murders, a journalist named Klaus Hartung publishes an article in Die Zeit, a weekly newspaper, entitled "Wider den linken Alarmismus" (Against Left-Wing Alarmism). The threat of a sudden shift to the right, says Hartung, was "a matter of course in the leftist culture" of the old West Germany. Since the pogroms in Hoyerswerda, "the left wing has restructured its defenses. Warnings are heard once again as Cassandras fill the horizon with predictions of approaching doom." Hartung denounces such predictions as "alarmist nonsense" and then goes on to praise right-wing ideologues for having "recognized the opportunity inherent in the societal vacuum and the potential for the new in the collapse of the old order." He then refers to the horrifying events in Yugoslavia. "Who could have believed before 1989 that a country in the middle of Europe would carry out a war of conquest and, unleashed by a National Socialistic ideology, set up concentration camps, and organize mass deportations and executions."

Enough! Various polls in the fall of 1992 make it clear that Hartung was mistaken about Yugoslavia and Germany. The atmosphere in Germany has changed, and the results of a poll funded by IBM are particularly terrifying. Approximately 30,000 young Germans between the ages of sixteen and twenty-four are prepared to act violently toward foreigners and refugees. The study classifies almost a third of adolescents as "thoroughly xenophobic or at least prone to xenophobic ideas," while 13 percent are politically "close to a fascist successor organization." Thirty-five percent of schoolchildren believe in a "Greater Germany that includes the Eastern Territories," and every third apprentice is convinced that "the Germans have always been the best."

The studies also show that the increase in extreme right-wing allegiances is linked to a strong tendency to deny the horrors of the Nazi era. Seventeen percent of the 4,300 adolescents from the states of Saxony and Saxony-Anhalt who were questioned considered descriptions of the Holocaust to be "greatly exaggerated." One fourth of all schoolchildren and 40 percent of apprentices accept the idea that the Third Reich "also had its good sides."

A poll conducted by researchers at the University of Cologne concludes that Germany's Jewish citizens once again live in fear. One fourth of all German Jews between the ages of eighteen and twenty-four feel "personally threatened." Barbara Distel, the director of the memorial at the Dachau concentration camp, remarks at the significant decrease in the number of visitors. In 1991 there were 30 percent fewer visitors. Distel blames the decline on the "revolutionary situation," and says that in Germany the expression "overcoming the past" is used increasingly to refer to the DDR and the Stasi.

Shortly after Rostock, a poll reveals that 37 percent of Germans believe they "have to protect themselves against foreigners in their country." Fifty-one percent are sympathetic to the slogan "Germany for the Germans," and 26 percent agree with "Foreigners out." These numbers go down slightly after the horrifying arson in Mölln and the government's first measures against neo-Nazi activities, but this isn't particularly reassuring. A significant portion of the population hold extreme right-wing opinions. Even Hamburg's Verfassungsschutz chief, Ernst Uhrlau, admits that the main issues for the nineties will be extremism, xenophobia, and nationalism. "More than twenty percent of young people sympathize with the parties of the extreme right. When this generation is established, it will have a greater—and completely opposite—effect upon our society than did the leftists after 1968.''

Uhrlau is behind the times. The issues have taken hold long ago—not only in parties of the extreme right, but at the very center of German society.

XI

THE INVOLUNTARY
DEMOCRATS

Since the Hoyerswerda pogrom of September 1991, I have been reading the newspapers with special care. I scan the pages with the small news items and comb through every article on the asylum debate. That's where I generally find reports of the latest xenophobic incidents and attacks. I get the impression that although the violence is becoming greater every day, the articles are getting shorter and shorter.

Here are two examples from November 1992, chosen at random. First: "Six youths attacked a home for asylum-seekers in Friedland (Neubrandenburg district) with stones. Property was damaged and the unidentified perpetrators escaped." Second: "In Lehrte, near Hannover, last night, rowdies threw a firebomb into a shelter for asylum-seekers. The inhabitants were able to put out the fire by themselves. Minor property damage was caused." I keep wondering, though, if property damage, or rowdy behavior, tells the whole story. It doesn't require an extraordinary imagination to picture what happened during those two nights. The refugees are awakened by young men yelling Nazi slogans. The children scream and cry, and everyone crouches on the floor to avoid being hit by the objects being hurled through the window. They smell smoke and see that a Molotov cocktail has exploded inside. Since the mob is waiting outside, they cannot go to the nearest telephone booth to call the fire department. A frantic chaos ensues in the shelter. Their desperate attempts to extinguish the fire are later collapsed into a simple news report that features such carefully chosen words as "minor property damage" or "arson." The perpetrators will be charged with these lesser offenses, if they are ever caught at all.

On the night of November 22, 1992, two Turkish girls, Yeli and Ayshe, and a Turkish woman, Bahide Arslan, burn to death in Mölln, in a fire set by neo-Nazis. Only then do the relevant state prosecutors' offices understand that the only difference between the almost 500 previous firebombings and the one in Mölln is that the latter was "successful." They start seeing them for what they are—murder and attempted murder—and begin to consider the production of Molotov cocktails as evidence of criminal intent. Only then does Attorney General Alexander von Stahl take control of the investigations. He had not previously been concerned with the danger of right-wing extremists to foreigners, only with their danger to the state, of which he found none. Now, after the events at Mölln, the words *"Heil Hitler"* at the end of the perpetrators' boasts is suddenly enough for the Federal Republic's highest prosecutor to infer an intent to promote the reestablishment of a National Socialist dictatorship.

Well over 2,000 racially motivated crimes were committed in 1991, and in the next year the number exceeds 4,000. Nevertheless, at the end of 1991, President Richard von Weizsäcker will emphasize that "This wave of violence does not signify a rebirth of racist or nationalist ideologies, but rather a crisis of human communication."

In the fall of 1992, the government is still firmly convinced that there is no evidence of an organized program behind the violence. The official analysis is that these are spontaneous acts committed by individuals or small, local groups. In *Der Spiegel,* psychology professor Reinhard Tausch says of the post-Hoyerswerda wave of violence, "The absorption of hundreds of thousands of immigrants naturally leads to distinct, stress-related reactions among those who live near large groups of immigrants. To portray such stress-related reactions as xenophobia is to ignore reality." The Verfassungsschutz doesn't disagree. An internal memo of the state security agency explains that

"The xenophobic skinhead generally comes from a broken family. He has no prospects and no societal recognition. His day is filled with boredom."

Attorney General Stahl, who could have sent a signal if he wanted, was also denying reality up until the deadly night in Mölln: "These attacks have nothing to do with right-wing terrorism. Right-wing terrorism is not a danger at present. The attacks are the spontaneous acts of overexcited, misled youths with a radical right-wing background but without any organization."

Politicians, scholars, security forces, and the courts are thus unanimous in their agreement that Germany contains many spontaneously acting, isolated xenophobes who are so distressed by boredom and the immigrants that they have no choice but to beat foreigners unconscious, or to death, and set fire to refugee homes. These acts naturally do not have any sort of political background, let alone an organizational framework.

Everyone in a position that reflects official policy either believes, chooses to believe, or wants to believe that there is no organization behind the mounting acts of right-wing violence. The judges, investigators, and police all influence one other in maintaining this attitude. Mölln has to happen before evaluations begin to change. Between the fall of the Wall and Mölln, thirty-one people died as a result of right-wing violence. Only then did the authorities react, as if they'd just discovered the existence of neo-Nazis in the republic. The documented desecrations of Jewish cemeteries at a rate of thirty to forty a year since 1980, the murders and attacks committed by skinheads in Hamburg in 1985 and 1986, the 1980 Oktoberfest bombing—all of this has been denied, repressed, and forgotten.

In the fall of 1991, after Hoyerswerda, public opinion became slightly more sensitized to racist incidents, and prominent Germans openly declared their sympathy for foreigners in the "I am a foreigner" poster campaign. Yet the courts still refused to take strong action against the perpetrators. Alcohol and youth were the most popular extenuating circumstances. When dealing with attacks on foreigners, judges suddenly discovered the rehabilitating effects of probation, and of as short a duration as possible. Of the many verdicts handed down, several in particular remain fresh in my memory.

In December of 1991, at the trial of three of the instigators of the Hoyerswerda attack (three neo-Nazi skinheads between the ages of twenty-two and twenty-eight), the court limits the punishment to eighteen months, to be served as probation, due to the mitigating factor of alcohol consumption. "It is not our place to judge the event's political dimension," the judge states repeatedly. The evidentiary hearing had revealed, incidentally, that a police car accompanied the three ringleaders during the entire riot, though the police did not intervene.

The first trial against violent right-wing criminals in the former East Germany takes place in November 1991, in Zittau's Youth Court. Eight defendants between the ages of eighteen and thirty-four stand before the court. Among them is the regional chairman of the Republicans; he is charged with disturbing the peace, bodily harm, and popular instigation. On Ascension Day they had invaded a hostel for children poisoned by radiation from the Chernobyl accident and injured their Soviet caretaker. The defense calls the incident a "boys' day out that went awry," and the court seems to agree. The sentences are light: a year for the REP chairman, fifteen months for two others, and probation for four more. "After all," says the judge, "this isn't a political trial." The defendants' political brethren, many of whom are present at the sentencing, are delighted.

In December 1991, Ernst Zündel, a major force behind the "Auschwitz lie," stands before a court in Munich. He calls himself a "revisionist" and denies that gas chambers existed in the Nazis' extermination camps. By now even the Federal Ministry of the Interior considers revisionism to be a serious threat. For popular instigation, incitement to racial hatred, and slandering the memory of the deceased, Zündel is sentenced to a fine of 12,600 marks. The court considers it a mitigating factor that "the overwhelming majority of Germans are so firm in their opinions that the defendant and his supporters pose no real danger."

On February 12, 1992, a nineteen-year-old skinhead who fatally stabbed an Angolan in Friedrichshafen am Bodensee gets off with five years' detention in a reformatory. The court convicts him only of "second-degree murder with qualified criminal intent"—the "qualification" being that "the victim's skin color significantly contributed to the crime." The judges themselves do not seem to understand that by accepting such a mitigating factor they have pronounced the ultimate racist verdict. The law in all its severity affects only those who murder "Aryans."

Two weeks later, the regional court in Koblenz is also trying a racially motivated murder. In December 1990, an eighteen-year-old skinhead in a small town in Rheinland-Palatinate had stabbed a seventeen-year-old Kurd in the back, killing him. He was sentenced to six years in a reformatory for "second-degree murder with qualified criminal intent." The skinhead had described himself to the police as the leader of a group of neo-Nazi skinheads, and the Verfassungsschutz had frequently spotted him at demonstrations and skinhead meetings in several regions. Nevertheless, the state prosecutor's office considers this crime the result of his "problems in school" and a life "of drinking and hanging around."

In my meetings with Kühnen, I learned that this is a calculated strategy. "Always say: 'I was drunk. I was bored. I was provoked.' Then you'll get off with half!" These instructions were given to skinheads in numerous meetings I'd attended. The police know it. The state prosecutors know it. The judges know it. Yet they still accept the hollow defense of drunkenness. The Koblenz court does establish a "certain xenophobic and racist, possibly also extreme-right, background" to the attack, but these ancillary motives were supposedly not the true motive for the murder. It had not been proven beyond a reasonable doubt that the defendant had "deep racist motives at the time of the stabbing."

In May 1992, ten young men stand before the court in Dresden. Six months earlier, they had set out on a hunt for foreigners and shot a man from Mozambique in the head at close range with a BB pistol. Afterward, half of the group masked themselves and broke into the apartment of a Vietnamese woman in the final stages of pregnancy. They bludgeoned the woman, kicking her in the belly. Later, her doctor called it a miracle that mother and child both survived. But the defendants, one of whom is a champion marksman, are in luck. They have a merciful judge, and every one of them leaves the courtroom a free man; the court decides on probationary sentences ranging from six to twenty-one months. Two of the skins had come from the West to Dresden for the sole purpose of founding the extreme-right Sächsischen Nationale Liste (Saxon National List), and another had been caught putting up an NSDAP-AO poster in the Dresden train station a day before the incident. But the court doesn't seem to comprehend extremist politics and racial hatred— only youthfulness and alcohol.

In September 1992, five skinheads are given juvenile sentences ranging from two years' probation to four years' detention. They had mercilessly kicked to death an Angolan man, Antonio Amadeu Kiowa, in Eberswalde in November of 1990. They had first met in a disco and then set off "to fuck up some niggers." On the way, they vandalized several cars while the police tailed them discreetly. Three plainclothes officers watched from a safe distance as Kiowa was set upon by his murderers. They continued to watch as the skinheads hit the Angolan with baseball bats, kicked him with their heavy boots, and jumped on his head. The skins let up only after he lay motionless in a pool of blood on the street. And only then did the police emerge from hiding and chase them off. Apparently it did not occur to them either to intercede or to arrest the perpetrators at the scene of the crime. Antonio Amadeu Kiowa never awoke from his coma. Nevertheless, instead of murder, the court in Frankfurt/Oder regarded this as a "typical youthful lapse," a grievous bodily injury followed by death. Moreover, the judges considered the political and social circumstances in the "five new states"* following reunification to be *mitigating* factors.

Also in September, a similar case is tried in the small town of Wittenberg. On the night of May 2, 1991, a mob of thirty to forty forced their way into a house inhabited by Namibians and threw two of them off the fourth-floor balcony. Both survived, but with serious injuries. The main defendant is convicted of attempted manslaughter—not attempted murder—and sentenced to six and a half years

*The official new name for East Germany.

in jail. His testimony incriminated the police; they had known in advance of the planned assault. "That evening," he said, "the police didn't make me feel like I was participating in crime." The subsequent investigations managed to locate only nine other participants.

At the end of November 1992, the Rostock district court gives six months' probation to a twenty-three-year-old man who'd thrown rocks at a refugee shelter and injured a watchman. Among the reasons for the judge's leniency is the fact that the police, with a "very lax attitude," had let the case sit around for over a year before taking action.

In the same month, participants in the Rostock pogrom of August 1992 are sentenced to juvenile detention or to enrollment in a course meant to teach proper societal behavior; the judges preferred to employ "educational means" on the youths rather than consider prevention or deterrence. But when a perpetrator vandalizes a police car or throws a stone at a policeman, the sentences become significantly more severe; and thus the physical inviolability of a refugee is judged to be much less important than that of a policeman.

How else to explain the events of the night of August 24? The police first retreated and then changed shifts while hundreds of violent extremists besieged a boardinghouse for foreigners in Rostock. The radicals did not stop in astonishment over this retreat, but celebrated their victory by storming the house, plundering it, and setting it on fire. The commanding police officers later claimed not to have known that the house was inhabited by 150 Vietnamese, who with a great deal of luck managed to save themselves by climbing out over the roof. According to the report of Siegfried Kordus, the Rostock police chief at the time, "The Vietnamese citizens in the neighboring house seemed to be less threatened than the police, who had appeared to be the group most hated by the intruders."

Jürgen Deckert, however, the senior police officer at the scene, contradicted Kordus. Deckert testified that "the police had an arrangement with the rowdies and were supposed to keep their distance." This quote appears in a police high commissioner's official report. Only in February 1993 does it become known that the Schwerin Interior Ministry had a copy of this report, suggesting the existence of a "truce" between the police and the rioters since September 1992. Yet during this time, officials had vehemently denied any such suggestions, and shortly after the incident, Interior Minister Seiters informed the press that what happened in Rostock was an example of the very first "cooperation between radicals from the left and the right." Upon further questioning, Eduard Lintner, under-secretary of the interior ministry, explained that the authorities reached this conclusion because "up to now the only known incidents of life-threatening firebombs have been in the context of riots led by criminals from the extreme left." He neglects to mention that since the new year there had been 405 attacks with firebombs and explosives, every one of them from the right, none from the left. Despite the ever increasing number of incidents, the federal interior ministry makes a simple, self-satisfied finding: "Our standard procedures have proven themselves in practice."

In the late sixties, the federal government developed a weapon to combat the terrorist Red Army Faction, and it has since been widely used to prosecute leftists: Article 129a deals with the actions involved in founding, joining, and supporting a terrorist organization. It is a powerful tool for investigators and prosecutors, since once the existence of a group is acknowledged, the entire group can be held responsible for the deeds of its individual members, thus making unnecessary the often complicated matter of proving individual participation in a crime. The article, as written, is by no means restricted to left-wing activities, but in practice it has rarely been directed against the right. Neither Hoffmann's martial-sports troop, nor Friedhelm Busse's Kommando Omega, nor Kühnen's Aktionsfront Nationaler Sozialisten, nor countless other groups have been prosecuted on this basis. Manfred Roeder and the members of his Deutsche Aktionsfront (German Action Front) are one of the few exceptions, and were convicted in 1982 under Article 129a for attacks on refugee homes.

In 1990 and 1991, the attorney general's office initiated a total of 297 proceedings under this law against alleged left-wing terrorists for "propaganda" and "support," and forty-one suspects were placed in pretrial detention—a fate spared right-wing terrorists. Although the incidence of racist crimes shot up in these two years, only six proceedings, involving a total of eleven suspects, are initiated against the right, and not a single rightist was prosecuted for issuing propaganda, although nearly every right-wing publication celebrated Hoyerswerda as a victory and new crimes and arson attacks were publicly urged before television cameras.

The studied neglect of Article 129a underlines what officials, clearly driven by political interests, repeatedly claim: that right-wing crimes are committed by *individuals,* and there are no national or international support networks for acts of neo-Nazi violence. Time after time, I see the same formula: "This is not a political trial."

The culmination of this constant denial of organized neo-Nazism is the popular individual-perpetrator theory, in which the criminal is preferably psychopathic and alienated from all groups. The case of Josef Saller is still fresh in my mind. One December night in 1988, this nineteen-year-old apprentice was "overcome" by the idea of setting fire to an apartment building in the center of Schwandorf. The building just happened to be inhabited mostly by Turkish families, and three Turks and a German died in the fire. The Schwandorf police suspected the possibility of arson but immediately denied reports of political motivations. The next day, investigators found a "Turks out" sticker on a neighboring building, and this led them to Saller, who was known throughout town as a right-wing extremist. On January 5, 1989, the apprentice made a comprehensive and detailed confession in which he stated his motive was "to annoy foreigners." This forced the police to revise their official version, and in a press statement issued shortly thereafter they claimed to be certain that "no other person was involved in the crime, and no right-wing radical group either knew of or incited the incident from behind the scenes."

The police maintained that Saller was the lone perpetrator even after a search of his home turned up numerous addresses and propaganda materials from the militant Nationalistische Front and the FAP, and even after his membership and high position in the NF became known. The police would stick to this theory through the end of their investigations, and the Amberg regional court finally accepted it as well. All contradictory evidence was systematically ignored. Envelopes found in Saller's home that contained propaganda written by a leading Austrian neofascist remained unopened until the assistant prosecutor demanded them. Train tickets indicated that Saller had attended the NF's fourth party congress in Bielefeld just before the crime, but the court took no notice of them. The NF and FAP leaders were never questioned about "Comrade Josef," as they would later call him in their publications, and his connections with the local Republicans were also ignored.

Josef Saller was finally convicted—not for murder, but for arson—and was sentenced to twelve and a half years in prison as an isolated perpetrator who supposedly "developed from loner into lone fighter." Since then, his name has appeared in the NSDAP-AO newspaper *NS-Kampfruf*'s list of "national prisoners." From his prison cell Saller gives interviews to neo-Nazi skinhead magazines like *Querschläger* (Richochet) and *Frontal* (Head-On). His "greatest political wish" is for a "Germany free of occupation troops and foreigners, in the Germanic–Prussian tradition, and for the borders of 1938, and for a Europe free of niggers, reds, and kikes," and "above all, the return of National Socialism."

Thus speaks a criminal without any background in the organized extreme right.

The Saller case raises other issues as well. The courts depend on the results of the police investigations, which in turn take their cue from the courts' attitude. Police chiefs in the East complain that they are unprepared for such incidents, and that the criminals they arrest are often released in a matter of hours. But they can't pass the buck quite so easily; in fact, they have played a major role in allowing the situation to escalate. Police officers have looked the other way, and not only during the murder of Antonio Amadeu Kiowa, in Eberswalde. Their behavior speaks for itself: when they consider the victim to be drunk, as they did during the murder of the Mozambiquan Jorge Gomandai, in Dresden, they neglect to apprehend the perpetrators at the scene of the crime. Police officers have known of planned attacks and refused to act, as in Wittemberg, where the two Namibians were thrown off a balcony. Police officers do not interfere with Gottfried Küssel, who, despite the fact that he was forbidden entry into Germany as of May 1991, travels openly throughout the country on "organizational activities." Police officers look on with indifference when, on October 3, 1992, approximately 500 supporters of the extreme-right Nationale Offensive raise their arms in the forbidden Hitler-salute in the center of Dresden. The salute, like other Nazi symbols, is punishable by up to three years' imprisonment.

Police officers have purposely spread disinformation—for instance, in the case of Sadri Berisha, a Yugoslav who was brutally beaten to death on July 9, 1992, by seven skinheads in Ostfildern, near Stuttgart. Despite comprehensive evidence to the contrary (including confessions), the police issued a statement to the effect that they were certain that the attack had no political significance. When, in November 1992, skinheads stabbed the Berlin printer Silvio Meyer after he criticized their patches, which read "I am proud to be a German," the police issued initial statements to the press about a "knifing" and fights within the leftist scene. Not a word about the right wing.

Federal authorities are also guilty of disinformation: at the end of October they kept secret the firebombing of Ravensbrück, the former women's concentration camp, for several days. The state prosecutor even forbade workers at the memorial to speak with the press. It seems that Britain's Queen Elizabeth was in Berlin on a state visit at the time, and the authorities wanted her to see only Germany's good side.

The Federal Ministry of the Interior is equally guilty. Since May of 1992 it has stubbornly refused to release to parliament any statistics about these occurrences and the subsequent investigations. Their justification is that they lack a special office to register the incidents. Such an office had, in fact, been proposed after the Hoyerswerda pogrom, but the federal ministries, along with the states, rejected the idea. A year later, after Rostock, a special office was again suggested as part of the "Urgent Program Against Extreme-Right Violence" presented to the public by Interior Minister Seiters. Nothing has yet been done.

The police have cause to reproach themselves. They allowed the

Rostock pogrom to escalate by retreating and then changing shifts at the most critical moment. Yet their superior, Mecklenburg-Vorpommern's interior minister, Lothar Kupfer, later declared: "The police did their duty. Not a single refugee lost so much as a hair."

I can still see the televised images of the terrified Vietnamese, trapped in the burning building. Why should the police intervene on behalf of the refugees when their boss says that the foreigners themselves provoked "the population's justified anger" by "camping out in the meadow and committing crimes in neighboring businesses and homes."

Why should the police take on neo-Nazis when Dieter Heckelmann—the commander in chief of the entire Berlin police force and a CDU senator—explains after the pogrom that "What was expressed in these manifestations of public sentiment in Rostock was not right-wing radicalism, xenophobia, or racism, but thoroughly justified discontent over the massive abuse of the right to asylum." Eckhardt Rehberg, the leader of the CDU faction in Mecklenburg, went even further and garnered tremendous applause when he remarked that "The foreigners are not familiar with our culture and customs and possibly don't even want to learn about them, and that disturbs our citizens."

Still, one man would break with the party line. Hans-Ludwig Zachert, chief of the federal police, declared that the Rostock riots had been "guided and organized." He was promptly censured. Eckhart Werthebach—the head of the Verfassungsschutz—and Interior Minister Seiters refute his claims, announcing in unison that it is absurd to talk about any organization.

And should the police reproach themselves for the failure of large-scale crackdowns if publicity-hungry politicians announce them to the press in advance? And are the police to blame for the fate of the *Nationalistische Front?* In November 1992, Seiters indirectly let slip news of the organization's impending ban a day early; he was subsequently "astonished" to learn that the NF had had the time to destroy incriminating material and that their leader, Meinolf Schönborn, was able to escape. Why should the police even look for organizational links when the attorney general of Saxony,

Jörg Schwalm, states that the incidents result "almost without exception from spontaneous decisions, usually made after drinking."

The cards are stacked against the police from the start. When it comes to attacks on foreigners, noticeably fewer witnesses turn up than for other serious crimes. As the Saar's police chief, Gregor Lehnert, elegantly describes this routine racism: "There isn't a great deal of identification with the victims."

In face of such a situation, even *Der Spiegel* is forced to speak of a "strange mixture of police incompetence and sympathy toward the perpetrators" that "encourages the rowdies to commit new crimes." The ambivalence of the police, however, is not surprising, given that up to 30 percent vote for the Republicans, the right-wing, law-and-order party. According to a study by their union, half of Bavaria's police officers agree with the REP's goals, and party chief Franz Schönhuber never misses an opportunity to express proudly his gratitude to "our comrades and friends in the police." REP regional associations in Hesse report that up to 15 percent of their members are policemen. Jürgen Schröder, who since October 1992 has been the state chairman for the Republicans in Rheinland-Palatinate, is a police detective, and he's not the only one in the party leadership.

Another situation for which no one wants to take responsibility turns up in February 1993. As a result of lax security checks, Berlin's Freiwillige Polizeireserve (Voluntary Police Reserves— FPR), with around 2,400 members, has become a home for violent criminals, child molesters, arms smugglers, and rightist radicals. Founding members of the FAP and members of martial-sports groups are also part of the voluntary police, getting eight marks an hour from government coffers while being allowed to carry weapons in public.

Perhaps we ought to be grateful for the unusual bluntness of someone like Andreas Schuster, chairman of the Brandenburg policemen's union. After criticizing the training and equipment of the police in the former DDR, he declares: "There will be a second and a third Rostock; they can happen anywhere."

It is important also to note that in December 1992, thousands of

German police officers demonstrated against neofascism and xeno-phobia. I am not speaking of them. I'm speaking, rather, of those who have apparently forgotten that we live in a democracy whose laws it is their job to enforce, as my colleagues and I had to learn.

On January 25, 1991, the Napoleon Bar outside of Frankfurt am Main is once again the rendezvous for the neo-Nazis in "Gau Hesse." Members of the Deutsche Alternative from "Central Germany" (the former DDR) are also present. But this particular meeting of around forty extremists is taking place in the presence of the police and a TV crew from the Hessian state television company. Heinz Reisz, the "show-Nazi" with the walrus mustache, is in the middle of his speech. Once again, he seems a parody of himself: "I am a Teuton and God save the teutonic missiles of our multinational faith!" he cries in a hoarse voice. Even the neo-Nazis grin at that one. Reisz lets loose with his stump speech—though without the *"Sieg Heil"* or the Hitler-salute, since the camera is running—and then, in his closing, reveals the reason for the meeting: "Long live the fight for Saddam Hussein, long live his people, long live their leader, God save the Arab world! Thank you."

A few days later, journalists Ulrike Holler and Herbert Stelz report on their television program that members of Kühnen's organization intend to form an international volunteer army to fight for Saddam Hussein. Five volunteers are already at hand, and they appear on national television. The two journalists had contacted the police, who, though they are present during the filming, see no reason to intervene. And the broadcast, on January 29, causes no uproar whatsoever. Everyone considers the neo-Nazis crackpots, and apparently neither the police nor the politicians could care less that they've pledged to fight for Iraq. The whole affair is practically forgotten within a few days.

The situation, however, takes a dramatic turn when the report is shown on Israeli TV on February 4. The broadcast coincides with a visit by Rita Süssmuth, speaker of the German parliament, who has come to Israel to demonstrate Germany's sympathy. She meets with anger rather than gratitude. Many Israelis are enraged that not only were the Iraqi missiles that threaten them made with German technology, but German neo-Nazis are now volunteering to serve

Saddam Hussein. Rita Süssmuth can do nothing but get upset herself.

Behind the scenes, the bureaucracy is propelled into unaccustomed action. A report commissioned days before by Frankfurt's chief of police is hastily finished and passed on to the Interior Ministry. The police chief recommends that a "counterstatement" to Holler and Stelz's news report be considered "because of the international resonance." He claims that the journalists' "primary motivation" had been "to bolster the stereotype of the 'monstrous' German, so popular nowadays among politicians all over the world." While Thomas Hainke in Bielefeld, Gerrit Et Wolsink in Amsterdam, and Gary Rex Lauck in Lincoln, Nebraska, coordinate the mobilization of mercenaries and slip squad after squad into Iraq with the "assistance" of Frenchman Michel Faci (alias "Le Loup"—"The Wolf"), the Frankfurt police chief accuses the journalists of having "staged" the meeting and paid the extremists "between four and five thousand marks." The sole source of this refutation is Heinz Reisz, who, on March 3, announces that he'd made his pro-Hussein remarks in order "to see what kind of men they [the police] are, to see if they'd fall for a hoax. I'd already tried this kind of thing in other TV spots, but this time it worked."

The local press blindly swallow all of the police chief's accusations, and promptly begin invoking such phrases as "checkbook journalism." Ulrike Holler and Herbert Stelz file a lawsuit to restrain the police chief from making his false claims, and on April 5 he issues a retraction. In a letter to the directors of Hessian State Television, he acknowledges "with pleasure" that his investigations "did not confirm the suspicion" that an honorarium had been paid to neo-Nazis," and he regrets "that the public discussion of this took place as it did." The press in Frankfurt report the police chief's retraction, but Herbert Stelz says he's still waiting for any discussion of the incident's political dimensions. He may have to wait a long, long time.

The authors of the police report evidently didn't know much if they could find "inexplicable" Kühnen's claim that, "if Hussein requested it, around three to four hundred members of his organization would stand ready for possible fighting.'' It is inexplicable, however, that despite busy telephone and fax correspondence between Kühnen's middlemen and the Iraqi Embassy in Bonn, the police could conclude that ''It cannot be said to what extent contacts with representatives of Iraq or other states or organizations from the Arab world even exist at this time.'' Thomas Hainke had begun to communicate with the Iraqi embassy via fax in July of the previous year. Kühnen told me that he'd visited the embassy himself in September 1990, and that Christian Worch had been chosen to negotiate with the Iraqis.

In April 1991, the police arrest Michael Kühnen, now fatally ill, in Thüringen. In the course of the arrest they find the draft of a treaty between the ''Anti-Zionist Legion'' and the ''Government of the Republic of Iraq.'' According to the treaty, the neo-Nazis wanted to support Iraq ''against the present aggression of Zionist and U.S. imperialist forces and to that purpose [contribute] an international contingent of volunteers.''

The Stockholm police chief is astonished when, in our interview, I am the first to tell him that either Copenhagen or Stockholm had been chosen as the meeting point for volunteers preparing for transport to Iraq. His German colleagues had neglected to inform him. The neo-Nazis' choice of cities can only mean that in Copenhagen and Stockholm it is logistically possible for them to safely house up to one hundred German volunteers for at least one night. This could be accomplished only with the help of similarly inclined neo-Nazis, since it is not likely that a hundred paramilitaries with combat gear would check into the Ambassador Hotel. ''If they were going to try that sort of thing,'' the lawman me, ''we would have known about it!'' He reflects briefly, then leans his head to the side. ''At least we would have known about it afterwards.'' This doesn't make me feel any better.

The draft treaty also says that ''after the first volunteers arrive,'' within four weeks ''up to one hundred additional volunteers from various Western countries (including citizens of the U.S.A. and Great Britain) will join the LEGION.'' These mercenaries would also be shuttled through Stockholm or Copenhagen. The two cities are also presented as possible locations for finalizing the treaty, but it is not certain whether a ceremonial exchange of signatures actually took place.

What is certain is that a few hundred mercenaries could not possibly have any military importance to Iraq. Why, then, one must ask, was Iraq interested in such cooperation to begin with? I spoke with Kühnen on the subject in September 1990—well before the Gulf War broke out. He had a plausible explanation: "From our point of view, it has to do with the old saying, 'The enemy of my enemies is my friend,' and for the Iraqis it's extremely useful on the home front. They can now boast in their propaganda that the entire world is *not* against them."

The international liaison men are Et Wolsink for the English volunteers and NSDAP-AO chief Gary Rex Lauck for the Americans. The entire operation is run by Hainke and three other activists, all well known to the authorities for related activities.

Rupert von Plottnitz, a member of the Hessian State Parliament, declares: "It seems to have entirely escaped the Frankfurt police chief that the police in a democratic, constitutional state have a duty to protect public safety and the rule of law against possible violations caused by the machinations of neo-Nazis like Kühnen. On the other hand, it is decidedly not within their rights to censor journalistic reports on such machinations or to label them politically biased." The only point to be added is that these unbelievable proceedings were not unique, but only one example of the methods used to silence troublesome journalists.

In Berlin, Jewish journalist Margitta Fahr was charged with utilizing unconstitutional symbols. On October 14, 1992, she had faxed a colleague information about neo-Nazi activities, including a Nazi sticker with a portrait of Rudolf Hess. The word *Hess* was written with SS runes. The police had obtained a copy of this fax— it remains unclear how they accomplished this—and used it to indict her.

But journalists weren't the only ones affected. Although rightist youths are generally set free immediately after their arrests for assaults and firebombings, two young men in Munich were detained for almost four weeks after they were accused of having ripped a jacket covered with Nazi slogans off the back of a right-wing extremist. The police explain that they wanted to "nip the battle between left and right in Munich in the bud."

In October 1992, when a group of French Jews brought a memorial plaque to Rostock and took part in a protest against the German–Romanian deportation treaty, the police behaved more diligently than they had during the pogrom itself. The group first went to City Hall and mounted the plaque, meant to be a reminder of the racist riots as well as the crimes of the Third Reich. Several demonstrators forced their way into City Hall and hung banners with the slogans "Germany, Don't Forget Your History" and "Gassed Yesterday, Deported Today" out the windows, and the police managed to detain four of them. When the other protesters removed these four from police custody, the police surrounded the demonstrators' bus and arrested them all. The state prosecutor initiated proceedings against forty-six of them for trespassing, and won imprisonment orders against three of them for freeing prisoners and resisting arrest. They spent nine days in prison. The memorial plaque at city hall was removed as soon as the Jews were arrested. A spokesman explained that the plaque was unacceptable, "as there has not been any racist violence in Rostock."

A flyer distributed at a Munich vigil to commemorate the eleventh anniversary of the Oktoberfest bombing also provoked an overzealous justice system. The flyer's controversial text suggested that, despite the abominable nature of the crime, the "partisan justice system" had intentionally neglected to make further inquiries into related perpetrators from the right-wing spectrum. Four distributors and the individual responsible for producing the flyer were fined for slandering government institutions.

A politicized judiciary was an essential feature of the Weimar Republic. The judgments in countless trials of that period speak for themselves. If one made public reference to a "republic of con men and Jews," he had to pay a fine of one hundred marks. But if in a political assembly one called a general a "butcher" and Hindenburg the "butcher in chief," he went to jail for six weeks. The same went for political assassinations. Between 1919 and 1922 there were twenty such murders from the left and 354 from the right. The total punishments meted out to the left amounted to ten executions, three life imprisonments, and a combined total of 248 years in jail; the sum on the right came to no executions, one life imprisonment, and approximately ninety years in jail. Only four of the left-wing murders went unpunished, as opposed to 326 of the right-wing murders.

The NSDAP fared similarly. In the spring of 1923, federal courts upheld the ban of the NSDAP, but after Hitler and Ludendorff's attempted putsch in November, the judiciary acted quite differently. Though Hitler was sentenced to five years' imprisonment, his "patriotic spirit and noble will" was noted by the court, which declined to apply the laws for high treason: "A man who thinks and feels as German as Hitler does cannot be convicted of high treason." He was released by mid-December 1924.

After Hitler's seizure of power, amnesties were granted to "national" criminals and the law was freely used as a political weapon. Judges' associations pledged loyalty to the Nazi leaders, and the SS and SA were granted generous legal room for action. The judiciary continued to function dutifully up until the final collapse of the Third Reich. In the spring of 1945, anyone who openly doubted the final victory was still rigorously prosecuted by special courts. The judiciary's final act was to destroy incriminating documents.

After the war, there was only a single attempt in the West to try to bring the Nazi judicial system to justice: fourteen former justices were brought to trial at Nuremberg. Only a handful were convicted, and most of those were already free by 1950; the last was released in 1956. A law passed in the Federal Republic in 1951 gave former justice officials the right to their old jobs, a decision that proved to be the keystone of the rebuilding of the justice system in West Germany. The continuity of personnel, which denazification was supposed to prevent, was now legally assured.

Forty years of repression and desire to forget have finally led to what may be called a natural amnesty for judiciary criminals, which is to say that most of the people involved have passed away. In 1989, even Hans Engelhardt, the federal minister of justice, found the situation disturbing. In his preface to an exhibition catalogue entitled "Justice and National Socialism," he wrote that this flight from the past was "the greatest blunder ever made by the justice system in the Federal Republic."

The investigation into the responsibility for the rapid and practically unresisted perversion of law after 1933 was pushed aside. Since "law is law" and "what was just then cannot be unjust today," the judges were exonerated. The legal system's strong esprit de corps took care of the more complicated cases; no judge condemned another judge. They preferred instead to settle a few old scores after the fall of the Wall and reunification.

On May 19, 1992, the eighty-six-year-old Gerhard Bögelein was sentenced in Hamburg to life imprisonment. He was convicted of having killed a senior Nazi military judge, Erich Kallmerten, in a Soviet prisoner-of-war camp in 1947. As a military judge on the Eastern front, Kallmerten had signed at least 176 death sentences against Germans, Russians, Estonians, Latvians, and Lithuanians. An attempt to try Bögelein in 1951 had failed, but a month after reunification, the ailing man was finally brought to trial. German unity made it possible to sentence Bögelein—who earlier had been sentenced to death by Nazi courts for desertion and opposition—while in all the time since the war, the West German courts have not condemned a single member of the infamous Nazi People's Tribunal, an institution that pronounced 5,234 death sentences in less than nine years.

The German courts, however, did manage to spare every one of the SS men involved in the murder of Ernst Thälmann, the chairman of the German Communist Party, in the Buchenwald concentration camp. The same courts recently stripped a man of the status of "being a German" because as a Wehrmacht soldier he had been taken prisoner and subsequently volunteered for the Polish exile army; the court in Koblenz found his wartime opposition a "denial of German nationality." As a consequence, his son, who had immigrated from Poland and wanted to take advantage of his German heritage, had his expellee's rights denied. Meanwhile, in December 1992, a controversy surrounded Peter Markert, an honorary judge in Bochum. His colleagues on the bench let him retain this post even though he produced a pamphlet entitled "Endorsement of Racial Collectivism" that states: "We don't want our grandchildren and great-grandchildren to be a bunch of half-Asiatics roaming around our homeland. . . . Because German blood is a very special sap, completely different from foul-smelling slime."

When people say that the German authorities are "blind in the right eye," it's neither an exaggeration nor a coincidence. It is the logical result of a very specific attitude, what Ralph Giordano, in his book *Die Zweite Schuld* (The Second Sin), calls "perverse anticommunism": "Professional, doctrinaire, and avowedly militant, West German anticommunism was forged in the furnaces of the Third Reich. It has absolutely nothing in common with a humane, democratically motivated rejection of the Soviet system."

The German secret service was a *de facto* offspring of a Nazi spy organization led by Reinhard Gehlen. Long before the war ended, he had already made contact with the American secret services. So it was no surprise that this association continued during the Cold War. Organisation Gehlen was renamed Bundesnachrichtendienst in 1955. There was no reason for him not to reassemble his former agents from the Gestapo.

Who would expect a secret service with such a history to even think about democratic values? Who will an old Nazi hire as an assistant or successor? A liberal, possibly even one who doesn't see the Russians as monsters and the peace demonstrators as communists? No, the enemy is always on the left. After all, the head of the Verfassungsschutz, Eckart Werthebach, himself points out that his organization is seen historically as a defense against communism.

A detailed discussion of the German secret services is beyond the scope of this book, but the Verfassungsschutz requires some comment. It produces yearly reports on extremist activities, and a close examination of these reports turns up revealing inconsistencies in the terminology used to describe these crimes; they refer to "murder or attempted murder" by leftists, but to "homicidal offenses" by rightists. The Verfassungsschutz is also much stricter with the left when it comes to registering individuals and organizations. The security service sees a particular need to register members of the peace movement, but lets key right-wing organizations such as HIAG, a federal association of former Waffen-SS members, simply slip by. Not to mention the fact that it took nine years before the Verfassungsschutz finally, in December 1992, began to keep tabs on the Republicans—in spite of the fact that it was common knowledge that the party had been infiltrated by ardent neo-Nazis and right-wing extremists since its foundation.

In this atmosphere, select groups were allowed to flourish. Conservatives love to dismiss them as "chaotic fringe groups" and, for the sake of simplicity—and obfuscation—lump the left and the right together. When, for example, Michael Kühnen's Nationale Sammlung was banned in 1989, the Interior Ministry's spokesman did not neglect to point out that the government was taking firm steps against both left- and right-wing enemies of the state. Yet attentive observers knew that extreme right-wing violence had already enjoyed years of official neglect. It is unclear why so many journalists and politicians from all points on the democratic spectrum have denied this growing danger.

It is also unclear why Bernd Wagner was dismissed from his job at the end of 1991. As director of state security in the "five new states"—the former East Germany—Wagner had the impudence to draw connections between neo-Nazis and established parties. He had likewise refused to toe the party line that viewed the neo-Nazis as nothing more than "aimless youth."

Wagner was forced out; the deniers won again. Only after the murderous attacks of 1992—and with great displeasure—would they be obliged to agree with Bertolt Brecht. Soon after the fall of the Third Reich, Brecht had warned:

The womb out of which that crawled
is fruitful still.

XII

The Fruitful Womb

"It would be funny if it weren't so horrible."
With these words, Enno von Lowenstern begins an editorial in the
respectable *Die Welt,* two days after the Vietnamese boardinghouse
in Rostock was set on fire. In the tradition of Nolte, Lowenstern
tries to diminish the severity of the crime by drawing false comparisons: "What happened in Rostock is something we have already
seen hundreds of times, from Brokdorf to Wackersdorf, from
Hafenstrasse to Freiburg."* He also suggests who is really responsible for events like the one in Rostock: "This constitutional state has
been systematically violating the Constitution for years. It has,
without any legal justification, doled out billions of taxpayers' marks
to tolerate and support individuals here with no rightful claims." So
ultimately the foreigners and refugees are to blame, because "No
people are more deserving of recognition for humane, constitutional, unfascist attitudes than the Germans. No people have been
so viciously denigrated by their own 'intellectuals,' orators, and
politicians." According to Lowenstern, "It is a terrible shame that
a rise in criminal incidents, rather than sheer reason, is dictating a

*References to demonstrations by environmental activists, peace protesters, and
opponents of nuclear power.

constitutional amendment. But regardless of the cause, we cannot maintain the present illegal situation."

So, if the criminals are right, they are right. Lowenstern has to wait only three months before the government narrows the definition of the constitutional right of asylum to the point of meaninglessness. The victims of Rostock, the Vietnamese, are also expelled. For years they were good enough to be "industrial workers" in the DDR, but now they are refused the same legal privileges enjoyed by the former West Germany's "guest workers." The federal court's brazen justification is that it can be assumed "with considerable probability" that they will not be punished in Vietnam.

Indeed, the atmosphere in Germany has changed drastically. While German business associations warn about the dangers posed to foreign investment and export markets by growing racism, individual companies threaten to move if refugees are housed in their vicinity. In Munich, in the fall of 1992, a twenty-three-year-old Indian woman, recently celebrated in the local press as the cathedral city's eight thousandth woman student, is assaulted and stabbed by three Germans. Meanwhile, during the nationwide broadcast of the Mölln victims' funeral, the Bavarian television audience sees only static. And Chancellor Kohl explains the Mölln firebombing in terms of a general increase in crime.

On the streets of Berlin, skinheads physically force ten-year-olds to raise their arms in the Hitler-salute, while attacks on refugees, foreigners, Jews, the handicapped, punks, and leftists occur every day, and with increasing brutality. There no longer seems to be any threshhold of restraint, yet the greatest worry of the politicians seems to be Germany's sagging image abroad.

Heinz Reisz of Langen, however, is delighted with the situation. He admits openly that his comrades' present goal is not to seize power—"That would be unrealistic"—but "to put enough pressure on the parties to force them to drift toward the right. And we've done that. Today the CDU and the CSU are making statements as far to the right as the NPD of twenty years ago."

Kühnen's successors in the NSDAP-AO advance organization

Gesinnungsgemeinschaft der Neuen Front (GdNF) also have reason to be pleased. Their newspaper, *Die Neue Front,* is published in the Dutch city of Delfzijl, and from there they hope to "carry the flame of the German Revolution from Rostock, Cottbus, and Dresden to Hamburg, Frankfurt, and Munich." With a firm "Keep Going, Germany," they celebrate the Rostock riots as "resistance."

Militant groups still don't stand a chance in elections, but extreme-right parties like Franz Schönhuber's Republicans and the Deutsche Volksunion, led by Munich multimillionaire publisher and real-estate mogul Gerhard Frey, get candidates into parliament. Even in the 1986 Bavarian state elections, the Republicans achieved a succès d'estime by winning 3 percent of the vote. After that, Schönhuber was a welcome celebrity guest at carnivals and fireworks shows or anniversary celebrations of rifle clubs and choral groups. He told the people what they wanted to hear: "Sham refugees out!" "We're not a welfare office for the Mediterranean." "We want to protect the German people's ecological *Lebensraum* against foreign infiltration." "We no longer want a television program of Dachau on channel one, Treblinka on two, and Auschwitz on three."

In Berlin's parliamentary elections of February 1989, almost 90,000 West Berliners vote for the Republicans. This result, 7.5 percent, not only sends eleven delegates to parliament, but also brings them half a million marks in electoral matching funds; the party uses the money to expand its organization and support its campaign for the European parliament. With 7.1 percent of the vote nationwide and 14.6 percent in their Bavarian base, the Republicans demonstrate that they are a force to be reckoned with.

The party was then shaken by internal quarrels, leadership battles, and a failed putsch against its chairman. Schönhuber skillfully explains the expulsion of disloyal members as "purification" and a battle against "extremism," but because of these troubles, the Republicans are not in a position to take advantage of the opening of the Wall and reunification. They do reach double digits in the Bavarian municipal election of March 1990, and are represented in the city councils of every major city. But in October they fall just short of winning a seat in the Bavarian state parliament with 4.9

percent of the vote. In the end, only 2.1 percent of the voters in the first Bundestag elections in reunified Germany support Schönhuber's party. But those numbers would change, and fast.

During the pause before the next scheduled elections, for the state parliaments of Baden-Württemberg and Schleswig-Holstein in 1992, the atmosphere is conducive to racist and anti-Semitic agitation. "We are fighting for a result in the double digits," the former SS man announces with customary bravado. His wish would be fulfilled. With 10.9 percent, the Republicans become the third strongest party in Baden-Württemberg. This represents Schönhuber's breakthrough, a solid four million marks for the party treasury, and a confirmation of the popularity of their issues. The next success comes in May 1992, during the first municipal elections in reunified Berlin. By now the media has grown so accustomed to the presence of the Republicans that even though they get 8.3 percent of the vote, newspapers around the country see no shift to the right in Berlin.

Franz Schönhuber can pat himself on the back. In just two years he has radically changed the image of his party. With their triumphs in Baden-Württemberg and Berlin they have shed the image of beery Bavarians in lederhosen. Intellectuals in jackets and ties dominate their June 1992 party convention in Deggendorf. "Foreigners out" has been replaced by an elegant plea for "cultural identity." After all, they want to be fit for mainstream society and for coalitions. Meanwhile, of course, their newly founded youth organization urges a "total rejection of a multicultural society," the "protection of the purity of the German language," and the "return of the Eastern territories." It also wants to eliminate school trips to "so-called memorials," since this "mass overcoming of the past" is "a crime against the souls of schoolchildren."

After Rostock, the Republicans win a solid 11.3 percent in the by-election for the Passau City Council, and Franz Schönhuber announces a "storm of new members" for his party, which at the time includes around 23,000 members. "Time is on our side," he adds.

Time is also working for the Deutsche Volksunion (DVU). In September 1991, the party, which was founded in 1971 by Gerhard

Frey, wins 6.1 percent in the Bremen state elections and reaches 10 percent in Bremerhaven, much better than their showing in the 1987 elections. The DVU now has around 26,000 members, and for the first time is able to form an official faction in a German state parliament. Half a year later, the party enters the Schleswig-Holstein parliament with 6.3 percent of the vote and celebrates this "victory for the righteous cause of the German people." In particular, the DVU introduces motions for "required community service for foreigners granted asylum," for "purifying school books of anti-German dirt and trash," and for providing schools with maps that portray "Germany in its rightful borders"—that is, including East Prussia, Pomerania, and Silesia. To this, Karl-Otto Meyer, a deputy representing the Danish minority, issued a furious response: "We will never again let ourselves be placed in a situation in which people like you and your kind can again put nooses around our necks. We will take action first."

With its 1.15 million marks in matching funds, the party finances its headquarters in Munich as well as its chairman's campaign trips to organize new local committees, especially in the new states. Two months before the Rostock pogrom, Frey and the DVU turned up in that city to agitate against the "flood of refugees" and the "Gypsy plague." DVU members mixed in with the Lichtenhagen Citizens' Initiative, which at the end of August urged the people "to take the asylum problem into your own hands." DVU members took care of the logistics for the rally that later developed into the pogrom. Once the groundwork is properly laid, the road from agitation to action is short indeed.

The so-called *Neue Rechte* (New Right) ideology, which has penetrated nearly all extreme-right parties and many conservative circles, is based on the Weimar-era *Konservative Revolution*—a group of young conservatives, nationalist revolutionaries, and racists who are considered to have helped pave the way for National Socialism. Their mentor, the constitutional lawyer Carl Schmitt, had fought the young republic's parliamentary democracy from the start, urging an authoritarian state ruled by an elite. A Nazi Party member and a protégé of Hermann Göring, Schmitt also published the influential *Deutsche Juristenzeitung* (German Jurists' Newpaper) in which he praised the Nuremberg race laws. The state, he said, had finally become "a means of national power and unity." Schmitt, who died in 1985, is enjoying a renaissance in Germany and beyond; his writings are also being reprinted and discussed in Italy and France.

Like Schmitt and his followers, the New Rightists consider liberalism the archenemy. "Freedom through order" is their motto; that is, an authoritarian state in which the individual must submit to the popular will. Nation, people, family, and order are the pillars of this ideology. Accordingly, the New Rightists support nationalist liberation movements and "ethno-pluralism," meaning isolated peoples living side by side. As part of their antiliberalism, they fight against what they term the "vodka-cola-culture" and "Western materialism."

Their main organ is *Junge Freiheit* (Young Freedom), an extreme rightist journal written primarily by students. The monthly magazine increased its circulation from an initial 400 to 35,000 within four years and plans to publish weekly as of January 1994. Its growth was greatly aided by the prominence of its guest authors, a mixture of CDU and CSU politicians, REP party officials, conservative professors, and more controversial figures such as David Irving. This "mix" gives the paper a reputation that contributes to easing of the mutual anxiety between conservatives, nationalists, and nationalist revolutionaries.

As part of its "antiliberalism," *Junge Freiheit* fights for what it considers Germany's complete sovereignty—including its "spiritual liberation." To that end, the journal has a special page entitled "Contemporary History," for which Alfred Schickel is responsible. Schickel is the head of the Research Institute for Contemporary History in Ingolstadt and is an enthusiastic historical revisionist. According to a tribute from the Sudeten German expellee association, he has succeeded in saving "historiography from the ghetto of the victors' histories." In his pages in *Junge Freiheit,* "the Auschwitz lie" is propagated and Germany's invasion of the Soviet Union is presented as an act of self-defense. This man, who also writes for a variety of other extreme-right magazines—was recently awarded the Distinguished Service Medal of the Federal Republic of Germany for his work against "ignorance, prejudice, and disinformation." That no one thought to criticize this travesty is in itself an eloquent expression of the state of the nation in Germany today.

Such successes were denied the German League for Nation and Homeland, an organization founded in October 1991 as a "rallying movement" by disappointed REP, DVU, and NPD members in a casino in Stuttgart–Bad Canstatt. When the men around Harald Neubauer and former NPD chairman Martin Mussgnung failed with the voters—while acknowledging with envy the triumph of the REPs and DVU—they dropped all restraint on militarism and looked toward direct action.

Their party organ *Deutsche Rundschau* (German Panorama) celebrated Rostock as the expression of "our people's natural, healthy impulses." "No state and no people can endure such immigration for long." "Our activities must encourage the people themselves to resist the unpopular establishment." No sooner said than done. In the Black Forest town of Villingen-Schwenningen, League members called for the formation of a "citizens' militia," and in July 1992 they conferred with officials of the Deutsche Alternative in the Brandenburg town of Gross-Gaglow about "concerted action in the future." In October they recruited for a "German Martial-Sports Initiative" in Solingen and organized a demonstration in Eberswalde "against left-wing parasites" together with the militant Nationalistische Front (NF).

"We make foreigners who live here feel as uncomfortable as possible," says Jürgen Rieger, a Hamburg lawyer and backer of numerous right-wing organizations, in describing NF's guiding principle at their national convention in the Hessian town of Niederaula in April 1991. In its "Ninety-Point Plan for Foreigner Repatriation," NF urges "the immediate deportation of foreign criminals," an "integration tax of 50,000 marks per year for every employed foreigner," a restriction of public housing "to Germans only," and the cessation of family and education allowances to foreigners.

It is worth recalling that nineteen-year-old NF activist Josef Saller, who burned down a house in Schwandorf in 1988—killing three Turks—later told police he had wanted "to annoy foreigners." The court, however, refused to take Saller's NF connections into consideration and judged him a "lone activist and perpetrator." In the middle of November 1992 two skinheads, apparently NF members, murdered a fifty-three-year-old man in a bar in Wuppertal because they thought he was Jewish. After beating him, they poured alcohol over him, set him on fire, and then dumped the corpse over the border in Holland. In recent years, NF members have also been involved in bombing refugee shelters in and around Bremen, and they have been at the head of Ku Klux Klan activities in the Westphalian town of Herford and in Königs-Wusterhausen.

The number of such NF incidents is rising so rapidly that they can hardly be classified, much less completely recorded. When Graeme Atkinson started to chronicle the atrocities for *Searchlight* in November 1992, he had to limit himself to listing the time, place, and type of damage; there wasn't enough room to mention, as is customary, names and circumstances. Still the list grows out of control, and must constantly be updated, since new riots and attacks are reported daily from all over Germany. "They're going crazy!" Graeme groans repeatedly as he sorts out the new reports and feeds them into the computer. The NF is nearly ubiquitous in the accounts.

The connection between aggressive, hateful propaganda and corresponding action is especially clear with the NF. They consider themselves successors to the SA, a "new, unified force of all revolutionary nationalists." Their members, who are required to contribute 5 percent of their gross income to the party treasury, do not want to be coffeehouse or beerhall nationalists, but real fighters. The party's campaign for "racial socialism" claims to be both anti-imperialist and anticapitalist—a position very appealing in the East once the Wall fell. The NF sees itself as a cadre organization made up of "cells" and "bases." In addition to indoctrination sessions and celebrations on Hitler's birthday, the group holds annual paramilitary training camps with names like "Young Columns on the March for the Fourth Reich." In June 1991, the NF tried to place itself at the forefront of the revisionist movement by organizing an international congress in Roding to spread "Auschwitz lie" propaganda, but the congress was banned.

Since the sale of their house on Bielefeld's Bleichstrasse, the NF have been based in Detmold-Pivitsheide. The army's exercise grounds at Senne are right next door, providing ideal conditions for spontaneous military training. The NF publishes an internal bulletin *Aufbruch* (Uprising) and a newspaper called *Revolte,* both of which openly applaud racist violence. Cartoons show skins stomping on a prone Turk. And as one reader, a juvenile offender in jail in Ottweiler, wrote in a letter to the editors, "This paper inspires me to get on my feet and join the battle!"

Rituals with fire, a favorite Nazi method of fascinating the masses, also play an important role in NF propaganda. The NF mobilized its supporters for the 1989 European parliamentary elections by reminding them to "Do your part to gather the wood that will build our fire." Summer solstice and new moon festivals are also part of the NF program.

NF general secretary Meinolf Schönborn's written call for "national commando teams"—'highly mobile cadres . . . to carry on the battle for a national Germany, with greater focus, efficiency, and success"—finally prompted the attorney general's office to investigate them on grounds of terrorism. But despite numerous house searches throughout the country, no evidence was turned up, and the NF was allowed to reorganize in time for the regional elections in Kelheim, Bavaria. Pedro Verela, leader of the Spanish neofascist CEDADE, marched at the head of the "Foreigners out" demonstration held in this pretty little town.

On November 11, 1992, Federal interior minister Seiters banned the NF—and this time searches produced not only propaganda material but also weapons, explosives, and a hit list. However, not a single NF member was arrested, and, thanks to an advance warning, General Secretary Schönborn was able to escape. Naturally, "respectable" NF supporters like Jürgen Rieger remained untouched. A week later, still in hiding, Meinolf Schönborn claimed that the NF was the "victim of the media's gigantic rape of our people, and of politicians submissive to the occupiers and foreigners." He declared the ban to be "utterly without effect," because "we are vindicated by history, we love Germany, we have the German people on our side. This ban will stir up *hate.*" Since the NF's Förderwerk Mitteldeutsche Jugend (Association to Advance Central German Youth) had been founded shortly before the ban, a replacement organization was already in place.

Two weeks after the ban, Interior Minister Seiters, who apparently had just discovered the existence of neo-Nazis, proposed stripping significant political rights—including eligibility for political office and freedom of expression—from Heinz Reisz of Langen and Thomas Dienel of Weimar. Thirty-one-year-old Dienel is head of the six hundred member Deutsche Nationale Partei (German National Party—DNP) and has excellent relations with Christian Worch. Considered psychopathic even by some of his own comrades, Dienel is always ready with a memorable phrase, especially if a camera is nearby. "No one was killed in Auschwitz—unfortunately!" booms this man for whom "there is only one Germany: the Germany extending from the Meuse to the Memel." He is also prone to make grand speeches in court. While defending himself in the Rudolstadt district court against charges of instigating public discord, he declared that "We will see to it that Turks, Chinese, Vietnamese, and Negroes no longer exist in Germany." When those sentiments won him two years and eight months in jail, Dienel's response was that "you can't ban opinions."

In his view, civil war is already raging in Germany, and he and his paramilitary troops—trained in explosives and hand-to-hand combat—have a mandate to do away with foreigners, refugees, and Jews in the country. Dienel proudly provides television reporters with videos of their training exercises, and announces on TV that they have "the police completely under control."

Dienel's great moment in Eastern Germany came after Michael Kühnen's death, when he became the DPN chairman for Thüringen. In the ensuing months he organized demonstrations in Halle, Leipzig, and Dresden with Christian Worch, Ewald Althans, Heinz Reisz, and Frank Hübner. In August he and Worch proceeded with the forbidden "Rudolf Hess March," which gathered about 2,000 neo-Nazis in Rudolstadt; it is no coincidence that within two weeks the Vietnamese boardinghouse in Rostock went up in flames.

Dienel had founded his DNP in proper style, on April 19, 1992, the day before Hitler's birthday. The character of this "radical national party" was apparent in the subsequent celebration of the Führer's birthday, and in flags covered with swastikas and Nazi-style graphics. Signed *"Heil Deutschland,"* the party's flyers speak of "racial murder through miscegenation" and blame "fraudulent black African refugees" for infecting Germans with AIDS. On the day of the party's founding, Dienel was already calling for underground activity to "fight the enemies within the country."

Dienel's favored ally is the Nationale Offensive (NO), which has shifted its focus toward Southern Germany and the East. The latter includes Eastern Germany, especially Dresden, but also Silesia, one of the "Eastern territories." Formed by discontented FAP members, this party was established on July 3, 1990, with former Bavarian FAP chairman Michael Swierczek as leader. Their motto is: "To go on the offensive is to stake everything, for the man who does not risk his life will never live! Attack!" and their program calls for repatriating foreigners, because "cultural mixing is national murder." They want to send drug dealers to work camps, commenting that "often not only is the drug Oriental, but so is the drug dealer."

Since the NO demands the reestablishment of the German empire in its "historic boundaries," they distribute stickers proclaiming "Germany for the Germans" and "Silesia Is Still German." NO activist Günter Boschütz bought a house in the Polish town of Dziewkowice (formerly Frauenfeld) together with NPD functionaries and turned it into the NO's Silesian headquarters. Since October 1991 he has published the monthly *Silesia-Report,* "the only purely German-language journal from Silesia for Silesia." Radio Silesia is also already broadcasting twenty-four hours a day from Zabrze (formerly Hindenburg) to "give several hundreds of thousands of Germans new faith in a future in their ancestral homeland, and to tell them that they have not been forgotten, betrayed, or sold down the river by Germany, but that they as Silesians are part of German culture.''

In all of their activities in Silesia, including setting up bilingual signs and restoring old German war memorials, the NO activists work closely with the federally funded Deutsche Freundeskreise (German Friends) in Poland and with the NPD's Germania-Reise (Germania Journey). The NO national treasurer is pleased to inform potential contributors that 1992 was ''a successful year,'' and that there would soon be a ''national headquarters,'' like the one in former Frauenfeld, in ''Russian-occupied East Prussia.'' In mid-December, the Polish authorities declare Günter Boschütz an undesirable alien and expel him.

This is only a brief survey of recent right-wing developments. Rolf Schmidt-Holz, the editor in chief of the newsmagazine *Stern,* sums up the state of the nation definitively in his editorial on December 10, 1992. ''You say, dear readers, that the politicians have failed dramatically? You're right. . . . There are no excuses left. We all see what is going on in Germany every day. We must take responsibility ourselves.''

If the candlelight demonstrations are enough is questionable. The fact is, it is high time for us to take responsibility, because the enemies of democracy are not playing around. In June 1990, a secret ritual is held in a remote clearing in a Bavarian forest, about an hour by car from Munich. It is one of Michael Kühnen's last accomplishments. He stands in full uniform, with brown shirt, black pants, and top boots before thirty or so similarly dressed followers, who stand rigidly before him in a straight line.

Kühnen expresses his regret that ''only so few made it through,'' since about a hundred followers were originally supposed to come. But he is proud that despite police persecution, the ''toughest of the tough'' are present to honor the memory of Ernst Röhm.'' The quiet of the summertime forest muffles all sounds. In the midday heat, most birds are silent; only the crickets chirp indefatigably in a nearby meadow. The neo-Nazis' arms fly up to give the Hitler-salute, then Kühnen strikes up the ''Horst Wessel Song'':

> With flags raised high and ranks close together,
> Storm troopers march with steady, quiet tread.
> Comrades, the men killed by reaction and reds
> March in spirit in our ranks. . . .

The thirty men sing earnestly and carefully, with no hint of a false note or a misplaced word. With subdued and solemn voices, they sing that they all "stand ready for battle" and that soon "Hitler's banner will fly over barricades" since "the bondage will last but a little while longer."

Then the *Bereichsleiter*—the head of the local *Gau*—calls forth a "Comrade Thomas." One of the men steps forward and stands at attention in front of Kühnen and the *Bereichsleiter*, his arm raised in the Hitler-salute. Once "admitted into the cadre," he shakes hands with both men and returns to his place. This procedure is repeated about ten times.

Kühnen then leads the comrades in an oath—not to him personally, since he knows that he will not live much longer. Nevertheless it fills him with pride to commit this cadre to the coming battle. "By my honor as a German," he recites and the men repeat after him, "I vow to serve the National Socialist German Workers' Party loyally and bravely. I vow to obey to the death the superiors assigned to me by the party. I swear secrecy toward all outsiders. May Germany arise and the Jew perish! *Sieg Heil!*"

The ceremony is over, and an SA stormtroop has been formed anew. Perhaps most frightening of all, this is not an exclusively German phenomenon but part of an international network.

III

INSIDE THE NETWORK

XIII

TRUTH WILL MAKE
YOU FREE

THE SA AND SS WERE DECLARED CRIMINAL ORGANIZA-
tions, in the Nuremberg trials, and their continuation and re-forma-
tion were strictly forbidden. This fact, however, doesn't hinder the
worldwide neo-Nazi movement from constructing cadre units modeled on these organizations, copying their ideology and structure.
This international network becomes visible only on very specific
occasions, when suddenly representatives from otherwise separate
parties gather in the same place to deepen old connections and begin
new ones.

In the summer of 1990 I had the opportunity to witness such an
event, one in which the leading figures from several countries
participated. Michael Kühnen had arranged for me to be invited, but
it was some time before I realized that this would be one of the most
important days in my investigation.

The people look as if they're about to pose for the group picture at
a great family reunion. Everyone is there—the old folks, the young
ones, the dear aunts and uncles, the married couples, even the
cousins from England. Yesterday was Great-Uncle Adolf's birthday,
and the old folks can still remember him perfectly. The entire family
celebrated, and a few of the boys are still hung over. Brother-in-law

Manfred brought along his videocamera. Old Uncle Otto-Ernst and Cousin Michael have quarreled, and Cousin Ewald has diplomatically seated them at different tables. Dear Aunt Christa has brought a cake, as always. Gottfried and his cousin Thomas are jokingly arguing about who's the best. Thomas's wound is bigger, but Gottfried has learned how to play guitar. Cousin Uschi is very excited; Cousin David, on whom she has a secret crush, is about to make a speech. And little Arno looks delightful in his new sailor's suit. He looks admiringly at Uncle Ekkehard, who always brings such wonderful firecrackers. But cousin Anthony from England is not doing well at all. He is in the middle of an identity crisis and insists that his name isn't Tony but Mickey.

This photo opportunity takes place at Munich's Löwenbräukeller on April 21, 1990. It's a big family: 800 "relatives" are throwing themselves a very well-organized party. The proprietors have even made arrangements with the police, who aren't part of the family at all. In Bavaria, there are strict limits on the very *far* right. These days, when neo-Nazis demonstrate openly with "Foreigners out!" slogans, the police intervene sharply. Competition from the right is not tolerated. After all, if you want to demand a "refugee-free zone," you can do it within the ruling Christian Social Union, the CSU.

If the Löwenbräukeller sounds familiar, it should; it's one of the biggest beerhalls in Bavaria. Ah, Bavaria! The land of Tyrolean jackets and dirndls, pork shanks and Oktoberfest. Where beer is a dietary staple, and where the mad King Ludwig II once ruled from his fairy-tale castle, Neuschwanstein. Large, high windows at the front of the hall let the daylight in, and the high-ceilinged room—with galleries, speaker's platform, and a side wing—holds the 800 people easily. Signs proclaiming *"Wahrheit macht frei!"* (Truth will make you free!) are held high by men in bomber jackets at the front of the speaker's platform.

The guests at the Revisionist Congress sit in the hall at large tables with blue-and-white tablecloths. They could be nice folks from next door. It's like a huge clan gathering. True, there are no children, but on the other hand, there are plenty of folk costumes. Two ladies in the beautiful white Pomeranian ones stand at the right of the hall, next to the tables with the books. Chicly dressed in rustic country-villa style and chattering excitedly, they look like the kind of women who would look after your pets while you were away on vacation. Elderly gentlemen with pipes and cigars cough gently as they speak confidentally to clean-cut young men; the boys have left their girlfriends at the table to watch over their beers.

Now and then people look over to the side of the hall, where young men in brown shirts and army pants are sitting. They have blackjacks in their pockets and are ready to intervene in case of any disturbance. Occasionally, they respond to these glances and polite greetings are exchanged. Young and old get along swimmingly here, since everyone has something in common. Armed with beer tankards, sausage, and sauerkraut, these ultra-Germans are waiting for a particular speaker, a special guest. They are waiting to hear a new version of history. New "truths" are in demand, for they are sick of feeling the burden of guilt on their shoulders: the guilt of the world war, the guilt of war crimes, the guilt of the Holocaust.

The burden will soon be lifted by the featured speaker, though he comes not from Bavaria, but from England, former archenemy. David Irving is his name. His books sell by the millions, all over the world, and they are published by prestigious houses like Ullstein in Germany. Ullstein's reputation did suffer a bit when Herbert Fleissner bought into the firm, since he is a well-known right-winger who owns shares in over twenty publishing concerns. His Langen-Müller Verlag published Schönhuber's *Ich war dabei* (I Was There). David Irving's Hitler trilogy, in which the author suggests that the Führer did not know that Jews were being gassed, was also published by a Fleissner imprint, the Herbig Verlag. But Ullstein is still considered one of the great publishing houses. Similarly, Irving's other publishers—Legenda in Sweden, Macmillan in London, Albin Michel in France—remain thoroughly respectable.

David Irving's books are thus read by many people who don't know about his true political identity. It is often mentioned that he's "controversial," but the people who buy his works apparently don't know much more than that. And how would they, when even

Chancellor Kohl gives one of his staff members a David Irving book for Christmas?* So it's not surprising that Irving's voluminous publications appear on the bookshelves of other unsuspecting souls, who are likely to assume that Irving is, if perhaps conservative, certainly a respectable historian. The Deutsche Volksunion's supporters know Irving quite a bit better. The man from London appears frequently and gladly (in return for a solid honorarium) at events organized by party chairman Gerhard Frey. There, to flag-waving and applause, he affirms that the English bombed Dresden—and that it wasn't even necessary.

Here among the family in the Löwenbräukeller, a day after the Führer's birthday, people are already set in their beliefs. Here Dresden is interesting only as a body count, a number to offset against "other" victims—for credibility. No, David Irving isn't going to speak of Dresden. Today the topic will be the Holocaust. In particular, Auschwitz. Majdanek, Sobibor, Belzec, Kulmhof, Treblinka, Chelmo, and many others have already been collapsed into that one place, Auschwitz—or, more precisely, the gas chambers there.

Irving's recipe, of course, is "Truth will make you free!," so everyone is waiting for him to speak. A plump man in a cardigan taps his knuckles nervously on the table. The buzz in the back of the hall grows louder when someone is spotted moving near the table with Irving's books. The minutes creep by. The tension becomes almost unbearable, even though everyone knows what David Irving is going to say. Michael Kühnen looks at his watch. Gottfried Küssel, his faithful follower, has not yet arrived.

Thomas Hainke, the "Gauleiter for East Westphalia-Lippe," gives me only a curt nod when I grin at him. He is on duty. He stands rigidly beside the podium, suitably dressed all in black with top boots. Head high, he holds up the black-white-red imperial flag. I consider asking him about his latest "battle wound," but David Irving has just arrived, so that will have to wait till later.

*From an article entitled "Ein Reich, Ein Irving" in the English *Independent on Sunday* (March 3, 1991): "Last Christmas, Chancellor Kohl gave one of his speech-writers a copy of Irving's notorious biography of Winston Churchill."

The opening bars of Richard Strauss's *Also sprach Zarathustra* sound from the loudspeakers. The horns roar mercilessly through the hall, and then the sound of applause mixes with the fanfare. David Irving strides down the aisle between the benches of the audience with the grace of a man used to applause. The only thing lacking is for the older ladies to grasp his hands and kiss them.

Irving wears a dark suit, and with his firm gaze and white shirt he radiates the air of sovereign competence needed to present his revision of history authoritatively. As a young man of twenty-one he was a steelworker in Germany, at Thyssen, and so his German is fluid and effortless. After a lengthy preamble, he proclaims, "I have the truth!"

But he prolongs the suspense by refusing to come right out and say what he means. "We know," he finally says, "and here I need only mention it as a footnote . . ." But it's this "footnote" that everyone is waiting for, and Irving knows it. The 800 people in the hall hold their breath until Irving liberates them: ". . . that there were no gas chambers in Auschwitz!"

Irving has to pause, since the cheering goes on and on. The joy of newly won innocence is in these cries, like the final climax after painful excitation. No gas chambers . . . no mass extermination . . . no guilt.

"Bravo!" cries a well-preserved pensioner with a scar on his cheek. In the middle of the hall people rise to their feet in a standing ovation. A woman with a perm and a lace collar blows her nose, shaking with gratitude and emotion. What joy, what bliss!

In this forum Irving couldn't care less whether or not he's taken for a serious historian. "So," he continues, "just as the gas chamber in Dachau was a dummy built in the first postwar years, the gas chambers that tourists now see in Auschwitz were built by present-day Poland right after the Second World War. The evidence exists, the grounds have been chemically analyzed, and we have now published the facts all over the world. And I can assure you, ladies and gentlemen, they will make quite a sensation. Our enemies will faint from the shock."

The promise to spread the message until the enemy faints elicits renewed ovations. And while the expressions of acclaim grow more individual, they are no less sustained. Irving waits silently at the podium for the applause to die down. Next to him, Thomas Hainke holds his imperial war flag with unaltered solemnity.

"There is only one truth," proclaims Irving in the voice of one enlightened, "and that is the total truth! Truth will make you free!" The 800 liberated listeners rise again in standing ovations. "Total truth" takes the place of "total war," just as "Truth will make you free" replaces "Work will make you free." It's exactly what they need. Onward against the enemy!

The "evidence" Irving mentions is anything but overwhelming, however. It is essentially based on the so-called Leuchter Report. The French revisionist literature professor Robert Faurisson had come up with the idea of scientifically "proving" that the gas chambers never existed. He looked for a "specialist" and came up with an American, Fred A. Leuchter, who describes himself as a "specialist in the design and production of execution apparatus" and has "worked on and designed the equipment used in the United States to execute prisoners condemned to die by cyanide gas." These qualifications were apparently sufficient for the revisionists to give him the title "engineer" and (for a $37,000 honorarium) send him to Poland in February 1988 with a "documentation team."*

Upon his arrival, Leuchter tramped around in the mud of the Auschwitz, Birkenau, and Majdanek extermination camps—places that have been left to the wind and rain for half a century—and took samples, which he tested for their content of Zyklon-B poison gas. As was to be expected, "the author finds the evidence overwhelmingly conclusive. There were no gas chambers for executions in any of these places. It is the strong professional opinion of this engineer that the alleged gas chambers at the inspected locations could neither have been used as execution chambers then, nor could they be seriously considered for such a function today."

*According to the research of the Anti-Defamation League (ADL Research Report, summer 1989, New York), Fred Leuchter's name does not appear on the list of accredited engineers in his home state of Massachusetts, where he would have to be registered in order to use that title legitimately.

He provides further evidence of his analytical capabilities in his report on the gas trucks the Nazis also used to murder Jews by locking them inside and funneling in the exhaust. According to Leuchter, "carbon monoxide gas was allegedly used. But . . . carbon monoxide gas is not a gas that can be used for executions. The author believes that the victims would all die of asphyxiation before the gas could come into effect." With this gem of sophistry, he concludes that no one was executed with carbon monoxide.*

Even the Leuchter Report's most outrageous declarations are topped by another "proof" offered by the revisionists to lie away the burden of the Holocaust: it is an "eyewitness report" called *Die Auschwitz-Lüge* (The Auschwitz Lie), by Thies Christophersen. This former SS officer writes that he didn't see any signs of mass murder at Auschwitz, where he was stationed. We will meet Christophersen again later, but today in Munich, in the Löwenbräukeller, he is nowhere to be found. There is a warrant out for his arrest in Germany.

Irving has finished his speech, but the meeting in the Löwenbräukeller rolls on. Many faces are already familiar to me. Ewald Althans, the ardent National Socialist who issued the invitations to this Revisionist Congress, is just now speaking with David Irving. They are sitting together on the stage. I have known Althans since my first (failed) attempt with Gerald Hess to catch Irving in Hamburg with a hidden camera. Althans was then, as now, working closely with Christian Worch.

By the time he was a teenager, Bela Ewald Althans was a member of Kühnen's FAP. At the age of thirteen, he had been hand-picked

*Leuchter is also praised by writers outside of the neo-Nazi hard core. Ernst Nolte stated his opinion in February 1990, in the radical-right journal *Junge Freiheit* (Young Freedom): "The Leuchter report is perhaps unconvincing. At the same time, it should encourage reflection," he says, adding that "if revisionism and Leuchter have convinced the public that 'Auschwitz' should also be an object of scholarly investigation and debate, then we must be thankful to them."

and systematically prepared for a leadership role by old ex-Nazis and Nazi sympathizers. One of his mentors was Princess Helene von Isenburg, who in the 1950s, through the ODESSA advance organization Stille Hilfe (Silent Aid), had helped Nazi war criminals escape justice, providing them with money and petitions to such personages as Pope Pius XII. The HNG later took over Stille Hilfe's operations. (Christa Goerth, the HNG's managing director, is also here today; I had met her at my first talk with Kühnen.) Althans received additional support from Otto-Ernst Remer, Hitler's bodyguard, who is also in the audience today. Systematically trained in Germany, Althans was also sent abroad. He speaks fluent English, passable French and Italian, and enough Spanish not to need an interpreter at CEDADE's meetings in Madrid.

In his mid-twenties, Althans corresponds closely to the Aryan ideal: he is tall and blond, with gray-blue eyes and well-proportioned features. He is also homosexual,* which in the Third Reich might have put him in a concentration camp, but he nevertheless considers Hitler "the most perfect man of all time." Althans is talented both as a speaker and as an organizer. He consistently demonstrates his organizational skills in his congresses featuring David Irving and other revisionists. In private life he claims to be a journalist and runs a firm called AVÖ: Althans Verkauf und Öffentlichkeitsarbeit (Althans Sales and Publicity Company).† In the spring of 1992, he shows exactly how he makes enough money to finance an office in Munich, complete with fax, portable phone, and computer system. He places an ad for "SPECTACULAR ACTION PHOTOS" in various newspapers. For a price of $5,000 he will provide the buyer with "action shots" of paramilitary neo-Nazis quenching their thirst for battle in Croatia as well as in Iraq during the Gulf War. These pictures, he promises, "have never been seen

*Althans is an exception among his crowd for openly standing by his homosexuality. From a letter to the editors of the gay magazine *Don und Adonis:* "I am a Nazi—so what? . . . My gay friends have also stood by me. After all, they always knew the truth."

†Depending on the client, AVÖ can also stand for Amt für Volksaufklärung und Öffentlichkeitsarbeit (Office for Popular Education and Publicity), as the Bavarian Verfassungsschutz notes in a 1991 report.

by the media before.'' He can also supply names and background information, and can even arrange personal meetings with mercenaries.

When he's not busy selling his pals to the media, Althans travels. His favorite destination is Toronto, where he visits a German–Canadian who, after discovering that there was serious money to be made selling neo-Nazi writings and materials (through his press, which is called Samisdat), announced that he was a revisionist. His firm's products include cassette tapes of speeches by Nazi greats. He signs his own literary efforts with the pseudonym Christoph Friedrich; his real name is Ernst Christoph Friedrich Zündel. He is responsible for a book entitled *Den Hitler, den wir liebten und warum* (The Hitler We Loved and Why). He was born in the Black Forest in 1939 and at age eighteen emigrated to Canada, where he became an advertising man, photographer, and an expert in retouching photographs. A virulent anti-Semite, Zündel has built up a worldwide network of similarly inclined ''anti-Zionists'' that includes both David Irving and an Englishman named Anthony Hancock.

The latter is present today in the Löwenbräukeller, but he is not completely at ease. Tony, as his friends call him, has brought along some of Hitler's watercolors and is now showing them at the press table. He is happy to let me film Hitler's artwork, but he gets nervous when I direct the camera at him. I ask him in English where he comes from. From London, he replies. And what organization does he belong to?

''I'm not connected with any organization, I just, um . . . I'm a sort of friend of a friend. . . .'' He stammers on for a little while.

I ask him if he's a collector.

''Oh, I am a collector of books and various things,'' he says.

When I ask his name, he hesitates briefly. Then he tells me, with a smile, ''Yeah, my name is Michael!''

He seems to be having trouble making up a last name on the spur of the moment, but I don't relent: ''Michael . . .?''

''Carter,'' he finally says.

''Michael Carter?'' I repeat the name. Fine. Anthony Hancock, alias Michael Carter, feels obliged to present himself as a marginal figure. ''I'm just a friend of a friend, you know, and I, um . . . I collect antiquarian books, books to do with World War Two, prewar . . . almost . . . I'm just a general collector. . . ."

"So you have nothing to do with the National Front?"

"No, no!" he says. "I'm just an independent . . ." Hancock has to think about what he could be. The story about collecting wasn't bad at all, so he repeats it: ". . . sort of, um . . . collector. I'm here for a weekend, nice time, days in Munich and all that, you know."

Shortly afterward, Hancock is arrested in England for forging checks worth millions and for forging a passport. His press near Brighton produces the infamous Holocaust denial pamphlet *Starben wirklich sechs Millionen?* (Did Six Million Really Die?), which is distributed in English, French, and German. Ernst Zündel, Althan's Canadian friend, takes care of distribution in Canada.

Althans has the knack of maintaining equally good relations with both the "moderate" right wing and with Nazis from the terrorist underground. It is a talent that is especially evident here in the Löwenbräukeller. Again and again, the waiters bring fresh trays of foaming beer into the hall where Althans's family is feasting. They sit there on the day after Great-Uncle Adolf's one hundred and first birthday, in cozy harmony, the old gentlemen and the firebugs.

Not all of them want to be in the family picture. The rather stocky gentleman with the goatee, for example. He waves his finger frantically when he sees my camera pointing in his direction and then ducks behind the men sitting between us. Later analysis of the film shows him to be Ekkehard Weil. Born in East Berlin in 1949, this former nurse has served several terms in jail for arson, assault and battery, and bomb attacks. After twice "reducing" his own sentences simply by not returning from prison furloughs, Weil moved to Austria. There he became friends with Gottfried Küssel. Küssel himself is a pretty brutal guy, but Weil displays his psychopathic readiness for violence openly, for all the world to see. One of his standard response to photographers is: "If you press that button you're a dead man!" Fortunately, I don't know any of this as I point my camera at him, so we're in luck. And my neck is still not broken.

In any event, I was on my way to the front of the hall, where the high society is congregating. To the right of the stage, for example, sits a white-haired, bespectacled man who looks like the stereotypical jolly good fellow. He had earlier been publicly welcomed by Althans, to great applause. It's Manfred Roeder, who is talking animatedly with his tablemates—to his left, a sweet young thing in a stylish lace blouse; to his right, a young man with dirty blond hair and a wool cardigan that really doesn't match his combat boots. Roeder himself, with his thin-lipped smile and unwrinkled suit, gives an impression exactly opposite of what he really is—an aging terrorist just recently released after years in prison. A fanatic Christian, he began with attacks on porn shops, reaching the high point of his career in 1980, when members of his band carried out numerous attacks with firebombs and explosives. After two Vietnamese were killed in a firebombing of a refugee home near Hamburg, Roeder was sentenced to thirteen years in jail, though he was set free after serving nine. The rehabilitating effect of his imprisonment may justly be doubted; his travels to meet with underground extremists, especially in England, suggest that more trouble will come from him.

Roeder suddenly stands up and waves to Tony Hancock, who smiles briefly and then disappears behind a pillar when he spots my camera. Tony, alias Michael, is still having an identity crisis. And he just hates to be photographed, which, of course, tempts me all the more. If he sits down at a table, thinking he's completely out of camera range, it doesn't take ten minutes before I unexpectedly appear in front of him, with lens poised. Thus I inch my way across the entire hall, past the family members chomping on dumplings and pork shanks, past beer steins and shot glasses, past whispering aunts and asthmatic uncles who perhaps once met Hitler up close and are still gushing about it today. We work our way past the skinhead with his middle finger in a cast, past Christian Worch, whom, naturally, I have to say hello to. Tony takes advantage of this brief exchange to scurry away. At the table in front, two skinheads are just now toasting each other with their beer steins. "ADF!" says one, and the other, who already has beer froth on his nose, repeats this standard Nazi toast. ADF stands for *auf den Führer*—to the Führer. Outsiders are generally told that it stands for *auf die Frauen*—to women.

People suddenly start bustling around in the front part of the

Löwenbräukeller. Tony Hancock finally gets a breather as I hurry forward. Three young family members are getting ready for the souvenir picture. They obviously *want* to be photographed. But it turns out to be just a propaganda stunt: they are posing in plastic donkey-head masks and holding a sign in front of themselves: "This jackass still believes everything he's told!" The subtext, to be sure, is that only jackasses believe the Holocaust lies—and I'm suddenly reminded of a well-known photo from the Nazi era. It shows a woman with a sign hanging from her neck that reads: "I am the biggest pig here and let only Jews come near me!" The SA had her photographed before making her and her Jewish boyfriend run the gauntlet—for the "crime" of "racial disgrace."

The association between the two pictures is intentional, of course. The idea was Michael Kühnen's. As early as 1978 he had Christian Worch and his followers parade through the center of Hamburg in donkey masks carrying posters that read: "This jackass still believes that Jews were gassed in German concentration camps!" The propaganda effects were enormous. Ten years later, Kühnen still boasted of it.

Here in the Löwenbräukeller the stunt is welcomed merrily, and even most of the photographers grin. Although three tables near the stage are labeled "Press," the majority of these journalists don't quite seem to belong to the democratic press. The man sitting next to me notices it too. He works for the Munich *Abendzeitung,* and after a quick look around he grumbles to me, "I think we're the only normal reporters here."

He's right about that one. The others are all part of the family. A middle-aged gentleman who was just laughing heartily at the "donkey photo" sits down at our table and looks at me with his strikingly bulging eyes before turning to his neighbor. As I fiddle with my camera, I hear him say, "Yes, yes. The bread I eat is the song I sing."

"And what kind of bread do you eat?" I ask eagerly, pointing my camera at him. I'm getting this remark on film!

"White bread!" he says and bursts out laughing.

I attempt an interpretation. "You mean, as opposed to black?"

"I already said it: white bread." He tries to hide his grin under his well-groomed mustache; he's really enjoying his joke. A man standing next to the table now grins as well. The two of them have been filming the entire time with their own videocamera. The colleague's name is Manfred Lating. He is in his mid-forties, short, and wears thick glasses. In his own words, he is documenting the atmosphere with his videocamera "for the Institute."

The "Institute" is based in Costa Mesa, California, near Los Angeles. Its full name is the Institute for Historical Review (IHR for short), and it is one of the most important organizations in the international neofascist network. Under the pretense of scholarly research, the IHR supports right-wing extremists, racists, and anti-Semites who try, through "documentary evidence," to free Hitler and the Third Reich of all guilt. Friends of the IHR include not only revisionists and neo-Nazis worldwide, but also members of the Ku Klux Klan, citizens of certain Arab states, and a number of Nazi war criminals, some still wanted. Their documentary "evidence" includes such spurious efforts as the infamous *Protocols of the Elders of Zion,* which in the 1920s were revealed as forgeries produced by the Czarist secret police. The Leuchter Report is also to be found in the institute's catalogue. Almost all of their "eyewitness reports" stem from perpetrators or collaborators who, naturally, categorically deny their crimes. The IHR denies even the crimes to which war criminals have personally confessed. The confessions were extracted by torture, they claim.

The IHR publishes, in numerous languages, a pamphlet called "66 Questions and Answers About the Holocaust." Question 14: "How many gas chambers were there in Auschwitz?" Answer: "None!" Question 53: "What evidence is there that Hitler knew?" Answer: "None!" The revisionists seem not to have noticed the contradiction, unless perhaps "knew" refers to the existence of concentration camps of any sort. The answer to Question 56 ("Is the Anne Frank diary authentic?") offers "extensive evidence" that the diary is forged; a study reveals that "portions were written with a ballpoint pen," and everyone knows that ballpoint pens didn't exist back then. That these "portions" consist of a note inserted later by a different hand is something the revisionists choose prudently not to reveal.

The Germans in the IHR are Dr. Wilhelm Stäglich, a retired lawyer, and the "historian" Udo Walendy, a former adult-education teacher and NPD member who has specialized in the "war-guilt question." Stäglich, who was recently stripped of his doctorate, is also in the Löwenbräukeller. Michael Kühnen gives me the tip: the gaunt man with the big nose leafing through some books near the exit—"That's him," Kühnen says. He also tells me that Stäglich "fought in the East. I'd say he saw quite a lot there. Executions and such. . . ." How nice for Stäglich to be among friends today who think that it all wasn't so bad.

Here in the Löwenbräukeller, Stäglich is clearly of the inner circle, and he shakes hands with Otto-Ernst Remer, who has already been greeted respectfully by many others. His wife, Anneliese, couldn't make it. She had to stay behind and take care of their book business. It so happens that the Remers supplement the retired general's pension by selling books, brochures, and such videos as *The Crucial Document,* which shows Fred Leuchter conducting his "investigations" in the mud of the concentration camps. (In order to avoid prosecution, a disclaimer at the end of the tape states that the film "does not dispute the Holocaust against the Jews." That could be a real faux pas here in the Löwenbräukeller, but in fact, everyone takes it for the fig leaf that it is; and anyway, Otto-Ernst regularly affirms his unswerving devotion to the cause with his journal *Recht und Wahrheit* [Justice and Truth]), where a recent essay, a revisionist view of Kristallnacht, culminates in this mad appeal to its Aryan readers: "Germans, open your eyes! The Second World War was not ours! It was an intentional plot by international Jewry, who manipulated hegemonic European interests against Germany in order to destroy our Teutonic will to self-assertion."

Otto-Ernst Remer's books even have their own stand in the Löwenbräukeller's foyer, where one can purchase his version of twentieth-century history, in condensed form, under the title *Kriegshetze gegen Deutschland* (The War Slander Against Germany). Jürgen Mosler, who designed the book jacket, earlier demonstrated his graphic talents in a repulsive cartoon video in which a caricature of a Jew changes into a death's-head to the sounds of a Jewish folk song. It is often shown as a warm-up before propaganda/indoctrination films like *Der ewige Jude.*

A personal enemy of Michael Kühnen, Mosler is the leader of the "anti-gay faction," and he is close to Otto-Ernst Remer—though, as Kühnen tells me, Mosler has recently "withdrawn more into private life." This change in lifestyle can be traced to his anxiety about the various indictments pending for him: for suspicion of forming a criminal organization, instigating public discord, and other crimes. In these matters Remer can offer him fatherly advice and guidance, being himself well-versed in the customs of the justice system. Remer, for example, is not above pleading for mercy, as in this 1989 letter to the Munich regional court: "As for the rest, I am calmly waiting to find out whether our 'constitutional judiciary' . . . will really manage to stick an old man like me into jail because of his advocacy of JUSTICE and TRUTH for his people."

Otto-Ernst Remer and Wilhelm Stäglich are now chatting with some of the family's nicer relatives. That round-faced man with the curly hair looks familiar . . . Of course! Wherever Remer shows up, the general's adviser and successor, Karl Philipp, is also sure to be. Philipp excuses himself, then joins Ewald Althans in admiring the doings at the edge of the platform, where Christian Worch's military men are arranging their signs: "Destroy What Destroys You!" and, of course, "Truth Will Make You Free!"

Philipp later joins Irving on the platform, and the two look down at the packed tables with satisfied expressions. The audience is finished with lunch and has moved on to coffee. In addition to representing Fiji Airlines and Solomon Airlines from his office in Frankfurt's West End, Philipp is a journalist whose credits include an article in the radical-right monthly *CODE* (number 4, 1990). This article contains several facts worth mentioning. In 1990, Dresden's commissioner of culture and chairman of the municipal council welcomed David Irving to his city with flowers. It was, he said, "an honor to provide the eminent contemporary historian with the great hall of the Palace of Culture for his speech on February 13." The speech, naturally enough, focused on the British bombing of Dresden. After forty years of antifascism, the neo-Nazis' prize historian is allowed to lecture undisturbed: "The Holocaust suffered by the Germans in Dresden was real. The one against the Jews in the gas chambers of Auschwitz is complete fiction." At the time, a warrant was out for Irving's arrest in Austria, where it is against the law to publicly deny the Holocaust (just as it is in the Federal Republic). Philipp wrote in CODE that he found the behavior of the Austrian authorities "strange." CODE's editor in chief, Ekkehard Franke-Gricksch, is also in the Löwenbräukeller. In the family portrait he'd be at the upper right, the fat man in the fancy suit. He even has real relatives in the family: Alfred Franke-Gricksch, a former high officer in the SS, was a leader of the Bruderschaft (Brotherhood), one of ODESSA's many auxiliary organizations which were active in the 1950s. Good connections seem to be important for the Franke-Gricksch clan, and CODE's list of supporters suggests that it provides many international connections to the radical-right network; it has editors in Argentina, Mexico, Canada, and the United States, among others. Victor Marchetti, for example, is listed as the journal's Middle East editor. Formerly a CIA agent, Marchetti has always been a fanatic anticommunist. Today he is a "journalist," and a staff member of the Institute for Historical Review.

Meanwhile, in the Löwenbräukeller, Karl Philipp is concentrating on the official business of the Revisionist Congress. He too is preparing to give a speech today. After all, he helped organize the event, though he would deny it, if asked. A bulletin from Ernst Zündel, however, informs all "comrades" to "notify me, Karl Phillips [sic] or Ewald Althans at your earliest convenience." At the bottom, Philipp's address in Frankfurt is given—a slip, actually, since he normally is careful to use an address in Bad Reichenhall for this sort of work. Revisionism, Philipp tells me, is rather bad for him financially.

Philipp possesses an astonishing capacity for self-transformation, as he demonstrates in his speech. The audience has just started their afternoon beer. Gauleiter Thomas Hainke continues to stand proudly beside the podium with his imperial war flag as Philipp develops from a small-town pastor into a foaming rabble-rouser. It is a metamorphosis the likes of which I never would have believed him capable.

"This country has never had so much freedom," he says, his voice trembling with hate, "freedom for hypocrisy, for lying, for depriving all Germans of their rights. Freedom for self-destruction and for child murderers." From the audience there is general agreement. The gentleman with the silk tie nods indignantly; his wife shakes her blond hair in disgust. But Philipp is ready with a remedy: "Nations all over the world are lining up to struggle against a homogenizing system of subjugation, and to demand their national identities."

The portly matron at the second table on the left almost chokes on her pie as Philipp continues: "The modern, so-called realistic politicians don't even realize that this trend has already overtaken them. And we are bringing forward a motion—a petition in the Bundestag—to buy these people a ticket. A ticket to Anatolia, or to Mozambique, or to wherever else . . . a ticket to the other side of the world!"

Philipp calmly accepts the enthusiastic cheers of his 800 listeners. His general is applauding him from his front-row table. When he exhausts himself clapping, Remer takes a little schnapps. Next to him is a young man whose obvious discomfort attracts my attention. While I'm filming the Führer's bodyguard, this pale-faced young man nervously fidgets in his seat, lowers his head, and raises his hand conveniently in front of his face. When, after several furtive glances, he's certain that I'm filming him, he stands up and tries in a British accent to make a few things clear. He and his companion come from England, he says in German, and he's been in Munich for three years. It's really a complete accident that he's here. "Look, I normally go to CDU events. It's a complete coincidence that I . . . ." he splutters.

I notice a patch from the British neo-Nazi National Front on his cotton sweatshirt. When asked about this he gets completely confused: "Oh, that's nothing. Um, I mean I just write for the National Front's newspaper." Of course, another journalist! (I later found an article of his in *Vanguard,* a paper devoted to the "advancement of British nationalism" by means of racist theories. He signs his article with the name I. S. Taylor and writes about the positive developments achieved by REP chief Schönhuber and the head of the French organization Front National in their attempts to unite the European right.)

This is exactly the gray—or rather brown—area in which "respectable" patriots and fanatic neo-Nazis walk side by side. Another example is Le Pen's trusted staff member Ivan Blot, who a year later will participate in one of Ewald Althan's neo-Nazi congresses; Blot even allows himself to to be photographed, as the March 12, 1992, issue of the newsmagazine *Stern* shows. The whole incident must truly irritate Monsieur Le Pen, since the Front National officially wants nothing to do with neo-Nazis.*

Organizer Ewald Althans's "comrade," an elegantly dressed young man with neatly parted blond hair, welcomes the "many guests from abroad"—from the Netherlands, "from the mountains, from Switzerland," from "the Eastern borderlands," Holland, Canada, and the United States.

The present Revisionist Congress in Munich's Löwenbräukeller thus emphasizes what most of the media and the authorities have either played down or failed to understand. Indeed, the few times this point has been raised, it has generally been used to distract rather than focus discussion. The fact is that neo-Nazism is not an exclusively German problem. It certainly has strong, deep roots in Germany, but it would be madness to dismiss the rising right-wing extremism in other countries. An international net of activists has developed. Every group and every individual cultivates contacts with like-minded activists in neighboring countries, to back each other up with propaganda or to shelter terrorists. All of the groups have a common spirit, distinguished by several features. Especially striking is their fervent advocacy of "law and order," despite the manifest criminal and terrorist activities originating their own ranks. The more moderate somehow justify their sympathy for attacks

---

*In 1987, Le Pen announced on French television that the Holocaust was a "detail" in the history of the Second World War.

against refugees while calling for maximum penalties for leftist acts. Anti-Semitism is always present in one form or another. Anti-Israeli "anti-Zionism" is always a start, where the unjust treatment of Palestinians provides an excuse to attack the Jews. If these "anti-Zionists" really cared about human rights, it would be irrelevant whether the Palestinians' persecutors were Jews or not, and they could cheerfully join Amnesty International. But it's not a question of human rights for them—it's Jews. Other variants range from "political" anti-Semitism ("We don't have anything against individual Jews . . .") to hard-core, rabid racial hatred.*

An exaggerated anticommunism in which leftists and liberals are summarily declared communists is also very common. In Europe, this serves as a pretext for denying guilt for the Second World War and for Nazi crimes. Hard-boiled anticommunists take great pains to equate National Socialism with the "criminal" DDR regime, stubbornly refusing to take into account that the DDR neither started a world war nor murdered millions in extermination camps. In this respect the neo-Nazi and the "conservatives" are often hard to tell apart. The urge to rehabilitate fascism by presenting its crimes as relative or by denying outright the Nazi crimes also links historians from the revisionists to radical neofascists.

The foundation of the right wing's ideology is racism in all its different forms—against foreigners, refugees, ethnic minorities, or everyone who speaks differently, has another religion, or simply looks different. These prejudices often are "scientifically" supported. Model racists are the American education scholar Arthur B. Jensen and the English psychologist Hans Jürgen Eysenck; the behavioral scientist Konrad Lorenz is also popular in New Right propaganda writings. The main themes, usually camouflaged as patriotism, are "national values" and "racial inequality." The Swiss neofascist G. A. Amadruz is the author of a book with the singularly provocative title *Ist Rassebewusstsein verwerflich?* (Is Racism Objectionable?)

*A good example of this extreme would be the Identity Church, which was founded in the early 1980s in the United States. Anglo-Saxons, it claims, are the "chosen people," while Jews are the daughters and sons of Satan, and nonwhites are not people but animals with a "somewhat human appearance."

It's been a long day here in the Löwenbräukeller, but after eight hours of solid propaganda, the congress will soon be over. An almost euphoric mood now spreads as the waiters remove the last dessert plates. A revisionist from Austria is making the final address of the day.

"Stand up in this hall!" he demands in a fiery voice. "All of you, stand up, up with you! Up, up, stand up and be courageous and bring forth a courageous deed. Stand up!"

Eight hundred chairs are pushed away. Like a wave flowing from the front to the farthest corner of the hall, the moderate ones and the radicals rise to their feet. Directly in front of me, the elderly, dignified gentleman with gray hair and glasses and his pretty wife look at each other briefly and then stand up as well. What will happen next?

The speaker urges the audience to go outside "into beautiful Munich" and show all the world why they came here: "We will not let them lie to us any longer, we want the truth, because truth makes us free, free, free . . ."

The skinheads and brownshirts can restrain themselves no longer. They thrust up their arms into the "resistance salute" and begin to sing the first verse of "Das Deutschlandlied":

Germany, Germany above all,
Above all else in the world,
When it fraternally stands together
To defend and to attack,
From the Maas to the Memel,
From the Etsch to the Baltic—
Germany, Germany above all
Above all else in the world!

Since 1949, the third verse alone, beginning "Unity and justice and liberty . . ." has been sung as the National Anthem of the

Federal Republic. The first verse, so beloved by right-wing radicals is banned.

Other voices join in. More follow quickly, and soon all 800, Germans and "guests" together, are singing what they feel: "*Deutschland, Deutschland über alles* . . ." With my camera I pan from the saluting skins in the wing over to the center of the hall, where isolated arms are also extended in the salute, including that of the respectable-looking gentleman right in front of me. Old loyalty has made his arm drift unstoppably upward until it presents a full Hitler-salute while, with emotion and fervor, he starts on the second verse: "German women, German faith, German wine, and German song . . ." Then his pretty companion, his own German woman, sees the lens of my camera pointing directly at them. In a panicked reflex, but too late, she pulls down his outstretched arm and hisses at him. There is now nothing left for this fervent German to do but bury his hands in his pockets and, like a scolded child, sing on with a slightly bowed head.

XIV

AUSCHWITZ IS THE
PROBLEM

WHY WOULD A SUCCESSFUL AUTHOR LIKE DAVID IR-
ving, or a literature professor like Robert Faurisson, spread the
myth of the gas chambers' nonexistence. With more moderate
views, these prominent revisionists could certainly lead more comfortable lives. Faurisson, for example, was attacked and badly injured by a militant Jewish group in Vichy in September 1989. So
why do they persist in denying this indisputable historical fact, a
crime to which thousands of victims and hundreds of perpetrators
have credibly attested?

There must be a reason that goes deeper than guilt or hatred, one
that forces us to confront such fundamental values as human dignity
and freedom of expression.

The principal text of Holocaust denial comes from the pen of a
seventy-year-old farmer. This particular farmer has bank accounts in
Copenhagen, Hamburg, Brussels, Vienna, Amsterdam, Johannes-
burg, and California. He was an SS officer at Auschwitz, and his
name is Thies Christophersen. He lives in Denmark, where he goes
by the name Tiis Christensen. His book, *Die Auschwitz-Lüge* (The
Auschwitz Lie) was quickly banned in the Federal Republic of
Germany, where it is against the law to deny the Holocaust.

The neo-Nazis continually denounce the ban of this and other revisionist works as an example of "the suppression of freedom of speech in this so-called democracy." The argument is insidious, as their invocation of democratic sentiments is completely insincere. The neo-Nazis would like nothing more than the immediate abolition of democracy. But when their freedom to spread malicious propaganda is endangered, they demand freedom of expression as their democratic right. In this too they misinterpret democracy, for the German Constitution also guarantees protection from public harassment—a matter of course in most democratic states, where human dignity is another fundamental right.

Free-speech absolutists such as the American Noam Chomsky— who is by no means right-wing—defend as a basic right the freedom of speech in which anyone can say absolutely anything. Their position unintentionally supports the strategies of terrorism; and the effects of unchecked hate propaganda is something we simply cannot ignore, particularly we Germans, who have already once endured the destruction of our liberal institutions by fascist extremists. Freedom of expression is not endangered when Nazis are forbidden their slanderous lies. A neo-Nazi is not punished for saying: "I like National Socialism. I hate Jews and intellectuals." Opinions cannot be forbidden. However, if he says, "There was no Holocaust. Stop with the historical lies, with the inventions of world Jewry," then he is liable to be punished by the state for using speech to manufacture new hate.

The Nazis do not dispute the Holocaust because they are ashamed of it. On the contrary, most are secretly proud of it. The revisionists who deny its existence have greater appeal for those who feel the guilt of the mass extermination as a burden. But both sides benefit: one lies shamelessly; and the other just as shamelessly believes the obvious lies, because they *want* to believe.

But guilt itself is not the real motive behind revisionism, which is suggested by Ewald Althans's remark that "Auschwitz must fall before man can accept what we want. The people all say, hey, that Althans, that's a nice guy, but Auschwitz. . . . This is the problem."

Given the Holocaust, Nationalist Socialist policies have no chance of ever winning broad popular support again. When people today think about the Third Reich, they think of mountains of emaciated corpses; mountains of eyeglasses, shoes, and hair from the murdered victims; of Jewish women, naked, holding their small children on the way to the gas chamber. *These* are the images that can still prevent mass fascination with parades, uniforms, cheering crowds. They are the images that bring us to the realization that such policies must never be reenacted.

This is exactly why the Holocaust is the number-one target of neo-Nazis and why they want to obliterate it from the minds of a potentially sympathetic population. It's purely a matter of tactics. They care neither about "the truth" nor "freedom of expression"—both of which they tout, for the moment. No, their single goal is to reestablish National Socialism.

The baseness of the "Auschwitz lie" itself goes even deeper. Christophersen's "eyewitness report" gives the impression that the Auschwitz concentration camp was a sort of reform school for recalcitrants in which the internees had it better than the supervisors. "In our weather station we had an SS assistant who once 'organized' a pair of silk stockings for herself.* As a result she was brought before a military court—for plundering. But the prisoners who worked there stole like magpies. I was frequently struck by how elegantly the prisoners were dressed. They did have to wear their prisoners' uniforms, but their underclothes, socks, and shoes were unblemished and first-rate. There was also no lack of beauty supplies. Lipstick, powder, and rouge were part of the female prisoners' kits."

It is difficult even to read something like this. A single picture of the emaciated bodies in the concentration camps, their eyes filled with terror, is enough to prove that this man is either mad or absolutely evil. Naturally, he regards himself as good-natured. "When we had a newcomer who showed up at the camp undernourished and thin, in just a few days he had a sleek pelt."

His personal slave—he notes that "lady's maid would be an

---

*In prison lingo, "to organize" means "to steal."

appropriate expression''—was a Polish woman he calls Olga. She was "extraordinarily eager to serve," but "As time went on this woman and her interminable chatter got on my nerves. Her eagerness to serve was too submissive for me, too slavish. I didn't like that. She was given a new job, one for which I didn't envy her. She was assigned to be a 'supervisor' in the women's camp and had to make sure that no unauthorized male prisoners came into the women's camp. Olga could scold wonderfully, and it was a pleasure to watch how she threw the men out of the women's camp. Her fellow prisoners called her 'Cerberus.' ''

The man who wrote this is the revisionists' chief witness. Irving, Faurisson, Zündel, and all the others refer to him. Thies Christophersen is a central figure of international neofascism, and that's why, in the summer of 1990, I decide that I have to speak with him.

Kühnen gives me the opening when he tells me that he's planning a meeting with Gary Lauck, the head of the NSDAP-AO in the United States. They will probably meet in Denmark where, "coincidentally," Thies Christophersen happens to live. But when I tell Kühnen that I'm interested in interviewing both Lauck and Christophersen, he demands 8,000 marks. Up to now I haven't paid a pfennig and wouldn't be prepared to, so I ask for time to think. When I discuss it with Graeme Atkinson, we agree that this figure is out of the question, and that nothing will probably come of it. But . . . if I were able to interview both Lauck *and* Christophersen, it might be a big step forward. "We're not about to finance their next event," Graeme says. "Let's be realistic: give him as much as it would cost you to fly to the States. After all, you'll save that much if you can get Lauck in front of the camera here."

A week later I meet Kühnen again and indicate my readiness to pay up to 3,000 marks—approximately what a trip to interview Lauck in Lincoln, Nebraska, would cost me. Kühnen stands firm. He wants 8,000 marks, all in advance.

We part without reaching an agreement, and three hours later I'm sitting in Graeme's apartment in Stuttgart. He rolls his eyes and says, "I saw it coming."

"And now?" I ask, discouraged. My finances are about to run out, and even 3,000 marks is a pretty big chunk for me.

Graeme pokes me in the chest with his index finger: "Tell him three thousand is all you can raise and he can take it or leave it. But you know each other well enough; he'll take it. And if not, that's all right too. Then at least you'll never have to blame yourself for having given them money."

But now I do blame myself. Looking back, I could kick myself for having done it. There is, I suspect, a difference between paying demonstrators "on the spot" for Hitler-salutes and Nazi songs in order to spice up the evening news and covering the travel expenses of an important interviewee, as I did, but money is money. To be sure, the "investment" produced worthwhile results. But it was completely contrary to journalistic ethics, and Kühnen bagged 3,000 marks for Lauck's travel costs.

Gary Rex Lauck was born in 1953 in Milwaukee, Wisconsin. He claims to have first felt "racial consciousness" at age eleven, and two years later he read, and "identified" with, *Mein Kampf.* By the time he was eighteen, he was calling himself "Gerhard" and was active in the neo-Nazi circles. Soon after, he became a cofounder of the NSDAP-AO, in Lincoln, Nebraska. Since then he has supplied his German "comrades" with propaganda, stickers, flags, books, audiotapes, videocassettes, as well as with money, organizational support, and contacts. Even though most activities are focused on Germany, the NSDAP-AO has members all over the world, but especially in Sweden, Austria, Hungary, Australia, and South Africa. Lauck allegedly sends funds to his German allies at irregular intervals through a Swiss bank account. He earns his money by selling Nazi devotional paraphernalia, through a company called R.J.G. Engineering, Inc., also located in Lincoln, Nebraska.

Lauck has connections with the Ku Klux Klan and with terrorist organizations like The Order. Issue 82 (1989) of Lauck's publication *The New Order* is dedicated to David Lane, the former Ku Klux Klan activist who is serving a 150-year jail sentence for murder, robbery, and other crimes. He was involved in the murder of Alan Berg, the Jewish radio talk-show host who was shot to death in 1984 in Denver, Colorado. They describe their terrorist activities as a "race war" against what they call the ZOG, or Zionist Occupation Government. In the same issue of *The New Order* is a piece by Lauck entitled "Action Program for Aryan Skinheads." In it, Lauck provides words of guidance for the "coming phase of the race war, when we'll fight man to man." As for now, he cautions, "all skins must hide their racist literature from their parents. Skinheads should not leave these things at home, but should deposit them in the safe apartments of older skins."

Lauck gives specific orders about guns. The skinheads should "hide their expertise, and store their weapons in remote places." There is special advice for beginners: "For starters, don't vote, don't buy Jew alcohol and dope, don't attend Jew movies, don't read Jew magazines and books." The indoctrination of hate must proceed with minimal interference from the liberal press—that is, "Jew magazines."

Lauck's last "professional" trip to Germany was in 1976, when he was arrested near Mainz with huge quantities of illegal propaganda and subsequently deported. In 1979 he was allowed temporary entry in order to testify in Michael Kühnen's defense. Several warrants for his arrest have since been issued for various offenses of the law banning National Socialist activity.

On July 4, 1990, I am in Denmark with a camera team.

Christian Worch has picked Lauck up at the airport in Copenhagen. They are careful to stay in Denmark, since Lauck is still wanted in Germany. I get a hint of the seriousness of this matter when Worch, while looking for Thies Christophersen's house, accidentally comes upon a German border crossing. With a panicked reflex, he pulls the steering wheel to the left and we turn, tires spinning and screeching, in the opposite direction.

We are close to the border in Kollund, not two minutes away from Thies Christophersen. We are gathered at the Albatross, a run-down pension whose most appealing feature is a magnificent view of the Baltic and the tiny brick houses on the other, the German, side. This is where the assembly is taking place.

Lauck is at least six-foot-three and has thick, dark hair that rebels against a part. With his walrus mustache and metal glasses, he looks rather like a harmless traveling salesman. His gray suit, boring tie, and black dress shoes complete the image of a good, if simple, man, but his speech to the assembled leaders and supporters of the NSDAP-AO shows him in another light. "I think that the Jews were treated a little too nicely in the concentration camps. Personally, I'd say that's a mistake we should not make again."

The applauding audience includes the neo-Nazi elite: Michael Kühnen, Gottfried Küssel, and Christian Worch, as well as Christa Goerth, friendly as always, and SS veteran Berthold Dinter, organizer of the "Rudolf Hess Memorial March" in Wunsiedel.* Next to him sits Günther Reintaler, alias "Hrouda," the *Gauleiter* of Salzburg. His trademarks are his dirty-blond ponytail and the Doberman that is always crouched around at his side; he compensates for a deformed hand with particularly aggressive behavior. In October 1990, militant antifascists set his BMW on fire; in the trunk of the gutted car, the police found a machine pistol with 390 rounds of ammunition, a 9mm pistol, and a shotgun.

I also recognize Tonny Douma (of the ANS/Netherlands), who once had put in a good word for me with Wolsink and who now acknowledges my gaze with a slight nod. Thomas Hainke, the boss skinhead from Bielefeld, has already shown me his newest wound: a cut on his upper lip, almost completely healed. Worch's wife, Ursula, attractive but cold, glares at me—she hates journalists. She prefers revisionists, like David Irving, with whom she has animated conversations at conferences. Later, rumors will suggest that Irving is one of the reasons she left her husband.

Tonight Lauck emphasizes the importance of division of labor. "Revisionism, for example. I think it's important. It's a good thing. But we can let the revisionist historians take care of it. They can do it better than we can. There may even be other jobs the nationalist-

---

*Dinter also publishes a small journal entitled *Wehr' Dich* (Defend Yourself). It contains "poems" with phrases like: "Blonde Annette in the eighth grade, her blood is of the German race . . . Zion is the only one to laugh, but just wait until Germany arises . . . then no one will yell 'Nazis out,' or else we'll break their bones . . ." (no. 8, 1990).

conservative groups can do as well or maybe even better than us. But there are also certain tasks that only National Socialists can perform.'' He doesn't say what these are, but his listeners get the idea. If in doubt, you can order one of Lauck's propaganda stickers. For example, ''Liberty or Revolution! End the Nazi Ban!'' On this one, a man wearing a swastika armband is shown lighting a fuse beneath a TV station with an audience inside.

Lauck is proud of his outlaw status: ''After twenty years, neither the Stasi nor the 'Verfassungs-Schmutz' has succeeded in getting rid of us. We're still here. And we're going to stay here. We'll fight right up to the end, if it takes one year or a hundred. We have more stamina than the Bonn politicians because we also have more idealism, more devotion. And we are more hungry for battle. *Heil Hitler!*''

Lauck speaks with a strong American accent, but his German is pretty good; interestingly, he has taken to speaking English with a German accent.

After the speech, I'm allowed my interview. He is willing to talk, so long as the questions are general. He confirms most of the facts Graeme and I turned up in our investigations. ''Of course'' members of his organization also belong to the so-called respectable parties. But when I ask him if any of his members are sitting in the European Parliament, he grows more cautious. ''I wouldn't say anything too definite about that. But you could naturally say, sure, if there is somebody there, it's certainly not a delegate on the left. You might ask: Who's the farthest to the right in parliament? And that's the man!''

''Is there anyone in the European Parliament that has ever belonged to your organization?'' Lauck turns taciturn; silence is one of the NSDAP-AO's statutes. ''No comment.''

But I already know from Kühnen that there might be someone: Harald Neubauer, member of the European Parliament since 1989. He has had a lengthy career in the extreme right: NPD, Aktion Neue Rechte (New Right Action), DVU, then Republican second-in-command, followed by election to the European Parliament. Though he left the REP after a break with Schönhuber, he will remain in the parliament until 1994.

A few months earlier, Michael Kühnen, upon hearing that Neubauer has been describing him as an idiot, subsequently lets loose and implicates Neubauer in front of my camera: "In the early and mid-seventies Harald Neubauer was an NSDAP-AO official in northern Germany and as far as I know also the *Gau* treasurer in Schleswig-Holstein."

But Lauck remains silent, even in the second part of the interview, when I seat him and Kühnen next to each other. Lauck won't go beyond "No comment."

This is too much for Kühnen, whose integrity is on the line. "I'd like to say something about this whole business. I know that Neubauer's a member." Lauck's face goes pale. According to the statutes of the NSDAP-AO, no one's present or past membership may be disclosed. Yet Kühnen continues:

"I've seen it with my own two eyes and I've had it confirmed by two comrades I was working with and who Neubauer was also working with at the time." Kühnen goes on to explain the situation. While Lauck can only wince, speechless at his colleague's complete lack of discretion, Kühnen explains that "there are and were individual cells that operated entirely independently, and there was a net of loose contacts that even worked on the *Gau* level—which corresponds pretty closely to the states in Germany today—and it was on this level, not local but regional, that this activity was taking place."

Period. He has spoken. Shortly afterwards, during a break in the filming—to reload the camera—Lauck turns to Kühnen. "And he's now with the Republicans? I had no idea."

"Yes," Kühnen says, "he's a hypocrite. And he was once damned grateful that we provided guards and supervisors. You can ask Wrobel about it, or Rohwer. But now he doesn't want to have anything to do with us, and that's why I see him as a political enemy. Even if he is still in the AO."

Rohwer was sentenced in 1979 to nine years in jail for founding a terrorist organization. An NSDAP-AO liaison man, he and Neubauer are demonstrably old acquaintances. Lauck is somewhat bewildered, but he quickly has to pull himself back together since the cameraman has put in a new tape. To Lauck's relief, we change subjects and speak, now in English, about one of his specialties. "I have no objections to Jewish people and their race and their culture surviving, but if they systematically try to exterminate my race, I will defend my race. If in defending my race I have to annihilate a few of them . . . fine. And if it's a matter of saving the last white man dying on this planet or having to kill the last Jew, it's bye-bye Jew . . ." His words sound memorized. "But when they systematically attempt to destroy my race, then I'm going to defend myself. And if it should be necessary to exterminate a couple of them—fine! And if it's a question of whether every last white man dies or whether we have to kill every last Jew, then it's 'Later, Jew!' "

I have no further questions for Lauck. For me, that kind of obsession doesn't arouse either curiosity or the desire to argue. All you can do with words like that is remember them, and remember that we must not give the Nazis any opportunities.

The situation becomes much more interesting when the door suddenly swings open and I hear the click of a camera. Lauck turns toward the door and says cheerfully, *"Heil Hitler,* Thies!" An old man stands there, a brightly colored hat on his head. A cane hangs from his arm as he fiddles with the lens of his mini-camera.

The first thing I notice about Thies Christophersen is a deep indentation, as big as a child's fist, at the bridge of his nose, right between his eyes. It's a war wound. "I'm not completely right in the head," he explains. "And you can see it." And *this,* I think, is the celebrated eyewitness? His left eye is also damaged; the lid sticks out a little too far on his long face, but it's easy to miss when he's got his glasses on. Once he takes off his hat, I see that he's half bald. The corners of his mouth turn down bizarrely when he speaks, and also when he laughs.

"Can we do an interview with you?" I ask him. Apparently Christophersen knows nothing about being filmed, and he acts surprised. When Kühnen explains that we're making a long-term documentary, Christophersen nods and stares admiringly at our equipment. Then Kühnen and Lauck are called away, leaving us alone with Thies Christophersen.

He takes the liberty of sitting in Lauck's chair. I somehow have the feeling that he doesn't quite understand that we're not neo-Nazis, since he addresses the cameraman and sound engineer as "comrades" as he inspects our camera. "Must be expensive, that kind of thing. Right, comrades? I have my own little one here," he says, using a word from Low German. He comes, after all, from the country, and his news-bulletin is called *Die Bauernschaft* (The Peasantry). He asks me what the interview's supposed to be about. When I tell him I want to discuss his book, *Die Auschwitz-Lüge,* he waves his hand dismissively.

"No, nothing about that."

"Why?" I ask, astonished he wouldn't want to discuss his greatest accomplishment.

"They just won't show it! It never works. We tried it already."

Now I'm almost certain that Christophersen thinks we're fellow neo-Nazis trying to sneak propaganda onto television. I decide to try again. "Don't worry, we'll manage it. No problem!"

He smiles at me indulgently. "Well, it can't hurt to try. The best thing is for me to say that all I want is the right to say my opinion. That always sounds good."

Bull's-eye! He thinks we're Nazis. And so it happens that Thies Christophersen gives us an interview that later causes him lots of trouble. He doesn't worry about contradictions, trusting that his "comrades" will censor whatever is necessary.

He begins by talking about his time as an SS officer in Auschwitz: "I was assigned to the horticultural division. That was done in Auschwitz because of the labor supply there. I was selective. In Birkenau I picked out my workers. I said: 'Which of you worked on a farm?' And then they came forward, and then I said: 'You and you and you—I'll take you.' Do you know how I did it? I looked at their eyes—whoever has white in his eyes is able to work." Christophersen laughs briefly at the memory of his own ingenuity. "But I also always had a couple of Gypsies with me, because Gypsies know how to make music."

I play my role of "comrade" to the hilt, even turning off the camera on occasion to ask if he thinks it's wise to talk about this or that. "In Germany they were trying to arrest me again," he says, "so I went into exile. Denmark is a very liberal country. Here you can be a Gypsy, you can be a Jew, and you can be a Nazi."

Since Kühnen could come in any minute and clear up the "misunderstanding," I need to get to the heart of the matter: the gas chambers in Auschwitz. "I'm now going to ask you a tough question," I say, giving him a significant wink. "Were there gassings or were there not gassings?"

"I didn't write anything about gassings in my report," he says. "But I did hear rumors of fire, that people were being cremated. And so I investigated all the fireplaces in the camp. I knew that there were crematoria. But I did not see any cremations and I did not know anything about them."

As always, no one knew anything, not even the SS officers in charge. Is Christophersen in contact with David Irving?

"I've known David Irving for many years," he says.

"What do you think of him?"

"He is constantly being attacked because he is an Englishman— and we don't like to hear it when he also talks about German atrocities. Which there certainly also were. But I admit, I am biased."

Christophersen appears increasingly helpless. He no longer knows what to say. But he feels he's among friends, and he lays himself bare. "I want to exonerate and defend us, and I can't do it with what we actually did. I don't deny that. But no defender with anything to defend will talk about what's incriminating."

Without noticing it, he's just denied the claims he made in his infamous book.

"They've even frozen my bank accounts, can you imagine that! But all of that doesn't affect me. I'll push on. I'd think of myself as having betrayed my friends if I recanted now, and that's something I've never done."

In September of 1991, our film *Wahrheit macht frei,* which includes Christophersen's revealing admissions, is broadcast in Sweden. It's an embarrassing moment for the Holocaust deniers. Within a few months, the film has been shown in most European countries. Now Christophersen has problems. In the December 1991 issue of *Die Bauernschaft,* he writes that "My statement was twisted into a completely opposite meaning. My later correction was never acknowledged.* The broadcast naturally caused me to receive several indignant letters from Swedish and Danish readers. It is a perfect example of the primitive frauds that our opponents are now forced to resort to in their distress."

Apparently he still believes he'd been interviewed by fellow neo-Nazis: "I never gave an interview to Swedish television. The correct story is that I once gave Herr Michael Kühnen an interview." As his "correction" continues, his memory gets completely muddled and he starts making things up: "I furthermore said that I might discontinue my work because of my age, but that I would think of myself as betraying my friends if I accepted their help and then did nothing in return. As for gas chambers, I said that they were there but only to get rid of lice. . . ."

So much for Thies Christophersen, the revisionists' eyewitness. His lighthearted remark about not being "completely right in the head" really said it all.

*Swedish television reports never having received any "correction" from Christophersen.

XV

THREADS IN THE NET

IT'S NOVEMBER 1989, SHORTLY AFTER THE WALL CAME down in Germany, and Thies Christophersen's friends are meeting in France, in the small Alsatian town of Haguenau. It's not the first time that neofascists from across Europe have gathered at the Hôtel National, whose proprietors have an excellent relationship with the extremists and have even sent Christophersen a letter expressing their regrets that he could not attend. He's keeping his distance because there is a warrant for his arrest in Germany and he's afraid the French police might capture and extradite him. Everyone here is sure that there are no police in the area, but why take unnecessary risks. Everyone is also confident that there are no eavesdroppers in this gathering: the press has been excluded, the host knows how to keep his mouth shut, and the participants are a sworn brotherhood.

Still, Christophersen is lucky not to have come, because agents of the German Verfassungsschutz and of the French interior ministry have bugged the hall. The host in Alsace was forced to cooperate, as in a B-movie. So the French and German secret services have the opportunity to hear David Irving, who before a select audience, and without the media around, can make revisionism sound quite amusing.

"And there was once also a one-man gas chamber!" he announces. "A one-man gas chamber with two soldiers who carried it around the Polish countryside, on the lookout for stray Jews . . ." Irving's audience titters expectantly. It's bound to get even better. "This one-man gas chamber, I believe it looked something like a sedan chair, but it was disguised as a phone booth." Everyone's waiting for the punch line, because this historian knows how to tell a joke. "So the question is, how did they get the poor victim to voluntarily enter this one-man gas chamber? Answer: there was a telephone inside. And it rang and then the soldiers said to him, 'I think it's for you!' . . ."

The men and women roaring with laughter include powerful figures in the international scene: Povl Rijs Knudsen, from Denmark, the "Führer" of the World Union of National Socialists (WUNS), who has excellent connections in South America; the Swiss Gaston Armand Amaudruz, a leader in the shadowy *Europäische Neuordnung* (ENO); Robert Faurisson; Professor Arthur Butz from Texas, author of the infamous *Hoax of the Twentieth Century* and a staff member of the Institute for Historical Review.

Individuals of rank and prestige in the German scene have also made the trip to Alsace: Christa Goerth, Christian Worch, Karl Philipp, and the lawyer Wilhelm Stäglich, who gives a lecture on how to promote "'Auschwitz lie" propaganda without breaking the law. Acting as master of ceremonies is Udo Walendy, the self-described political scientist and former NPD man.

Faurisson welcomes an unexpected guest from Canada: "It is a complete surprise to see my very special friend Ernst Zündel here. If I had known he was coming I would have brought a present." This is the German–Canadian who publishes neo-Nazi articles under the pseudonym Christoph Friedrich, and who, when he is on trial, sometimes comes to court dressed as a concentration camp inmate. Zündel thanks Faurisson for his warm greetings, and calls the professor his "master."

The other star of this event, along with Irving, is Robert Faurisson. The Frenchman used to try to pass himself off as a leftist, hoping this would lend added credibility to his revisionist ideas. That didn't work very well, so today he frequently compares himself with Galileo. Among neo-Nazis he is considered a genius, and no wonder. After his brilliant idea of commissioning the Leuchter Report in 1988, he already has something new up his sleeve: "We want to launch an international campaign, together with Ernst Zündel. I've prepared an outline for it." Faurisson has drawn up a list of questions about the "Auschwitz lie." The plan is for as many sympathizers as possible to present these questions, always in the same prescribed form, "to certain media personalities, politicians, lawyers, and policemen" in order to keep the debate alive.

The entire Fall Convention passes smoothly. The eavesdropping policemen do not intervene, not even when Ernst Zündel, to thunderous applause, lets loose with his slanderous tirades: "Why should we, upright German men, dirty ourselves in this slime, in this pigsty, in these demonic base lies about our people that this pack of Jew rabble has spread. I am sick and tired of it."

The convention comes to a successful end, and the whole affair would probably not have interested anyone else if Otto Riehs, the Sudeten German snake collector, had not been such a video buff. Along with Ernst Zündel's private team, Riehs immortalized the Haguenau meeting on video. Like a professional, he included shots of the exterior of the hotel and several broad shots to convey the mood of the assembly.

Otto Riehs had already so kindly introduced me to "the Führer's bodyguard," and now he would prove himself extraordinarily helpful a second time. In return for a promise not to "do anything stupid" with the material—and fifty marks to cover his expenses—he agrees to duplicate his videotape for me. Thorough German that I am, I even have him write me a receipt stating the terms.

Thus the French broadcast of *Wahrheit macht frei* in December of 1991, which includes material from Riehs's "home movies," startles everyone concerned. The Alsatian populace reacts to the film with outrage. The proprietor, fearful for his reputation, exposes the police monitoring operation. And the Nazis realize they have aroused the special interest of the authorities. But the police are the most disturbed of all. An official declares that the broadcast has ruined their investigation and they will now have to start all over again. According to an AP report, the Renseignements Généraux (the French police intelligence service) concluded from their own recordings only that Faurisson and Irving could be identified as revisionists and anti-Semites. It is open to question whether such massive bugging was required to reach such an obvious conclusion. The Alsatian Jewish community certainly sees it differently. They justly demand that in the future the authorities "do everything possible to prevent such assemblies, which violate French law."

Professor Robert Faurisson has many friends abroad; more, indeed, than he has in France. One of them is Ahmed Rami, who lives in Stockholm. It's been almost twenty years since he arrived in Sweden as a political refugee from Morocco, where he claimed to be one of the officers who plotted to assassinate King Hassan. The coup failed and almost all of the conspirators were executed, but Rami was able to escape. In Sweden he continues his struggle against "other kings," as he puts it, quickly making it clear what he means. His first priority is to spread anti-Semitic propaganda, presented under the ever-popular cover of "anti-Zionism." But his Stockholm radio station, Radio Islam, has grown to become a vehicle for Holocaust deniers in addition to Jew-haters from all over the world. In 1989 he is sentenced to a brief jail term for "incitement to race hate."

He obviously must have had some interesting cellmates, since of late he has been chatting with genuine neo-Nazis on Radio Islam. One of his favorite guests is Tommy Rydén, whose Kreativistens Kyrka (Church of the Creator) was modeled on the American Church of the Creator and thus belongs to the anti-Semitic Identity Church movement. This group has close contacts with VAM (Vit Ariskt Motstand—White Aryan Resistance), a small but dangerous organization whose name reflects an American neo-Nazi group, the White Aryan Resistance. VAM consists of fifty to sixty activists; after numerous murders, bombings, and raids on banks—and, once, even a police station—at least half of VAM's leadership are behind bars.

Yet the Swedish Nazi scene still has sufficient personnel in the spring of 1992 to provide Ahmed Rami with two skinheads as bodyguards. The occasion is Faurisson's visit to Stockholm, and the skinheads are visibly uncomfortable in their suits and ties. But at his press conference, Faurisson declares: "I have nothing to do with neo-Nazis!'' Nevertheless, despite his neo-Nazi bodyguards, a group of determined antifascists convinces Monsieur Faurisson of the wisdom of a quick departure from his favorite Stockholm bar; fearing the thrashing that awaits them out front, the two skinheads spirit the Frenchman away through a rear exit.

Faced with such determined resistance in liberal Sweden, Rami takes great care to cultivate good contacts abroad, including Muammar al-Qaddafi in Libya and Islamic fundamentalists throughout the Middle East. In the United States, the NSDAP-AO newspaper *The New Order* listed Rami alongside other neo-Nazi activists as a ''White Power Prisoner,'' a martyr for the cause of National Socialism, while he was serving his jail term.

In the summer of 1991, I meet with Ahmed Rami in Stockholm. I try to make sure that Rami knows as little as possible about me. We have almost completed our film *Wahrheit macht frei,* and I don't want to take any chances. After a brief greeting we agree to talk in English. The camera is already running. ''I am a revisionist,'' he says good-naturedly, ''and I am happy to be a revisionist.''

''But you claim,'' I say, getting down to business, ''that you don't have any contact with neo-Nazis?''

''No!'' He looks at me with astonished brown eyes, as if I'd just proposed something obscene. Rami is a small man with a friendly face, and his forehead furrows deeply when a conversation takes an unpleasant turn. I decide to help him a little. ''Maybe you know the name Ernst Zündel?'' I'm hoping he'll deny it, since I have evidence of their connection.

But Rami must not consider Zündel a neo-Nazi, because he replies, ''Yes. But I never met him. When I was in Munich, he was arrested. I didn't meet him, never. But I respect him.''

So Rami, too, was at the Revisionist Congress Althans had sponsored this year in Munich, where the police commendably fulfilled their duty with Ernst Zündel. I need to get a clearer idea of his opinion of Zündel. ''He is a neo-Nazi!'' I tell him. He starts to respond, but I haven't finished yet: ''And an anti-Semite!'' Now Rami begins to defend Zündel, but I interrupt him again. ''He talked about a 'pack of Jew rabble'!''

Rami frowns. ''Are you sure?'' he asks, perplexed.

The only thing I'm not sure of is whether he has completely understood me. After all, English is a second language for both of us. When I ask if he understands what I'm saying, Rami says no. So I tell him again, word for word, what Zündel said in Haguenau. This still doesn't seem to make an impression.

Now Rami is interested in something else: "Can I ask you—are you Jewish?"

"No," I tell him, getting more and more annoyed. As if you had to be a Jew to find Zündel's slanders repulsive.

Rami has apparently decided to set me straight. Since his English isn't good enough for the purpose, he switches into Swedish and my colleague translates. Rami doesn't even look at me as he instructs my colleague, "You can tell him that there weren't any gas chambers."

"But there were!" I say, astonished, as his declaration is translated for me. "I was there. I saw them with my own eyes!"

Rami shakes his head. He raises his index finger as he complains to my colleague about my impudence. "I must be permitted to say that he is not telling the truth. He hasn't seen anything. He's simply lying. But I don't want to condemn him for it. I consider him to be the victim of brainwashing. I've often thought that we should establish a counterindoctrination institute to help Jewry's victims."

I look at my Swedish colleague, who has finished translating and now looks back at me helplessly. He is a thoroughly decent man, almost personally ashamed for what he has just translated. I nod to him and we call it a day.

For the moment, a "counterindoctrination institute" is not possible. So Rami and his comrades must resort to other methods in order to propagate their "Auschwitz lie" among the people. An example of this is found, once again, in beautiful Bavaria. A full-page ad appears on April 30, 1991, in the *Münchner Anzeiger* (Munich Advertiser). The ad has been taken out by the J. G. Burg Society, an organization dedicated (says the ad) to "carrying on the life's work of the Jewish publicist J. G. Burg in reconciling Jews and Germans on the foundation of truth." The bulk of the page is devoted to a long interview with Ahmed Rami, who, according to the ad, reaches "a total of 700,000 listeners four times a week" in

Stockholm through Radio Islam. The journalist's name is given as Joachim Gross. He takes pains to make his questions sound antifascist, but they are deliberately ineffective. "Doesn't that sound as though you're defending Hitler's National Socialism?" Gross asks, as Rami babbles on about how the German people have been "stripped of their rights." Then comes Herr Gross's red herring: "The fact is, six million Jews were systematically and cold-bloodedly gassed."

In this the revisionists' handwriting is clearly discernible. The figure "six million" indicates *all* the different victims—the ones gassed, shot, beaten to death, poisoned, starved, worked to death, and so on, as part of the "Final Solution"—but once the revisionists establish that not nearly so many as six million were actually *gassed*, they boast that they have revealed "the first exaggeration." Next, the reader is presented with a string of spurious, unverifiable claims, all of which are logically dependent on a false charge of "Jewish exaggeration." Fragments of official statements from respectable institutions are cleverly worked into the argument. With details taken out of context, further "contradictions" can easily be demonstrated. The next step is then to introduce the Leuchter Report to "prove" that gas chambers as such did not exist, while continuing to play with the numbers to work them down toward zero. But they don't go all the way to zero. Yet the revisionists do not deny the existence of the concentration camps themselves, and are cunning enough to allow that "natural mortality" would have killed between 40,000 and 300,000.

This is exactly what happens in this interview with Herr Gross. Rami even reduces to 15,000 the number of those killed at Auschwitz. When Gross asks why anyone would "invent" the gas chambers, Rami says, "There's a lot of money involved. You could see it during the Gulf War. The Israelis had barely put gas masks over their faces before the money started to flow from Germany."

Gross feigns indignation: "I will not tolerate such talk. The Jews still suffered under Hitler, even when you consider the truth."

"Even when you consider the truth?" Who, I wonder, is this Joachim Gross? I reach for the telephone and call the *Münchner Anzeiger*. The editor in chief knows immediately what I'm calling about. They published "that," he says with Bavarian charm, because they thought it was good.

"What?"

"Well, the thing about Auschwitz," he mumbles.

I don't let up. "What about Auschwitz?"

"Yes, well, that it, um, wasn't *like* that."

"That *what* wasn't like that?"

"You know, about the gassing."

"Now who, exactly, is Herr Joachim Gross? Could I speak with him?"

Noticeably relieved, the editor in chief answers that Gross isn't in the office at the moment, but that he is "a very good journalist" who writes for major daily newspapers.

I'm about to hang up when, by chance, I notice the address at the bottom of the ad for the J. G. Burg Society: Bad Kissingen! That's where Otto-Ernst Remer lives, the Führer's playful bodyguard. Suddenly something clicks, and I ask the *Münchner Anzeiger*'s editor: "Is Joachim Gross's real name Karl Philipp?"

Bingo. All he can come up with is, "I really can't tell you that. After all, I don't even know who you are."

It's only one thread in the net of hate: a net of thousands, working in different ways toward the same goal. Various methods, but with one identical fanaticism.

XVI

THE LINK MAN

THESE CONNECTIONS BETWEEN AHMED RAMI AND
Swedish neo-Nazis are only one example of the smooth cooperation
between revisionists and terrorists. The connections work through
personal contacts, but there is also an internationally organized
underground. This network shelters terrorists, like the Italian
Roberto Fiore and others involved in the 1980 bombing of the
Bologna train station, who later hid out with English "comrades."
Further contacts exist in England: so that even though the Italian
authorities are after Fiore, and *Searchlight* has exposed his identity,
he is not extradited. Perhaps Fiore's knowledge of the Fatah's
Lebanese training camps is too important. In 1983, the German
right-wing terrorists Walther Kexel and Ulrich Tillman, after
bombing a series of American institutions in Germany, also found
refuge with English "comrades" before they were finally caught.
When Kühnen was on the run, he hid out with Mark Frederiksen
in Paris. Other fugitive right-wing terrorists have relied on Swiss
"comrades."

This network of "safe houses," which crisscrosses Europe, depends for its smooth operation on the work of reliable "link men."
One of the most important of these lives in Amsterdam. He's had
combat experience as a "soldier of the Führer," and on the condition that I do not ask him about his contacts, I am permitted an

interview. After placing a telephone call and supplying the code "January 13," I speak with Gerrit Et Wolsink. I accept his terms and we agree on a date.

"What were the best years of your life?"

Wolsink doesn't move. It's as if he's paralyzed. Then he pulls himself out of his memories and says, "The war years were the best, yes."

We're in Amsterdam; it's the summer of 1990. Wolsink's apartment is overflowing with furniture and flowers. He has made himself comfortable on a plush sofa. A black dog occasionally trots past our legs, and a cheerful canary chirps behind us. I have politely refused coffee. Sitting on a sofa to the right of Wolsink are Eite Homann, the swastika-tattooed head of the Netherlands *Gau,* and Michael Kühnen, who arranged our meeting. Richard van der Plaas has just left the apartment in a frantic rush, refusing to be filmed under any circumstances; he is a leading member of the Dutch Centrums-Demokraten, which, like the French Front National or the German Republicans, continually insist that they have no neo-Nazi connections.

I glance at my notebook, where I've written what I already know about Wolsink. He was born in 1926, and even as a child he loved military games. At sixteen he falsified his age and volunteered for the Wehrmacht, then the SS and the Reich Central Security Office. He was also a member of the Brandenburg Division, a collection of zealots and violent thugs originally transferred for disciplinary reasons. The Branderburgers were mostly sent on suicide missions, and primarily in the East to fight partisans, which generally involved horrible atrocities. Entire villages were "eradicated." During the Ardennes offensive—the Battle of the Bulge—the Brandenburgers were sent behind enemy lines in enemy uniforms to set up ambushes. On the command of SS section-leader Joseph "Sepp" Dietrich, they summarily executed over a hundred American prisoners of war near Malmedy on December 17, 1944. Wolsink's final rank was *SS-Hauptsturmführer* (the equivalent of captain).

He looks just as I remembered him from our first meeting, with a "musketeer"-style beard, jughandle ears, and piercing eyes. Although he claims to have severe stomach problems, he has a cigarette in the end of his long holder and is savoring the smoke as I ask him: "So then you were on missions with the Brandenburgers . . . undercover, sometimes in enemy uniform, as special commandos . . ."

Wolsink nods. "Yes, for the most part." Homann and Kühnen look at him admiringly, and I decide to ask if he was one of the SS killers.

"Did you also carry out liquidations?"

He leans his head back. "Hmm . . . Talking about that is still a complicated matter, since they're seen as war crimes." Wolsink now is hesitant. "Er . . . I don't want to make excuses, but . . ." His cigarette glows even though he hasn't taken a drag. He murmurs to himself and turns to the side. He has always looked me straight in the eyes, but now he's looking away, looking around the room. Then suddenly his gaze is on me again. "If I did it," he says cautiously, "then it was only . . . then it was only as a mop-up action, to protect the lives of German soldiers." He pauses very briefly, then says, "In order to continue the war."

Wolsink wasn't convicted of war crimes, as he himself has written, "thanks to a lack of evidence, a false name, and false date of birth."* In 1946, a second court sentenced him to eight years for his membership in the Brandenburgers, but a year later he was set free "on the condition that I participate in the 'Cold War,' under allied command," because of his knowledge gained as a sabotage and terror specialist with the Brandenburgers. "I received the approval of my highest postwar commanding officer, Section Leader Dietrich, for this activity." For his new, Allied employers Wolsink took part in "various actions in the Soviet sphere—modeled after the Brandenburgers." Wolsink was also secretly active in the Werewolf Movement—Hitler loyalists who were supposed to carry out terror and sabotage against the "occupiers" after the war. This was largely a failure, but the construction of the ODESSA network, camouflaged as the Netherlands HIAG, progressed with remarkable suc-

*From the Nazi underground paper *Die neue Front* (no. 65).

cess. Officially, Wolsink worked in the hotel business. On the side, he built up the Dutch division of the Viking Youth and was active in the Northern League, an international neo-Nazi organization. Otherwise he restrained himself. Later, he found "the Negro and Arab problem too racially threatening" and joined the NVU (Nederlands Volks-Unie), but left it again in 1986. Since 1985 he has been affiliated with the ANS-Niederlande.

The number on Wolsink's NSDAP-AO membership card is 688463, and today he is an international coordinator for the organization, with contacts in South Africa, Australia, and the United States. His most important contact in the United States is James K. Warner of Louisiana, a KKK member. In 1971 Warner founded an organization called the New Christian Crusade Church (NCCC). This organization soon developed a subsidiary: the militant Christian Defense League (CDL). Both organizations are part of the Identity movement. The CDL has contacts with, among others, neo-Nazi and former KKK grand wizard David Duke, whose recent unsuccessful gubernatorial campaign in Louisiana nonetheless won him 44 percent of the vote in the primary and 39 percent in the general election. Wolsink is also an honorary member of the strictly clandestine, militantly terrorist British National Socialist Movement (BNSM).

International activities, such as the task of assembling mercenaries for Iraq, are skillfully coordinated by Wolsink. He sees himself as part of the underground, which is why he was reluctant to talk, even with Kühnen's recommendation. He is not informative, and it seems to me that I had better be satisfied simply to have gotten him in front of the camera. Still, his activities during the Cold War interest me. "After the war you worked for the Allies," I say. "But weren't they really the enemy?"

Wolsink looks at me with big, watery blue eyes; his glasses make them seem even bigger. "My precise choice was either to be dead—or to be free and working in approximately the same direction—"

"Against communism," I cut in. Wolsink shakes his head. That much was obvious.

"And what you have done as a twenty-one or twenty-two-year-old . . . ."

"It meant a better life. And then I could also get back to my Nazi work at once." As it was for Klaus Barbie (the "Butcher of Lyon") and other top Gestapo and SS officers, the Cold War was a blessing for Wolsink, a gentlemen's agreement in which it was tacitly understood that he would continue his Nazi activities.

"I always did my part, and back then I didn't have much reason not to, either." Wolsink smiles smugly. The memory of his cooperation with the "enemy" still amuses him today. I ask what kind of work he did, but Wolsink refuses. "I can't talk about that. You'll have to take my word for it. It just wouldn't do."

"So you still can't even talk about those missions, not even today?"

Wolsink closes his eyes briefly. Then he shakes his head. "No. It wouldn't do."

"Why not?"

"Surely you understand that it's still going on."

XVII

THE INCOMPLETE PUZZLE

WOLSINK'S SHADOWY POST-WAR ROLE IN "WORKING for the Allies" left me rather baffled. I knew, for example, from John Loftus's book, *The Belarus Secret,* that in addition to helping East European Nazi collaborators find safe havens in the U.S. and elsewhere, the Western Allies had set up units for sabotage and subversion behind the Iron Curtain after the onset of the Cold War.

Nevertheless, there was little evidence of similar operations in Western Europe. Within three months of the meeting with Wolsink, however, his reluctance to clarify his statements about this "work for the Allies" took on new meaning.

In Italy, on October 17, 1990, details of a clandestine NATO group known only by the code-name "Gladio" began to emerge from a probe into right-wing terrorism by Venetian judge Felice Casson, and from Italian government inquiries into the Red Brigade's murder of Premier Aldo Moro and the role of the Italian secret services.

Giulio Andreotti, then the Italian prime minister, admitted that a secret army of anticommunist guerrillas still existed, and had for more than forty years. Andreotti had served as Italian defense minister from 1959 to 1966, and had been personally involved with underground structures established for the purposes of organizing rear guard resistance in the event of a Warsaw Pact invasion of

Western Europe. It turned out that Gladio, with an estimated strength of 1,000 people in Italy, was only the Italian arm of a paramilitary front extending across the whole of Western Europe, including even neutral Sweden and Switzerland.

Andreotti's confession detonated a political bomb. Gladio—the Cold War's best-kept secret—was also known to Italian President Francesco Cossiga, who confirmed that he had dealt with the organization in 1967 during his own term as defense minister. However, as recently as August 1990, Andreotti told the Italian Parliament that Gladio had been wound up in 1972, and NATO spokesmen at the headquarters in Belgium likewise denied the organization's existence.

The mention of Gladio's NATO connections and NATO's adamant, even frantic denials immediately touched off journalistic investigations in other countries that, often with the help of former NATO and CIA insiders, soon revealed why this matter was so delicate. In Italy, for example, it became known that Gladio was also active in internal politics. Roberto Cavallero, a former Gladio member, told the Italian news magazine *Panorama* that he was trained to prepare groups that, in the event of an advance by left-wing forces, would fill the streets, creating a situation of such tension as to require military intervention. He also claimed that other members of Gladio—working with Italy's security services counter-intelligence—had infiltrated the Red Brigades, who murdered Aldo Moro, the architect of a 1978 pact between his Christian Democrat party and the still powerful Italian Communist Party. Cavallero's statements matched remarks made by Moro, in letters written during his captivity, suggesting that the secret services could be implicated in an attempt to destabilize the country.

These disclosures also gave rise to a welter of accusations that Gladio counted among its connections the shadowy P2 Masonic lodge, headed by long-time fascist Licio Gelli. Gelli had meetings—organized by the CIA—with Alexander Haig, Nixon's chief-of-staff and later NATO Supreme Commander, at the U.S. Embassy in Rome in the early 1970s, to discuss the need to restrict the power of the Italian Communist Party. One former NATO official charges that the U.S. spent nearly $100 million on a secret project called

"Stay Behind," which was designed to prevent a communist take-over at all costs.

Cavallero acknowledged Gladio's links with P2, which had fi-nanced rightist terrorists like the NAR (Nucleii Armeti Rivolu-tionari—Armed Revolutionary Cells), whose members bombed the Bologna railway station in September 1980. Later, members of both P2 and groups close to the NAR admitted that the bombing was designed by Gladio to force the political axis to the right. Thus Gladio connected Italy's ruling conservative Christian Democrats to some of the country's most violent and lawless fascists. Overseeing the whole operation were SISMI, the Italian military intelligence organization; SISDE, the Italian civilian intelligence organization; and SIFA, the Italian equivalent of the CIA.

The eruption of the Gladio scandal had international dimensions. In other countries, authorities began to concede that similar opera-tions had been devised for the same purposes—anti-communist sabotage—but not necessarily using fascists as key personnel or as weapons in internal politics. In the Netherlands, Premier Ruud Lubbers acknowledged that a Dutch version of Gladio, for which Gerrit Et Wolsink could conceivably have worked, did indeed exist and that its size had recently been subject to a review. In Greece, Yannis Varvisiotis, then defense minister, declared that the CIA had launched a similar network under the code-name "Sheepskin," but that it had been dismantled in 1988. Similar admissions followed in Portugal, Turkey, and France where, according to Defense Minister Jean-Pierre Chevenement, it had "only recently been dissolved."

However, it was in Germany, Belgium, and Sweden that investi-gations of Gladio produced the most significant results, and revealed the greatest parallels to the Italian experience. In Germany, for example, it emerged that ex-Nazis—some of them SS members from the post-war Bund Deutscher Jugend (BDJ)—had been the first recruits. A former senior CIA officer with knowledge of the entire NATO operation told Graeme Atkinson that the U.S. Office of Policy Coordination, a CIA front, had "incorporated lock, stock, and barrel the espionage outfit run by Hitler's spy boss Reinhard Gehlen." He explained that Gehlen was the spiritual father of "Stay Behind," and that West German leader Konrad Adenauer was fully aware of his role. Upon Germany's accession to NATO in May 1955, Adenauer signed a secret protocol with the U.S. in which the West German authorities agreed to refrain from the active legal pursuit of known right-wing extremists. "What was not so well known," the official continued, "is that other top German politicians were party to the existence of secret resistance plans, including the then German state secretary and former high-ranking Nazi Hans Globke."

In fact, the whole secret operation drew almost all its personnel from former SS and Waffen-SS men during the early post-war years, men who were then trained by the British Secret Intelligence Services (SIS). Later, the entire operation was absorbed into the West German intelligence service, the Bundesnachrichtendienst. At the end of 1990, the independent television program "Stern" highlighted some of the key plans of the German Gladio, including possible assassination of left-wing politicians in the event of a Soviet invasion. High on the list were two leading Social Democrats: Herbert Wehner, party chairman in the Bundestag (and an ex-communist whom the Nazis had never forgiven for escaping to the Soviet Union), and the mayor of Bremen, Wilhelm Kaisen.

Among those involved after the war—when the Gladio infrastructure was still being created—was ex-*Übersturmführer* Hans Otto. But "the prize catch," declared the former CIA man, "was Klaus Barbie, who functioned as a recruiting agent for ex-Nazis and members of the BDJ." The veracity of this dramatic accusation has never been confirmed, but documentary evidence in the hands of the British Parliament's All Party War Crimes Group—established in 1986 to bring Nazi fugitives in Britain to justice—shows that Barbie was in close contact with both the British and American secret services after the war.

It has also been amply confirmed that Swedish neutrality was violated from the early 1950s, when the United States installed a "Stay Behind" program, using former Swedish Waffen-SS men who had fought in the Finnish–Soviet war and, later, on the Eastern front. The choice of ex-Nazi Waffen-SS men was logical, since they alone in Sweden had the necessary mixture of anticommunist virulence and combat experience. In Belgium, too, "Stay Behind" recruited fascists as well as extreme-right elements within the police and armed forces.

The Gladio affair is important above all because it demonstrates the willingness of state authorities to collaborate for their own purposes with the most violent and hate-filled enemies of democracy. The precedent for this should be a cautionary footnote to all anti-fascists, democrats, and victims or potential victims of fascism: the extent to which the Nazis were encouraged and supported, prior to 1933, by "democratic" politicians, "democratic" army officers, "democratic" academics, "democratic" policemen, and "democratic" bankers and industrialists was revealed only after the final defeat of the Third Reich in 1945.

Gladio may well be the expression of a similar phenomenon today. But this time nobody can claim not to have been warned.

Afterword: To Soothe the Soul

WE OFTEN SPEAK ABOUT HITLER WHEN WE REALLY
mean the Third Reich. That alone is a fundamental error. How can
we know what would have happened if Hitler hadn't existed? Other
right-wing radicals were also attempting to attract the disappointed
and the aimless. Perhaps one of these others might have won the
masses over with the same simple, brutal methods. While it's also
said that Hitler was at first not taken seriously enough, that too is
misleading. It wasn't simply Hitler but the entire radical right that
was treated too lightly, just as many dismiss neofascism today.

When we talk about the "aimlessness" of radical-right youth
(who are sometimes as much as twenty-five years old), perhaps we
should recognize that they do have an aim, and that it's an extreme
right-wing aim. In 1992 alone, twenty people were murdered by
neo-Nazis in Germany; others remain hospitalized, in critical condition, even as I write this. Meanwhile, those who deny and those who
incite continue to speak with terrifying assurance about the "refugee
problem" while the mob burns down refugee homes almost undisturbed, preparing to treat this situation in the spirit of the Nazis.
The government expresses its indignation by banning several advance organizations—though only after determining whether these
were, as they claimed, legitimate political parties. And, of course,

now that the constitution has been amended, life will become more difficult—not for the Nazis, but for the asylum seekers.

In the seventies, when politicians and industrialists were terrorized by the radical-left Red Army Faction, the official reaction was different. The government was so concerned about the welfare of potential victims that police stood on every corner—I remember it perfectly. The government even declared a state of emergency. When the threat came from the left, those in power made bizarre, misleading, and dangerous comparisons. In 1984, on the occasion of a radical-left demonstration, Dr. Helmut Kohl declared: "There is no difference between the Nazi barbarism and the terror propagated by this mob." This quote is taken from *Ein Deutsches Jahrzehnt* (A German Decade), a festschrift published in 1992 to celebrate the chancellor's tenth year in office. Evidently, Kohl's advisers and media consultants still consider this an apt comparison. When ruling politicians protect themselves by any means possible while simple people are abandoned to brutal attacks, then democracy is only being discussed, not practiced. And it is simply unconscionable that, in November 1992, Chancellor Kohl referred to a "state of emergency" caused not by murderous right-wing radicals but by the "flood of refugees."

For many, the main problem seems to be Germany's image abroad. Here we have a band of professional apologists ready to step forward to defend that image. In January 1993, a grateful reader wrote *Der Spiegel* that Angelo Bolaffi's essay "soothed the soul." This reader's gratitude would seem to be representative, since other letters to the editor express similar sentiments.

"The times in which Europe could punish the unpopular Germans simply by referring to historical guilt are now past," wrote Bolaffi, a professor in Rome, in his essay in the December 14, 1992, issue of *Der Spiegel*. "Perhaps Europe should consider whether it would not make more sense to imitate the German example instead of fearing it. Wouldn't it be more sensible to look for the secret of Germany's postwar economy and political stability instead of just watching it with worry and suspicion?"

This sounds liberal and open-minded. But what was so mysterious about the German "economic miracle"? It was massive support from the United States, and the good will of the other victorious powers, that initially made the Federal Republic's rapid recovery and economic growth possible; this aid was largely intended to strengthen the country as a buffer against the Communists to the east. And, incidentally, it was not only the German work ethic but also the large-scale employment of "guest" labor from Italy, Spain, and Turkey that made this "miracle" possible.

None of this interests Bolaffi, who begins his essay by stating that "An anti-German syndrome is spreading through Europe—a genuine allergy to the new reality of unified Germany." He immediately identifies the responsible parties: "European leftists, including Germans but mostly Italians, have played a special role in this orgy of unkind speculation and outright distortion." He adds that "The left is showing Germany the same intolerance that it has shown Israel. This attitude comes dangerously close to racism." Then Bolaffi, who teaches political philosophy at La Sapienza University, goes even further: "It almost seems as if the left wishes that the so frequently decried 'German danger' really would become reality again." The neo-Nazi terror, he explains, "is a case of self-fulfilling prophecy, of outright political masochists who are trying to find an enemy— and, if necessary, to create one." Apparently, without the leftists, especially the Italian ones, there would be no skinheads, neo-Nazis, right-wing terrorists, or radical-right members of parliament. If indeed these perverse accusations "soothe the soul," whose soul are they soothing?

"When the cemetery in Dachau is desecrated," Bolaffi finally admits, "there is certainly reason for sorrow and concern." But Bolaffi's "concern" is a straw man, and he qualifies his "sorrow" in the next sentence: "Nevertheless, the old disinformation campaigns against Germany don't help anyone, and hatred helps even less."

What disinformation is he referring to? The claim that human rights are no longer guaranteed in Germany, where Japanese firms instruct their employees to wear dark suits in public so as not to be confused with refugees? Can only a Bolshevist conclude that the German justice system is blind in its right eye? And it's not just the justice system; and it's not just in Germany.

Bolaffi and his kin come up with hollow platitudes like "hatred helps even less." Where, after all, does hate come from? Even Bolaffi notes that 50,000 Italian neofascists recently marched through Rome. Italy also brutally deported the Albanian refugees, and there is just as much racism in Italy as in Germany. It was in France that the word *detail* was first used to describe the Holocaust, and where suspected Nazi war criminals were not prosecuted. Since the general amnesty, it's no longer possible in France to say anything about the tortures and massacres in Algeria. In France, young skinheads march on May 1 past *their* Führer, Monsieur Le Pen. The list goes on and on. . . .

Hate comes not from a single country but from all over the world. This book is not just about the German people as individuals, but also, and predominantly, about German politics as a whole. It is only by truly understanding its own politics that Germany can reach understanding and friendship with other democratic countries. That, along with warning against rightist extremists, is the goal of this book. It is dedicated to all those individuals who do not falter, who believe, above all, in humanity and who have the courage of their convictions.

As for Germany's image and reputation abroad, this was salvaged by the hundreds of thousands of people who, in the winter of 1992, demonstrated against hate with candles. One can only hope that their beliefs are firm and, above all, that their spirit will spread to the politicians.

ADL   Anti-Defamation League of the B'nai B'rith (USA)

ANS/NA   Aktionsfront Nationaler Sozialisten/Nationaler Aktivisten (National Socialist Action Front/National Activists)—banned in West Germany in 1983 (Germany, Chile)

ANS/NL   Aktionsfront Nationaler Sozialisten/Gau Niederlande (National Socialist Action Front/Gau Netherlands) (Netherlands)

AVÖ   Althans Verkauf und Öffentlichkeitsarbeit, *or* Amt für Volksaufklärung und Öffentlichkeitsarbeit (Althans Sales and Publicity Work, *or* Office for Popular Education and Publicity Work)

AZA   Anti-Zionistische Aktion (Anti-Zionist Action)

BDV   Bund der Vertriebenen (League of Expellees)

BM   British Movement (UK)

BNSM   British National Socialist Movement (UK)

*All organizations are German or West German unless otherwise noted.

BND	Bundesnachrichtendienst (Federal Information Service)
BRD	Bundesrepublik Deutschland (Federal Republic of Germany)
CDL	Christian Defense League (USA)
CDU	Christlich-Demokratische Union (Christian Democratic Union)—center-right German political party
CEDADE	Circulo Español de Amigos de Europa (Spanish Circle of European Friends) (Spain)
CIA	Central Intelligence Agency (USA)
CIC	Counter Intelligence Corps (USA)
COBRA	Comité Objectif Entraide et Solidarité avec les Victimes de la Répression Antinationaliste (Objective Committee for Mutual Help and Solidarity with the Victims of Antinationalist Repression) (France)
COFPAC	Committee for Free Patriots and Anticommunist Political Prisoners (USA)
COTC	Church of the Creator (USA)
CSU	Christlich-Soziale Union (Christian Social Union)—right-wing German political party; Bavarian partner of CDU
DA	Deutsche Alternative (German Alternative)
DDR	Deutsche Demokratische Republik (German Democratic Republic)—the former East Germany
DFF	Deutsche Frauenfront (German Women's Front)
DL	Deutsche Liga für Volk und Heimat (German League for Nation and Homeland)
DNP	Deutsch-Nationale Partei (German National Party)
DSU	Deutsche Soziale Union (German Social Union)
DVU	Deutsche Volksunion (German People's Union)

ENO	Europäische Neuordnung (European New Order) (Switzerland)
FANE	Fédération d'Action Nationale Européene (Federation for European Nationalist Action) (France)—now forbidden; reorganized as FNE
FAP	Freiheitliche Arbeiterpartei (Free Workers' Party)
FDJ	Freie Deutsche Jugend (Free German Youth)—former Communist Party youth organization (DDR)
FDP	Freie Demokratische Partei (Free Democratic Party)— liberal German political party; presently in coalition with CDU/CSU
FN	Front National (National Front) (France)
FNE	Faisceaux Nationalistes Européens (European Fascist Nationalists)—successor to the banned FANE
FPÖ	Freiheitliche Partei Österreichs (Austrian Freedom Party) (Austria)
GDNF	Gesinnungsgemeinschaft der Neuen Front (Community of Partisans of the New Front) (Germany, Netherlands, Belgium)
HIAG	Hilfsgemeinschaft auf Gegenseitigkeit, Bundesverband der ehemaligen Soldaten der Waffen-SS e.V. (Mutual Aid Society, Federal Union of Former SS Soldiers) (Germany, Netherlands)
HNG	Hulpkomitee voor Nationalistische Politieke Gevangene (Aid Committee for Nationalist Political Prisoners) (Belgium)
HNG	Hilfsorganisation für Nationale Politische Gefangene und deren Angehörige e.V. (Relief Agency for National Political Prisoners and Their Dependents)
IIIR	Institute for Historical Review (USA)

JU   Junge Union (Young Union)—CDU youth organization

KK   Kreativistens Kyrka (Church of the Creator) (Sweden)

KKK   Ku Klux Klan (USA, Canada, UK, France, Germany, Sweden, Norway)

NA   Nationale Alternative (National Alternative)

NAR   Nucleii Armati Rivolutionari (Armed Revolutionary Cells) (Italy)

NCCC   New Christian Crusade Church (USA)

NF   National Front (UK)

NF   Nationalistische Front (Nationalist Front)—banned in 1992

NL   Nationale Liste (National List)

NO   Nationale Offensive (National Offensive)

NPD   Nationaldemokratische Partei Deutschlands (German National Democratic Party)

NS   Nationale Sammlung (National Union)

NSDAP-AO   Nationalsozialistische Deutsche Arbeiterpartei—Auslands- und Aufbau-Organization (National Socialist German Workers' Party—Foreign and Development Organization)

NVU   Nederlands Volks-Unie (Dutch People's Union) (Netherlands)

NWD   Nationaler Widerstand Deutschlands (German National Resistance)

ODESSA   Organisation der Ehemaligen SS-Angehörigen (Organization of Former SS Members) (Germany, Austria, Italy, Switzerland, Sweden, Yugoslavia, Syria, Egypt, Chile, Argentina, Brazil, Bolivia, Mexico, and others)

P2   Propaganda Due (Propaganda Two) (Italy)

PDS	Partei des Demokratischen Sozialismus (Democratic Socialist Party)—successor to DDR Communist Party
PEU	Pan-Europa-Union
RAF	Rote Armee Fraktion (Red Army Faction)—banned
REP	Die Republikaner (Republicans)
RSHA	Reichssicherheitshauptamt (Reich Central Security Office)—formed in 1939
SA	Sturmabteilung (Storm Troopers)—formed in 1921
SED	Sozialistische Einheitspartei Deutschlands (German Socialist Unity Party)—DDR Communist Party
SPD	Sozialdemokratische Partei Deutschlands (German Social Democratic Party)—center-left political party
SRP	Sozialistische Reichspartei (Socialist Reich Party)—banned in 1952
VAM	Vit Ariskt Motstand (White Aryan Resistance) (Sweden)
VAPO	Volkstreue Ausserparlamentarische Opposition (Extraparliamentary Opposition of Loyalty to Our People) (Austria)
VMO	Vlaamese Militanten Orden (Belgium)
WAR	White Aryan Resistance (USA)
WJ	Wiking-Jugend (Viking Youth) (Germany, Austria, Netherlands, Sweden, Denmark)
WUNS	World Union of National Socialists (Denmark [headquarters], UK, Germany, Austria, Italy, France, Spain, Argentina, Chile, Bolivia, USA, Canada, and others)